The Old Order Changeth

The
Old Order Changeth

A Novel

BY

ARCHIBALD MARSHALL

New York
Dodd, Mead and Company
1919

CONTENTS

v

CONTENTS

The Old Order Changeth

CHAPTER I

THE SALE

AT first sight one would have thought that some sort of fête was in progress. On the great stretch of level lawn in front of the house stood a white marquee, with flags flapping at either end of it. The September sky was brightly blue. It was just the day for a flower-show, or a Primrose League festival, and just the place.

The house was one of those enormous country palaces that make one wonder what sort of life those who built them can have had in mind for themselves. It had the dignity of size and proportion, but little beauty otherwise. In front of it was about half an acre of gravel; in front of that a squared lawn of about an acre; and in front of that again, on a slightly lower level, and divided from the lawn by a balustrade, was a formal garden of a desolating ugliness, covering about two acres. The box-edged beds were disposed in a vast and complicated pattern, and . each contained some plant chosen for the colour of its leaves or flowers, and for its low and tidy habit of growth.

With that two-acre carpet expensive ugliness ended and beauty began. The open ground was flanked with the graceful growth of huge beeches, through which the carriage roads approached the house on either side. Behind it the woods, now just beginning to show their autumn variety of colour, rose in a wide amphitheatre, and the white stone house with its many windows looked out across the levelled ground on to a wide-sweeping expanse

3

of meadow and woodland, that ended only with a line of low hills thirty miles away.

The great house not only of a parish but a county, Kemsale had been accustomed to extend its amenities to all sorts of festive and patriotic demands. The marquee was not hired for such occasions, but was kept until it was wanted in one or another of the buildings, as extensive as a village, that existed for the service of the house. Then it was put up by some of the small army of men employed about the place, and after it had served its temporary purpose taken down again, and the grass carefully rolled and watered, so that its billiard-table smoothness should not be marred by the least irregularity of colour or surface. The lawn was not even used for games, the ground for which was elsewhere. To keep it and the gravel smooth, and to fill and tend to the contorted beds of the carpet garden, so that at certain seasons of the year, during the greater part of which the house was shut up, its design should be coloured, occupied the attention of many men. They lived by this work, and those of them who had families fed and educated them on the money they were paid for it. Some of them occupied cottages on the estate, with little gardens of their own, as unlike as possible to the one that they laboured six days in the week to tend. So that the lawn and the carpet of Kemsale may be said to have been endowed with houses and land as well as with money. And yet, of those who had paid the price of all this steady labour, that had gone on for years and years, hardly one had ever rested his gaze with pleasure on its results, though many had done so on the lovely stretch of country that lay below and beyond. It was kept up because it was there, and had always been kept up. And the scores of rooms in the great house, all richly or comfortably or

conveniently furnished, the greater number of which their
owners never visited, were also kept up, and endowed
again, as it were, with regular well-paid service, for the
sake of the few occasions in the year in which they were
filled or partly filled with guests; and because they were
part of the state attached to such a house as this.

But now, at last, on this bright September day, all the
complicated and expensive machinery that had been
kept oiled and wound up through generations was in
process of disintegration. The marquee on the lawn
indicated festivity, it is true, but as far as it concerned
the great house it was a festivity sadder than any
mourning. Those who had eaten and drunk in it, and
were now spreading over the lawn and overflowing with
admiring comment into the untrodden walks of the carpet
garden, were the birds of prey that had settled upon
Kemsale. They had been invited to settle on it, and fed
and filled as a reward for doing so. They were to pick
it clean of all it contained, and leave it staring in its large
emptiness over the wide country of which it had been the
crown and centre, until some sort of machinery should be
put into it again, and it should reflect a life that might
in some respects resemble the old one, but could never
be quite the same.

Kemsale was being sold up—lock, stock, and barrel, as the
phrase goes. This was the third day in which luncheon had
been spread in the great marquee for the benefit of those
who had come from all over the country to bid for its
hoarded contents; and the sale would last for three days
more, with increasing competition and excitement amongst
the buyers, as the catalogue worked slowly down from
the upper floors to the valuable "lots" from the
lower.

The upper floors—even the great range of attics behind

the balustrade of the roof—had already yielded surprises
in plenty to the buyers, though few bargains; for this
sale had been too widely known and too eagerly anticipated
to serve the bargain-hunters. The house, as it stood, had
been furnished from roof to basement for over two hundred
years, and the basis of its furnishing had been the contents
of a much older, though smaller, house, the place of which
it had taken. In the course of subsequent additions to its
stock of household gear, good things had receded from
places of honour, and taken up posts of retiring usefulness
instead. Sometimes they had been discarded altogether,
for no more than a reparable weakness, and relegated to
lumber rooms, until now the long years had brought them
to light again, more valuable in their partial destruction
than when they had left the hands of their makers, strong
and whole. Servants' bedrooms had yielded their scroll-
backed chairs, their mahogany tall-boys, toilet-mirrors,
brass fenders, and copper coal-scuttles, which had been
put into them new two hundred years before, as the ordinary
furniture of the time, and had come out old, to enter on a
new career as articles of price, fit for the best rooms of
other houses. From the broad corridors and hive of rooms
on the second floor—bachelors' rooms, nurseries, rooms of
dependents above the rank of servants—had come a rich
succession of treasures amongst the steady flow of old and
solid furniture. The engravings alone would have formed
an embracing collection—mezzotints bought at the time of
their publication for a few guineas, kept, perhaps, in port-
folios for a time, then framed by the score and hung up
to decorate bare walls, and afterwards forgotten, now selling for scores and hundreds apiece; etchings picked up by
some dilettante of the family making the Grand Tour, and
treated in the same way—Albrecht Dürers, Lucas Van
Leydens, Rembrandts, Marc Antonios amongst them; deli-

cate prints in coloured stipple after eighteenth-century
artists who would have been forgotten but for the repro-
ductions of their work, now more valuable than the original
paintings—all these had been the normal yield, and their
total price had run up to many thousands, though the list
had been hurried through for the sake of richer treasures still to come. There had been great store of old
china too, lotted and catalogued from these upper floors,
every piece of it of value, and some here and there of
great value; old cut glass; old clocks; old inkstands and
trays and writing-table toys; old dressing-table sets; old
carpets and rugs and curtains, faded and worn, but eagerly
bid for. Each room had become richer as the years had
passed, as more important rooms had been refurnished,
and their superseded contents moved up to the less important. The things from the upper floors alone would
have set up a dealer in antiquities for life, and filled his
shop to overflowing.

That is the light in which they were looked at by those
who competed so eagerly to possess them. They would
come to be scattered all over the country, and so scattered
would give infinitely more pleasure to their numerous
purchasers than they had given to their old owners. And
yet, in truth, as each was knocked down and its price
entered up by the busy auctioneer's clerk, virtue was
slowly and inexorably departing from these inanimate
things. They had come together through long years, filled
their natural place in the furnishing of a noble house,
given to each of its many rooms its own character. They
had had life, made up of old memories and associations,
and that life was dissolving. However carefully and lavishly the house might be filled again, it could never have
the meaning that these things had given to it.

Now, on the third day of the sale, they were coming

down to the rooms of the first floor, and here there were things to be sold more valuable than had been sold before, and more bound up with the intimate lives of those who had used them. A gong boomed out from the porch in front of the house; the figures that were spread out on the lawn and in the garden came flowing towards it. With well-fed alacrity they settled themselves behind the long tables in the ball-room, while the auctioneer slipped into his high seat under the musicians' gallery, and two men in baize aprons brought in a large mirror which they carried round the space left between the tables.

"Now then, gentlemen, we'll go on where we left off, page twenty-five in the catalogue: From the Blue Boudoir, Lot 494, Fine Gilt Chippendale Mirror. What offers? Oh, come now, I hope the good lunch you've enjoyed hasn't blinded your eyes. This is a collector's piece, gentlemen. Famous waterfall design, Chippendale's best period, and not a scratch or a mark on it. Probably bought from the maker himself, and been hanging here ever since. That's better; but let's take the business seriously, gentlemen. We've got a lot to get through."

At this time a carriage was driving up the long road through the woods that led from the east gates. The tall bay horses trotted up the gentle slope that rose all the way to the house as if it were level ground. The coachman and footman wore liveries of black cloth with dark green facings. The whole equipage was well turned out, in a sober but highly polished sort of way, as if in the particular establishment to which it belonged fine horses and easy carriages were the chosen means of conveyance, and not an old-fashioned survival destined to give way to motor-cars when they should be worn out. It belonged to Edward Clinton, Squire of Kencote, ten miles away, who had driven fine horses all his life, and up to his present age of seventy-one had never ridden in a motor-car, nor intended to.

He and Mrs. Clinton were in the carriage, and with them was Lady Grace Ettien, the Squire's kinswoman, who had been born in the house to which they were driving, thirty years before, and lived in it the greater part of her life. It was not a pleasant drive for any of the three of them, in spite of the glory of the autumn woods and the softness of the sun-soaked air.

Grace Ettien was a sweet-faced woman, tall and slender, with features rather too much of the aquiline type for beauty, but pleasant to look on for all that. She sat on the back seat of the carriage. The Squire was recovering from a sharp attack of rheumatism, or he would have been driving his phaeton, as he still preferred to do when he went abroad. He sat in his corner, his white beard spreading over his buttoned-up shooting-cape, the skin under his eyes a little loose, but his cheeks firm and fresh-coloured still—a big, handsome old man, only a trifle out of repair for the moment, and by no means yet to be considered in his fit place leaning back against the cushions of a carriage driven by a servant. Mrs. Clinton, although her hair was as white as her husband's, looked a good deal younger than he. Her face was fresh-coloured too, as became a woman who had lived all her life in the country. The Squire had been a stay-at-home since his youth, and she had stayed at home with him, although at times she would have preferred not always to stay at home. She was rather short, and might have been considered dumpy, but that she held herself erect, even sitting in her carriage, and had a look of energy, both mental and physical. Her face was round, and very kind. Just now, like that of her husband, it showed deep concern.

They had been discussing the sale to which they were

driving, and certain of the circumstances that had led up to it; but the Squire, who did not consider that when a thing had been said once it need not be said several times more, now broke out again.

"'Pon my word, Kemsale ought to be ashamed of himself. It makes my blood boil to come here and think of what has happened and what is happening now. I shan't come into the house, Grace. I don't think I could. To think of what it used to be in your grandfather's time, and now *that* going on in it! There's only one word for it: it's criminal. Criminal."

Kemsale was the title by which Lord Meadshire had been known until he had succeeded his grandfather, ten years or so before. He was known to his friends and relations as "Kem," but the Squire was much too angry with him to use any such abbreviation at present.

Grace Ettien leaned forward. "Poor Kem!" she said. "I know he feels it, Cousin Edward. If he is here, and you see him, don't make it too hard for him."

"Feels it!" snorted the Squire. "I should think he did feel it. No man in his position has a right to behave as he has done. When your grandfather was alive he was the chief man in the county; and his father and grandfather before him. Actually—ten years ago—the owner of Kemsale was Lord Lieutenant of Meadshire. And now! Kemsale sold up! Sold up! And the Marquis of Meadshire no better than a beggar. Pshaw! It doesn't bear thinking about."

He threw himself back in his corner of the carriage. He had been talking like this during the best part of the long drive, and as the horses were trotting up the last rise that led to the house the two ladies may have hoped that he had exhausted the subject, painful enough to them, for the time being. But he still had something to say, something that he had been searching for during all his long repetitive tirades, that would sum up what he felt about this startling disintegration, that would bring it into the sphere of morals, and justify the deep-seated dismay with which he regarded it.

"Kemsale has been using what doesn't belong to him," he said, and his hearers knew that his words had a meaning deeper than the literal. "Property.in his position is a trust, and he has broken it."

The carriage drew up before the porch, as it had drawn up many times before, bringing its occupants to pleasant private or semi-public gatherings very different from this one. The two ladies alighted from it. The Squire looked with pained disgust upon the litter in front of the house, the vans and carts that were already beginning to take things away, and the men who went to and fro, with no respect for the sanctities attaching to such a place as this, laughing and talking and smoking, as if the downfall of a noble family were a mere incident in their customary activities. The Squire had an impulse almost of rage towards them; these things were so very real and so very important to him. He got out of the carriage, assisted by the footman. "I can't sit still here," he said angrily. "I shall walk about outside. If you want me, I shan't be far off."

He went off, leaning on his stick, without further words, and the two women, looking after him for a moment, turned and went into the house.

With a frown at the marquee, in which eating and drinking were still going on, the Squire made his way across the lawn towards the carpet garden. He had no desire to review that conventional hideosity, but below it there were other beautiful gardens, the privacy of which might remind him of all that was passing away, and solace the actual pain that he was feeling. But when he came to the balustrade the steps and slopes that he would have to negotiate deterred him from going farther in this direction, and he made his way slowly round to the stables which flanked the house to the west.

As he went under the archway that led to the great stable-yard he felt an additional pang. He had loved horses all his life, and as a boy and a young man he had so often trodden these stones with light step, eager for the busy life that had its centre here. The stables of Kemsale had been kept up on a scale greater even than those at Kencote, important as those had been. There had always been something interesting and exciting to see there, and in his youth he had never visited the house without visiting the stables. It was the old associations that had brought him to them now, rather than any desire to see what might be going on; for the Kemsale horses had already been sold, and he anticipated no pleasure from visiting the place where they had been.

The pang he felt was not wholly, nor perhaps in the main, on his own account. He had been too fortunate in life to dwell on past happiness with the half-sweet half-painful longing which visits those whose days have declined to dullness. His own satisfactions would hardly be touched by the withdrawal of Kemsale from his orbit. Nor did he wince in sympathy with the man who had had all this and had thrown it away. As far as that went the punishment was just and fitting. It was the break-up of an institution that he felt so deeply, and above all the surprising suddenness with which it had come about. Ten years of folly and lavish spending, and all this state and circumstance, so admirably indicative of honourable condition, had come tumbling down like a house of cards, when it had seemed to have been founded on an impregnable rock. If that could happen where the place had been so high and so apparently well-guarded, was there real safety anywhere? He did not tell himself that his own old line was in danger. There was none visible there, either in his own time or in that of his immediate heirs. But full confidence had been sapped. He felt the same sort of discomfort that many people must have felt after the *Titanic* disaster, when they stepped on board a great ocean liner, no longer with a sense of safety so assured that it need not even be dwelt upon. Kemsale, with all that it had meant in this little corner of the world and in the country at large, had come to an end. The Marquis of Meadshire had his title left to him, and very little else in the world besides; and what was his title worth, unsupported by the land that had given it virtue? Not so much as his own ancient Squiredom. He found it impossible to grasp the magnitude of the catastrophe. It was like a nightmare, so monstrous as to bring a sense of its own impossibility even before the waking. Surely such things as this could not be! If they were allowed, then nothing could be expected to stand firm. He saw rocks all around him, although for him and his there were no rocks anywhere within sight, and his course was over clear and smooth waters. His perplexity increased; he was very deeply troubled.

" Hullo, Edward! Glad to see you about again. Pretty dismal sort of place this to come to nowadays, though."

He looked up to see the man who was at the root of his perplexity standing before him, with a friendly smile on his face, and he grew so red with shame and anger that the smile faded away, and Lord Meadshire looked down on the ground in confusion.

But only for a moment. He looked up again and laughed. " Why, any one would think that it was you who was being sold up, to look at you," he said. "Surely, my dear Edward, if I can put up with it, you can."

He stood before him in a long frieze motoring coat, his goggles pushed up on to his forehead underneath his dusty cap. The long grey raking machine that had brought him many miles in an incredibly short space of time was still throbbing behind him with its bonnet open, and his *chauffeur* was doing something to the engine. It added enormously to the Squire's furious disgust with him that he should stand there looking like a *chauffeur* himself, or at least obviously in accord with the oily stinking machinery that was taking all the dignity out of progression in these modern days. But something in his look as he had turned down his glance for that brief moment prevented his breaking out against him, as otherwise he would have done. He turned his back instead, and limped out of the yard, his stick striking the cobbles sharply.

Lord Meadshire threw a glance at him, and then, with the smile that was seldom absent from his face, took off his coat and threw it into the car, and followed him, unhooking his goggles as he did so.

He was a man of rather more than forty, and looked his full age. He was tall and heavily built, with rounded shoulders and long thin legs. His face was amiable and had once been handsome, but it was blotched now, and stamped with the mark of intemperance. His voice, as he called after his cousin, was husky.

"Wait a minute, Edward. Are you going in to the sale?"

The Squire turned round sharply. "No, I'm not," he said, and was about to add more, but Meadshire broke in on him: "Well, I don't know that I want to either. I suppose you brought Grace over. How is the dear girl? It's a jar for her, this sort of thing, isn't it? Still, we shall both be much better off in the Herons' Nest than ever we were here. Have you been over there lately, Edward? It's all finished now, and ready to put the things into. It will be as pretty a little place as ever you saw, when we've finished with it."

He spoke without a trace of awkwardness, and as if he were quite unaware of the antagonism that was seeking an outlet in his cousin's mind. They were walking slowly along the path that bordered the lawn towards the south.

"The Herons' Nest!" said the Squire contemptuously. "A cottage suitable for an artist or some such fellow, and all you've got left out of all this!"

Meadshire would not let him go on. "Well, if you come to that," he said, in the same easy tone, "I think it will be a precious sight nicer to live in than all this." They had come to the balustrade overlooking the carpet garden. "Look at it," he said, laughing. "All that ugly nonsense has been kept up for years and years, at a vast expense, and what good is it to anybody? We shall have a garden we can make something of in the Herons' Nest."

"The new toy!" snorted the Squire. "And how long will you keep it, I wonder? At your rate, you'd eat it up in a day, if——"

"If!" Meadshire caught him up quickly. "There are two very big ifs, my dear Edward, in the way of my eating it up. The first is, as you know quite well, that it belongs to Grace, and not to me, and the second is that I've turned over an entirely new leaf."

The Squire was getting more and more incensed against him. "How many does that make, I wonder?" he asked bitterly.

"I don't know. About the hundred and fiftieth, I should think. But the others have all had this absurd place hanging on to them. Now, at last, I've got rid of it there'll be a different state of things altogether."

The Squire stopped and regarded him from under heavy frowning white brows. " I sometimes think you've got no sense of right and wrong at all," he said. "You talk as if you had nobody but yourself to think of, and your place in the world were nothing. Kemsale has gone on for hundreds of years, and every man that has held it has played his big part here. And now you—*you*, with your selfish ways—you've thrown it away, and talk of it as if it were nothing. Bah! You make me feel positively sick, Kemsale."

Meadshire became a little more serious. " Now look here, Edward," he said earnestly, " you've got to look facts in the face. I've played the fool; yes, I know. But I've had a run for my money, anyhow. You talk—you always have talked—as if I'd come in for a magnificent property and chucked it all away in a few years. You know very well that I came in for a white elephant. If I had lived here at Kemsale as quietly as my old grandfather did when he was over eighty I could just have kept the place together and no more."

"At any rate you *would* have kept the place together, as it was your duty to do; and you might have played the part that your grandfather played, and played so well. Instead of which——"

" Instead of which I go about stealing ducks. Yes, I know all that. And I tell you I couldn't have played the part my grandfather did, even if I'd wanted to. The fact is that he skinned the place, and you know it perfectly well. I'm not blaming the old boy. He spent his money in the very way that suited him—cutting a big figure, and all that. You could do that on land, and land only, when he was a young man, and you couldn't when he was an old one. We've had nothing but land, and that sort of thing was bound to come to an end sooner or later. It came to an end with him. Who raised the first mortgage on Kencote? Eh?"

The Squire made no reply to this question, but looked on the ground in his turn. There came before him things that he never willingly thought of. He had been brought up at Kencote by his grandfather, a man who had thought about little but sport, and in spite of his wealth and long descent had chosen to live the life of a plain country Squire. His grandfather's sister had married the Marquis of Meadshire, and the present Marquis's grandfather was her son. During his boyhood Edward Clinton had been taught to regard Kemsale as something very stately and very honourable, but only accidentally allied to the more modest pretensions of such a house as Kencote. In his youth he had mixed more with the great world than his grandfather had ever done, and the sense of a considerable difference had lessened. But there had always remained the feeling that his cousin was a great man, with the sort of social greatness that he himself best understood, and it had come as a great shock to him, not many years before that cousin's death, to be asked to lend his assistance in raising money for him on Kemsale. He himself had inherited money from more than one source, but he had looked upon it all as attaching to Kencote and its wide lands. He hated to think of Kencote, which had supported the Clintons in their modest state for generations, being bolstered up by money from outside, and the knowledge that Kemsale, which was not so bolstered up, could no longer support its more elaborate state was a painful and disturbing thought.

He shook himself free of it. "A mortgage is nothing," he said. "It's your criminal folly that has brought this about. You ought to have thought of the line. You ought to have married long ago."

Meadshire's face changed. "Oh, that's another question altogether," he said. "We won't go into that now. Well, I think I'll look in and see how things are going. I hear they're getting record prices. I'd no idea there was such a lot of stuff in the house. Hullo! Here's Grace! Well, my dear, have you got the things you want?"

CHAPTER II

THE CONTEST

LADY GRACE came quickly over the lawn towards them. She smiled when she saw her brother. " I didn't know you were here, Kem," she said. " Cousin Edward, they are bidding the things up in an extraordinary way. We have been able to get nothing we decided upon yet. I want you to tell the man to go higher still for some that are coming. The limits we gave him are not enough."

One of Meadshire's crowning follies had been to raise money upon a Bill of Sale, which had included everything that the house contained at the time. It had been for a large sum, but not nearly so large as the treasures of Kemsale were still worth, even with the most valuable of them already sold by their owner. Edward Clinton had advanced money to clear off the Bill of Sale, so that his cousin might at least get the benefit of the open market. But the arrangement had been made hurriedly at the last moment, and instead of withdrawing the things he and his sister had wanted to keep Meadshire had let them go in with all the rest. It may have been part of the turning over of that new leaf, of which he had spoken, that had led him to do so. " They are yours up to a certain value," he had said to his cousin. " If we see that they are likely to fetch a good deal more, we can buy back more. If not, we'll do with a few. You've been very good, Edward; but I don't want you to give me the things."

And, indeed, there had been a sort of pride and independence in his spendthrift career. He had probably never asked a friend to lend him money; he had certainly never asked Edward Clinton, who was his sister's trustee, and a strict and rigid one. The Squire had made the offer about the Bill of Sale, and Meadshire had accepted it as a business arrangement, and for his sister's benefit as well as his own. The things she would want could be bought in too. It would only be making two bites at a cherry to have them valued and withdrawn, and there wasn't much time. He wanted to get the beastly business over and done with.

But it seemed there was a difficulty about buying things in at any reasonable price.

" But we gave him a limit half as much again as the things were likely to fetch," said the Squire. " The fellow must have muddled it."

" There is one man that bids against him," said Grace. " He seems determined to have what he wants, whatever it goes up to. Fortunately, there has been nothing I want very much so far; but they will soon be coming to my own rooms, and I want you to tell our man to go higher still, if it is necessary."

All three of them went across to the house. Grace had her catalogue with her, and showed them the prices at which some of the things they had marked had been knocked down for. They seemed extravagant, and far beyond the rate at which other things had been sold, although prices were universally good.

They went into the great room where the sale was being held. It was as full as if it had been a London auction-room, and in fact all the dealers from London were there, or their representatives, and buyers from all over the kingdom besides. There were also a great many people

from the country around, and the Squire noted with a frown
the presence of several of his friends and acquaintances.
He thought that they might have kept away, out of
delicacy; but there seemed no particular reason why they
should, since it was to be supposed that the more people
there were to bid for the things put up for sale the better
it would be for the sellers.

A man from the county town of Bathgate had been
commissioned to bid on behalf of Lady Grace, and of
the Squire himself, who had marked down a few " lots "
to be transferred to Kencote. He joined them when they
entered the room, in some excitement.

" He says he's got his orders, sir, but he won't tell me
who he's bidding for. I been trying to make some sort of
arrangement with him."

" Who is it? What are you talking about? " asked the
Squire impatiently.

He pointed out a man to whom a " lot " had just been
knocked down at a high price. " I've found out who
he is," he said. " He comes from a very respectable firm
in London. He's acting under orders, but it can't be for
his own people. They'd never pay the prices he's running
up to. He's acting for a private buyer."

The Squire bent his frowning gaze upon the man. He
seemed to be of an innocuous type, and rather nervous
besides. He was bidding again, for a little chintz-covered
easy-chair out of one of the bedrooms, and other dealers
were laughing at him and running him up. It could have
been bought new in any shop for two or three pounds, but
it was knocked down to him for five pounds ten, and there
was laughter and a disposition to cheer as the hammer
fell.

" Lot five hundred and ten, marble-topped rosewood
washhandstand," said the auctioneer. " A fine solid piece

this, gentlemen. I won't have it brought in. Shall we start at three pounds? "

There was a bid of ten shillings, at which price fine solid pieces of this description are occasionally acquired, by mutual arrangement between dealers, at private sales. But this sale was too well attended for the machinations of the " ring " to have scope. Somebody bid a pound, and somebody else thirty shillings.

" That's no price for an article of this sort, gentlemen," said the auctioneer. " Now then, Mr. Waller, two pounds? Thank you. Two pounds. Two pounds. Any advance on two pounds? "

" Run him up," said Meadshire. " Let's see how far he'll go. Go on, quick."

" Two pound ten. Thank you, Mr. Giles. Two fifteen. Three pounds. Three pounds five. Three pound ten. Any advance on three pound ten? "

" It isn't one of the pieces you wanted, sir," expostulated Giles. " It's not worth—Oh! "

Meadshire had given him a sharp dig in the ribs. The auctioneer's eye was on him.

" Three pound fifteen. Four pounds. Four five. Four ten."

The Squire's agent faltered at ten pounds, but the light of battle was in Meadshire's eyes. " Go on," he adjured him, and he took it up to fifteen, with increasing excitement on the part of the onlookers.

" Don't be a fool, Kemsale," said the Squire angrily; but Meadshire took no notice of him. " Stop at nineteen fifteen," he whispered to his man.

But Waller, now in a painful state of confusion, stopped before that, and the washhandstand was knocked down to Meadshire's agent at eighteen pounds five shillings.

Meadshire swore, and then laughed. " We've broken

him, anyhow," he said. " He can have the rest out of this room."

Waller seemed very unhappy. He was a short, nervous-looking man with a dark pointed beard, neatly dressed, and of a class rather above that of most of the dealers around him. Probably he was a member of the firm that had been entrusted with this important commission. His purchases had already run up to a high figure. He did not look like a man who would show any resource in an auction-room battle, and evidently shrank from the amused notice that his exploits were bringing him.

He rose from his seat, and, looking round, seized upon another dealer with whom he conferred over his catalogue. Then he hurried from the room, passing close to where Meadshire and the party from Kencote were standing.

Meadshire followed him into the hall, where there were men passing to and fro with articles for the sale-room.

" Where's the telephone? I want to get to the telephone," cried Waller to all and sundry.

" In that room there," said a man with a green apron, pointing to a door.

Waller was hurrying towards it when Meadshire stopped him. " Wait a minute," he said. " What do you want the telephone for? "

Waller started nervously and stopped, and then frowned. " What's that to do with you, sir? " he asked. " I suppose I can use the telephone if I like? "

" I don't know that you can," said Meadshire. " This isn't a public office."

One of the old servants of the house, who for lack of instructions had been hanging about the hall in a miserable sort of way, came up.

" The telephone ought to be at the service of buyers,"

said Waller angrily, " especially of big ones like my firm.
It's very important that I should telephone to London. I'll
pay for the trunk call, of course."

" What do you want to telephone about? " asked Meadshire again.

" I want—— But who are you, sir? What business of
yours is it what I want? You seem to me to be taking a
great deal upon yourself."

" Oh, if you're going to talk like that! " said Meadshire,
turning away. " You can tell the gentleman who I am,
Cooper; and he's not to use any of the telephones in the
house."

Meadshire went back into the sale-room and hid himself in a corner. Waller came in almost immediately, and
as if he wished to escape notice. He looked furtively about
amongst the crowd, which was now fairly thick, and made
his way through it to where the man who had been bidding
for him sat. Meadshire peered over heads and saw him
giving this man earnest instructions. Waller then took his
place at the table and the man pushed his way through the
crowd towards the doorway.

Meadshire went out into the hall before he could reach
it. " There's a big fellow in a bowler hat coming out," he
said. " If he wants to use the telephone, let him; but don't
tell him who I am."

He went into the room off the hall, which had so far
undergone little change. Only the numbered labels stuck
on to the furniture indicated that its time for disintegration was coming. It was rather like the waiting-room of
an old-established club, with a turkey carpet, massive
mahogany furniture, and portraits in mezzotint on the dark
walls. Meadshire took a book of reference from the
writing-table and seated himself in an easy-chair by the
window.

Waller's lieutenant pushed his way into the hall and went up to Cooper with half-a-crown ostentatiously displayed in his fingers. " I say, mate, I wish you'd put me on to a telephone," he said. " No need to tell the Governor about it, you know. It's between you and me."

The half-crown changed hands. Cooper saw no reason, in view of the possible scarcity of such presents in the future, why he should not accept one for doing his duty. " I'm not sure there isn't somebody using it," he said. " But you can go in there if you shut the door after you, and don't say I told you."

He turned away with a grin, and the man, thinking how easy it was to get what you wanted if you went the right way about it, went into the room.

He found a middle-aged person in a rather shabby serge suit turning over the leaves of a large red book. " Have you finished with the telephone, mate? " he asked cordially. " 'Cos I want a trunk call."

" I'm not using it, thanks," said Meadshire.

He looked undecided for a moment. " I got leave to use it from the people of the house on rather a private matter," he said. " *You'll* understand. If you wouldn't mind——"

Meadshire looked up with bland amiability. "I don't mind in the least," he said. " Go ahead; " and returned to his book.

There was something about him that made the man hesitate again. He had thought at first that he was some one like himself, who had made his way in here in the general confusion. Now he thought that he might be somebody connected with the house, and it might not be wise to ask him to leave the room, or indeed likely that he would go.

" Oh, well," he said, " I suppose you won't want to listen

to a private conversation, and perhaps you'll have found what you're looking for by the time I get my call."

He rang up a London number and then hung about the room with one hand in his pocket and the other pulling at his moustache, his eye fixed doubtfully upon Meadshire.

Meadshire laid down his heavy book, and looked up at him with a pleasant smile. "Things seem to be fetching a big price," he said. "*I've* never seen a sale like this before. Have you?"

Then he must have some connection with the trade, after all. The man's face cleared. "It's surprising some of them," he said. "There's a little sitting down at the Meadshire Arms there of an evening amongst the biggest of 'em, but they don't seem to have much to work on. It's the public coming in that spoils things. Did you ever see anything like the bidding for that washstand, and that there little easy? It's crool, I call it. Pos'ively crool."

"I expect Waller knows what he's up to," said Meadshire. "He belongs to a good firm."

"Ah, now, that's just it. I've nothing to say against Waller. I've known him for a good many years, and in his own line he's a good man and deserves to get on. There's nobody in the trade as'll spot a fake sooner than Waller; or sell one either. He's worth money to the firm. and they didn't lose by giving him a partnership. But when it comes to an emergency Waller's likely to lose his 'ead. He's in an emergency now, and he don't know whether to follow instructions or use his judgment."

"I suppose he's been instructed to buy in certain things, and given *carte blanche*."

"Well, I wouldn't take such instructions if it was me. There's no sense in it. A customer tells you he wants certain things and there's no limit. D'rectly other people get to know that they run you up for the fun of the thing.

It's what 'appened with that there washstand. Waller was quite right to let 'em 'ave it, but he didn't do it in the proper way. He should have left off with a snap, as if he'd meant to give 'em one, 'stead of as if he was frightened by 'em. Then the laugh would have been on his side, and they wouldn't 'ave tried it on again p'raps. Then he comes rushing out to telephone for further instructions, and runs up against 'is lordship, not knowing who he was, and gives 'im lip, and of course 'e's told politely that the telephone ain't at 'is disposal. I said I'd do it for him. I don't mix myself up with no lordships; I tip the flunkey be'ind 'is back and the thing's done."

The telephone bell trilled sharply. He hurried to it. " That you, Colt & Horn? Oh, yes, trunk call; put me on to them as quick as you can, there's a good girl."

He turned round with the receiver to his ear. " I know pretty well what they'll say," he said, " 'specially if it's old Colt. Oh—— Hullo! Colt & Horn? That you, Mr. Colt? I'm speakin' from the sale at Kemsale, on be'alf of Mr. Waller. They're runnin' 'im up, Mr. Colt, like anything. 'E wants to know if 'e's to bid regardless, according to instructions, or exercise 'is own discretion. He's 'ad to pay—— What? Yes. Yes. Well, he knows all that, Mr. Colt. But he says the instructions were explicit, and he doesn't like to go behind 'em without 'aving it quite understood. Yes. Yes. Well, it ain't going to be as easy as that, Mr. Colt. 'E's just as likely as not to be run up a hundred pounds for a thing that's only worth five. They're in that spirit, you know. If he's not going to be at liberty to let 'em in every now and then—— What? Yes. Yes. Well, I think you had better do that, Mr. Colt. Then it won't be your responsibility. Righto. I'll 'old the line."

He turned round again. " He's going to telephone to

his client," he said. "That'll put him right, whatever happens."

"Who is his client?" asked Meadshire.

"Ah, that'd be telling, wouldn't it? But to be quite honest with you, I don't know. I fancy from what Waller told me, it's somebody who's going to buy the place when it's put up. At any rate the things he buys are to remain here for the present. He's bought 'alf the 'ouse, as far as I can see."

"Well, look here. Tell Mr. Colt that there are some things that were left in the sale by mistake, and the family of the late owner wants to buy them in. If he'll come to an arrangement about them they won't run him up."

His tone had changed. The man looked at him with a trace of his former suspicion. "Oh, you've got to do with the family after all, then. I thought from the way you spoke you belonged to the trade."

"Well, this is trade business, isn't it? Go on. Tell Colt what I say; or let me speak to him."

The man grumbled, but did as he was asked, not without delay and difficulty from the telephone. "Oh, Mr. Colt, sorry to trouble you again. There's a cove 'ere acting for the family. Better ask if he can 'ave some of the things he wants. Eh?"

He turned with a grin. "Old Colt don't mince his words when he's annoyed. You oughter told me what you wanted when I first got through to him."

The end of it was that a message was sent to Waller that he'd had his instructions and was not to play the fool.

"Did he tell his client what I told you?" asked Meadshire.

"Yes, and got a flea in his ear for bothering him. He'd been told what to do; if he couldn't do it there were plenty

of other people who would. Well, I'll be getting back to
Waller."

He hurried from the room, and Meadshire followed him
more slowly. He felt suddenly angry. He had had his
fun, and because he had been intent on his fun he had
missed his chance. Some of his anger was directed against
himself. But as he went back into the sale-room he determined that he would fight this unknown personage, who
seemed to have made his decisions somewhat prematurely.

He was going to buy the whole place, was he? Con-
found him! Meadshire had already refused to consider
an offer for the whole place as it stood, which had been
made to him through his solicitor. He had not wanted
some rich fellow to walk in and take possession of Kemsale
just as it was. His mind was a swirling mass of contra-
dictions about Kemsale. He was relieved to get rid of
the burden of the great useless house, but prepared to
hate anybody who would take it off his shoulders and pay
him for it. He had already sold valuable pictures, and
other rare things, out of it, at different times, received what
amounted in the aggregate to a handsome fortune for
them, and got rid of the money with a light heart. You
couldn't afford to keep family portraits that would sell for
ten thousand pounds apiece in these days, or articles of
vertu that you hardly ever looked at. When the Kemsale
tazza had been sold at Christie's for seven thousand pounds,
Meadshire had said: " Now there's a thing that has cost
us a pound a day to have in the house. Perhaps I've looked
at it once a year. That makes three hundred and fifty
pounds a look. It isn't worth it." But most of the money
had gone to redeem past loans and their colossal interest,
and the rest had been carried by Pickles, a horse that had
run second in the Cesarewitch instead of first.

There are people who want money for its own sake;

there are others who want it so, that they can acquire possessions; there are others again who want it so that they can spend it on the amusements of the moment, and with these the spending of money often becomes an amusement in itself. Money burns holes in their pockets; they can't bear to have it lying idle, or even saved up for an occasion on which they may have a use for it. These are of the sort who light their pipes with banknotes in the early days of a gold-rush, or break all the bottles in a bar, and pay for them afterwards. Meadshire would have been quite capable of performing either of those feats. He had committed many hardly less foolish, and had gained satisfaction from them. Nobody knew where all his money had gone; he did not know himself. He had kept race-horses, but chiefly because racing will get rid of money almost faster than any other pursuit. He had no love for horses at all; his tastes were mechanical, where they had any room to grow, under the shade of that vast obsession of spending. They were hardly even extravagant, apart from the necessity of getting rid of money. He dressed like a *chauffeur,* and not the smartest sort of *chauffeur* either. He had fallen under the influence of drink at an early age, but he did not care for expensive wines, although he preferred that the friends he entertained so lavishly should always drink them; nor particularly for expensive food. He had really been at his happiest in the early days of motoring, when there was always some tinkering to be done whenever you took out a car. During this time he had actually lived within his income, seemed to have lost his unhappy taste for drink, and begun to look like a young man again. But the phase had not lasted; the ruling passion was too strong. His father died, and he inherited money that had come from his grandmother. He ran through that, and was deep in the mire again, when his grandfather died. Revenues by that time had begun to shrink, but there was more than enough for a careful man to have played as big a part as Marquis of Meadshire as any of his forbears. Meadshire had no wish to play that sort of part, and it had taken him only ten years to bring his house to the ground, with nothing to show for it but a series of follies.

But was he so ready to give up that place in the world of which he had made light? As far as it rested on possessions he laughed at the idea of its affecting him in any way.

But he would have nobody living at Kemsale, surrounded by the family gods of the Meadshires, if he could prevent it.

The sale had reached Lady Grace's rooms.

" The West Boudoir, gentlemen. Lot 542. Axminster pile bordered carpet, twenty by eighteen. What bids? "

Wall roused himself, and his re-entrance into the bidding aroused a hum of amusement. The carpet fell to him.

So did the curtains for three tall windows, after both had been bid up to more than their sale value.

The Squire was now fussing and fuming, and the light of battle was in Meadshire's eyes.

" But I don't mind those things much," said Grace. " It is my writing-table I want chiefly, and the china; and especially the pictures. I must have the pictures, if I can't get anything else."

" Lot 544. Buhl and ormolu writing-table. Period Louis Quinze. What offers? "

Waller was determined to have that. So was Meadshire, and the bids rattled up without pause till they reached two hundred pounds. Then the Squire made himself heard. " It's perfect folly," he said angrily. " Grace, you had better be content with the portraits, if they are determined to have all the furniture."

But Meadshire had already prodded his man up to three hundred pounds.

Waller got it at five hundred and twenty. Meadshire was now furious and lowering. " He shall pay through the nose for everything," he said. " And when we come to the pictures we'll break him."

Waller mopped his brow and bid doggedly for one thing after the other, paying enormous prices for everything, but getting everything at the end. A sort of hush had come over the room, and only the two voices were heard sharply answering one another, while the auctioneer looked on impassively, and when the other voice ceased, knocked with his hammer once, mentioned Waller's name and the price, and went on to the next lot.

Poor Grace saw her cherished possessions go one after the other—all the delicate pieces of china that she had got together here, the water-colours that she loved, the gold and silver and tortoiseshell toys of a woman's pretty room. She had removed the things that had actually been given to her, her own books amongst them, but all the rest had always been considered hers, and only her scruples had made her leave it, to be thus haggled over in shameful publicity. Long before the contest was over she would have given up everything rather than go on with it. All these grinning open-mouthed people knew what the struggle was about now. She stood in sight of them, a woman whose shy privacies were invaded. And her brother in his enraged advocacy of her cause only added to her distress. He had moved up to one of the tables and stood over the man who was bidding for them, all but taking the bids out of his mouth. Everybody now knew who he was, and regarded him with open curiosity. He should have kept away altogether, in this hour of his disgrace. But he was making himself the most prominent figure in the room.

They came to two tinted pencil drawings of Grace's grandfather and grandmother. They had been "taken" soon after their marriage, and showed a handsome gay young man and a sweet-faced girl, with a look of Grace herself. They were by a well-known artist of the time, who had also painted the later full-length portraits of the same pair which hung elsewhere, but hardly so successfully. The drawings had their value, but it was not an extravagant one. Fifty pounds apiece would have been a good price for them.

They were put up together, and were run up to a hundred in advances of ten pounds. Then up to five hundred with a sudden jump into fifties. The onlookers stared open-mouthed. The bids had followed one another without a moment's hesitation on either side.

Waller faltered and looked round furtively at his adversary, as if imploring him to have mercy on him. Meadshire's face was red and scowling. He had pushed his agent aside, and stood at the end of the table glowering over the crowd of buyers as if he would have annihilated the lot of them. The party from Kencote were now quite in the background, hidden by the crowding mass of spectators.

Waller bid five hundred and fifty. Meadshire rapped out "Six hundred," himself. Waller paused again. The new voice, gruff and loud, aroused a general murmur. There was some giggling encouragement of Waller to go on; but there were more voices advising him to "let him have 'em."

The auctioneer raised his hammer. "Seven hundred," said Waller, before he could let it fall.

"Eight hundred," came from Meadshire, in a voice louder than before.

Waller paused and looked around again, meeting nothing

but rows of faces with every eye in them bent upon him. The auctioneer raised his hammer again.

" Nine hundred."

" A thousand."

Waller hesitated a moment, shrugged his shoulders, and returned to his catalogue. It was a confession of defeat. The hammer fell, and Meadshire pushed his way through the crowd and stalked out of the room, pursued by a volley of cheering, which put the finishing touch to his fury.

CHAPTER III

LITTLE KEMSALE

LITTLE KEMSALE lay just outside the village that clustered about the west gates of the great house. It was the great house in miniature, built at the same time, and of the same white stone. It stood in a clearing of the beech wood that rolled down the hill behind it, but though on a considerably lower level than the great house, of which it was a sort of appanage, it was still above the level of the country that faced it, and commanded a fine spreading view. A soft sloping lawn, much more attractive than the flat rectangle of the great house, divided it from the road, which ran under a sunk fence high enough to preserve its privacy. It merged on either side into the russet-carpeted shade of the beeches. Originally the carriage drive, going in at one gate and out at the other, through the trees, had led to a door in the middle of the façade, but at some period that arrangement had been altered. A hall had been made and a porch added on the west; and the east drive had been done away with. So now the gravel that lay between the house and the lawn, masked by shrubs from the drive, made a pleasant place to sit out on. The dining-room on one side and the drawing-room on the other, with the room that had once been the hall between them, all had tall windows reaching nearly to the ground. They were spacious well-proportioned rooms, and in the summer, with their easy access to the quiet garden and their wide south-ward view of blue country, very attractive. So they were in the winter, when they were close-curtained and lamp-lit, and surrounded by the deep stillness of the country night. In the daytime their large expanse of glass gave them an air slightly bleak, though they caught whatever sun might be shining. The front of the house was much overgrown by creepers, and its likeness to the great house, many of the points of which had been copied in its exterior, was lessened by them. People driving by, seated high enough to catch a glimpse of Little Kemsale, found it worth looking at as a specimen of the small country houses of England, which are often so much more attractive than the big ones. Wistaria, clematis, Banksian roses, ceanothus, and other flowering or evergreen plants framed all its windows in their several seasons; the lower ones were provided with gaily striped awnings; great tubs of agapanthus, azaleas, hydrangeas, pink geraniums, stood along the broad space of carefully rolled gravel and on the edge of the lawn. Hammock chairs and wicker tables might be seen invitingly grouped there, and the observer might sometimes surprise a tea party, half in and half out of one of the open windows.

Such an one, as he drove on along the shady road that curved round the shoulder of the hill, might have found himself wondering whether the owners or inhabitants of such a house were appreciative of their happy lot, or fitted to enjoy it. Those who have that embracing taste for houses, so that they can scarcely pass one with any attractions, large or small, without imagining themselves living in it, are apt to forget the Horatian dictum that a change of sky does not bring about a change of mind. Perhaps the majority of those who live in the houses that they are inclined to envy are not appreciably the happier because of their surroundings. The troubles of unrequited love, ill-health, debt, disappointed ambition, and all the pack of worries incidental to daily existence are not sensibly lightened by the possession of a beautiful house. House-envy-ing, as a pursuit, can only be carried on satisfactorily by imagining the mind permanently attuned to its surroundings; and it is a pity that the agents cannot guarantee that the amenities they have to offer in the way of peace and comfort shall operate within as well as without.

Nevertheless, there are some to whom the possession of a house in which they can take a pride and pleasure, be it large or small, is a constant, every-day enhancement of life's interests, and at this time the occupants of Little Kemsale were amongst them.

They were a Captain and Mrs. Douglas Irving, who had already lived there for two years, and hoped to live there for the remainder of a lease of seven, fourteen, or twenty-one years, and longer still if they should be permitted. They had youth, health, and a sufficiency of income; two small, naughty, but most engaging children; and tastes and habits which could all be gratified by the manner of life they had chosen.

Douglas Irving was in the middle thirties, and his wife in the late twenties. He had retired from the Service two years before upon the death of his father, who had left him a fortune of between thirty and forty thousand pounds, after having told him persistently ever since he had first mentioned the subject that he might expect about five hundred a year and not a penny more. It was about what the old gentleman had spent himself, living in rooms in London near his club, ever since the death of his wife in Douglas's childhood. He may have saved the rest until it had rolled up to the respectable sum mentioned, or he may have amused his leisure with investments that had turned out luckily. At any rate, there was no doubt about the money, and Douglas Irving could never think of the day in which he had learnt of what had come to him without a glow of memory.

It had made such a difference to him. He had always been hard up, and had always hated being hard up. At school he had had less pocket-money than other boys, at Sandhurst and in his regiment a smaller allowance than his fellows. And he had had no happy home life as a child, except for the first few dimly remembered years in India, when his mother had been alive. He had been sent home to an aunt who had married a clergyman with a living in a poor London suburb, and little to supplement it with, and he had spent his dreary school holidays there for the most part, and some of his leaves, when he was too " broke " to amuse himself elsewhere.

He had enjoyed soldiering, and especially the two years he had spent in South Africa, when he had been enabled to put straight his already slightly dislocated finances. He had been a very young subaltern then, and had developed a military keenness that had somewhat evaporated later on, when he had settled down to a pottering life in a garrison town. Then he had obtained a five years' billet as adjutant to a Territorial regiment, and that had been better, for he had had more money to spend, and opportunities for sport, in a friendly county. But he was already " dipped " again financially when he fell in love with the only child of a lady, the widow of a clergyman, who lived in the seaside town nearest to the one in which he was quartered. It was an eminently suitable match, the girl's birth being about on a level with his own; his father had made no objections to it, but had offered to increase his allowance by a hundred pounds a year, if the girl's mother would make her a like allowance.

It would just " run to it," and he thought himself very fortunate, though his debts, about which he said nothing, somewhat dimmed the bright prospect. He thought him-

self more fortunate still when he discovered that his *fiancée*
had about three hundred a year of her own, and would
have rather more than double that when her mother died.
He seemed to have come into wealth unlimited, or at least
to have the happy prospect of furnishing a charming little
country cottage and living in it in the most ideal fashion.
His tastes already inclined to a quiet, domestic, country existence, with as much country sport to salt it as could be
obtained on the least possible expenditure; and he was very
much in love with the girl he was going to marry. He had
loved her when he thought she had nothing, and did not
love her the less because her small income enabled them
to start their married life in a way that delighted both of
them together.

But the debts soon began to overshadow their happiness.
The two children came, one a year and the other two years
after they were married, and even without them it is doubtful whether the scale upon which they lived in their pretty
creeper-smothered bandbox would have enabled them to
keep their heads above water. Beatrix Irving had a head
for management, but little experience. Their income was
about the same as hers and her mother's had been, and they
lived in a smaller house, though in a more elaborate way,
with much entertaining of men friends, and many little
extravagances such as she had had no previous experience
of. She trusted her husband with the apportionment of
their income, and never exceeded the allowances for the
spending of which she herself was responsible; and she
did not like to suggest to him any curtailment of the expenditure which kept him so gay and happy that the little
house was full of sunshine for her, in spite of the shadow
that was creeping over it. Then the children came, and she
was too much occupied to take upon herself the initiation of
a different scale of expenditure altogether, which would

soon have become absolutely necessary but for her mother's death.

This was a great grief to her, and her health, after the birth of her second child, was not good for a time. She allowed herself to drift with the current, and only mildly opposed the taking of a larger house during the remaining year of her husband's adjutancy. They had already out-grown their cottage, and the house was a very nice one. If they liked it they could stay on there, for Douglas Irving had already decided that he would not go back to his regiment. He was very sympathetic with her over her unexpected loss, but " in a way " it was " providential," and with the addition of the handsome old-fashioned furni-ture and effects that his wife had inherited, and their increased income, his own genuine sorrow was assuaged by the inauguration of the new house, and also by the ability to settle old accounts.

But the shadow soon closed over the new house, as it had closed over the old one. There was a stable and a large garden to keep up, to say nothing of the nurseries, and not nearly enough money to do that and all the rest with, unless the money had been carefully husbanded, which it wasn't. The appointment came to an end, and there was so much less income. They let their house and went abroad for a year. Then Colonel Irving died, all the difficulties were swept away, and a new and most delightful life opened up before them.

Such had been the history of this fortunate young couple up to the time of their settling at Little Kemsale, and perhaps Beatrix Irving realised exactly how fortunate they had been. Her husband yielded to her in no way in gratitude for the change that had now come over their life and prospects, and felt it all the more because his past presented itself to him as a perpetual and undeserved struggle against adversity. If he had seen it in its true light, it had been nothing but a succession of generous chances such as come to very few spendthrifts. For there was no doubt that Douglas Irving was a spendthrift, although not of the neck or nothing type of Meadshire. He was of our second sort—those who want money for the sake of possessions. He loved a house and its contents, and the power of adding to them. That was the necessary background of his life. And he wanted money for the sake of opportunities, not to throw away, as Meadshire did. In fact, when he came into his compact little fortune, he suddenly became careful about money. Many spendthrifts have that contradictory faculty. The Meadshires would gaily dissipate in a year a sum that would keep them handsomely for the rest of their lives, with no disturbance of mind as to what should come after. The Irvings would never know a happy moment in dissipating a fortune, unless they had some hopes that another would follow it. They do not dissipate fortunes at a stroke; they eat into them. And all the time they writhe under the troubles of debt, and are well aware that nothing they seek to enjoy is worth the price they pay for it, or is enjoyable at all unless it has the quality of permanence.

So Douglas Irving conceived of himself as having thoroughly learnt his lesson, by a series of awkward strokes of fate, and by long periods of life in which his enjoyments had been almost completely spoilt by the consciousness that he was heading for catastrophe. He would indeed be a fool if he overspent an income large enough to afford him everything he really cared about in life, when there was no longer any prospect of that income being increased. Of course, he could have done very well with twice as much, and it was necessary to be careful. But a wise man cuts his coat according to his cloth, and if the cloth is long enough even finds some satisfaction in the process. Irving now kept his accounts carefully, and took a good deal of pleasure in doing so. He even saved money every year—not very much, but enough to give him the comfortable feeling of living well within his income and providing for Jimbo's education. His pass-book was no longer a reproach, but a beneficence, and it was exciting to enter into an occasional little speculation—always with the " margin," never with money allotted to other purposes. He had turned over a new leaf altogether, and shuddered at the thought of the old ones; and it seemed extremely unlikely that he would ever jeopardise his present substantial happiness by reverting to his old carelessness about money.

An extra piece of luck had befallen him at the time he had taken Little Kemsale. Meadshire had suddenly decided that he would let his shooting. It was part of his fantastic way of doing things that he decided everything of this sort in a hurry and without any reference to other decisions. He would not let Kemsale with it, and Little Kemsale he had already let about a month before. His agent was in despair, and came to Irving to ask him to sell back his lease. " How on earth can I let eighteen thousand acres of shooting without a house? " he asked. Irving refused to surrender his lease, but thought he might help him otherwise. He knew of a rich bachelor who was on the look-out for a shoot; if he took this one he might work it from Little Kemsale.

He ran up to London, full of eagerness. His friend came down with him and surveyed the prospect. Eventually an arrangement was come to by which Fanshawe, the rich friend, and two others took the shooting. Irving was to manage it for them and they were to pay their share of expenses whenever they and their friends came down. The arrangement was to be made for three years. Meadshire objected to this, but gave way suddenly when negotiations were on the point of breaking off altogether.

The result, as it affected Irving, was that he had all the fun of a big shoot at no expense whatever, and practically saved his rent besides. It may be imagined that he did not love Little Kemsale the less because these sporting amenities had become unexpectedly attached to it.

On an October evening, about a month after the sale at Kemsale, Douglas and Beatrix Irving were walking home together. They had been to interview keepers about the arrangements for the next day, for their friends were coming down that evening for the first big manœuvre amongst the pheasants.

It was a lovely mild evening, with an illusive air of spring in it. They were both in the highest spirits. Things were going so well with them, and there was not a care on the horizon. And they both looked forward to the entertainment immediately ahead. The house would be crammed to the uttermost, and both of them enjoyed that thoroughly.

They swung along the road at a sharp pace, chattering about the coming pleasures. Beatrix had entirely recovered from her weakness of some years before. She was full of health and vigour in these days, and was almost as much in the open air as her husband. With her slim figure, in its cleanly cut tweeds, she looked no more than a girl. Douglas was straight and spare too, and still kept his look of youth, although he was approaching his thirty-fifth birthday. He was a good-looking fellow, of the well-set-up military type, with crisp gingery hair and a close-cut moustache to match, over a mouth full of strong white teeth. He had never known a day's illness in his life, not even a twinge of toothache. The gods had showered their gifts on him, and it must be said that at the present time he was grateful to them, though he did not recognise the full measure of their lavishness.

The two of them lingered in the garden, under a sky of amber and jade. They were as keen on the garden as on everything else at Little Kemsale, and just now there were borders being reconstituted and flowering shrubs planted. Douglas slipped his arm into his wife's as they examined the long double border that led through the middle of the garden behind the house, and found fault with what had been done while they were out. They were the best of friends, these two. Their continued pleasure in one another's society was another gift of the gods, but one which they took as a matter of course.

They had tea in Douglas's room, which had been built for a billiard room when the house had been rearranged. It was not big enough for a billiard-table and the furniture of a comfortable sitting-room besides, so he had made a library of it, for he read a good deal, and liked buying books and arranging them on his shelves. He had bought a good many at the sale at Kemsale, and brought his bookshelves round to a return that jutted out into the room, by the door. The work had just been finished, and all the books, new and old, arranged to suit the extension. And two or three of the prints that he had also bought from Kemsale were hung on the back of the new bookcase, which was covered with red canvas to match the walls of the room. Douglas was enchanted with the effect. The masking of the door made the room, which was large enough to benefit by such an arrangement, ever so much cosier. The handsome binding of many of the books from Kemsale added to the appearance of the well-filled shelves. He sat on the cushioned fender in front of the fire, with his hands in his pockets, and looked round him with deep satisfaction.

" It's a great success, isn't it? " he said. " The only

thing about it is that the room is so jolly now that there's nothing more to do to it."

That was the fly in the ointment. The pleasure of " making " a room, to those who have those tastes, is keener than the pleasure of living in it.

Beatrix laughed. She liked " nice " things, but was without the driving acquisitive taste. " We shall have enough books now to keep us quiet for a long time to come," she said.

Douglas rose and went up to the shelves. " I don't know," he said. " There are a good many we haven't got that we ought to have. I rather wish I had bid up for that Pentland Stevenson."

" Oh, my dear boy, it went up to a terrific price; and you've got all Stevenson."

" Not quite all, and not in a good edition. That one is sure to go up in value still further. That's the best of buying good editions. They're jolly to have, and you can sell 'em for more than you gave, if you want to. I say, it's jolly getting this whole set of ' Punches,' isn't it? Fancy having them all bound in red morocco like that! I must ask Meadshire where it was done. We shall have to get the new ones bound in the same way."

" I don't suppose he knows," said Beatrix. " It would be done by the groom of the chambers, just because it had always been done in that way; and probably Lord Mead- shire never looked at them. It's perfectly appalling the waste that went on in that house. There was nobody to check anything."

Douglas returned to the fireside, where Beatrix was now busy with the tea-table. Meadshire and Kemsale were perennial sources of conversation.

" In a way," said Douglas—this was a very frequent opening of his—" in a way, I can understand Meadshire being quite relieved at getting rid of a great overgrown place like Kemsale. You might almost say it was never really his. It was chock full of jolly things, but they had all been put there by somebody else. He just lived amongst them, when he was there, and didn't care a bit about them."

"I'm not sure that he didn't. He was very keen on getting the things that he and Grace wanted for the Herons' Nest, and furious when they bid up against him in that extraordinary way."

"Well, that's just what I say. The Herons' Nest is their own, in a way that Kemsale never was. Of course they take tremendous interest in it, and in everything they put into it. It even gives Meadshire something to do that he enjoys, though it isn't one of his chief tastes—that sort of thing—and he'll probably get tired of it when it's all done."

"Poor Lord Meadshire!"

"He's nobody's enemy but his own. You were going to say it; I know you were."

Beatrix paused, looked slightly indignant, and then laughed, and Douglas bent down to her and kissed her. It was one of the amiable habits of this couple to take each other up in this way when any obvious remark seemed about to be made.

When the tea was nearly over, the two children rushed in like a tornado. Woozle, whose baptismal name was Emily Beatrice, had reached the tooth-shedding age, but was otherwise of exceptional and, as it seemed to her father, even of super-earthly beauty. She had very dark eyes and hair, and a pair of reedy brown legs, of which her afternoon costume displayed the greater proportion. She hurled herself at her father, who had just time enough to put down his teacup in order to receive the assault, and he hugged her and rumpled her and turned her over his

shoulder and back again in a way that made her shriek
with joy, and then threw himself into his deep easy-chair
with her on his knee.

In the meantime Jimbo, who was all white sailor suit, blue
eyes, and lacquer-coloured hair, had been turning somer-
saults in the middle of the room, with vociferous demands
for notice between each event. When he had nearly upset
the tea-table his mother caught him, laid him wriggling
across her knee, and essayed to slap that part of him which
seemed to have been made for the purpose; but failing in
this intention pulled him upright and hugged him instead.

" You'll spoil that young ruffian before you've done with
him," said Douglas.

" You'll spoil that little minx long before you've done
with *her*," retorted Beatrix. " We are both very unwise
parents. Now then, Jimbo, tell mummy everything you
have been doing this afternoon with Lizette, in French."

" Which mummy won't understand," said Douglas.

CHAPTER IV

THE SHOOTING PARTY

THE shooting party arrived with a cheerful bustle in comfortable time to settle themselves for dinner. It consisted of John Fanshawe, a large good-humoured rather lazy bachelor of no occupation; William Bradgate, who had been in Douglas Irving's regiment and was now of the Stock Exchange, with his wife; and Charles Wesbrook, a successful hard-working barrister, with a slow smile and a confidential manner. There were also of the party the Rector of Kemsale and the agent to the Meadshire property, both of whom were to shoot with them on the morrow.

The Rector was a cousin of Meadshire's—the Honourable and Reverend James Compton. He was not clerical, either in manner or appearance—a very tall thin man of about forty, with sleek black hair well brushed back, and a cynical type of face permanently decorated with an eyeglass. He had no particular love for his work, and no particular aptitude for it, but did what had to be done in the way of duty conscientiously, and was well enough liked by his parishioners. He was a bachelor, and reputed rich, both from the emoluments of his living, which were substantial, and from private sources. He lived in some style and considerable comfort in his charming rectory house, from which he hunted regularly throughout the season. Apart from sport, he was something of a recluse; it was not very often that Beatrix Irving could get him to accept an invitation to dinner, and he hardly ever dined out at any of the country houses round about. He was an omnivorous

48

reader, and if he could ever be induced to talk, in congenial company, exhibited a mind stocked with all kinds
of knowledge. He seemed to forget nothing that he had
ever read, and had marvellous powers of assimilating and
collating his knowledge. But he made no use of it, had
never published a line, or written anything except some
quite ordinary sermons. Douglas Irving was a little
afraid of him. With his encyclopædic knowledge, he was
a wet blanket upon his own facile excursions into the field
of mental culture, and did not respond too heartily to
friendly advances. But he was rather proud of him too,
and recognised to the full his remarkable abilities. " That
fellow knows more than any fellow I've ever met," he
would say to those to whom he wished to exhibit him. " You
try him on any subject—I don't care what it is—and you'll
find he knows more about it than you do. Jolly good man
on a horse too," he would usually add, " and knows all the
country like a book. You'll.never find him far behind
when it comes to the end of things."

Captain Herbert Fuller, Meadshire's agent, was a small,
compact man of about sixty. He was rather a pathetic
figure to those who knew of his life and immediate surroundings. He had married rather beneath him, and his
wife had been trying to persuade everybody ever since that
she had married beneath her. She was extravagant, in a
yellow-haired towny sort of way, and had a daughter of
one and twenty whom she was training to follow in her
footsteps. They lived in a converted farmhouse, which
would have been an ideal country home if Mrs. Fuller had
had any idea of how to make it so. But there was no comfort or enjoyment inside it, at least for the poor little
peaceably minded Captain Fuller, who was obliged to spend
on it the whole of his hardly earned income, and had constant ado not to exceed it. Mrs. Fuller went by the name

of Tottie behind her back, and all the ladies of the neighbourhood regarded her as a scourge. Some of them were sorry for her daughter, Irene, agreeing that she had not had much chance; but she was dull and slow at the best, and by this time she had been generally given up, as material to be worked upon. Mrs. Fuller had been making ludicrous attempts during the past five years to marry her to the Rector, who could hardly bring himself to be civil to either of them. Poor little Herbert, as Captain Fuller was usually called, would never have been allowed to dine at Little Kemsale *en garçon* as he was now doing, and Beatrix Irving would never have spoilt such a party by asking his women folk, if they had been there to be asked. But, fortunately, Tottie and Irene were amusing themselves shopping in London, and poor little Herbert, with his neat little grey moustache and sharp decisive speech, was quite ready to expand to his small limits, and play his part in a company consisting chiefly of men.

"Well, Kemsale is sold," he told them, standing before the fire in the drawing-room, and looking sharply from one to the other. "I had the news this afternoon. But I can't tell you who's the buyer yet."

"Oh, I can," said Bradgate. "I heard it in the City this morning. It's Armitage Brown. Douglas, my boy, if you play your cards well, you'll get tips that will put money in your pocket all the time."

There was a general exclamation. This was news indeed, and gave matter for discussion during the greater part of the dinner to which they now went in.

Every now and then there arises on the horizon a man of business who captures the imagination of the whole country; a man who stands for brilliant success and opportunities for unlimited wealth. Armitage Brown was that man at this time—a self-made man, as most of them are,

a keen and masterful financier, with some big affairs to his
credit, and as yet no trail of deluded victims hanging on to
his operations. And indeed there seemed to be no reason,
in his case, to anticipate the ultimate downfall that not
infrequently overtakes these Napoleons of finance. His
operations were large and bold, but they were clean and
sound enough, or at least had attracted none of the criticism
that would have been eager to pounce upon them if there
had been any points to direct itself against. And the
public at this time was cautious about such operators, and
apt to be suspicious of them. The last one had gone down
heavily, and dragged thousands with him. Armitage Brown
had a difficult path to tread, but so far he had trodden it
without a slip.

Bradgate had a good deal to say about him. "He's
more like one of the big American fellows, the Carnegies
and Pierpont Morgans, than our Jabez Balfours and
Whittaker Wrights," he said. "He's got the eye for it;
sees money in everything."

"The rubber boom started him, didn't it?" asked
Wesbrook.

"Oh, he'd made a pile long before that. But he probably more than doubled it over rubber. All his things
were sound, too; that's what gave him his reputation.
And he made another scoop when the slump came; he knew
his markets. He's a wily bird, Mr. Armitage Brown.
He'll be a big little man one of these days, bigger than he
is now."

Most of the company round the dinner-table were anxious
for news of Mr. Armitage Brown on his private and
domestic side, which would affect them more than his public
—his wealth being taken for granted. But there was
very little news forthcoming.

"I've seen him in the City," said Bradgate. "He's a

middle-aged fellow with a heavy jowl and a stubby moustache, nothing very remarkable to look at. I don't fancy anybody knows much about him in his happy home. He seems to have kept that dark, so far."

"He has a great big house out at Hillgrove," said Wesbrook.

"Ah, yes, in the suburbs. And now he's ready to cut a dash as the country gentleman. You'll be having some changes here, Douglas, my boy."

Poor little Herbert had been soaking in the information afforded with an ever-lengthening face. "I hope he won't be trying new-fangled experiments with the land," he said.

"Of course he will," said Bradgate. "You'll be taught your business, Fuller. I bet he'll make the land pay, too, whatever experiments he tries."

Poor little Herbert's face grew longer still. It seemed possible that under the circumstances he might not be there to learn his business over again. And if he were dismissed, what chance had he, at his age, of getting another job?

"Then we know now who it was that bought all that furniture at the sale," said Beatrix. "Of course, if it was a man as rich as that, he wouldn't mind what he paid for it."

This was a new light. It moved the Rector to speech. "I don't imagine I shall get on with a man like that," he said slowly.

The rest looked at him. This was important.

"Meadshire telephoned to his agents," he went on, "that he wanted to buy in a few family things, and Brown, or whoever it was, told them to buy them all the same."

"Yes, that's Master Armitage all over," said Bradgate. "What he wants he's going to have."

"What about the shoot?" asked Fanshawe.

"Well, he can't turn us out of that this season. I don't suppose we shall get it again, though. Master Armitage will want to learn to shoot himself. I don't suppose he's ever done such a thing before. When's he coming down, Fuller?"

Poor little Herbert came out of a painful reverie with a jump. "I don't know," he said. "I just heard that the sale was complete—the house and all the farms."

"What an appalling prospect!" said the Rector.

His tone brought a short pause. It showed him to have considered the news in its entirety, and to be pronouncing upon it. His character and position were such that the way it struck him gave food for conjecture as to future developments.

"It will make a good deal of difference to all of us," said Douglas.

Mrs. Bradgate broke in. She was a lively pretty little woman, some years younger than her husband. "You ought to have a lot more fun than you did when Lord Meadshire was here," she said. "You can't say that *he* is much loss."

There was another pause, such as to cause her to look round to see whether she had said something that she ought not to have said. She met her husband's eyes directed towards her with humorous tolerance. "Oh, yes, you've put your foot in it all right," he said. "Mr. Compton is Lord Meadshire's cousin."

The slight tension was relieved. Compton laughed with the rest. "You needn't mind, Mrs. Bradgate," he said. "I don't in the least. My cousin's follies have been as annoying to me as to everybody else."

It was not quite what he might have been expected to say. Opinion towards Meadshire was tolerant at this time. He had at least paid the full price for his follies, and should be considered immune from criticism until he committed further ones. Besides, as Beatrix Irving had said with such originality, he was nobody's enemy but his own, and he had certainly never acted with enmity towards any of those present.

Poor little Herbert came up loyally to his defence. "He was a very good landlord," he said. "Lots of landowners who wanted more money out of their estates could have done all sorts of things to get it or save it that he never did. Everything has been kept up, till the last minute."

Perhaps some of the dislike that Compton felt for the persecuting Tottie extended vicariously to that lady's husband; perhaps he merely resented a hint of contradiction. He looked at the speaker not at all amiably. "He never gave a moment's thought to his duties as a landlord," he said. "You know that as well as I do. He just let everything slide."

Poor little Herbert was taken aback by this direct attack, and subsided, fingering his moustache. Douglas Irving came to his rescue, amiably, but with a shade of nervousness. "He knew that he could safely leave everything to Fuller," he said.

Compton turned to him. His face was pale, and his jaw set. "I've kept pretty much to myself," he said, "while all this business has been going on. I've been bottling up what I feel about it. Now I'll tell you, straight out. I think that for a man in Meadshire's position, the way he's dealt with this property is a betrayal of trust. Everybody is inclined to pat him on the back now, and say he's done the right thing. He was in debt, and he's given up everything. What right had he to give up everything? If a general in the field gets into a mess, are you going to pat him on the back if he slinks out of it and gives up his troops?"

He threw himself back in his chair. The pause that followed was very awkward indeed. He had spoken with heat, advancing a disconcerting point of view. No one wanted to blame Meadshire; no one wanted to discuss the ethics of landowning.

Mrs. Bradgate broke the silence. " I feel very sorry for poor Lord Meadshire," she said feelingly.

There was a moment's tension, and then everybody laughed, except Compton, who glared at her.

"Now we are going to have this company promoter foisted on us," he went on. " He'll ride roughshod over everything and everybody. Nothing will be the same as it was before. And that's what Meadshire has brought us to."

No one in the room had heard him talk like this before, or indeed express himself with warmth upon any subject whatever. Douglas Irving was impressed by his manner to vague discomfort.

"Oh, well, perhaps he won't be so bad," he said. " He won't want to upset people."

Compton made no reply, except a shrug of the shoulders.

Charles Wesbrook entered the lists in his slow deliberative way. " That sort of thing is going on all over England," he said, " the old men going out and the new men coming in. It doesn't work so very badly. The new men make mistakes occasionally, but they learn, and before you know where you are, they're the old men in their turn."

Compton roused himself again. Evidently, anything but complete accord with his opinions irritated him. " It's only the people who are bred and born to it who know how to deal with land," he said dogmatically. " Every time a property passes from the hands of those who understand land, and comes into the hands of those who don't, the country goes back."

Nobody was ready to draw fire upon himself by disputing this proposition. Mrs. Bradgate did so by inquiring: "That's what you call High Toryism, isn't it?"

She asked the question with engaging innocence, her head a little on one side and her limpid eyes fixed sweetly upon Compton's face. He replied, rather sourly: "It's common sense, which I suppose is the same thing," and then everybody else laughed, once more.

Later on in the evening, when Compton and Fuller had gone home, and the rest of them were round the fire in Douglas's room, the little lady was accused of pulling the Rector's leg.

But she would not acknowledge it. "You always laugh at me, Bill, whenever I try to take part in a serious conversation," she complained. "I believe you think I'm a fool."

"We don't, Mrs. Bill," said Fanshawe. "We think you're a very clever woman. I say, Douglas, that parson of yours is what you call high and dry, eh?"

"I'm a Tory myself," said Wesbrook; "but I hate intolerance."

"He didn't show up very well to-night," Douglas admitted. "He's an extraordinarily clever fellow, really; and a jolly good man on a——"

"It doesn't take much cleverness to repeat all the Tory gags," interrupted Wesbrook. "That's about all he did to-night."

"Oh, well," said Douglas; "he's rather a bore on politics, I admit. But get him on any other subject—I don't care what it is—and there's no fellow who knows more."

"If he thinks in that way about Mr. Armitage Brown," said Beatrix, "they won't get on very well when he comes here."

"As he's so keen on people doing their duty," said Wesbrook, "I should say that a parson's duty is to keep on good terms with his squire."

"I suppose he'll still look on Meadshire as his squire, if he's going on living here," said Fanshawe.

"Well, he's his own squire—in a way," said Douglas. "He bought the patronage of Kemsale from Meadshire, to prevent his selling it elsewhere."

"Then in that case I should think he'd make himself a thorn in the side of Master Armitage," said Bradgate. "I shouldn't be too ready to take sides if I were you, Duggy. Armitage Brown is as rich as Crœsus, and if he's decided that his time has come to set up in an enormous house like Kemsale, there'll probably be some fun going."

The advice fitted in with Douglas's inclinations. "Of course I'm sorry to see Meadshire turned out," he said. "But after all, he's sold the place and got his price. The new man ought to have his chance. It will be rather exciting, finding out what he's like."

"Lord Meadshire is furious at his stopping him getting the things that he and Grace wanted at the sale," said Beatrix. "I don't think he will give him a very warm welcome."

CHAPTER V

ARMITAGE BROWN

On a Sunday afternoon at about this time, Mr. Armitage Brown and his wife and son and daughter were drinking tea in the morning-room of Hillgrove Towers.

Hillgrove Towers was a castellated mansion which had been profusely erected in the middle of the nineteenth century on the site of an older house. It stood in about twenty acres of beautiful grounds, on the side of a hill overlooking the country to the south of London, from the heart of which it was divided by three or four miles of suburbs, which already hemmed it in on three sides and were fast pushing out beyond it on the fourth. The trams ran along the road upon which its lodge gates were situated; Armitage Brown's motor-car deposited him at his office in the City in less than half an hour from the time of his stepping into it at the front door of the Towers, and had been known to come home from a late theatre, when the streets were clear, in a quarter of an hour.

But inside the high walls that surrounded the property there was complete seclusion, and except for the sooty coating on the trunks of trees and the leaves of shrubs, you might have been in a garden in the heart of the country. It was very opulent, in the way of great ranges of glass-houses, elaborate effects of tender flowers in the summer beds, and very carefully tended lawns; but there were sylvan recesses within its limits besides, and a tree-enclosed paddock or two, and a large lake on the lower ground.

These *rura in urbe* are becoming increasingly rare in the immediate outskirts of London. At the time that the pretentious " Towers " had taken the place of the pleasant old rambling house that had stood here, this one had been actually in the country; and a little bit of the country was still preserved within its walls. But outside them there was nothing but a waste of little houses, running in rectangular streets over the ground where there had once been meadows and arable fields belonging to the old house. A few such places have lately been preserved from the fate that has overtaken most of them by the rise of motor-transport. Rich people who like space around them, but have no further leanings towards country life, might be expected to compete eagerly for the possession of them, where they have been made almost as accessible as South Kensington or Campden Hill. But there remains a sort of stigma on suburban life, even where it has almost ceased to become suburban, and few families that inhabit such places as " The Towers " remain in them for more than a generation.

The Browns had lived here for nearly twenty years, and now they were ready to move on. They were a case in point.

Armitage Brown was a self-made man, but he was not sprung from the lowest classes of the community. He had no difficulty with his h's, and had never eaten with his knife. His father had been in business in the City, in connection with produce of some sort, and had even left him some money. He had an elder brother who still carried on the paternal business, and did well with it. Armitage Brown had left school at fourteen and entered a stockbroker's firm, first as office-boy, then as clerk, then as authorized clerk. For ten or twelve years he had remained obscure, one of the many thousand young men

who work in offices in London, and go home every night
to some unknown dwelling-place, in which they live a life
completely separated from that of their working hours.
The degree to which the one life is subordinated to the
other will usually give the degree to which any one of
these young men has it in him to raise himself out of
the ruck.

Armitage Brown married early, on a very small income,
and his three children, one of whom died in infancy, came
quickly, one after the other. He might, at this stage, well
have been immersed in the little interests and anxieties
of his home life, as are many thousands like him. The
difficulty felt by such men as he is often in finding just
that first small sum of money which they can use as a
lever in raising themselves out of the salaried class. To
that extent he had handicapped himself by his early marriage, for the whole of his salary was swamped in current
expenses.

But he was learning, and watching for his chance all
the time. He saw it, and asked his father for money, which
was refused him. He never forgave this, not even when
his father died and left him a couple of thousand pounds.
That sum was nothing to him then. A tenth of it would
have saved him three years of poverty, if he could have
had the use of it at the right time.

It was for three years that he waited for the next chance,
but in the meantime his salary had increased, and his
home expenses had not—not by a penny. His wife knew
nothing of the business side of his life. For all the information he gave her she might have expected him to remain
a poor clerk all his days.

He came home one evening and told her that they could
afford to move into a larger house and keep three servants

instead of one. He was his own master now—had been for a month and more—and was doing well.

Exactly how well he was doing she had not the slightest idea of. Things had begun to march at last. He was only twenty-five, but it seemed to him that he had passed a long lifetime of struggle, with all the chances against him.

The years of watching and waiting, and the ultimate success, from which he never looked back, had, in fact, set their mark on him, and far more than he knew. On the one hand, he had wonderfully perfected his knowledge and judgment, had learnt patience and strong self-restraint. There had been many times when a speculation, hardly even risky, would have put him where he aimed at being. But he would not risk what he had—his reputation, the assured basis of his home—ever so slightly. When he struck, it was with the certainty of succeeding. This holding back of himself, through what seemed at his age long years, while the spirit of adventure in him urged him to make use of his fast-maturing powers, was an achievement of character.

On the other hand, the splitting up of his life into two, begun at that early age, marked the price which most men who make a strong assault upon wealth have to pay for their success. His working hours were full of interest; his home life was stunted and incomplete, for lack of money spent on easing the wheels of its machinery. Ease and enjoyment, these would come later; in the meantime he withdrew his mind from desire of them.

If he could have made his wife a partner in his ambitions no harm need have come of this. But he knew, with the sharp instinctive knowledge of character that was already beginning to develop in him, that she would not agree with him in sacrificing some years of their youth to the chance of large wealth in the future. She was a shade more gently nurtured than he, and while she bore uncomplainingly the poverty to which he condemned her and her children, as well as himself, because she thought it unavoidable, it is doubtful if she would have forgiven him if she had known that he was depriving her of the small yearly sum that would have taken off her shoulders the worst of the burden. He never did tell her that he had been saving money during the greater part of those hard years. She never looked back upon them with pleasure, as so many people who have become rich are able to do on their early days of poverty, except perhaps upon the first year of their married life, before the children began to come. The struggle had marked her too deeply. She only wanted to forget it.

Nor did she know, when they moved to the larger house, and her authorized expenditure was multiplied by four, how small a proportion it still bore to what her husband could have afforded. He set aside money for his home on terms that were almost cold-blooded, although he was a kind-hearted man by nature, and loved his wife and children. He would certainly have said that it was for them he was working, and believed it; and it would have been true with regard to the money that he allocated to the expenses of living. He allowed himself no pleasures that they did not share, and his meals in the City, when he was scraping money together, and was of an age when the body calls out for nourishment, were more meagre than theirs. Also, they would have all that they wanted in the future. But he would have kept them, and himself as well, on their almost starvation allowance for an indefinite time, if there had been any practical object to serve by doing so. There was none, when he did make the increase. The few hundreds a year that he allotted to living expenses counted as nothing in the turnover of his operations. It was what he could afford without being hampered by its loss. He fixed it by that standard. It was put aside and not thought of again. It was for his wife to deal with it.

At this stage, then, he had already reached the point at which the making of money was his chief object, and not any of the things that money could buy. He enjoyed the increased comfort of his home, but only in a very minor degree beside the enjoyment he obtained from his work, and his now increasing opportunities in it. He rather guarded himself against interests outside his business, from the feeling that the time had not yet come for him to divide them, in however small a degree. His evenings were apt to be dull; he came to the beginning of the week's work with much the same pleasurable anticipation as most men come to the end of it; and the annual holiday was acute boredom to him. His home was a place to rest in; he wanted no society but that of his wife and children, and was gradually unfitting himself for society, except that of men with whom he could talk business; he never read anything except what might have a bearing upon business; he had a mild liking for music and pictures, and thought that he might develop those tastes later on, when he should become very much richer and should have more time. He did not see that he was impairing all his capabilities for enjoying life outside the doors of his office, and that the more money he should make the less he would be fitted to use it except as a lever to make more still.

Probably the two years they spent in the semi-detached villa which was their second home was the happiest period of his life. The severe restrictions of the early years, which had irked him, although much less so than his wife, were over, and he had absolutely everything that he desired in his home. And in the much fuller life that he lived in pursuance of his schemes, the glow of excitement was over everything—more so than in later years, when success was a fact beyond all hazard, and expectation embraced only the operation of the moment, and not the large future.

And yet, even at this stage, he would never have admitted that the skill with which he played the game of finance, and the success he might have in it, were the only things he really cared about. To acknowledge that would have been to depreciate the coin for which he worked so hard to the value of a counter. No; he was to use it some day, or the overplus of it; but the using of it would need a whole new set of desires and occupations, and these would have to be created. It was a prospect that infused no warmth into his imagination. He would like to be a rich and powerful man, living in a big house—at least, he supposed he would like it. But there was no hurry; that could all wait.

He was under thirty when he bought " The Towers," and his expenditure rose from hundreds to thousands. Those thousands had no more actual significance in the strategy of his dealings than the hundreds had had. He had gone beyond the point at which he could measure the satisfaction to be gained from existence in such a house by what it cost him. It might be said that, judged by any practical standard, it cost him nothing.

But he did gain some genuine satisfaction over dealing with large sums of money in this way, for the first time. The feeling curiously resembled the spendthrift satisfaction in getting rid of money for the sake of getting rid of it, of which instance has already been made, but rested on very different grounds. Its basis was an attempt to touch the measure of possession, hitherto little tested on this side. Henceforward there would be no limits to the acquisition of anything that he might desire to have— the desires themselves being contained within reasonable bounds by his previous training of himself. Cost need not be counted, and indeed the satisfaction would have departed if it had had to be. The things that other men struggled hard for, as an end in themselves, and made themselves anxious about, he could now take, with no more forethought, as far as price was concerned, than is necessary for the buying of a toy in the street.

That he could hardly expect to enjoy them when he had got them, as much as if he had been obliged to scheme for them, did not occur to him. He did enjoy possession of " The Towers " as much as he had left himself capable of enjoying anything outside the main interest of his life. Its largeness and pretentiousness suited what taste he had in such matters, and it pleased him again to write a thumping cheque for its sumptuous furnishing, after he had given his wife *carte blanche* in that respect. She was encouraged to run the house on a lavish scale, and he did the same himself with gardens and stable, but exercised his grasp of detail there, to the extent of not being imposed upon by servants. Otherwise everything was to be of the best, and he came to take a mild pleasure in his forcing-houses and conservatories. It amounted to no more than a stroll round them with a cigar, on Sundays or summer evenings, and a pride in the show they made. He knew the names of very few of the flowers banked there in gorgeous masses, and nothing at all about their growth; all that was left to his gardeners. When the house was once furnished his interest in it ceased. He took for granted what was in it, and never thought of adding anything, though his wife was at liberty to buy what she liked.

After a time he began to buy pictures. He bought them nearly all out of the yearly exhibitions at the Academy, and occasionally in sale-rooms, but bought none of an earlier date than the latter half of the nineteenth century. In time he acquired a large and representative collection of modern British art on its more obvious side, and had paid in the aggregate a very large sum for it. For many years this collection represented all his expenditure outside the keeping up of his home; and he was growing richer and richer, though he had not yet reached the point at which his name had become a household word.

Perhaps that was what he was unconsciously striving for during those years—to take a recognised place amongst the big men. Work must have some end in view if it is to keep its salt, even though that end may not be definitely envisaged. He had no ambitions towards any larger life outside his business hours to which his money could help him, and, denied an outlet there, his energies could only lead towards wide recognition, if they were to lead anywhere. When the recognition came, when his name became known everywhere, and hardly a newspaper was published without some mention of it, a change in his way of living seemed already to be indicated. He was to be carried on. to embark on new and untried waters, and it was not without surprise that he learnt now that his own untrammelled will was no longer the sole shaper of his course.

It was not likely that his wife's development under the influence of sudden and then increasing wealth should have followed the same course as his. Her interests had scope in what to him was only the permanent and unchanging background of his life, his own vital interests lying quite apart from it. In their second home, where she was able to throw off the constant burdensome anxieties of the days of their poverty, she began to make a life for herself. She was still young, rather handsome, rather stupid, but very eager for her place in the sun. She was domestic enough to find her chief pleasure in looking after her children and her house, but she also enjoyed the intercourse that she had with the people who inhabited similar houses to their own around them. She made no intimate friends, and what real sociability she had in her expended itself upon her own and her husband's immediate relations. What she liked was the mechanism of sociability, the "calls," the "At Home" days, the formal gatherings. For these she dressed herself and decked her house.

When they moved to "The Towers," her life expanded largely, but was still contained within limits essentially narrow. Her children were older now, and she left them a good deal with nurses and governesses. When she learnt that she was at liberty to spend what to her was unlimited money, she gave herself seriously to the question of dress. There was hardly a day in the week in which she did not drive into London to "shop." The hours she spent with dressmakers and milliners were the stirring hours of her life. And she spent much money on expensive appointments for the house, but never bought anything of real artistic value.

"The Towers" was in quite another quarter from that in which they had lived formerly, and she dropped all her old acquaintances completely, and filled their places with the people who at that time lived in Hillgrove. This was not out of snobbery, from which she was comparatively free, but simply because a circle of acquaintance was necessary in order to exercise the pseudo-social activities that went with such a house as "The Towers." The people who lived in similar, or rather smaller, houses immediately around were those amongst whom she must now play her part and her former acquaintances were cut. She wanted friendships as little as before.

Armitage Brown had bought "The Towers" when Hillgrove had already begun to deteriorate as a residential suburb. Through the years that followed, one by one the larger houses disappeared, to make way for the streets of small houses that were Hillgrove's ultimate fate. The wastage of people whom Mrs. Brown could ask to her house, and to whose houses she could go, went on very fast, and she had absolutely no reserves on which to draw elsewhere. It was a very rare thing for her husband to bring a business friend home with him, and if he occasionally dined with one of them in London, he did not take her with him. Not for years did she enter a house as large as her own, or indeed any house belonging to rich people, outside Hillgrove.

When they had lived at "The Towers" for about twelve years they went to the Riviera for a holiday. It was the first time that either of them had ever been abroad; and it was the first time that Armitage Brown had ever enjoyed a holiday since his boyhood. His enjoyment was of a mild enough order. He liked the sunshine, and the bright life, and the change of food. He was just beginning to feel ever so slightly the strain that his unremitting concentration upon business had brought him. He was in the mood to lie fallow for a few weeks.

But to his wife the experience was a revelation of what life might be. The clothes alone would have filled her mind. She had always been a peacock amongst jackdaws, or at best amongst pheasants. She had dressed herself from fashion papers and show windows, not from other women. But here there was something to observe, something to emulate. And she saw how much she had yet to learn. Strong ambition awoke in her. She had the figure, and the type of face, and the genius for it; and, of course, the money. Another year, if they came to this place— and she was determined that they would—she would shine in it as brightly as she had shone amongst the women of Hillgrove.

They made some acquaintances at the smart hotel

in which they stayed. Her husband made them more
readily than she did. He was already known as a rich
man, and a rich man has no difficulty in making acquaintances. The men with whom he went over to Monte Carlo,
or with whom he smoked and talked in the lounge of
the hotel, or on the terrace overlooking the sea, found
him companionable. He was interesting on his own subject, and as his own subject was money there were plenty
glad enough to listen to him.

With her it was different. She had no warmth of nature
to make up for her total lack of experience of the sort of
life lived by the women with whom she foregathered. She
had the sense to use a large silence and to learn much from
their talk. But her silence did not commend her to them,
and whenever she did speak she stamped herself as suburban, or else as a stiff bore. The men who were inclined
to cultivate her because of her good looks found her quite
irresponsive. She wanted notice, but not the sort of notice
that demands any return.

The net result of this visit was a door opened to her in
Prince's Gate and another in Kensington Palace Gardens;
and she and her husband spent a Sunday in August in a
house that one of their new acquaintances had taken on
the Thames.

Next year they went South again, and Armitage Brown
bought a villa at Cap Martin. He bought it just as it
stood, furniture and all, and paid a price for it that made
talk when it leaked out. They had dined in it one evening,
and sat out on the terrace after dinner amongst the orange
trees, looking over the moonlit sea to the fairy lights of
Monte Carlo. What little romance Armitage Brown retained in him was stirred. Such a place as this would be
much more agreeable to retire to for a rest than a noisy
hotel. And they could have the children there, and they

and his wife could live there for a few months every year instead of a few weeks, while he went backwards and forwards.

He asked his host, whom he knew in business, whether he would sell the villa. His host laughed at him and said he had only just bought and furnished it. He offered him a high price for immediate possession, which was refused. He offered him a much higher price, which was also refused, with some irritation. He offered him an extravagant price, which was accepted. His friend walked out and he walked in, taking over the staff of servants and everything in the villa except the clothes of its former occupants. Then he went home to England and brought out the children, while his wife slowly woke up to the fact that a new era had commenced for her.

She was completely happy in it. Dull-witted as she was, she quickly and instinctively learnt what was expected of her. She had nothing to offer except lavish entertaining, but that she offered, and it was enough. She was shy of small parties, in which she would have to talk and show the hollowness of her sociability. But if she could ask people in numbers big enough to amuse themselves she understood how to do all the rest. The easy-going crowd ate her elaborate dinners, and praised them. This praise, coming to her ears, made her happy.

"The Towers" was dull after Cap Martin. The savour had gone out of her suburban entertainments, to which she had great difficulty in attracting her newer acquaintance. She asked her husband to move to a house in London. It was the first time she had ever initiated any desire of her own, having been content hitherto to act within the limits he had assigned her, and he refused, in some surprise that the request should be made. By and by he asked her why she had made it, and then told her that he had

no intention of giving up his leisure to a round of dull
gaieties. He did not mind while they were at the villa—
he had nothing much to do there—but when he came home
from his work in the City he wanted to be quiet, to stroll
and sit in his garden, to eat his dinner, and go to bed
early. "The Towers" suited him. He had no idea of
giving it up.

She accepted his decision, but looked forward to its
alteration some day, from force of circumstances. She
saw the trend of things in what affected her as clearly
as he did in the realm of finance. She had a clearer idea
than he of what an attraction his wealth was to all sorts
of people whom he made no effort to attract. She also
saw, which he as yet did not, that as he became increasingly
known, it would be impossible for him to bury himself
outside his hours of business for the greater part of the
year. She endured, and bided her time.

It had now arrived. Armitage Brown was a name in
everybody's mouth. Its owner must take the place in
the world that was expected of him. It seemed a natural
step in the great campaign to which he had committed
himself, although in its earlier stages he had not thought
that it would involve his private life.

CHAPTER VI

HILLGROVE TOWERS

It was a family party that sat about the tea-table at Hillgrove Towers on that Sunday afternoon. Armitage Brown, with his stubby dark moustache and his rather heavy face, was of the type that always looks middle-aged. He was still a few years short of fifty, but had not changed much in appearance during the last ten or fifteen years, and would not change much for ten or fifteen years more. The look of grim power which his face wore during his business hours was absent from it when he was at home. He did not usually even take the lead in conversation. He was content to leave that to his son and daughter. But he was undoubtedly master in his own house, as he was master in most positions in which he found himself.

His son, Alfred, had reached the age of five-and-twenty in a manner agreeable enough to himself, but somewhat disappointing to his father. He had some of his mother's good looks, and some of her tranquillity of manner; but his face was intelligent and alert, and he was ready with his tongue, which she had never been.

He had been sent, as a day boy, to a private school at Hillgrove, being taken away from it during the Riviera sojourns and sent back again on the return to England. A public school education had not been within his father's experience or designs at this time, but after desultory years under tutors, and in " families " in Switzerland and Germany, he had been sent to Cambridge. This had suited him admirably, but his previous lack of steady training, and his inexperience in English games and sports, had not prepared him for any very strenuous life there. He went through his three years as an amiable slacker, but developed a taste for the arts. He sang, and played the piano, quite nicely, acted at the "A. D. C.," dabbled in water-colours, and contributed to various undergraduate journals. He was clever in everything he took up, but lacked application in everything.

When he left Cambridge, after a very long Long Vacation, he was introduced to a stool in his father's office. But that was a failure from the very first, and he only occupied it for a year. Then he read for the bar, but professed himself sick of the law in a few months, and proposed to become an artist. He went to Paris, enjoyed himself exceedingly, but did very little work, having soon discovered that no amount of work was likely to lead him anywhere. He developed a taste for writing short stories in the French manner, one or two of which were published in English magazines. That was the stage which he had now reached. He was engaged in literature, and might have been engaged to some purpose if he had had to make his living out of it.

His failure to follow in his father's footsteps had not seriously disturbed Armitage Brown. His business was not a great organization that would need a successor. It was almost entirely personal to himself, and would disappear on his death or retirement, if there were nobody with similar gifts to his to carry it on. As his son was obviously lacking in those gifts, it was waste of time to train him to the work. Much less than a year showed up the unlikelihood of his ever making money on his own account, and as there was no actual necessity for him to make money, he was only kept at it for that time to make quite certain of his inability. After that his father did not care much what he did, as long as he did something. The traditions in which he himself had been brought up demanded that, but he did not adhere to them very strictly. He was quite aware by this time that any work his son might be doing was only a pretence. He had left off expecting anything of him, except perhaps that he should comport himself fittingly as the son of a very rich man, upon whom whatever fame or honour he himself might attain to would eventually descend.

It was not an arduous part to play, but unfortunately Alfred showed no greater capacity for it than he had shown for the intricacies of finance. He had no fixed allowance, but was encouraged to ask for any money that he might want. He asked for very little in comparison with what he might have had. If he was not much of an artist, he was an expert in getting all the fun possible out of an artist's life, which does not involve the spending of a great deal of money. He wandered about the Continent of Europe a good deal, very often on foot, and shunned the places frequented by the rich. He could very seldom be induced to visit the villa at Cap Martin, but stayed frequently for weeks together at "The Towers," for he was fond of his parents and of his sister, and was little disturbed in his private pursuits there.

He was a greater disappointment to his mother than to his father. He was a very presentable young man, and she would have liked to drag him about with her and show him off, incidentally relieving herself of the burden of talk, which was the one fly in the ointment of her activities. But he looked upon her life with absolute horror, though his affection for her and his good-humoured tolerance of all eccentricities prevented his showing it in any way that might have wounded her. He chaffed her about it, and she took the chaff without resenting it, or perhaps understanding it. They were good friends, but she felt that he did her no credit, when he might have done her so much.

Her daughter, Katharine, did her none either. She was a year young than Alfred, but seemed older. In appearance she took after her father, who had neither the build nor the features that would translate themselves into feminine beauty. She was short and square, and if the truth must be confessed, plain. But she had a lively, energetic way with her, and was a general favourite— would have been so even if she had not been known as the daughter of a millionaire.

She had a good head too. If she had been born the boy and Alfred the girl she might very well have fulfilled all her father's hopes, and Alfred would at least have afforded a figure to which his mother might have extended her own taste in dress. It was heart-breaking work trying to dress Katie. She looked just the same in anything, and had no taste whatever of her own for clothes. It was some consolation to Mrs. Brown that she liked going about. But that was because she liked making friends, which was not the aim of her mother's peripatetics. So even there there was not much that they had in common. Mrs. Brown sometimes felt that she had been hardly dealt with, both in her son and in her daughter. But Katie and her father got on well together. She was the only person to whom he sometimes talked of his business schemes, apart from those who were directly interested in them.

Armitage Brown's elder brother and his wife made up the party. Uncle James was an active, cheery man of about fifty. He had prospered in the world to the extent of being able to live in quite a nice house at Reigate, drive a motor-car, and take at least two days a week off his business to play golf. He was not in the least jealous

of his brother's success, which fact makes of him rather
a remarkable person.   He sometimes consulted him about
an investment, but that was the extent of their business
dealings with one another, and they were all the better
friends because of it.   His only trouble in life was that
he had no children.

His wife—Aunt Millie—was a bright little lady, very
well suited to him.   She was the only person outside her
own family for whom Mrs. Armitage Brown felt any
affection.   She had been kind to her in the days of her
poverty, when she herself, as a young wife, had been
very much more comfortably situated; and Mrs. Armitage
had never forgotten it.   She felt at home with her, as
she did with few people, and showed at her best, never
taking her stand upon the riches that had heaped themselves up around her, nor latterly upon the place she
was making for herself in a world from which her sister-
in-law was cut off.

Whether Aunt Millie viewed the rise of a woman so
inferior to herself in character or intelligence with the
complete equanimity displayed by her husband in the case
of his brother may be doubted.   But she showed as little
jealousy as he did, unless jealousy was shown by her
steadfastly refusing to receive anything from the hands of
her sister-in-law that she could not return.

Poor relations!   Judged by the standard of Armitage
Brown's great wealth, Uncle James and Aunt Millie were
poor relations.   It is a difficult part to play, but they
played it so well that their course of life was almost as
much an achievement in its way as his was.   They were
always welcome at " The Towers," and their rich relations
liked going to them at Reigate, and in fact went there
more often than to any other house.

They were talking of the coming changes.   Alfred,

stretching his long legs from a low chair, his teacup in his hand, was treating them in a spirit of levity which his mother felt to be in questionable taste, but had no weapons to silence.

"We are going to blossom out as lords of the soil," he said. "Our men-at-arms have dislodged the defenders of the bold Marquis, and the banner of the Browns now floats proudly from the battlements. I've forgotten what device it bears, but it will show up very well."

"Alfred is talking his usual nonsense," explained Mrs. Brown. "Kemsale is not an ancient castle. But it is a very large house and will take a great deal of furnishing."

"It has about sixty bedrooms," said Alfred. "It's just the house we've been looking for. We hate feeling cramped. We shall be able to find you a corner sometimes, Aunt Millie."

"I was wondering, dear, whether you would care to come down with me to help get the house in order," said Mrs. Brown. "They will begin to pack up here next week, but I shall send most of the servants down, and there is enough furniture still in the house for you and me and Katie to be able to picnic there till the rest comes. And we shall be able to see what more is wanted and come up and buy it."

Aunt Millie considered for a moment. The prospect would have been alluring to any woman—a large house to furnish and unlimited money to do it with. Would she be departing in any way from her rule by accepting the invitation?

Alfred broke in before she could reply. "My dear mother!" he exclaimed. "You can't possibly do it. Think what you owe to the county! Supposing the vicar were to call and find you on your knees with a duster in your hand, cleaning out the cellarette!"

"Don't be foolish, Alfred," his mother rebuked him. "Many of the rooms are completely furnished, and of course there will be servants to do all the actual work. We shall only have to see where the things from here are to be put, and what more is wanted. I hope you will be able to come, Millie. If it is fine, I should propose to motor down on Tuesday week. We should be there quite alone, and of course nobody would be admitted to the house."

Aunt Millie said she would come if James would do without her; and James, who had been talking to his brother, said that he should enjoy a bachelor existence for a week, or even longer.

"I read about the sale," he said. "Some of the things fetched enormous prices. Did you buy much there, Armitage?"

Armitage Brown never answered a direct question without considering what his answer should be. His wife replied to this one. "Armitage wanted to buy everything as it stood," she said, "as we did with Les Glycines. It would have saved a great deal of trouble, and he was prepared to pay any price that might have been asked. But when I saw how the house was furnished I was not altogether sorry that the offer had been refused. We can do better than that."

Alfred laughed. "I paid a surreptitious visit to the future home of our ancestors," he said, "while the sale was going on. Nobody knew that I was the rightful heir in disguise, except the gentleman who was bidding for us. By the by, father, I told him to buy one or two little pictures I thought rather nice. I thought you wouldn't mind."

"I don't mind, Alfred," said his father. "If you had

done what I asked, you would have gone down before, and picked out anything that was worth having."

" I rather wished I had when I got there. I had no idea what the house contained, though all the very valuable things had already been sold at Christie's."

" Everything was very old-fashioned," said Mrs. Brown. " Handsome, of course, a great deal of it, but to my mind the best modern furniture is far preferable. What we have here will brighten the house up wonderfully, but it will not go very far, and there will be a lot that we must get."

She spoke with deep satisfaction. She had a glorious time in front of her, with an excuse for plunging deep into the rich stores of the most modern furnishing shops. Her perceptions, which had mastered the art of dress and the presentation of food, had not yet led her to any understanding of what was considered " the thing " in furnishing. That was all that she really cared about, but she cared about it so much that if she had realized that the age of admiration for new gilt splendour was over she would have despised it herself as sincerely as anybody, and speedily acquired a taste more in accordance with the time.

Aunt Millie, who, although quite content with the modern furnishing of her own house, had absorbed some of the prevailing appreciation of old good things, thought it surprising that her sister-in-law, with her larger opportunities, should have acquired none of it. But Mrs. Brown's opportunities had been curiously limited, and her observation was as sluggish as possible except where her emulation was aroused, and then it was acute. She had got as far as big sofas and easy-chairs covered with loose gay chintzes, instead of tight satin and plush, but that was about the limit of her newly-acquired taste. The room in which they were sitting had these, and an abundance of flowers besides, but it also had a large gilt consol-table, crimson silk curtains under heavy gilt cornices, and for ornament, marble statuettes, great vases of modern china, and clocks and candlesticks of elaborate ormolu. She had seen with amazement the beautiful restful rooms at Kemsale, in which the more intimate daily life had been lived for generations. Her eye had entirely failed to take in their high subdued values. They had contained none of the things which she regarded as necessary for rich furnishing —no gilt, very little mirror, no bright colour. Indeed, she " could do better than that! "

" I liked the house as it was," said Armitage Brown quietly. "And there must have been a lot of valuable stuff in it, judging by what it fetched. But I leave these things to the wife. She knows a good deal more about them than I do."

He spoke with a smile, and without the least intention of sarcasm. He thought that she did know better than he did in such matters, and did not care enough about them to press his own mild preference for more sober surroundings.

" But you bought a good deal, didn't you? " asked Uncle James.

" We bought a lot of the bedroom furniture exactly as it stood," said Mrs. Brown—" the rooms that had been most recently refurnished. They will do very well for the present, and I can furbish them up by degrees. There were such a lot of them that it would not have been very amusing to take them all in hand at once. And Armitage liked the library as it was. We bought that."

" Ah, then we shall have something to read," said Alfred. " That's encouraging."

" We did not buy the books," said his mother. " They were mostly old and shabby."

" I did tell them to buy most of them," said her husband.
" The shelves must be filled with something."

" Oh, well, we can have the oldest of them rebound."

Katie spoke for the first time. " I don't believe the
house will be half as nice as it was," she said sturdily.
" I'm a very modern person myself, but I do like old
things, when they seem to belong. I've got two lovely
rooms of my own, Aunt Millie. I think they belonged
to Lady Grace Ettien. They were delightfully furnished,
in an old-fashioned faded sort of way. I knew I could
never get them so nice again, so I asked father if he would
buy everything in them and leave them exactly as they were.
I don't think they contained anything very valuable."

Her father smiled at her. " They were the two most
expensive rooms in the house," he said. " I paid a fortune
for them. But I don't mind if you like them, my dear! "

She expressed her surprise. " I am sure there was
nothing there that ought to have cost a lot," she said.
" However, if they did, I shall like them all the better."

" A chip of the old block," said Alfred. " Perhaps Lady
Grace Ettien wanted them herself, and ran them up."

" If she had wanted them they wouldn't have been there
for sale," said his father. " I believe there was a mistake
about a pair of drawings, but those they seem to have got.
I was worried about them in the middle of the sale. I
had given my instructions, and I was annoyed. My people
wanted to enter into a lot of explanations afterwards, but
I wouldn't have it. You didn't want the drawings particularly, did you, Katie? "

" I rather liked them; but I suppose they are family
portraits. I can do without them."

" Aren't you going to have the house done up before
you go in? " asked Uncle James.

" We thought we would wait until we go to Cap Martin,"

said Mrs. Brown. "Then we shall know better what is wanted. Besides, Armitage wants to sell 'The Towers' now, and we must have somewhere to go."

"I've got an offer that isn't likely to be repeated," said Armitage. "They're going to cut it up for building. If they can't have this place at once, they'll buy another."

He spoke without a shade of feeling of the place that had been his home for nearly twenty years. But Mrs. Brown showed some. "Hillgrove has become impossible," she said. "It is quite time we left it."

Alfred sighed. "Hillgrove suits me," he said. "I am so afraid I shall fail in my behaviour at Kemsale. Will the heir of all the Browns be expected to hunt, father? They do that in the country, don't they—foxes, and stags, and things?"

What a disappointing son this was! His mother would have liked him to hunt—in a well-fitting red coat.

"Any golf links handy?" asked Uncle James.

"No, but I am going to lay some out in the park," said his brother. "I am going to take up golf myself."

This was entirely a new departure. "I want exercise," he explained. "I shall give it a trial. You must come down and teach us, James."

"Not me," said Alfred. "I refuse to play that debasing game. Father, you must buy me a horse, and I will ride him in secret until I know how. Then I will go out and hunt the fox. I feel quite sure that that will be expected of me."

"Do you know any people in the neighbourhood?" asked Uncle James.

"There were a Captain and Mrs. Clinton who had the villa next to Les Glycines last year," said Mrs. Brown. "She was rather delicate, and I did not see much of her;

but they dined with us once. They live a few miles off.
I believe he is some connection of Lord Meadshire's."

"Lord Meadshire is still living at Kemsale, isn't he?"

"His sister is. I don't know whether he is going to
live with her."

"I believe he is what is called a rotter," said Alfred.
"But it is to be expected that the county will rally to
him. The ancient and baronial family of Brown will
have to be very careful how it behaves."

"You talk great nonsense, Alfred," said his mother.
"We shall have our own circle. We shall not be dependent upon the people around, though we shall be quite
ready to make friends with them."

"I don't know much about English country life," said
Alfred. "But I should say it would be more a question
of their making friends with us. We are rich but new,
and they are reported to look with suspicion on the
combination."

"I am quite sure we shall find plenty of people to make
friends with," said Katie. "And at any rate there will
be the villagers. It will all be perfectly delightful."

CHAPTER VII

A MOMENTOUS INTERVIEW

The new millionaire did not take up his residence at Kemsale, after all, until the late spring. Mrs. Brown found that the house needed a great deal more " doing up " than she had supposed. Electric light had to be installed, drains overhauled, plumbing modernized everywhere, bathrooms added. And painting and decorating was needed throughout, according to her standards, and must precede furnishing, unless the work should be all done over again, in an intolerable muddle.

When she came to a practically empty house, instead of one that contained the accumulations of two hundred years, she found herself out of her depth. The furniture from " The Towers " hardly seemed to count, in the enormous and repeated spaces of Kemsale, nor did the large purchases that they had made at Kemsale itself. And the idea of expecting necessary adaptations and structural decorations of such a house to be finished in two months was seen to be quite impracticable. It would be nearly a year's work to reconstitute Kemsale afresh. The builders and decorators were given six months; they charged heavily for the speeding up, but fulfilled their contract.

The Browns took a furnished house in London for the winter, and until they went to Cap Martin after Christmas Mrs. Brown was engaged nearly all the time with the firm of upholsterers to whom she had committed herself. She learnt a good deal during those weeks, and began to be doubtful about her wisdom in allowing so much that had been in Kemsale to go out of it. But suggestions were naturally made with diffidence to a lady who hardly ever asked the price of anything except to fix upon something that cost more, and the firm was quite willing to adapt its taste to hers when she made it known what her taste was. Besides, she was worth an extra one per cent. dividend to the shareholders in buying at full price the most expensive things out of stock that had been superseded, and was cumbering up warehouses. Kemsale was the last very large private house to be elaborately furnished and decorated in Victorian style. Even hotels now wanted their Tudor and Jacobean and Georgian chambers. The presiding genius of the firm, when he learned what a big business this was going to be, took the matter in hand himself, and derived a great deal of interest—and profit—from evolving a definite idea out of the chaos of the Victorian style. When all the work was finished he went down to Kemsale and chuckled over the result, walking through the blue drawing-room, and the pink drawing-room, and the yellow drawing-room, and the other shrines of his art. " I don't believe there's anybody else could have done it," he said to himself. " It isn't hideous at all. It has character—the character of the people who are going to live in it, and a little bit of mine."

When all the papers were signed and all the money paid that transferred Kemsale to its new owner, Captain Herbert Fuller was summoned to London for an interview with Armitage Brown. The little man obeyed the summons in nervous trepidation, which the energetic promptings of his wife to behave as if he valued himself and "keep his end up" had done little to allay. So very much hung upon that interview, and as he sat in the corner of a third-class carriage on his way to London, and fingered his neat little grey moustache, he vacillated be-

tween the extreme of hope and the depths of dejection.
If only the interview were over, and he were coming back
again with everything settled, one way or another! It
would be a relief to know the worst. He had his full
share of pluck, and he thought he could face it, black as
it looked. But if he *should* be able to persuade this new
rich man, who couldn't be expected to know much about
land agency, that the natural thing for him to do was to
keep on the agent who had looked after the property for
the last fifteen years—well, he would have had a fright,
but no man need be the worse for that. At any rate, he
would do his best to fight for his job, but as he told himself so, he realized with a sinking feeling that there was
not likely to be much opportunity for fighting. Such a
man as he supposed Armitage Brown to be would probably
have made up his mind already.

It was odd that one man should have so much power
over the life of another. To this man whom he was going
to see, the income that would make all the difference between
comparative affluence and desperate poverty for three people
represented nothing at all; and yet he would take it away
if it suited him to do so without a thought of what its
withdrawal would mean. How was it that he, Herbert
Fuller, who had worked diligently and faithfully all his
life, should be dependent upon the decision of a man who
had gained immeasurably more for a much shorter period
of work? He could not quite make it out, but there seemed
to be something wrong somewhere.

He was rather surprised at the appearance of the office
in which such wealth as Armitage Brown's was dealt with.
It was on the first floor of a narrow house in Lombard
Street, and the little outer room contained only one clerk,
and hardly room for more. He was taken at once into
the great man's sanctum, which was a good deal larger,

but very ordinary in its appointments, and showing no signs at all of the wealth of its owner.

Armitage Brown rose from his desk to shake hands with him, and his secretary left the room as he did so. " I'm pleased to see you, Captain Fuller," he said. " I want to settle everything with regard to the estate. I'm going to America to-morrow, and when I get back I shall be too busy to attend to it for some time. I can spare you five-and-twenty minutes."

Poor little Herbert gasped. He had come with a bagful of papers and memoranda, and had expected to be closeted with his new employer for the rest of the day at least— as a preliminary.

Armitage Brown had given him a searching look as he shook hands with him. Probably in that instant he had summed him up, and made up his mind as to the man he had to deal with. The capacity for forming lightning judgments of that sort had been one of the factors of his success.

" I'm not going into details," he said, with a glance at the bag that Fuller was nursing on his natty serge-covered legs. " I'll ask you what I want to know, and you must answer me as concisely as you can. Then I'll tell you what I want done. What was the net return on the whole property last year, and the year before? "

How poor little Herbert blessed his life-long hobby for figures, during the fusillade of questions that followed! It had been his pleasure to take out statistics of every sort and kind connected with his work, and with other subjects in which he was interested, and he had sometimes rebuked himself for giving too much time to them, where their actual usefulness was questionable. Armitage Brown asked many questions that no man who knew anything about estate management would have thought of asking, and no agent would have been expected to answer off-hand. But Captain Fuller answered them all, with only an occasional reference to a page of his neat memoranda; or, where they could not be answered, explained the reason sharply and concisely.

It was exhilarating. It reminded him of his long-past days of military *viva voce* examinations. And the man who was cross-examining him had something military in his sharp direct manner. His own was sharp and direct too, where he was sure of his ground, as he was here. He did not know that his questioner felt an increasing respect for him as he sucked his brain, and made his own notes on the pad on his desk; nor that his briskness was causing him to appear as a younger man by ten years than he actually was. Still less had he any idea that the thought that had passed through Armitage Brown's brain, as he had shaken hands with him and thrown him that searching look, was, " You won't do at all. I must get rid of you. Too old, for one thing."

Armitage Brown actually smiled at him when he had asked his last question. " Well, you know your work, Captain Fuller," he said, as he leaned back in his chair.

It was his way to praise, with a single short phrase, when he was well served, and to blame in the same manner when he was not. But he did not blame twice.

Poor little Herbert felt as if he could have gone down on his knees to him. Surely he wouldn't have said that if he had not meant to keep him on.

As for his knowing his work—well, it was rather like the examination room again. He had been " put on " in the subjects he had got up. The weaknesses had been left undisclosed.

For there were weaknesses, and he knew them better than anybody. He had not been bred to the work, nor even brought up in the country. His knowledge of farming was inadequate, though he had done his best to improve it. His first agency had had to do mostly with town property, and he had been lucky to get his second, at Kemsale. He would hardly have kept it had not the Lord Meadshire who gave it to him been an old and a very kind-hearted man, unwilling to make changes. And he was liable to be imposed upon by tenants, and knew that too. More money had been spent on their behalf than a careful landlord would have considered necessary in these latter days. In the matter of farm and cottage buildings Kemsale was a model estate, and Herbert Fuller knew what he was about when the details of building were in question. But the expenditure on this head had not been justified by the rent-roll, however well and economically the work had been done.

How could Armitage Brown know that? Fuller was startled by his saying, immediately after his word of commendation: " The place doesn't seem to have been run to pay. I suppose you had your instructions. The housing and so on was the chief thing."

Fuller hesitated long enough to cause a sharp glance to be directed towards him. " The old Lord Meadshire liked everything of that sort to be done as well as possible," he said. " This one has left it pretty well to me; but he never complained of anything I did in that way."

" Oh, well, I'm not complaining either. If that's the tradition I shall keep it up."

There followed another string of questions, as to bricks and mortar this time, and they were answered with the same crisp efficiency as before.

Again came the smile and the word of praise. " One would think you had been brought up to the building trade, Captain Fuller."

" I served in the Royal Engineers, and after that I had a good deal to do with planning and building. It always interested me, though of course it isn't the chief thing in a land agent's job."

He felt obliged to put that in. A man like this mustn't be deceived.

" Well, I'm inclined to think it may interest me too. At any rate, until I come down and take the reins, you'll understand that you have authority to do what you think necessary in that way. Do what you've done before, in fact. That point's settled, and we needn't recur to it."

Then he was going to be kept on. There seemed no doubt about it now. He felt himself bathed in a warm glow; but he had to collect himself sharply for what was coming now.

" When I said that the place hadn't been run to pay I didn't mean that I regarded the outgoings that we've been talking about as unreasonable. As far as that goes I certainly shan't be behind Lord Meadshire in keeping up the property, or improving it where improvement is wanted. It's not my way. But I shan't be content with three-quarters of one per cent. on the capital I've put into it, either, and that's about what it seems to have averaged lately, leaving out of account the letting of the sporting rights. By the by, that arrangement comes to an end this year, doesn't it? "

" At the end of the season."

" And that's when? I don't know anything about sport."

" It ends on the first of February."

" It ends there for good, then. You understand that? "

Captain Fuller had been prepared to discuss the point at leisure. But all he said was, " Oh, certainly."

Armitage Brown looked at his pages of large-scrawled notes and figures, then turned sharply to Fuller.

"How would you suggest making the place pay—say three per cent.?"

Poor little Herbert's jaw dropped. The weak place was exposed now, with a vengeance. In commerce, Herbert Fuller would have been a confidential clerk in a hundred thousand—accurate, conscientious, untiring, trustworthy; but he would never have made a penny of money on his own initiative. And landowning is nothing but a branch of commerce, if it is to be judged by percentages on capital. To be asked coolly what he would suggest to multiply his returns by four, when it took him all he knew to maintain them at their present level, was to turn him from ready, confident speech to a hesitating confusion that seemed likely to destroy all the good he had so far done himself.

But Armitage Brown knew his man now, or thought he did. He laughed shortly at his face of dismay. "Well, I don't know that you should be asked to pronounce on what isn't your business," he said. "You've carried out a system. It wasn't for you to alter it." He referred to his notes again. "You've told me how much land is pasture, and how much is—what do you call it?—arable. Tell me how dairying is carried on on the property."

Without the guidance of leading questions, the information given was not so clear or exhaustive as it had been. There was one large holding consisting chiefly of grassland on the outskirts of the property, near the terminus of Ganton, where dairying was carried on on a considerable scale. Armitage Brown began to ask him questions about that, when Fuller had floundered through his account of how things were done on the home farm, and on other farms where a herd of cows was kept. He asked about markets and freights and the times of trains, and the proportion of labour to the land, and of the herd to the acreage, and many other things of which Fuller knew little or nothing. He felt miserable again now, and began to experience a sense of unfairness, and to consider whether he should not put in a protest.

But Armitage Brown virtually put it in for him, and met it. "Well, I suppose that isn't your business, either," he said. "I'm not trying to puzzle you, Captain Fuller. You must remember that I know almost nothing about land and how it's held. I don't think I ever realised, what I see now, that the tenant does pretty well what he likes on his farm, and the agent's business isn't exactly to overlook him—to know more about it than he does himself, in fact. Can you get up a subject, Captain Fuller?"

The questions generally came sharply, after a speech that had tended to relieve previous tension. Poor little Herbert was beginning to feel the strain. Under pretence of blowing his nose, he passed his handkerchief across his brow. Perhaps it would be better to make a clean breast of it.

"The fact is," he said, "I'm not a practical farmer. I've learnt a good deal about it, of course, and I know good farming from bad, and a man who's likely to do well by his farm from a man who isn't. And I've always run the home farm myself, with a bailiff, on satisfactory lines, I think. But if you were to put me down in a large farm, and tell me to make a handsome profit out of it, I don't believe I could do it. I haven't been trained to it. I don't want to sail under false colours."

He felt relieved at having said it. He would have everything open and above board, and stand up to the worst if the worst was to come.

Armitage Brown looked at his watch—an action that was not reassuring. But he spoke at once. "I understand all that," he said, "but it isn't exactly what I asked. Take

this subject of dairying now. I read a pamphlet the other
day that fell into my hands about dairying as it is carried
on in Australia, on a very large scale. It interested me.
And I suppose there's information to be got about how
it's done in Holland, and in other countries. If I got
together for you whatever has been written on the subject,
with returns and reports and so on, could you master them,
so that whatever questions I asked you you'd be able to
answer, just as you answered the first lot of questions I
asked you?"

Fuller plucked up courage. " Yes, certainly I could do
that," he said boldly. " I did it once with the question
of fruit for the old Lord Meadshire. It's exactly what
I'm fit for."

" I think it is, Captain Fuller; I think it is." The words
brought balm. " And it is what I shall want from you.
I'll tell you now that I shan't be content to carry on the
business of the land at Kemsale in the old-fashioned way.
I shall want to make experiments, and see if more can't
be done with it. The responsibility for them will be mine,
and you won't have to worry yourself about it. If I fail,
it will be my fault and not yours. All you will have to
do will be first of all to collect information for me, and
then see that what I decide is carried out. We'll begin
on those lines with this dairying question. Get together
all the information you can—I'll send you down books and
papers—and let me know exactly what the process would
be—alterations necessary and so on—to try it on a large
scale at Kemsale. It may not be feasible; that I shan't
know till I'm primed. But we'll talk it all over when I
come down in the spring. That's settled then. Now
you've told me about the tenancies on which the farms
are held. Take a note of these instructions, please. Where
they are yearly, renew them till next autumn. Where

there's a year's notice required, give it, as from this autumn, if that can be done. In the case of the two farms that are vacant, take them over yourself—but I suppose you've done that already."

"Some of the farms have been in the same hands for a number of years, Mr. Brown."

It was the old order crying out to the new. Armitage Brown's face hardened slightly. "I don't propose to be hampered by those considerations," he said stiffly. "At the same time I'm not going to turn off anybody that I can use. You can let it be known that the notice is only intended to give me a free hand. I'll consider each case in detail when I come down next year."

There was no time except for lightning decisions. He had already opened his mouth to make his next speech, when Fuller said: "I should like to use my discretion in that matter, and tell certain of the older tenants that the notice is purely formal."

Armitage Brown frowned. He had given his orders, and was not accustomed to have them questioned. Fuller saw the frown and it stiffened him. He was ready to obey orders, but not in the manner of a servant. His tone was as decisive as the millionaire's as he said: "You told me just now that you knew nothing about the tenure of land. There's no time to explain things. I'm ready to do what you want, but you'd much better let me do it in my own way. It will come to the same thing in the end."

The little man would not have cared for the moment if he had lost his post straight away. He was not going round to tenants who had held their farms at Kemsale for generations with a curt notice of dismissal, unless he took his own along with them. There was loyalty in these matters.

"The notice isn't purely formal," said Armitage Brown. "Whatever I decide to do with the land, I don't intend to run it on the old lines. If the tenants who are there already choose to work on my lines, they'll have the chance, those of them that I think suitable. But it's just the old-established ones that are most likely to make difficulties."

"Do you want me to tell them that you're going to make these experiments with the land?"

"Of course I don't want that. It's understood that anything I've said to you is confidential."

"Then what's the good of upsetting them beforehand? Instead of coming down to find your way prepared for you, you'll get nothing but friction that could just as easily be avoided."

"Supposing I say that things must be done in my way when I've indicated plainly what that way is to be, Captain Fuller?"

"Then I'll ask you to get somebody else to do them, Mr. Brown. All the knowledge I have is at your service. If you can't make use of it, you can't make use of me."

Armitage Brown's face suddenly lightened. "Well, I'm not such a fool as not to see that," he said good-humouredly. "I think I shall be able to make use of you very well, Captain Fuller. Have it your own way, then, for the present."

As the little man travelled home that evening, sitting in a corner of his third-class carriage, and fingering his moustache, he was full of happiness. He smiled constantly as he went over the points of the interview. At one time the smile left his face and was succeeded by a look of consternation. "By Jove!" he said to himself. "He didn't give me notice; I gave it to him. Thank goodness he didn't accept it." Then he laughed.

CHAPTER VIII

BARTON'S FARM

HERBERT FULLER reached home that evening in time for dinner. His wife was standing at the door as his cart drove up. "Well, what's the news?" she called out in her high-pitched voice, as he pulled up his horse.

He did not answer her at once, anxious as he was to tell her that the news was good; and as he stepped down from his seat, she said, with sharp vexation, " Didn't you hear me speak? Why can't you answer? "

" I couldn't tell you before him," he said, indicating the groom, who was now driving round to the yard. " The news is good, my dear. I'll tell you about it if you come up while I change."

" Well, that's something to be thankful for," she said, " if it really is good, and you're not only kept on temporarily. But you don't want to dress to-night, and it's cold upstairs. Come in here; I can tell them not to lay the table for ten minutes."

She led the way into the dining-room, where there was a bright fire burning. It was the only comfortable thing in the room, except a shabby easy-chair, which was supposed to be Fuller's, but which his wife more frequently occupied. Dressmaking had been going on, and every table and chair was littered, not only with the materials and implements for such work, but with accessories to indoor life, and outdoor too, that it was too much trouble to put into their places. It was a large, rather low room, with a great oak beam running across it, small-paned windows on two of the walls, and a cavernous hospitable hearth. It would have made a delightfully comfortable general sitting-room if there had been the slightest attempt at keeping it in order; but if the maids tidied up in the morning their work was always undone by the time the evening came round. The drawing-room was the room of state, not used except for visitors, who were never allowed to enter this one. So it didn't matter what it looked like.

Herbert Fuller looked round it with distaste. He was cold and hungry; it was a quarter to eight, but the dining-table was cluttered up with a sewing machine and a disorderly pile of feminine gear. His wife was in her day clothes—a soiled blouse and an old skirt—and as she had appointed to herself a day of retirement, she had not troubled to dress her hair properly. Only he would see her, and he didn't matter.

Perhaps he was a little exalted by his late success. He did occasionally assert himself against the tyranny to which he was subjected in his home, and did so now. "Why isn't dinner ready?" he snapped. "The room looks like a pig-sty. And if you're not going to take the trouble to make yourself look decent for the evening, I am."

He marched out of the room and up to his dressing-room, from which he was immediately heard to shout downstairs for hot water. There were no bells in the house, and the mistress being what she was, the servants frequently neglected their most ordinary duties.

Mrs. Fuller was fully capable of dealing with a revolt of this sort. The easiest way would have been to follow her husband upstairs, "row" the maid who had neglected her duty, and make some sort of excuse for the state of things to which he had come home. Or if not the easiest way, to her, it would have calmed him down instantly, and he would have told her all she wanted to know, and he wanted to tell her.

For she had, in fact, gone through a very anxious day. As she had been cutting out and stitching and working her machine, she had been visited by sundry very cold fits when she thought of the possibility of her husband losing his position. There was next to nothing to fall back upon. He had about a hundred pounds a year of his own, and she had nothing. And he was getting on. She knew as well as he did that if he lost this job he would almost certainly not get another. She had been able to put all thought of the future aside as long as they were where they were, and muddle away what was quite a good income without allowing him to put by a penny of it. But if the income should suddenly cease! There was no getting away from the thought now.

As she stitched and turned the handle of the machine, and snapped at her daughter when she made some remark that disturbed her train of thought, she imagined her husband giving in meekly to the man who had his fate, or rather her fate, in his hands, showing himself weak where he ought to be firm, and "uppish" where it would be better to give in. That was the way he dealt with her, although she would not have acknowledged it; and she despised him for it. If only she could have been there to stiffen him! She quite thought that she could get her own way with any man, as she got it with him. She thought nothing of his cheerful conscientious service, nor hoped that his new employer might recognise it, nor sent out her sympathy to him in his anxiety and in the test that he was undergoing. She only thought of him ignominiously failing to make himself out something that he wasn't, and felt anger and contempt against him for his deficiencies in an art that to her was second nature. If he

came back to tell her that his place had been assured him,
she would rejoice for her own sake, but would not allow
him to take any credit for it. She actually made up her
phrases beforehand. " Well, I'm glad he didn't see through
you." Or if he showed himself particularly pleased with
the way the interview had gone, " Oh, I dare say you flatter
yourself you got the better of him. We shall see what
happens later on." If the news were to be that he was
to remain on for a time on trial, she would gird at him
and ask him what he supposed they were to do when the
time came to an end. If it was to be dismissal, supersession,
then she would employ all her bitterness upon the poor
little honest man, who had only erred in not taking a firmer
stand against her, for the sake of their joint security in
the future. She would gain some immediate relief of the
black terror that would settle upon her, by seeing him hold
his head in his hands in misery under the lash of her
tongue. He would do that; he would not stand up to her;
and she would be goaded by his abject submission to still
further flights of vituperation.

Now she hesitated for a moment as he walked out of the
room. She did want to hear what had happened. Should
she make some half-contemptuous advance that would draw
it out of him? The hesitation was only momentary. He
had said that the news was good; details could wait. A
look of spite came over her face.

Her daughter came into the room. She had on a new
evening gown, in which she had been arraying herself
for the last half-hour. Herbert Fuller always dressed for
dinner by choice, the habits of his youth and his orderly
precise ways demanding some sort of recognition of the
evening meal as dividing off the day. His wife usually
compromised in a draggled tea-gown, which she threw on
over other clothes in a few minutes. She hated the trouble

of dressing, unless it was for "company," when she would spend hours over it. But occasionally she would take it into her head to appear in full costume when they were alone, especially if she had something new that she had not had an opportunity of wearing outside. Her daughter was taking after her in all these whims and habits.

"Why didn't you clear up before you went upstairs?" she asked angrily. "You leave it all for me to do. Any one would think I was your servant, to go trapesing about and picking up all your mess. Put the things away at once, and tell them to keep dinner back for half an hour. I'm going up to dress."

"You're surely not going to take half an hour, mother, are you?" asked the girl. "It's just eight o'clock, and I'm as hungry as a hunter."

Among the good points that had not yet been driven out of her, this girl had an equable spirit, and was not easily put out by her mother's eccentricities of temper.

"Oh, yes, I'm going to *dress*," said Mrs. Fuller, her annoyance against her daughter overcome by her annoyance against her husband. "Your father has come home so perked up by his visit to the great man that he won't look at us in anything but our best clothes. If he doesn't like waiting for his dinner while I put 'em on, he can lump it. Tell them to serve up at half-past eight, and if cook gives notice, tell her she can go. I'm sick of her impudence."

She was going out of the room when Irene asked: "Is it all right about father's job?"

"Oh, you'd better ask him," she said on the stairs, "especially if you want your nose bitten off. *I* don't know anything about it, and don't care."

Irene shrugged her shoulders, and began to clear the table, putting the things down on the chairs or anywhere

where there was room for them, without any attempt at reducing the room to order. She was a tall well-made girl, with a face neither plain nor pretty. Her new frock was over-smart, and looked cheap at the same time. Her mother spent too much money on her own clothes and too little on the girl's; but the neck and arms so liberally displayed were firm and smooth, and she moved with youthful litheness. Perhaps she was justified in feeling that her new frock was a sort of refuge against the cantankerousness that was apparently going to be the note of the evening.

She went out and gave the orders that she had been bidden to give, even to the extent of telling the cook that she could go if she liked, and then came back and took some almonds and raisins off a dish on the sideboard, and settled herself in the big easy-chair to nibble at them, and read a novel which she picked up from the floor, where she had thrown it after lunch.

At the stroke of eight her father came briskly into the room. His spurt of irritation had died down; he was looking forward to his dinner, and to regaling his wife and daughter with the full account of his experiences.

His face clouded again when he saw the table still unlaid. "Why on earth isn't dinner ready?" he asked. "It has struck eight and they haven't even laid the table."

"Mother put dinner back to half-past eight," said Irene. "She has gone up to dress."

She spoke lazily, leaning back in her chair, and looking up at him.

He was too loyal to say anything in criticism of his wife to his daughter, but stood irresolutely in front of the fire, his face troubled and vexed.

"Well, I shall go into the den till it's ready," he said.

" I hope it won't be later than half-past eight, for I'm confoundedly hungry. I had lunch at one, and no tea."

"I expect mother will be some time," said the girl. " Why don't you have a whisky and soda and a biscuit? "

She did not offer to get them for him, or to vacate the chair that was supposed to be his. " I think I will," he said, and went to the sideboard, where there was a spirit tantalus and a siphon of soda water.

" Is it all right about the job, father? " Irene asked, as he came back to the fire.

" Oh, yes," he said shortly. Then he added: " We've got another chance. We shall have to begin to be a bit more careful now."

This did not interest her, and she returned to her book. Presently, after he had looked down at her, he said: " Well, I shall go to the den till dinner is ready. I have some papers to look over."

" There isn't a fire there," she said, without raising her eyes from her book.

The den was as neat and tidy as the dining-room was the reverse. On one side of it was a small carpenter's bench and a metal-turning lathe, with tools on a rack above them, all in their places. Writing-table, book-shelves, nests of drawers, everything showed the occupation of a man to whom orderliness was almost a passion. There was a hearthrug, but no carpet on the floor. An old wooden gate-backed armchair, with no cushions in it, stood by the fireplace. The other chairs were of the common Windsor pattern. There was no attempt at comfort in the room, but its neatness made it look actually more comfortable than the dining-room.

Herbert Fuller drew the curtains, lit the lamp, and after a moment's hesitation put a match to the fire. He deposited his bag of papers by the side of the writing-table,

and then sat down in front of the new crackling fire, with
his glass in his hand.

He was not greatly disturbed by his wife's spiteful
counter-attack. His mind was too simple and direct even
to recognise its pettiness. She would keep him waiting
half an hour, or perhaps longer, for his dinner. His annoyance on that account would not be added to by her
sailing into the room in elaborate evening costume, and
saying that she hoped she was smart enough now. But
her attitude stiffened him in a decision he had come to,
and that he had hoped to be able to carry out with her
co-operation. If she was not in a mood to give it, then
he must take steps to enforce his will, as much for her
sake as for his own.

Money had flowed through her fingers like water. He
was eminently capable himself of using an income to the
best advantage, and again and again he had made estimates
and apportionments which, if they had been kept to, would
have enabled them to live comfortably and save a considerable sum every year. But the years had slipped by
and nothing had been saved. She seemed incapable of
husbanding her resources in any way. She would neglect
her household accounts for weeks together, and when they
came to be added up and found greatly to exceed the sum
that had been laid down for them, all her excuse would
be that she " supposed they must have enough to eat."
She invariably exceeded her dress allowance, but " never
had a stitch to wear." She hated the discomforts of debt,
and took great credit to herself for this feeling. It did
not prevent her from running up bills, but it brought her
to him with them when they were large and pressing enough
to disturb her. Then the money that he had scraped
together to invest would be paid away, and she would
promise to be more careful, but accept no blame. These

were the only occasions upon which he could make himself felt at all, and then never without fierce recriminations and disclaimers from her. The only saving clause in the situation was that Barton's Farm, which was the name of their house, was not large enough for her to expand their way of living beyond a certain point. She could spend half as much again on their hugger-mugger existence as a careful housewife would have needed for a well-appointed house, but its bounds did put some sort of limit to her expenditure inside; and outside, in gardens and stable, his own careful management gave them what was necessary on the most economical terms.

Barton's Farm was not the official agent's house, which was considerably larger. They had occupied it as a make-shift when they had first come to Kemsale. The only appreciable success that Herbert Fuller had had in his incessant struggle against over-expenditure was that he had never allowed himself to be persuaded, or bullied, into moving into " The Limes." Even his wife, insanely un-practical as she was, and contemptuous of his expostula-tions, had never found an answer to his argument: " If we can only manage just to keep our heads above water here, what chance shall we have in a house like that? " To the fortunate accident of " The Limes " having been tenanted at the time they had come to Kemsale, they owed it that they had, so far, kept their heads above water.

But now the time had imperatively come when more than that was wanted, and it was on the means of bringing it about that this active, honest little man, who felt younger than his years, but was beginning to see them drawing to a close, cogitated, as he sat hungry and still rather cold before his smoky fire.

It was twenty minutes to nine when the dinner bell at last rang. The extra delay had irritated him to the point

of making him feel himself a martinet, and when he went
into the dining-room he was determined to carry out the
decisions he had made, with no nonsense allowed. His
wife was already seated at the table in what looked to
him like a ball-dress, and a very expensive one. She wore
all her jewels, and had dressed her brass-tinted hair elaborately. The process had, curiously enough, driven away
the effervescence of her ill-humour. She had kept him
waiting for his dinner for nearly an hour, which would
"teach him"; and now, if he chose to behave himself,
he might deliver his budget of news without being more
snapped at than in normal conversation.

"Well, I hope this is grand enough for you," she said
as he came in.

"It's a bit too grand for my taste," he said, as he sat
down. "But at any rate it looks clean."

It must be admitted that this was rude; and the maid
was standing at his elbow, and would certainly report the
speech to the enraged cook.

No more was said until she had left the room, when there
was an explosion.

"I meant what I said," he snapped in answer to it—he
could snap, too, at times. "And as for saying such a
thing before the servants, it's nothing to what you allow
yourself to say before them if you're annoyed."

"Oh, please don't quarrel, children," said Irene lazily.
"I want to hear about the great Armitage Brown."

Her father was already a little ashamed of his speech,
and of pursuing a quarrel before her; and his spurts of
temper died down quickly and left no sulkiness behind
them. Mrs. Fuller was still furious with him, but her
gown seemed to demand behaviour more "lady-like" than
she was accustomed to adopt in the home circle. She sat
stiff and offended while he told of the cross-examinations

to which he had been subjected, and the success with which he had met them. " That taste of mine for statistics has turned up trumps," he said. " I suppose in a business like his they have to use them a lot more than it's necessary for us to do. Anyhow, it seemed to be exactly what he wanted."

It seemed to her as she listened to his account of the earlier stages of his interview, which was broken off while he was carving and the maid was in the room, that he really had succeeded in bluffing the great man into thinking him of more value than he was; and it suited her better to believe in that sort of success than in the possibility of his having shown qualities to earn it. She grew interested in his account of the interview, seeing in it a contest in which he might easily have broken down, but apparently hadn't, as in the end he had kept his post. When he suddenly halted, she allowed herself to unbend so far as to ask a question. He had begun to tell them, with a laugh, and a "By Jove! though," that at one period of his interview he had actually said that if he couldn't have his own way in a certain matter he should ask Mr. Armitage Brown to find another agent, when he bethought himself that he must not say too much about changes that might be coming.

" What did he want you to do? " she asked.

" Well, don't say anything about it outside, but notice has got to be given all round. It's often done when a new landlord takes a property over—just a matter of form, till things are settled all round. What I told him was that some of them might not understand that, and it would make trouble unless I had authority to say that it wasn't intended to turn out old tenants, like the Davises and the Pettifers, for instance. He's a man who's accustomed to do things in a pretty high-handed way, and he didn't like it when I interrupted him to say what I thought about it. He said—oh, you should have seen his jaw set as he looked at me—he said, 'And suppose I say that when I say a thing is to be done in a certain way, it's got to be done in that way, Captain Fuller?' 'Well, then, I'll ask you to get somebody else to do it, Mr. Brown,' I said."

He took a sip of wine, enjoying the memory of his triumph. He was warmed and fed now, and had talked himself into equanimity.

"You really said that to him!" exclaimed his wife. She had had no idea that he had it in him to bluff to that extent, and had no idea now that he had not been bluffing. The revelation removed from her mind questions she had intended to ask about the notice to the tenants. If her husband could get the better of the millionaire in that way, what might not she herself be able to effect with her far greater powers?

"Yes, that's what I said. I think he had only meant to see what sort of answer I should give him, for he took it with a laugh, and told me to do things in my own way. I should say he was a *straight* fellow; hard, perhaps, and likes to have his own way, but——"

"But you can get round him. Well, that's good hearing, I'm sure. And you seem to have hit upon the way to do it, luckily for ús. But I shouldn't give him notice every time you want your own way, if I were you. You might give it once too often. Besides, I don't suppose your way would be any better than his, or so good. It's your business to keep in with him. What about *her?* Did he say anything about what's going to happen up at the house?"

"Yes, I was coming to that. It's one of the best things I've got to tell you. Mrs. Armitage Brown is coming down next week to begin to get the house in order. He's been suddenly called to America, and when he comes back they're going to the Riviera till April. He's got a villa there. He likes to go off in January, and——"

" Oh, you've talked enough about him. What about her? "

" I was just going to tell you. There'll be a lot to arrange, getting the house into order again. I fancy he thinks it will be a bigger job than she does; and running it afterwards, too. He asked me questions about that, and I told him that the old lord had had a secretary who was kept pretty busy with accounts and overlooking things generally, and that I thought it hadn't paid not to have one lately. I said I'd do what I could in the Estate Office, but——"

" Surely you didn't offer to take on all that extra work for nothing! Why, Mortimer had three hundred a year, and his rooms and keep in the house. Well, you *are* a fool! "

He looked annoyed for a moment. " I wish you'd let me finish," he said. " I was going to say that in the end he offered me another hundred pounds a year, and an extra clerk in the office, to take over the house accounts."

He had meant to lead up to it by repeating the conversation that had passed. He had felt the offer to be a generous one under the circumstances in which it had been made, and its effect would be that at last he would be in a position to save. But as it had been forced out of him, it fell flat.

"Well, upon my word! " she exclaimed. " A hundred a year for doing the work that old Mortimer got what was equal to five or six for! And you let him get the better of you as much as that! I thought we should have a different story before long."

He looked downcast, but defended himself with some irritation. " Mortimer was a relation; it was quite different," he said. " And a great deal went on in the old lord's time that people not in his position won't want.

Mr. Brown asked me about Mortimer's duties as secretary,
and when I told him some of them he laughed, and said
he shouldn't mind spending money on living comfortably
at Kemsale, but he didn't see himself spending it in that
way; and of course there's no denying that, rich as he is,
he won't fill anything like the position that old Lord
Meadshire did. Besides, he's got his own secretaries, and
you may say that half Mortimer's job will be done by
one of them. No; I should have been quite ready to take
the household accounts into the office, if he'd given me
another clerk. It was his own suggestion that he should
give me the extra hundred, and a clerk as well. It will
pay me handsomely for the extra work I shall have, and
he offered it in a nice sort of way. 'Well, I can't expect
you to save me money and get nothing out of it yourself,'
he said. 'How would it be if I increased your salary by
a hundred a year? Would that suit you?' I said I hadn't
expected anything of the sort and thanked him, but he
said I'd nothing to thank him for; he should save much
more than that by having things looked after by a careful
man. I thought that was generous. I believe it's true,
of course; but it isn't everybody who'd have said it, and
it showed that he'd taken my measure."

"Yes, he seems to have done that all right," she sneered,
"getting two people's work out of you for a little more
than the price of one. Still, it will just make the difference. There'll be no excuse for not getting into a decent
house now. You say you've got to give everybody notice.
That'll make it easy to shift that old cat out of 'The
Limes.'"

CHAPTER IX

GARDEN NOTES

SOMEWHERE about the middle of November, when work at Kemsale was in full swing, Alfred Brown came down for a few days' visit, and was so pleased with his surroundings that he stayed for a month, in spite of the carpenters and painters and plumbers that were all about him, and the absence of the sun, which he loved.

The sun was not completely absent, even during those weeks of November and December. On his first arrival it shone mildly for three days together, in a sweet belated Indian summer, and he told himself that he had never before realised how lovely the English country was. He was one of the many thousands of Englishmen who are entirely ignorant of what rural England is like except in the summer; but before he went back to London he had grown to love even the cold wet days, and to congratulate himself upon having acquired a new and valuable artistic impression.

Part of the charm of country life in the winter depends upon the kind of shelter to which one returns as dusk falls. Alfred considered himself fortunate in this respect. His sitting-room was the old steward's room of Meadshire days, which with most of the offices of the house had been bought in with all their effects standing. It was on the basement floor, and partly below the level of the ground outside. But it had two large windows, one facing south and the other east, and whenever there was any sun shining he

used to come down in the morning to find the room flooded
with it.

But he liked still better to come back to it in the evening, when the faded red curtains were drawn, and a piled-up
fire was blazing on the old-fashioned hearth. He would
change his wet boots for slippers, and ensconce himself in
a deep chair with a book and a pipe, and taste to the full
the delights of undisturbed peace and bodily comfort.

He would chat to the elderly lady who came in to lay
the table for his dinner. She and her husband were care-
takers, old Meadshire servants, who knew well enough
how a gentleman ought to be looked after; and he thought
he had never been so well served in his life. She had
taken a fancy to him, and he to her. She told him many
tales about "the family," and he liked to hear them, but
would sometimes confuse her by asking whether she didn't
really think it rather funny that a person like himself
should be in their place. "Now if you want to tease me,
sir," she would say, "I shall send Lizzie or my husband
in to wait on you"; or "It's because I think you'll do
very well that I like to have speech of you"; or "When
we're all in order you won't be seeing much of me; you
must talk sensible." But she would never admit that she
accepted the new order as a satisfactory substitute for the
old; nor could she hide what she felt about the downfall
of all that she had been brought up to. "Ah, it's a sad
thing to think of his lordship and her ladyship coming
down to live in that little Herons' Nest," she would say,
"and her so much looked up to and so suitable for living
in a great house like this, if I express myself right."

He began to be interested in her ladyship, in a way that
may be said to have been sentimental, although not in
any degree lover-like, because he had learnt that she had
reached what to a very young man is middle-age in the

other sex. She represented a romantic state which had
now suffered eclipse. He saw quite clearly, under the
influence of old Mrs. Parmiter's backward-looking talk,
that however much money might be lavished on Kemsale
in the future, it would never again be what it had been in
the past. Lady Grace had taken something away with her
that could not have been bought, if she had been willing
to sell it. Her influence was still over the wrecked house,
especially in those two quiet upstairs rooms which had
been hers. Comparing what was being made of the rest
of the house with those two rooms, or even with the solid
unpretentious comfort of this one that he was using, he
could only see in it irreparable loss, and came by degrees
to value more highly still the virtues that had gone out
of it. And even if the house could have been kept intact,
heavy gain as that would have been, its spirit would still
have departed; it could not have been supplied by those
who were going to live in it.

He asked about the Herons' Nest, and received an
impression that made him hope some day to know it intimately. It was about a mile away. Its situation, as
described by Mrs. Parmiter, hardly fitted in with the observations he had made of the country around. It stood
amongst pines on the edge of a rocky gorge; he imagined
a scene such as may be seen in Swiss mountains. There
had always been some sort of rustic cottage there, used
for picnics and such retirements; for it might actually
have been said to be in the grounds of Kemsale, approached
as it was by long shrubbery walks, and only recently fenced
off. Some years before, the cottage had been rebuilt,
greatly enlarged, and furnished for residence, though it
had never been continuously occupied. It had been left
to Grace for life by her grandfather, with some acres of
ground, which included the whole picturesque gorge, the

waterfall, and the heronry above it. Upon her death it would revert to the estate, and Meadshire had refused to sell its reversion. So there, in the very heart of the eighteen or nineteen thousand acres, were about thirty that were alienated. The price for the whole had been reduced on that account, but Meadshire had been obstinate about it.

When it had been decided to sell Kemsale, the Herons' Nest had been still further enlarged, to make Grace's home of it. And Meadshire had decided that he would make it his home with her. " I'm not denying it's a very pretty place," said Mrs. Parmiter, " and her ladyship is making it prettier still, with gardens and all. If all was as it should be here, with his lordship married and living in the great house, as his forbears have done before him, then it would be a very suitable place for her ladyship, as long as she didn't marry herself, dear heart! But as it is——! "

Alfred took an early opportunity of surveying this Naboth's vineyard, as it was likely to become to his father. From the road all that could be seen was a stream that had already lost some of its impetuosity, passing under an old stone bridge, and a little way from the bridge a gate, flanked by a rustic lodge, and a road leading through trees to much higher ground. A little farther along, after a corner had been turned, a bold scarp of rock could be seen, which soon softened into the thickly wooded slopes that were the usual feature of this long range of hills. All the rest was hidden from sight, and approached from other quarters the place was still hidden by its banked masses of trees. Only towards the summit of the hill, where the heronry was, the ground was a little more open; and the way in which the little river had cut its way through the rock could be seen at another point outside the new high fence. The occupants of the Herons' Nest were at least assured of complete privacy within the limits of that fence.

Alfred heard about Lady Grace and the Herons' Nest
from Mrs. Parmiter on the evening of his arrival.   He
heard more about them the next morning, when he
went out in the soft November sunshine to explore the
gardens.

He would much have preferred to go about unnoticed.
He was as far as possible from wishing to take up the
position of heir apparent to all the new splendour that was
being created about him.   He was so constituted that it is
probable he had never yet thought of himself as some day
succeeding to it all; otherwise he would certainly have
made some effort to reflect his own taste in the reconstitu-
tion of the house, for he could hardly have imagined himself
living in the sort of place it was going to be, as its master.
In the mood of his youth it would be irksome to him to
be tied to any house, least of all to the gorgeous palace
that his parents were creating for themselves.   He had
not even reached the point at which he wanted any sort
of resting-place of his own.   All he wanted was his freedom; and a couple of rooms that he could make himself
at home in, when he wanted to be with his family, were
all the anchorage that he needed.

But he was not able to dispense with attention.   He
had not seen much of the garden before he was joined by
the head gardener, who offered to show him round.

" I don't want showing round," he said; " thank you
very much.   I want to wander at my own sweet will.   I
say, this looks pretty beastly."

He was standing on the steps that led down to the
carpet garden, now bare of all its plants for the winter,
and showing only its intricate design of squared box
edging, raked soil, and rolled gravel.

The gardener's face darkened.   He was a Scotsman,
with a temper that he did not control when dealing with

his subordinates, although he did his best in that respect, otherwise, where he judged it politic to do so.

"The plants have all been taken in for the winter," he said. "It looks quite different when it is bedded out."

"Yes, I've seen it bedded out, and I didn't think it looked much better than it does now. I hate bedding out, especially on this scale."

"Well, it's a matter of opeenion," said Mackenzie dogmatically. "The carpet garden at Kemsale has always been considered a feature, and I may say that for the twelve years I've had to do with it it has lost none of its reputation."

He spoke rather disagreeably. He was "trying it on." He was of the class of old-fashioned gardeners extraordinarily capable within their limits, who take in no new ideas, and fight against all interference from their employers. At their most tyrannous, they regard the gardens which they are employed to overlook as their own, and expect those who own them to be content with their use as pleasure grounds. They are getting rarer with the growth of the taste for amateur gardening, but Mackenzie was an advanced specimen, and was prepared to go to all lengths to dominate the people who were now to pay him his wages. To all lengths short of losing his place, that is; for he was enough aware of the changes in gardening taste to be doubtful of getting another that would suit him. He had formed his opinion that the people he should now have to deal with would be just of the sort to be kept in their place, and he had also determined the lines on which it should be done. He had better begin at once with this very young-looking son, who did not look in the least formidable.

"I hear Lady Grace Ettien is making a very original garden at her new house," said Alfred. It had occurred to him that it was odd that she, who had presumably had the direction of what had been done in the gardens of Kemsale of late years, should have tolerated this expensive piece of ugliness, which offended his artistic eye, although he knew nothing of practical gardening. That was why he brought her name in.

He had aroused a hornets' nest. Grace had been the stumbling-block in the way of Mackenzie's complete autocracy. He had had to give in to her, and had done so without showing how much he resented her interference, so that she had only laughed at his cantankerousness, and taken his opposition to each and all of her plans as natural in an old servant. He had succeeded in confining her activities to the lower part of the garden, and her own unwillingness to spend money on it had confined them still further. But a greater cause of offence against her still was that she had not asked him to go with her to the Herons' Nest, but had taken his second in command, with two of the under gardeners. He would not have gone if she had asked him, and in this he was almost alone of the army of indoor and outdoor servants at Kemsale. He felt that his secret disloyalty had been found out when she left him where he was without a word, and the offence rankled deeply.

"You may call it gardening if you like," he said contemptuously. "Her ladyship's at liberty to play about as she pleases. She never knew what gardening was, and never will."

"Didn't she like this sort of thing?" asked Alfred quickly, indicating the bare beds near which they were still standing.

"No; she——"

"Well, I don't either. Now, I'm going to explore. Good-bye, for the present."

An hour later Alfred stood on the steps overlooking the two acres of carpet garden again. In the interval he had acquired the glimmerings of a delightful new occupation.

" I wonder if I could do it," he said, reflectively scratching his chin. " I think it would amuse me to try."

The next morning he wrote up to his father's London office, asking that a cablegram might be sent to him: " May I make some alterations in garden, and dismiss head gardener if necessary? Reply direct Kemsale. ALFRED."

The answer came the next day. It consisted of the single word " Yes." Armitage Brown liked to save money on cablegrams.

Alfred had already sent to London for books on garden design and found others in the library that helped him. He spent his evenings making elaborate plans for transforming the flat oblong on which the carpet garden was laid out into a formal garden of the most approved style. There were to be arcades and alleys of yew, fountains and tanks, if water could be provided, knots and parterres, treillages and statuary—every feature, in fact, that would have been found in every mediæval garden, and a good many besides. He was unhampered by any knowledge of the habits of flowers, or of the time it would take for his plans to mature; but he enjoyed himself exceedingly and finally produced a plan that did great credit to his artistic taste, and not a little to his capacity for assimilating knowledge that could be acquired from books.

On the second evening of his studies—he had as yet only made tentative sketches of the plan that was forming itself in his mind—Mrs. Parmiter informed him that Mr. Mackenzie wanted to see him.

" Ask him in," said Alfred.

Mackenzie was in a temper, which he made no serious effort to disguise, except by keeping his voice to a comparatively respectful key.

"I've come to ask, sir," he said, "if you'll be good enough to give me orders if you require anything from the houses."

"Certainly," said Alfred genially, "unless I take it into my head to pick something for myself. I picked a bunch of grapes this afternoon. Is that what you're referring to?"

"You'll excuse me, sir, but as long as I'm head gardener here, things can't be done in that way. My orders are to send up so much vegetables and flowers and fruit to Berkeley Square, and the grapes you picked were intended to be sent off to-morrow. If——"

"Oh, I'm sorry for that," said Alfred. "But there seemed to be several hundred bunches of grapes ready to be picked in the different houses. It's unfortunate that I should have hit upon the very one. How do you know them apart?"

"I've got my work to do," said Mackenzie in a tone slightly higher than he had used before, "and I'm quite ready to do it, as I understand quite well how, having lived in the highest families all my life. If I'm interfered with, I can't expect to give satisfaction. I had my instructions from her ladyship—I should say from Mrs. Brown—and I've got to carry those instructions out."

It may have been Alfred's imagination that he had made his mistake purposely, and corrected it on a note of contempt. At any rate it aroused his anger; but he did not show it.

"Well, you may take it from me," he said, "that Mrs. Brown won't mind in the least which particular bunches of grapes are sent up to her; and that seems to be all that you need worry about. If any complaints are made, you're quite at liberty to put the blame on to me."

"Then, sir, I shall make a complaint. I know my duty, and what's expected from men in my position— I dare say a good deal better than you do. Ever since I was 'prenticed as a boy, I've worked in the gardens of the nobility——"

"Yes, you told me that before," Alfred interrupted, "and it doesn't interest me at all. You're not working for the nobility now, and it's quite possible that you may have to adapt yourself to some changes. Now you've made your protest, and I've given you my answer. I don't look upon the houses or anything else in this place as yours, and as long as I'm down here I shall take what I like out of them."

Mackenzie was almost choking with rage. "If that's the way I'm to be spoken to, I shall give notice at once," he said, getting out his words with difficulty.

"I shouldn't advise you to be in too great a hurry," said Alfred. "If you do give notice, it will probably be accepted. I'll say good-night to you now."

When Mackenzie had taken himself off, with no further words, Alfred grinned to himself. "I don't believe any of the nobility could have done it better," he said. "Impudent beast!"

Then his face changed. "It's rather a shame to goad him on," he said, "when I hold all the trumps. I'm not going to kick a man out of his job if I can help it."

He wrote to his mother to tell her how matters stood. "All the servants that you have taken over seem to be a nice lot, except this fellow. He wants to tyrannize, and if you leave him to me I'll put him in his place, so that you will have no trouble with him when you come down. On his own lines I should say he was an excellent man, and you don't want to get rid of him if you can help it." He then went on to tell her about his garden plans. "It's the greatest fun in the world," he wrote. "The heir of all the Browns has taken very kindly to country life, and you may have to put up with his presence in the ancestral castle more often than you bargained for."

Now the head gardener at "The Towers" had comported himself in exactly the same way as Mackenzie proposed to do, and it had suited Mrs. Brown admirably. She took no interest whatever in the processes of gardening, and as long as any orders she might give as to what was to be brought into the house were obeyed, all the rest was left to his discretion. She had interviewed Mackenzie in a stately sort of way during her short stay at Kemsale, had given the orders which he was ready to carry out, and left all the rest to him. He had rubbed his hands and chuckled to himself after the interview. But he had none the less misread Mrs. Brown.

There was a strain of arrogance in her composition, which had been heightened by the wealth at her command. She had envisaged herself reigning at Kemsale with undisputed sway. She had been quite sincere when she had intimated over the tea-table at "The Towers" that it would be the part of the people living about her to cultivate her, not hers to cultivate them. Whatever her social success had been, she had owed it greatly to this calm dependence on her position as a woman much richer than others. She hunted no tufts, but enough tufts had hunted her to make her believe that all of them would, of any amongst whom she should be placed. If not, she would do without them. She did not know enough about country life to imagine a different kind of intercourse from that with which she had made herself familiar on the Riviera. Money would surround her at Kemsale;

money would draw the people she would want to know; money would do everything for her.

But there were little doubts and hesitations at the back of her mind all the time, and perhaps Mackenzie had divined some of them. Certainly he had " tried it on " with her, and cleverly enough, insinuating information as to how things were done in the establishments of the high nobility, and taking it for granted that she would like things done in the same way. So she would. And he was right too in thinking that much that he told her was news to her, as it very well might have been if she had known a good deal more than she did, for his assumptions had been preposterous. Where he was entirely wrong was in thinking that she had been awed into subjection to him, and that her haughty acceptance of his statements had been the mere veneer to hide it. He was quite ready to play up to her haughtiness, if he could have his own way in everything. But his way happened to suit her. Money was no object; he could spend as much money as he liked, if he obtained the right results. He was to supply the best of everything that was wanted; how he did it was his own affair; she did not want to be troubled with details.

When Alfred's letter came by the same post as Mackenzie's formal complaint, she was coldly angry. She had half suspected Mackenzie of trying to work upon her with his references to the "nobility," skilfully as he had used them, but thought she had shown him by her manner that he could not impress her by those means. The same reference in his letter was not the least of his mistakes. Furthermore, one of her troubles about Alfred had been that he was too easy with servants. She wanted him treated, as the son of the house, with the same machine-like deference she demanded for herself; and how could

that be expected when he seemed to prefer to make friends
with them? This man must have made himself extraordinarily offensive if Alfred had taken notice of it. His
complaint to her was a gross impertinence, practically
demanding of her that she should humiliate her son on
his behalf.

As for Alfred, it delighted her that he should have taken
up this new interest that would attach him to Kemsale.
She wanted him to play his part there, and a big part.
The alteration of a garden was not much, but it was
something; and the rest might come to be built upon
it. He had said in his letter that he liked the place, and
the life of the country, much better than he had thought
he should. She would see him hunting and shooting with
his neighbours after all, and doing her credit as neither
her husband nor her daughter could. This new taste of
his must be encouraged for all it was worth.

She wrote and told him to do exactly what he liked
with his formal garden. He had hinted at certain ideas
for it that he had rejected because of expense. She
would be responsible for anything that it might cost, and
she asked him to write further about it, so that she might
interest herself in it too. She had not hitherto cared
much for gardening, which, however, everybody nowadays
seemed to be going mad about. If he were going to take
it up, she should like to do so too. At the end of her
letter she wrote: " I have written to Captain Fuller asking him to dismiss Mackenzie, and find another man who
knows how to obey orders."

CHAPTER X

THE HEIR APPARENT

It must not be supposed that Alfred Brown, even in the early days of his stay at Kemsale, had been confined to the society of Mrs. Parmiter. However lightly he himself may have taken his position as heir apparent to the transferred glories of his house, it was of importance enough to others to bring them about him with attentions that at first he would rather have been without. He was not, however, of an unsociable habit, and before his month at Kemsale was far advanced he was glad to have houses to go to and people to talk with.

Captain Fuller he fell in with on the first morning, immediately after he had come in from his exploration of the garden, for Fuller was keeping an eye upon the workmen engaged in the house, and spent some time there every day. Fuller, acting upon instructions, asked him to luncheon. He refused for that day, but finding that he should have to accept some time or other accepted for the next. Barton's Farm was the first house in which he was entertained at Kemsale, and Mrs. Fuller's satisfaction was deep and sustaining.

When Mrs. Brown had come down to Kemsale with her sister-in-law, Mrs. Fuller had been all over her. The phrase may be a vulgar one, but Mrs. Fuller was a vulgar woman. Aunt Millie saw it; Mrs. Brown did not. But then Mrs. Fuller took a great deal more trouble with Mrs. Brown than she did with Aunt Millie. Aunt Millie was a poor relation, in her eyes, because she never put

123

herself forward, and was always very quietly dressed. And such women as Mrs. Fuller find it difficult to disguise their contempt for poor relations. She did her best in this instance, because Mrs. Brown was evidently fond of Aunt Millie, but her best only amounted to an occasional address, in which patronage was at least as much apparent as courtesy, and she would have been surprised to learn how closely the bright but quiet little lady had taken her measure.

Mrs. Brown was not at home to visitors during her brief sojourn, but as she had to be in constant communication with Captain Fuller, who had immediately entered upon his new duties in connection with the house, it was not possible to escape the attentions of his wife. These had been most skilfully brought to bear. Mrs. Fuller had made herself useful; she had made herself pleasant; she had burnt incense of a delicate aroma; she had made good her footing. After the three days' campaign, wearing but exciting, she was entitled to congratulate herself upon the success, as far as Mrs. Brown was concerned, of the tactics in which she placed such reliance. She had bluffed herself into being accepted as something other than she was.

Her knowledge of dress had done most for her. In this she could not have deceived Mrs. Brown, however hard she had tried. But she really knew. She had been a dressmaker—a lady dressmaker, of course—say a *modiste*. She did not seek to hide it. She had been poor, and "one must do something."

And since she had lived at Kemsale her husband's position had given her opportunities for lynx-eyed observation. She could reproduce the manners of the *élite*, if the effort required was not too long sustained. She could be quiet and self-possessed in the grand style, or in close

imitation of it. She could assume natural manners, extremely unnatural to herself. She could create the effect
of being in her native air when in touch with great wealth,
but of being quite unashamed of her own state of comparative poverty. She knew well what a bad card fulsomeness
is, and restrained her persistent inclination to play it.
Her flattery was of the most delicate kind, and her only
mistake was in not exercising it towards Aunt Millie, who
might possibly have been taken in by it, but, as it was,
saw right through her as if she had been made of glass,
and was only restrained from saying so by considerations
that concerned her own rather difficult position. She was
strong in her determination not to allow herself to be
influenced by her sister-in-law's riches; she would say
nothing to warn her against a woman whom she saw to
be influenced towards her by nothing else, for fear of
being misunderstood.

So Mrs. Fuller had her triumph for the time being.
When Mrs. Brown left Kemsale she thought of Mrs. Fuller
as an agreeable, well-connected woman, who had rather
thrown herself away, but had made the best of it, and
would never presume upon the intimacy to which she
seemed entitled. She asked her to propose herself for
luncheon in Berkeley Square if she should happen to be
in London. They might, perhaps, have an afternoon's
shopping together. And they would be seeing more of
one another when she settled at Kemsale in the spring.

Mrs. Fuller's reward seemed assured when Alfred, on
his introduction to her, amiably told her that he had
heard about her from his mother, who had rather hoped
to have seen her in London before this. His speech exhibited a shade more cordiality than his mother's had
done, and seemed to imply a willingness towards cordiality on his own part which made Mrs. Fuller very happy.

The more members of the family she could draw into her circle the stronger her position with her patroness would be. Alfred, at least, should return to London with golden accounts of her.

As for the match between him and Irene, upon which her thoughts had, of course, been busy, great care must be exercised at the present time. She saw now that the Rector had been too patently pursued. It had been proved to be so much more effective to cover up all signs of pursuit, while none the less eagerly pursuing. The same subdued note as she had used with Mrs. Brown would be imperative here. Alfred must never suspect that Irene was being thrown in his way. She must be her mother's precious treasure, destined for great things, but with no thought of finding them, so to speak, on the premises. She thought she could do it, if Irene played up; and she'd better.

The luncheon, though simple, as became what was no more than a farmhouse, was well served. The room looked what it should always have looked—the bright, tidy, cosy living-room of a modest but well-cared-for home. It drew admiration from Alfred, who had a taste for domestic simplicity.

" Well, it is rather nice," Mrs. Fuller admitted, looking round upon it as if she saw it for the first time, " but it isn't quite what we've been accustomed to. We came here for a few months, and have stayed for fifteen years. We shall be sorry for some things to leave the old place, but——"

" We're not going to leave it," interrupted her husband doggedly. He had fought her over this day in and day out ever since he had brought the news of his increase of income. And he would go on fighting against any unscrupulous attack she might bring to bear upon him.

Only the flicker of an eyelid showed Mrs. Fuller's annoyance. "Ah, that's a little matter of friendly dispute between us," she said, with a smile. "But I shall get my own way in the end."

Irene was quiet during the progress of the meal, and hardly spoke except when she was spoken to. This was chiefly from laziness, but her air of indifference towards the much-dowered young man fitted in admirably with her mother's ideas. It drew Alfred to go a trifle out of his way to include her in the conversation, and Mrs. Fuller thought she detected a dawning interest in him which was almost more than could have been hoped for at this very early stage. When he suggested that they should all go out somewhere in the car, and the two ladies went up to prepare themselves, she said to her daughter, with suppressed excitement: "My dear, you're behaving splendidly. Don't let him see yet that you're in the least interested in him."

Irene looked at her with her large eyes, and went into her room without speaking. She drifted up to a looking-glass and surveyed herself. "I'm *not* in the least interested in him," she said. "Nor in old Compton either. I wish mother would leave me alone."

They drove far afield, and touched the bounds of the estate at many points, but hardly went outside it. The progress was made semi-royal by Mrs. Fuller. "All these roads and lanes thread your father's property," was the note of her pointings. "All these rich meadows, fat ploughlands, deep woods, meandering streams; all these snug farmhouses, pretty cottages, churches, vicarages, manor-houses, and villas are his." And from beneath it all peeked out the consciousness: "And they will all be yours some day."

Fuller sat in front beside the *chauffeur,* and turned

round every now and then with a word of explanation. Alfred sat on the back seat opposite to Irene, who, lulled by the soft air and swift motion, and the after effects of a luncheon rather larger than she was accustomed to, found it difficult to keep her eyes open, and impossible to arouse herself to conversation. Alfred occasionally addressed a word to her, and looked at her frequently, with a good-natured expression which Mrs. Fuller translated into admiration. It was all going as well as it could be expected to go.

They had come into a long stretch of straight road, at the other end of which appeared a black figure on a horse. "Here comes the Rector," said Fuller, turning round.

"Oh, stop him," said Mrs. Fuller eagerly. "It will be a good opportunity to introduce him to Mr. Alfred." He was to be called so, she had explained with friendly emphasis, to distinguish him from his father.

The car, which was going at a considerable pace, began to slow down; the black figure came trotting along the road towards it. Mrs. Fuller leaned out, and the Rector's face darkened as he saw who it was that was about to stop him. He could hardly avoid reining up, as the car had come to a standstill, and the lady was so very insistent. He took off his hat without a smile, and looked at her inquiringly.

"Oh, Mr. Compton, I want to introduce you to Mr. Alfred Brown, who has come to stay here for a few days."

Compton said: "How do you do, sir?" still without a smile, and then trotted on, with his face disagreeably set.

"He didn't seem violently anxious to know me," said Alfred, whose first impulse was to salve over the affront to the lady's feelings.

But Mrs. Fuller, besides being not altogether unaccustomed to such affronts in that and other quarters, had

fulfilled her object, which was to display herself and her
daughter in intimate contact with the heir apparent. " Oh,
you never know how to take Mr. Compton," she said
lightly. " I suppose he's been cubbing, a long way from
home, and feels hungry. He'll call on you now he knows
you are here. We don't care for him much ourselves, but
of course you have to keep in with the parson of your
village to some extent."

" Well, I bain't terr'ble wrapped up in parsons myself,"
said Alfred. " I don't much care if he doesn't call on me."

" Of course, he's not quite like ordinary parsons," said
Mrs. Fuller. " He's the brother of a peer, and all that
sort of thing. He's quite a person to know in this part
of the world, though he shuts himself up a good deal.
One has to make allowances for him."

Alfred began to feel a doubt as to whether Mrs. Fuller
wasn't, after all, rather a tiresome sort of person. She
seemed to be a bit of a snob. No woman who respected
herself would have taken the man's rudeness in that way,
or have run the risk of meeting with it if she knew that
it might be offered. That he was " the brother of a peer,
and all that sort of thing," should not have been considered a palliation. It certainly should not be as far as
he himself was concerned. If the Rector did call on him,
which seemed unlikely, he would not see him, or return
his call.

He was, in fact, angry, though he showed no signs of
it. He was aware that there might be some feeling against
people like himself and his parents taking the place of
people like the Meadshires, which was one of the reasons
why he had kept himself somewhat aloof from the dis-
cussions and preparations that had gone on in his family
with regard to Kemsale. He was not going to spoil his
happy freedom by settling himself in a position where

"all that sort of thing" was of such importance. It was of none whatever to him. Most people claim to be indifferent to rank, but Alfred really was so. He was ready to make friends with all and sundry; he was incapable of resting himself upon the accidents of his own birth with those less fortunate than himself, or of paying court to anybody because of the accidents of theirs. The whole question of rank and wealth, as it affected a man, was a nuisance. The jolliest companions he had known had had neither. So it had come to pass that he had rather kept out of the way of those who were gilded with "all that sort of thing." They might be as jolly as anybody; he had come across those that were; but more probably their standards would be different from his. Better not run the risk. There were plenty of others in the world.

And now Mrs. Fuller had let him in for a snub from a person of the suspected class, and had taken it for granted that he would swallow the snub because of the class. He was as much annoyed with her as with the person who had dealt it.

He dropped the Fullers at Barton's Farm as dusk fell, and refused to come in to tea. He was already rather tired of the Fullers, and wanted to get back to his cosy room and his garden designing.

He was not, however, to enjoy his solitude just yet. As he got out of the car, Douglas Irving was just turning away from the door.

He introduced himself. "Fuller told me you were here for a day or two," he said. "I thought I'd look you up, and see if I could do anything for you. You can't be very comfortable here with all this mess about."

Alfred was rather pleased to see a man near to his own age than any he had talked with for the last few

days. And there was something about Douglas's frank
and natural address that attracted him.

"Not comfortable?" he echoed. "You come in and
see."

They were standing before a side entrance, more frequently used than the main one. Alfred led the way
through a hall and passage full of the ladders and gear
of the decorators, and down a flight of stone stairs to
the echoing basement. He threw open a door. "There!
What can you want more comfortable than that?" he
asked.

A fire of logs was burning on the hearth; a lamp was
on the table, and lighted candles on the high chimney-
piece. The curtains were close drawn; toasted muffins
were keeping up their circulation on an old brass grid in
front of the fire, and a copper kettle was purring on the
hob. The invaluable Mrs. Parmiter had even put Alfred's
felt slippers to warm against the fender, although he was
not accustomed to wear them, except in his bedroom.
She had a genius for creating an atmosphere.

"It looks like a poem by Cowper," said Douglas. "Who
would have thought there was a room like this in this
barrack of a place?"

Alfred had thrown a searching look at him when they
had come in to the light. He was not quite as young
as he had thought, but he felt inclined to like him extremely.
Young men do take sudden fancies to men older than
themselves. Douglas Irving, with his military bearing
and his well-cut country clothes, had all the air of belonging to the class upon which Alfred was accustomed to
look askance, but he forgot all that, and pressed him to
sit down and make himself at home. Tea would be in
directly.

"I've had tea," said Douglas, "but there weren't any

muffins. How do you do, Mrs. Parmiter? Got somebody to look after again, eh?"

Douglas talked about shooting. Alfred began to fear that his type was too pronounced to afford probability of common interests, in spite of the reference to a poet not usually read by sportsmen. He laughed when he himself was invited to shoot. "I've never fired a gun in my life," he said. "It's a bit late to begin now."

"Not a bit," said Douglas. "You'll certainly want to shoot if you're going to live here. Come out with me some morning quietly; I'll lend you a gun and put you up to it. You'll be as keen as mustard when you've brought down your first pheasant."

"It's most awfully good of you," said Alfred. "Perhaps I will some day, but you'll find me an awful duffer. I've never gone in for sport; never wanted to; I've had all sorts of other things to do. Still, if you'd put me in the way of it, I might give it a chance."

Douglas did not quite know what to make of him. He had not expected Armitage Brown's son to be like this. He had pictured a young man either inclined to give himself airs because of his potential command of money, or inclined to subservience through not being quite sure of himself. But this young man had thanked him with warmth for his offer, without a trace of subservience, and had admitted his ignorance of what a purse-proud young man would prefer to be thought to know something about. He was "all right" too, according to Douglas's standard—boots not quite thick enough for country wear, but collar and tie correct, and suit such as anybody might wear who didn't care to go to the expense of having his tweeds made in Savile Row. His manner and speech were "all right" too. He was, in fact, a "gentleman."

But still, there was something about him that didn't

exactly fit in with the ordinary public school type, whose
virtues and limitations alike such men as Douglas Irving
feel most at home with. The sons of self-made men are
sent to big schools and turned out to pattern; and if
possessing no salient characteristics of their own are in-
distinguishable from the sons of fathers who are not self-
made. Their address to their fellows is as careless and
as unenthusiastic; they don't " swank "; their tastes, habits,
and appearance are woven on the same loom. But this
young man did not conform in all respects. There seemed
to be a thread of originality woven into his tissue, and
originality is suspect until it is known on what grounds it
rests. Still, he was inclined to like the fellow. He was
very heavily gilded, which might induce liking or the
reverse, according to circumstances. If he were not himself inclined to protrude the gilding it would not make
him the less likable.

" What have you been doing with yourself, if you haven't
had time for sport? " Douglas asked.

" Oh, painting and writing a bit, and wandering about
generally. I tried the City for a year when I came down
from Cambridge, but it didn't suit me at all. I suppose
you might call me a sort of Bohemian."

He said it with an engaging smile. He wanted to stand
well with this older man, and doubted whether his sym-
pathies would extend as far as any sort of Bohemianism.
Cambridge had been thrown in as a sop to his supposed
prejudices in favour of a conventional career.

Douglas was entirely satisfied. The ground was cleared.
His own tastes were not Bohemian, but they were artistic
within limits. He would never have chosen those interests
of his as an opening for conversation, but he was quite as
ready to talk about them as about sport. They got on
well together after that. Douglas stayed for an hour,

and Alfred promised to dine at Little Kemsale the next evening.

"Oh, Douglas, I think he's a dear," said Beatrix, when the dinner had been duly eaten, and Alfred had gone away at a late hour of the evening. "He's not a bit spoilt."

They went back to the library. "You'd hardly expect a fellow of that parentage to turn out as he has," said Douglas. "He seems to be bored by it all. I must say it's a great feather in his cap that he takes it as he does. It makes one like him extraordinarily. If the rest of them are like that, we shall have some very jolly new neighbours."

"I don't think they are. At least, his mother isn't, if she's anything like Tottie's description of her. A high and mighty lady, as one might have expected."

"Really, Tottie's the limit!" exclaimed Douglas. "It's plain she's got her claws into this youth. Wants him for Irene, I suppose."

"I think he sees through her all right. I like him for not saying things against her. Douglas, Mr. Compton seems to have been awfully rude to him."

Douglas considered this. "Of course he hates the Browns coming here," he said. "But surely he can't be meaning to cut them altogether."

"It looks like it. But I suppose it was Tottie and Irene he really shied at. Can't you see how Tottie would behave? 'Here's somebody much better worth getting hold of than you are.' That's what would stick out of her."

Douglas smiled and pinched her chin. "How uncharitable you are," he said. "What should we do without our Tottie? But I do think it's a bit too bad of Compton, all the same. You couldn't have a nicer fellow than young Brown is—modest and bright and clever. Oh, I think he's an acquisition. I expect Bill and the rest of them

will like him. I'll teach him to shoot, and he shall come
out with us when we have a quiet day. I expect he'll be
asking *us* to shoot next year. May as well make friends
with the Mammon of unrighteousness, anyhow."

"I shall tell Grace how nice he is," said Beatrix. "I
wonder if Lord Meadshire will call on him."

"Not he," said Douglas. "He's got his knife into
the Browns and everything and everybody connected with
them."

CHAPTER XI

THE CHANCEL PEW

On Sunday morning Alfred went to church, which was not his usual practice. But here in the country it seemed to be part of the delightful leisurely progress of things. You got up in the morning with a sense of the day being different from other days. You marked the difference by the clothes you put on. You had sausages for breakfast, if you were looked after by a Mrs. Parmiter. After breakfast it was almost your duty to idle until church time, and the idleness was pleasant, as it would not have been if you had felt you were wasting the morning. Church was a mild excitement, tuned to the key of the day. You met people, going and coming, whom you knew; you saw them and other people at a new angle, and joined with them in various acts of at least some social significance. The cigarette that you lit immediately you were clear of the churchyard was better than other cigarettes, and you would be quite ready when the time came for your luncheon, or early dinner, which with a Mrs. Parmiter at the helm would certainly include roast beef.

And so on throughout the day—slight changes in occupation and in consequent outlook, which brought you to the end of it with renewed zest for the usual activities of the week. But to taste the full flavour of the day you must go to church, at least in the morning.

Alfred went rather early. He had been at Kemsale five days now, and it had begun to dawn upon him that he was expected to play a part. The indications had been subtle but pervasive, and there had been nothing as yet to alarm him. But in his general ignorance of what might be expected of him he was inclined to be watchful, and it had occurred to him as he was dressing that there might be some question of a squire's pew, which he would be expected to occupy. He had no intention of occupying a conspicuous position of any sort, and thought he might escape the risk of being asked to do so by slipping into the church ten minutes or so before the service began.

He did so, and found himself alone there, except for the sexton, who was pulling at one of the ropes that hung in front of the closed west doors, and two old women in black bonnets, with their heads close together, in a pew near him. There were six crisp loaves of bread on an old coffer that stood against the north-west wall of the church, and before any one else entered four more old women came and joined the first two, one of them advancing a surreptitious finger towards the loaves as she passed them. They were the recipients of Cope's Charity, Cope having been in his grave for the last two hundred years or more, and being therefore responsible for at least sixty thousand attendances at divine worship on the part of the successive old women who had carried off his loaves during that period.

Kemsale Church dated from the fourteenth century. It was of noble proportions, and its great square tower was a landmark for miles around. Its interior had points of interest here and there, but its character had been much lessened by an elaborate restoration that it had undergone some fifty years before. It was too large for any congregation that was ever likely to gather in it, except on the occasion of a Meadshire wedding or funeral, and the seating that had been put in left broad open spaces which to some extent redeemed the havoc it had undergone.

Alfred seated himself in as retiring a position as he could find, but there was none in which he could not be seen by any one entering the church, except a large double pew behind a carved screen in the chancel. This was probably the pew that went with the house, and he thought that, after all, he would have been more comfortable in it than elsewhere.

But did it go with the house? A few villagers had trickled in, but he had not been in the church more than three minutes before a middle-aged man with a red face, followed by a tall thin lady with a pale one, entered and walked straight up the nave to take their places in this pew. Alfred had no difficulty in identifying them as Lord Meadshire and Lady Grace Ettien, and felt some surprise at the stare with which Meadshire surveyed him and the frown that showed itself when he had evidently identified him in turn. Lady Grace had also looked at him, and as she had followed her brother up the aisle she had blushed and seemed ill at ease.

Alfred took it that they—or rather Meadshire—had heard that he was at Kemsale, and had come early to church for a similar reason to his own, to occupy the position they wished. Supposing they had found him already in the chancel pew! He smiled when he thought how their respective desires fitted in. And then he felt rather serious. Was this man, whose property his father had bought at a high price, going to take up a position of hostility towards them for no other reason than that they were the purchasers of what he had had to sell? If so, surely this was rather a small way of showing it. It did not occur to him until later that the laying claim to what had obviously been the Meadshire family pew might be a considered act of aggression which the new owner of Kemsale would be invited to fight. It was quite possible that the rights to the pew did go with the house, and had been bought with all the rest. He hoped his father would not consent to fight at all on such a question, but it was disturbing to feel that enmity was to be shown from the first by people who, so far as he knew, had no reason to show any.

The school children clattered in, and up the wooden stairs to the gallery; farmers and their wives and families, cottagers, little shopkeepers from the village, began to fill the pews.

The Rector came in, and passed close to where Alfred was sitting. He allowed his gaze to rest upon him for a moment and went on to his vestry. It was made plain, in some indefinable way, that his failure to give him any sign of recognition was not because this was not the time or place to give such signs, but because he had no intention of giving them at all.

Miss Merriman came in—a short, grey-haired lady in old-fashioned attire, whom Alfred knew to be the present occupant of " The Limes." She was well off, and much given to good works. She was accompanied by three young girls in the most elaborate London attire, who caused considerable attention amongst the congregation, and seemed to enjoy it, although all three of them behaved beautifully, and sang psalms and hymns in such a way that everybody listened to them. They were members of some Actresses' Guild in which the good lady was interested. She often produced week-end visitors of an unconventional description. She had once brought six London flower-girls to Kemsale Church, shawls, large-feathered hats, and all; but they had also behaved very well.

The Irvings came in, Woozle held firmly by her father and Jimbo by his mother, so as to subdue any untimely exuberance of spirit.

The Fullers came in, and upon seeing Alfred, who had by this time realized that he had taken up a position not usually occupied in that assembly by a man with a gold ring, Mrs. Fuller paused, and issued whispered instructions to her husband to invite him to a seat with them in the middle of the church.   He refused the offer, somewhat annoyed that it should have been so ostentatiously made.

He regarded the Rector with some interest, as he went through the service, and occasionally turned his gaze upon the pair in the chancel pew, who were in full view of the church when they stood up.   Here were two people, if not three, out of those who were ostensibly gathered together to perform an act that implied peace and charity between them—two people, if not three, who had put themselves into a position of hostility towards him, a stranger, and had not scrupled to show it in this place— had even made use of this place to show it in.   Like many who confess to no creed, Alfred had a deep respect for the spirit of Christianity, wherever it showed itself, and could not but think it odd that people who made public profession of their beliefs, and amongst them one who had set himself apart to teach them, should show so little.   The sense of personal enmity, which he had done nothing to deserve, disturbed him, who was so ready to show goodwill to all men.   It spoilt the serenity without which, careless as he was, he would not have cared to take part in a church service.   It destroyed the sense that he would otherwise have enjoyed in such a church as this, of a little company of people, most of whom knew one another in their daily lives, gathered together, on the day of rest, in peace and concord.

The Rector read the service in a monotonous, conventional tone, and the lessons in the same way.   His sermon was short and academic, showing no signs of the wide

knowledge with which his mind was stored, or indeed of
any qualities above the ordinary, either of head or of
heart. It was difficult to imagine him moved in his actions
or impulses by principles other than those which any
decent-living, well-educated Englishman of no religious
faith whatever would acknowledge. Perhaps his faith
gave him some hope for the future; probably he found
in it support for some of the opinions he had formed on
mundane affairs. It did not seem likely to be of much
use to any one but himself.

Lord Meadshire occasionally sang a line or two of a
hymn or a psalm, but spent most of his time looking about
him. Alfred thought that his presence in church might
have been dictated by his wish to " set an example," and
smiled as the thought occurred to him. But as a matter
of fact he had come very seldom to church when he had
owned Kemsale, and if his retention of rights in the
Meadshire pew should depend upon his occupying it regularly, was unlikely to persist in the struggle.

The attitude of Lady Grace was different. She was
devout and collected, and never once, when she was in
view of the congregation, did she look towards them.
Alfred watched her with interest. Her profile, which was
all he saw of her face, did not attract his artistic sense.
It seemed to him indicative of long descent, with its high-
bridged nose and arched eyebrows, and he wondered idly
why no such facial signs showed themselves in her brother,
whose appearance would have led no one to guess the
fact of his birth. But the aristocratic type—if there really
is such a thing—is not beautiful in itself, and Grace was
already past her first youth. Alfred, whose own youth
was strong in him, regarded her almost as elderly.

And yet she attracted him. Her expression had sweetness, subdued as it was. It seemed to have sadness too.

He felt a quick sympathy with her. She was "getting on." She would probably not marry. If the immensities of Kemsale had been her native air, as they never could be that of those who were to take her place, and if she could not now look forward to breathing it elsewhere, then she was to be pitied, as her brother was not. And if she cherished a grudge against those who had dispossessed her, she might be forgiven for it.

But as he observed her, it came into his mind that she, at least, bore no grudge. Her meek downcast eyes were not those of a woman who hugs a grievance. And if it was the case that her brother had marched up to that chancel pew with the idea of pushing a claim, the look of her as she had followed him seemed to show that she had not done so in his spirit of aggression. Alfred's mind lightened as he eliminated her from the list of those who had already made up their minds to dislike him and his. Perhaps they would be friends some day. It seemed absurd that they shouldn't be, living so close together, in a place where they would be obliged to meet now and then. Kemsale had been rudely disrupted, and was being reconstituted in a fashion that would give it an altogether new character. But it was its old character that was beginning to make itself felt with Alfred, to the extent at least that, having come down for the shortest possible visit, he was now inclined to throw out roots, as he had never before done in any place in which he had lived. And so much of Kemsale's old character was connected in his mind with this gentle lady, who had hitherto lived all her life in it. Yes, decidedly they would make friends, if it were in any way possible.

The service came to an end, and the congregation filed out, ready for the next process that marked the day for what it was. This was, immediately, greeting of friends

and acquaintances in the precincts of the church, and
walking away in conversation. Alfred manœuvred so as
to emerge from the sphere of silence with the Irvings, and
not with the Fullers. In the porch Beatrix asked him to
lunch with them.

"Bless you for being so prompt," he said. "I will
come with the greatest of pleasure."

Mrs. Fuller almost pushed her way out. "Oh, how do
you do, Mr. Alfred?" she said in a voice that carried, and
was intended to do so. "You are coming to lunch with
us, aren't you? You mustn't be left to mope by yourself
on Sunday."

Alfred regretted the impossibility, and she was going
on to ask him to supper, but broke off to say: "Oh, I
want to introduce you to Lord Meadshire and Lady Grace.
Do just wait a moment. They will be out directly."

She made a motion almost as if she would have laid
hands on him; but he pretended not to hear her, raised his
hat and walked on with the Irvings.

She came after him, and renewed her request. She
could not bear to be deprived of the exiguous triumph of
bringing the old and the new together publicly. It was
awkward, because they were in a stream of people. But
by the lych gate it had thinned enough for Alfred to be
able to say without being overheard: "I'd really rather
not, Mrs. Fuller, thank you all the same."

He could not altogether keep the annoyance out of his
voice; but she was too eager in her desire to keep him
to notice it. "Oh, don't be shy," she rallied him. "They
won't bite you."

Now he was angry. "I'm not at all sure that they
want to know me," he said. "Mr. Compton evidently
didn't." Then he left her, and joined the Irvings.

The stream of people had now left the churchyard.

Irene, quite indifferent to her mother's desires, was waiting for her, reading the inscriptions on the tombstones that came within her view. Herbert Fuller, who was church-warden, had not come out yet. But as Mrs. Fuller joined her daughter, Meadshire and Grace appeared under the porch.

She greeted them with a warmth that was met by Grace with politeness, by Meadshire with joviality. He found material for constant amusement in "Tottie" and her ways. "How are you, Mrs. Fuller, how are you?" he inquired, wringing her hand. "Aren't you going to say 'How do you do,' Irene? By Jove, you look more fetch-ing than ever. You've been buying clothes, both of you. I know you have."

Irene allowed herself to smile, though she was not amused. There had been a time when a higher alliance even than that with the Rector had seemed to be indi-cated for her. But, misunderstanding so many things, Mrs. Fuller had never really misunderstood Meadshire's attitude towards herself and her daughter. Bright visions, half-formed, had to be given up. He was not serious. Besides, he was too old, and "unsteady" besides. It would never have done. She had spoken of it regretfully, to people at a safe distance from Kemsale. He had seemed to be attracted, but she had felt obliged to put a stop to it. He had taken it well upon the whole, and they had remained friends. Irene, fortunately, had not suffered; she had not cared for him "in that way," although, of course, they had been great friends ever since she had been a little girl. Her heart, she thought, was engaged elsewhere, and in a quarter which promised a far more satisfactory development; she could not say anything more about that at present, but if it "came off," it would be all that could be wished.

" Oh, Lord Meadshire," she said. " I did want to introduce you to young Alfred Brown, who is here for a few
days. He is such a nice young fellow. We have been
seeing a great deal of him."

Meadshire dropped his chaffing manner. " Thank you,
Mrs. Fuller," he said, frowning, " I don't want to be
introduced to young Alfred Brown. If you had done so,
I should have told him so."

The Rector and Herbert Fuller came out of the church.
" Oh, but I'm sure you would like him," she pleaded. " He
really isn't half bad; quite a gentleman, which you might
not have expected. Oh, Mr. Compton, good-morning. We
were just talking of young Alfred Brown. You were really
rather rude to him the other day, you know. But I suppose you were too much taken up with your deep thoughts.
Shall you call on him? I think he expects it, you know."

" I've no intention of calling on him," said Compton,
and went off along the path that led to the rectory. Meadshire and Grace were already at the lych gate, where a
powerful car was waiting for them. Meadshire never
walked if he could help it, or had himself carried anywhere under about forty horse-power.

" Well, really, people don't seem very agreeable this
morning," said Mrs. Fuller. " Any one would think they
hadn't been to church at all. Irene, *did* you see those
chorus girls with old Mother Merriman? I could hardly
take my eyes off them. I call it a disgrace bringing people like that into a church. Well, I've done *my* best
to bring people together. What's up with them, Herbert?
Aren't they going to have anything to do with the
Browns? "

Herbert could not inform her. He looked worried.
The almost forcible occupation of the chancel pew boded
trouble, in which he would probably be involved. She

had not apparently noticed it, and he said nothing about it to her.

"Well, I don't know that it much matters," she said, after a pause of consideration. "The Browns are *our* friends, anyhow; and the others don't amount to much now—except for their titles."

CHAPTER XII

MORE GARDEN NOTES

WITH great manipulation of cartridge paper, compasses, T-square, and water colours, the great plan for the formal garden had been finished. The Irvings had expressed warm interest in the project. Formal design had not come within their scope, but planting of all sorts had; perhaps their experience would be of value. They were invited to come round by Kemsale on their way home from church, and examine the result of much planning.

They walked through the ground-floor rooms before descending to Alfred's appointed retreat. Decoration had already been set in hand here, at the same time as structural alterations were going on elsewhere. The blue saloon, pink saloon, and yellow saloon were already nearing completion. Alfred said nothing as he piloted them through the echoing spaces. And neither Beatrix nor Douglas said anything, although they would willingly have made comment if they could have found anything appreciative to say.

It was left to Woozle to express an opinion, which she did in the following concise phrase: " I think it-th puffickly beathly."

All three of them looked at one another, Douglas and Beatrix with a quick deprecatory glance at Alfred, before falling upon Woozle to rend her, Alfred with his head on one side, inquiringly. Woozle escaped the rending. All three of them burst into laughter, and laughed for a long time.

"Nothing more need be said. Now we'll go downstairs and look at my plan," said Alfred.

The plan proved to be of such interest that they decided to take it on to Little Kemsale to study more at their leisure. On the way there they looked at the carpet garden, soon to be dispossessed. "If you like to say that this is 'puffickly beathly,'" said Alfred to Woozle, "I shan't blame you."

But Woozle said she had liked it when all the flowers were there, and Jimbo put in a sudden claim to having once walked over one of the beds, to see if it was really like a carpet.

"He did, the bad wicked man," said Beatrix. "We had to tell Mackenzie, the head gardener, and he was very angry with us, wasn't he, Jimbo?"

"So was you," said Jimbo, quick to see the change of attitude. "But you're not angry now."

She embraced him. "You'll ruin that child," said Douglas, as he took advantage of her example to embrace the too-entrancing Woozle.

"I think Mackenzie will be angry with me when he's told what is going to be done," said Alfred. "It will be broken to him to-morrow morning."

"That's a gentleman you've got to keep under your thumb," said Douglas, "unless you want to live all your life under his. Poor Grace Ettien did. She had to fight for everything she wanted to do. Let's go through the lower garden. It's only a little way further. She did some jolly things there; but everything she planted had to be got through him—for the sake of his commission, I suppose—and even then she had to keep a sharp look-out that he got the right things, and planted them right."

They went down through the lower terraces and slopes,

charmingly arranged to afford mild surprises, sun here and shade there, vistas and glimpses, beauty of flower and foliage, green spaces, and above all that sense of peace and seclusion which a well-planned English garden should always offer, even when all its trees are bare.

"Dear Grace!" said Beatrix regretfully. "Her garden is like her, sweet and gentle."

The speech pleased Alfred. "I think it's the best thing here," he said. "I hope mine will be half as successful."

A few late roses were still blooming. The pomp of crimson and bright pink was over; these were faint in colour and delicate in scent. Alfred cut half a dozen of them for Beatrix—all the perfect ones that the bushes could show. They, also, seemed rather like the quiet gentle lady whom he had just seen at her devotions. These lower gardens were another part of Kemsale that kept their flavour amidst all the ruthless change, and should keep it still, if he had his will. His own changes, he prided himself, would have the effect of building up on the basis of the old, which was beginning to appear to him such a priceless though easily dispersed treasure.

What he felt about it all was expressed both by Douglas and Beatrix.

"You know, in a way," said Douglas, with a laugh, "the carpet garden seems more in keeping with what's being done in the house than all this does."

"Grace always hated the carpet garden," said Beatrix. "She would be very interested in your plans. I wish we could get her to see them."

"Isn't Auntie Grace coming to tea this afternoon?" asked Woozle, with her toothless lisp. "She gen'ly does on Sundays."

"I expect she will," said her mother. She did not say

anything further, having observed the little comedy in the churchyard.

There was still time to go round the garden at Little Kemsale before luncheon. Alfred, who would hitherto have considered that a garden, at a time of year when nearly all its flowers were over, could have no interest for anybody, was beginning to have a dim idea of the absorbing interest of the autumn and winter planning and preparation. " I believe I shall take to this," he said. " But there seems to be a terrific lot to learn. Tell me candidly now how far my ignorance has affected the plan I've made."

" We'll go all through it this afternoon," said Beatrix.

Douglas was more direct. " The plan's all right as far as it goes," he said. " But it's only half done. I suppose you'll hand it over to Mackenzie to carry out. Well, he'll get the yews planted, the beds dug, and all that; but what are you going to put into them? If you leave it to him it will be the carpet garden over again, which will be ' puffickly beathly.' "

The plan had simplified itself to broad alleys and arcadings of yew, with wide spaces of lawn, and here and there box-edged beds and borders. There was to be a stone-edged lily tank in the wide central space, and a fountain jet at each end of the main transverse alley. When Alfred had written to his mother—whose reply was to be expected the next morning—he had had in his mind a more elaborate framework to his garden, with higher boundary walls, wrought-iron gates above and below, and at each corner little Renaissance pavilions, with flagged patch connecting them. But as he had worked out this idea throughout the whole of a long evening, he had found himself losing his zest for it. It would be very expensive. He had little doubt about being authorized, and even encour-

aged, to spend as much as he wanted to spend over it.
It was not that that damped his ardour. It was his own
protest against depending upon the lavish use of money
to bring happiness and interest in life that was rising in
him. He had never done it before. He had been surrounded by wealth all his life, and had instinctively recoiled from it as a danger to true contentment. He had
always been happy, except when he had been sitting at his
desk in his father's office. He had had a few qualms occasionally as to whether he had a right to make himself so
happy, since he was doing nothing, or very little, that
would lead him anywhere. His father's character lived
in him to that extent. But such doubts had troubled him
little as long as he was not resting himself upon the golden
pinnacle that was there for him if he wished to occupy it.
If he were to leave his simple, inexpensive way of life,
and begin to think about what pleasures he could obtain
by the spending of money, his contentment would vanish.
He felt it, though he did not analyse his feeling. Not to
spend more money than he could help, not to think about
money at all, was his way of keeping himself unspotted
from the world.

Directly he threw over his elaborate plan, his pleasure
in designing his garden returned. The other would have
been interesting, and, in comparison with what was now
being done at Kemsale, and even with what had been
done in the past in the way of expensive improvements,
its cost would have been negligible. But, somehow, it
was not for him to set it in hand. And Lady Grace's
garden, as he liked to call the lower slopes, had shown
him that it was not necessary to spend large sums of
money in order to get gracious and charming effects.
Great skill was necessary, as he was beginning to see, but
he thought it would not be beyond him to gain that skill;

he had already gained a good deal by his studies. At least let the skill come first, and let not ignorance be plastered over by great spending.

He was a trifle dashed when Douglas, with the plan spread out before him, and all three of them ready to give it their undivided attention, said: "Of course, you know, this is going to cost an awful lot."

"But I've kept it very simple," Alfred expostulated. "They'll have to lay water on for the fountains, but bar that and the bit of stonework, it's nearly all of it yew."

"Yes, but it will take thousands of yews, and you'll want them a good size, I suppose. You won't want to wait twenty years before you get any sort of effect."

"That's where I'm ignorant," said Alfred. "But if that's all, I don't think it matters."

"Ah, well," said Douglas, "then if I were you I should get trees as big as possible. If they are carefully looked after when they are planted they'll come together in a couple of years, and you'll get your effect almost from the first."

He had given his warning, and was relieved of responsibility. He had not really supposed that cost would matter, and meant to recommend the planting of well-grown trees that would cost at least ten shillings apiece, even if bought in thousands. It would be jolly to take a hand in an affair of that magnitude, and he was inclined to envy one who could garden on a scale so much larger than was permitted to himself.

Alfred was relieved too. The actual cost of the garden was not the question with him. There was no such thing as actual cost in such matters as this, so far as his father was concerned; would not have been even if he had kept to his more expensive design. Armitage Brown would have paid the bill for either without thinking about it.

It was the difference between spending money on dead
stone and brick and mortar, and spending it on living
growth that seemed to matter. He would be prepared to
order yews of the largest size that could be transplanted,
and as many of them as was necessary. That was ordinary
gardening as he envisaged it. That it was gardening with
a golden spade in Douglas's eyes would have troubled him
but a little if he had known it. His own secret protest had
been obeyed. He was gaining his pleasure from the simpler of two ways.

The colloquy was long and interesting; catalogues were
produced, lists made, sheets of notes scribbled. Alfred
began to regard a nurseryman's catalogue with new eyes.

" I shan't be able to do this myself, you know," he
said. " You'll have to help me."

This was what Douglas wanted. He leaned back in his
chair and played with his pencil. " Well, I'll tell you,"
he said judicially. " If Mackenzie were the right sort of
gardener, you wouldn't want much help, when you'd decided what things to get, and where to put them. But
you'll have him against you all the time, and the fact of
the matter is you don't know enough yet to see that he
does what he's told. Besides, this is going to take all winter, and I suppose you won't be here all the time."

" No," said Alfred. " I wish you'd overlook it for me."

" I will with the greatest of pleasure," said Douglas.
" Beatrix and I both will. She's jolly good at colour. We
shall enjoy it awfully. But you'll have to put us right
with Mackenzie. He'll have to get the actual work done,
or let us have men to do it. He'll be furiously up against
us, of course; but I shan't mind that if I've got undoubted
authority."

" Come up to-morrow morning," said Alfred, " and we'll
initiate Mr. Mackenzie into his new duties. You won't

have any trouble with him. He's going to do what he's told, though he doesn't know it yet."

They had been talking and planning for an hour. It was now past three o'clock. There came a slight pause, and Alfred suddenly remembered that Lady Grace was probably coming to tea. His heart beat a trifle faster at the thought. He wanted to see how she looked and spoke. But Beatrix had not asked him to stay to see her. He supposed he had better be going.

He was just rising to take his leave when the throb of a motor was heard outside. "That must be Meadshire," said Douglas.

"Well, I think I must be going," said Alfred. "I'll take the plans and the catalogues. It will amuse me to work it out more in detail, as we've arranged it. And you'll both come up about ten to-morrow morning."

The door opened and Meadshire came suddenly into the room. "Excuse me for walking in," he said jovially, and then he saw Alfred and his face dropped.

"Good-bye, then; to-morrow at ten." Alfred was out of the room before any one had time to speak. He took up his hat and went out at the hall door. Meadshire's powerful car was gently simmering outside, and Grace was sitting in the front seat alone. Their eyes met as he passed, and he dropped his with a blush as he fumbled at his hat-brim. He thought to himself as he went down the drive that he must have appeared in an odd light to her, but hoped she had not misunderstood his nervousness, if she had noticed it.

"Oh, you've had that young man here," said Meadshire, when the door had closed behind Alfred. "He seemed to be in rather a hurry."

"I suppose he didn't want to meet you," said Douglas.

"Well, I don't want to meet him," said Meadshire. "So

we're both suited. Look here, Grace wants you both to come up and see the garden. Bring the kiddies up too; I know you can't bear to be parted from them."

Beatrix went upstairs. "I say, Meadshire," said Douglas, "what have you got against young Brown? He's——"

"I've nothing against young Brown," interrupted Meadshire, "except that he's the son of old Brown. And I'm not going to have anything to do with any Browns of them all. No more is Grace. We're going to keep ourselves to ourselves in our quiet humble way, and they can cut their dash here for all they're worth. That's to be the note, Irving, my boy. If you want to make friends of them, do, by all means. But don't follow Tottie's example, and try to bring us together, for it won't work."

"It'll be jolly awkward," grumbled Douglas. "How can you help meeting them sometimes? If you come here when this chap happens to be here, what are you going to do? Are you going to be rude to him?"

"Oh, dear, no; that isn't my way. I'm one of the politest fellows that ever lived. When I do meet him I shall be quite affable, though possibly with a shade of distance."

"But I suppose you'll cut him when you meet him again, if it's out of doors."

"I shan't do that either. You don't know me, Irving. That's what I complain of. It would be making too much of him, for one thing. I shall nod affably. If I happen to be in a particularly affusive mood, as I sometimes am, I shall even remark that it's a fine day—always supposing that it really is fine. I shouldn't tell a lie even for the sake of young Mr. Brown."

"Well Compton was pretty rude to him the other day."

"Ah, that's different. Jim Compton hates a fellow with a fair moustache. Besides, he's a disagreeable fellow himself; he's made himself devilish disagreeable to me lately. If he doesn't look out I shall leave off going to church."

"Well, I suppose if you have made up your mind not to make friends with these people, you've a right not to. I'm hanged if I think Compton has. They've done him no harm—you either, for that matter—and the parson of a place ought to be on good terms with his parishioners."

" I'm inclined to agree with you, Irving. If Jim makes himself unpleasant to them, you let me know. I'll talk to him. Ah, here you are, all of you. Come along or we shall lose the daylight."

Alfred had Mackenzie summoned to his presence immediately after breakfast the next morning. Mackenzie arrived in his most aggressive mood. He had received a letter that morning from Berkeley Square with further instructions as to sending flowers and fruit. " Mrs. Armitage Brown wishes," it had begun, and he had taken it to have been written by that lady herself. He could hardly have expected that it should contain a reference to his own complaint. The fact of its being written at all seemed to show that she had " knuckled under." Very likely she had written to Mr. Alfred with instructions that so valuable a servant must have his own way, which did not in the least soften him to either of them, as such characters as his can only use a concession to demand more. Perhaps the young gentleman had sent for him in order to climb down. If so, he would not make it easy for him. He would use the opportunity to push his advantage, and " show who was master."

" Good-morning, Mackenzie," said Alfred cheerfully. " I've been employing myself the last few days in making a plan for the carpet garden. I've sent for you to show it to you, and see how we can best set about it."

The plan was spread out on the table. Mackenzie

hardly deigned to glance at it. " The plan for the carpet
garden is already prepared," he said. " It'll be what it's
always been for the spring planting. I should have set
it in hand last month, if I hadn't been three men short.
I shall begin planting this week."

Alfred took his stand in front of the fire. " I don't
think you quite understand me," he said. " There's not
going to be any more carpet garden. It's going to be
done away with. The space is to be planted afresh,
chiefly with yews, according to a plan I've prepared."

" Do away with the carpet garden!" exclaimed Mackenzie. " Why, it's been a thing people have come miles
to see, and I've got prize after prize for it. There's not
a finer one to be seen in the whole of England."

" Well, you see, it won't amuse us particularly to see
you getting prizes; you can get them for something else.
Anyhow, the carpet garden is going. That has been decided on, and——"

" And may I ask, sir, who has decided on it? Am I
to take my orders from you, or from Mrs. Brown? I
just ask, because I want to know exactly where I stand.
If I'm to do my work here to satisfaction, I'm not going
to be interfered with at every turn, and I'll say so at
once to save further trouble. I felt it my duty to make
a complaint of the way you interfered with me the other
day, and I've had a letter this morning from Mrs. Brown
giving me instructions to go on as I've been accustomed
to. I know well what's expected of me, and——"

" Wait a minute," said Alfred. " What did you say you
had heard from Mrs. Brown?"

" I had my instructions, following on the letter I wrote,
making complaint of you interfering with me in a way
I won't be interfered with if I'm to stay here and give
satisfaction. I'm not going to serve two masters, and that

I tell you straight, young gentleman. I make no doubt that Mrs. Brown understands me very well, or she wouldn't have written as she did. I dare say, if the truth were known, you've had a letter from her yourself."

"Have you seen Captain Fuller this morning?" asked Alfred.

Mackenzie, who had worked himself into a cold ugly passion, was arrested by something in his tone.

Alfred took a letter from the mantelpiece. "I did hear from my mother this morning," he said. "I wrote to her about this plan I've been making. She doesn't mention you till the end of the letter. Perhaps you would like to see what she says."

He handed him the sheet. Mackenzie took it and read it. It deprived him of all speech. He could only look up from it and roll his eyes, and look back again.

"It's time we understood one another," said Alfred. "You've miscalculated the situation altogether, you see. I'm not inclined to stand too much on my dignity, but really, you know, it was a precious piece of impertinence your writing to complain of me to Mrs. Brown. You see what *she* thinks of it; and I don't see how you can have expected her to treat your complaint in any other way."

Mackenzie had somewhat recovered himself. His aggressiveness had disappeared. It was of the sort that flourishes vigorously until it is met by its like and then wilts away. "I never expected to be dismissed for trying to do my duty," he said. "I think you might have given me credit for that, sir. I don't believe there's a head-gardener in the country who has kept up the show that I have here."

"I've had nothing to do with your getting turned off —so far," said Alfred. "I told my mother that I thought you'd do very well, if you could bring yourself to take orders, instead of expecting to give them. At least, I didn't put it quite like that, but that's what it comes to. What she has written to Captain Fuller is the result of your own letter, which I warned you against writing, if you remember. The question is, *are* you prepared to take orders?"

Mackenzie saw a gleam of light. There was no doubt about his prospective dismissal. He had read the contemptuous reply to his ill-advised complaint with his own eyes, and had seen at the same time that it was in a different hand from that of the letter he had received himself. The lady had not been so much impressed by him as he had imagined. She had not, in fact, been impressed at all. No member of the "high nobility" could have kicked him for his impertinence with a loftier stroke. But perhaps this young man, who had, after all, turned out to be master, might be worked upon to avert the stroke. He seemed to have a touch of softness. Mackenzie was quite ready, immediately, to take his orders. He had the hectorer's complementary quality of servility. If he could not be master himself, he would truckle to a master. It was only necessary that mastery should exist somewhere, instead of give and take, which he could not understand.

"The question is," said Alfred, "*are* you prepared to take orders?"

"I'm sure, sir, I've always done my best to give satisfaction. I can only say——"

"I don't think you have done your best to give satisfaction. You certainly haven't given it in the way you've spoken to me. Look here, Mackenzie, it's no good holding out; you've got yourself into a mess. If you go out of this room now, you'll get your dismissal directly Captain Fuller comes up, and you'll richly deserve it. You understand that, don't you?"

"Well, sir, I dare say I've been a bit too free, and I'm sure I'm sorry for it. I've always been accustomed to have my own way within limits, and they've been understood by those I've served, and——"

Alfred made a movement of impatience. "Oh, if you're going on in that way," he said, "I'll have nothing more to do with it. You can go, and be hanged to you. There are dozens of men can be got to fill your place."

Mackenzie finally touched earth. "If you'll get me kept on, sir," he said, "I'll do everything I'm told, and you'll never have reason to complain of me again."

"Very well," said Alfred. "On those conditions I'll get you another chance—one more chance, mind, and only one. This garden is going to be run for the benefit of the people who own it, and as far as I shall have any concern with it, I'm not going to be bothered by having to fight you at every turn. Now I'm going to turn that beastly carpet garden that you're so proud of inside out. It's going to be set in hand now, and Captain Irving is going to look after the planting of it. He's due up here now, and we'd better go out and talk it over on the spot."

"Am I to take orders from Captain Irving, sir, when you're not here?"

"Yes, you are, unless you'd prefer to take the one you'll get from Captain Fuller."

It was a bitter pill, but Mackenzie swallowed it. "Very good, sir," he said.

CHAPTER XIII

THE VOICE OF KENCOTE

THE tea encampment was set in the shade of the great cedar on the lawn at Kencote. It was still early in May, but a burst of continued sunshine had seemed so to insist that summer had already arrived, that the fact had been temporarily accepted. A rug had been spread under the Squire's chair, as a sop to his fears of rheumatism, but the ground was as dry and hard as if the month were August, and the grass was beginning to look parched. Ungrateful mortals were already crying out for rain, but, until it should come, the boon of spring sunshine, hot days, and delicious cool evenings were theirs to enjoy in their non-agricultural moods.

The great stucco-covered house dozed in the afternoon sun; the trees in the park cast their shadows across the grass, and the herd of Alderneys stood in their shelter, lazily flicking the flies from their creamy flanks; bees hummed about the spring flowers that seemed to show an air of surprise at finding themselves overtaken by high summer. There was a large peace in the garden at Kencote, which seemed to have settled upon the group under the cedar, for none of them looked as if they had a care in the world, or had anything to do but enjoy themselves in the sunshine.

Nor, for the moment, had they; but there was not one of them that would not have represented himself or herself as leading busy and useful lives.

They were a family group. There were the Squire, who had a large landed estate to look after, and his eldest son

Dick, who actually looked after it. Mrs. Clinton had her household, her villagers, and an increasing number of grandchildren to interest her. Virginia, Dick's charming and very faintly American wife, had no children, but she had Dick for a career, and wanted no other. Cicely Graham, the Squire's eldest daughter, who lived at Mountfield, four miles away, had a family of four, in the nursery-governess stage. She was very pretty and young-looking, but matronly in her ways and in her thoughts. There was not so much money at Mountfield as there was at Kencote, and she had to " manage." So had Jim, her husband, who owned a house rather too big for his means, and both of them managed very well. Joan, a much younger daughter, was Countess of Inverell, which gave her enough to do in itself. She was a bright lovely creature, treated still as a child in her old home, in spite of the bundle of lace and cambric belonging to her that slumbered peacefully in the shade of another tree a little way off. And finally, Frank, the youngest son, but some years older than Joan, had returned only that morning from the other end of the world, in whose waters his ship had been stationed for the past three years. It was to welcome him home that the little party was gathered together—all of his brothers and sisters who were within reach.

There were three more of them: Humphrey, a widower with no children, who had been in Australia for the last four years sheep-farming; Walter, a fast-rising physician in Harley Street, who had married Jim Graham's sister, and had six children; and Nancy, Joan's twin sister, the wife of Colonel Spence, with two bundles of lace and cambric similar to Joan's one. There were thirteen grandchildren in all, in whom ran the ancient vigorous Clinton blood. They were the source of great pride to the Squire, whose one cause of complaint against their parents was that he had never seen them all collected together at one time beneath the roof of Kencote.

It all seemed a little strange to Frank, but most delightfully familiar as well—the leisured gathering under the cedar, the peace, the spaciousness, the complete absence of struggle or anticipation. He was thirty-one, already making his mark in his profession, and as keen as possible on its varied activities. But he felt like a boy again, coming back from school, or from the *Britannia*, full of pleasure at being at home once more, where there was never any change, and no change was ever wanted. Changes there had been, later, with all of them growing older, and now all but himself married; but not in the basic life of Kencote, which went on as it had always gone on. Every time he had come home, after his periods of absence, he had thought at first that the changes must make a difference; but he had very quickly adjusted himself to them. He was in the process of adjustment now. His father looked a good deal older than when he had last seen him. He had lived such an active life, and had lived it for so many of his years in the same place and in the same way, that he seemed to have stood still in age. But age had marked him now. He was an old man. And yet, while he looked for the signs of it, Frank was already losing the impression. There was so much that was familiar in his tones, and in the turns of his mind, as they exhibited themselves in his talk. His mother was older, too, but not yet, as it seemed to him, an old woman, though she was nearing seventy. The adjustments to be made in her case were small. Neither did Virginia or Cicely seem much older, nor Jim Graham, with his slow solid ways and speech. But Dick did. He had been smart and slim and soldierly up to the age of nearly forty. He was smart and soldierly now, with his well-knit frame, upright carriage, and ex-

pensive inconspicuous clothes. But he was slim no longer.
He had become much more like his father; the Guardsman
was becoming merged in the country gentleman. He had
seemed to have the perpetual gift of youth; now he was
middle-aged.

But it was towards Joan that Frank's eyes most frequently turned, and when he looked at her he usually
ended by smiling and sometimes by suddenly laughing.
This was when he caught her eye, and she would laugh
with him, having divined in what respect the change in
her amused him, and being somewhat amused by it herself.

In appearance she had scarcely altered since he had last
seen her. She still looked a young girl—she was not
quite twenty-three—though there was that subtle change
in her that comes of wifehood and motherhood. She was
beautiful and happy, as she had always been. It was
what she now represented that struck Frank as so irre-
sistibly comic. She and Nancy had been small children
when he had first gone to sea. On his successive homecomings, they had been first bigger children, then mis-
chievous school-girls, then grown up, but still michievous,
and liable to stern rebuke if they outstepped the large but
well-defined limits of feminine liberty as it was understood
at Kencote. So he had left them last. And now Joan was
a great lady, at home in the most exalted circles, her comings and goings of importance enough to be chronicled in
responsible newspapers, and the mother of the extremely
important bundle of lace and cambric already referred to.
It wanted getting used to—more than the new aspect of his
father as an old man, and his brother as a middle-aged
one, especially as she was to be seen now in her old familiar
surroundings, and not in her new glories.

The changes were greater this time than they had been
on former homecomings, but already the level easy change-

less life of Kencote was obliterating the sense of them.
And yet they pointed, as they had never done before, to
much greater change. That could not now be expected
to tarry for many years longer. The Squire was seventy-
two, still strong and hearty when he was perfectly well, and
as a rule he was perfectly well. But at seventy-two a man
has passed the allotted span of human life. So much that
Kencote meant to Frank, who had spent his happy childhood and his happy holidays in it, depended upon him.
When he died there would perhaps be less change than
is usual upon the death of a rich man. Dick would step
into his place at the great house, and Mrs. Clinton, if she
survived her husband, would go to the Dower House, where
Dick and Virginia lived now. That would be all, on the
outside, except that Frank would exchange his handsome
allowance for his younger son's portion, and be thence-
forward "on his own." But it was just there that the
great change would be felt. Dick was conservative enough
in all his ways, and Virginia would originate little apart
from him, but they would not live at Kencote in exactly the
same way as the Squire had lived. And if they did, still
the house would not be Frank's home in the same way as
it had been before, welcome as he would always be in it.
It was the sense of shelter, of fatherhood, that would be
lacking. Frank had never been in the least intimate with
his father, and his home thoughts, during his long absences,
had centred around him less than any member of his family,
and far less than around his mother. But the fatherhood
was there, with all that it meant in the long-established
home of which the Squire was the head. Frank had had
a slight pang upon seeing him much aged. It was the
shadow of the end, not very long to be delayed.

There was one slight change in the atmosphere—but
perhaps it was only temporary—that struck Frank as they

sat and talked round the tea-table. Though remote, in its quiet corner of the country, Kencote had always taken to itself the air of being closely connected with all that was going on in the great world—not the great world of politics, except in so far as politics were connected with names, or of thought, which was not one of Kencote's obsessions, but of social activity. For the greater part of his life the Squire had stuck to his acres as closely as any country gentleman of the seventeenth or eighteenth centuries. But his wide relationships and the connections of his rich youth had brought him a sense of personal contact with much that was going on in the world from which he had largely cut himself off, and he liked to discuss it all and feel that he was still part of it. And Dick had been very much part of it during his nearly twenty years of soldiering; so had Humphrey, who had been in the Foreign Office before he had acquired his Antipodean interests. They had brought home all the news, and from the conversation that had gone on, chiefly amongst the men, you might have thought that Kencote was one of those great country houses which only their immediate surroundings and their distance from London differentiate from a house in Mayfair.

But Humphrey was on the other side of the world and Dick was becoming bucolic. The talk now was of local interests, and although those interests were connected with the world outside the county of Meadshire, they were not discussed except from the local point of view.

The downfall of Kemsale was an old story. Everything had been said about it, and said many times over, that concerned Meadshire's follies and wickedness. He was wiped out now; it wouldn't much matter what he did in the future, except as it affected dear Grace, who had stuck devotedly to him. And Kemsale had been wiped out with him, as the chief seat of aristocratic importance in the county. From that point of view it had disappeared as completely as if it had been burnt to the ground. That it had not been burnt to the ground, but still existed to the outward eye what it had always been, only made of it a large country house like any other, with no character except what its new owners should give it.

Frank would have welcomed more information as to its downfall, which was a somewhat startling fact to one who had been brought up to the Kencote view of Kemsale. But he generally listened to the talk around him when he first came home without taking much part in it, except to ask an occasional question. He was listening to it now, and forming his own impressions.

The question was of the Armitage Browns, now settled, at least for a Whitsuntide visit, at Kemsale. In what manner were they to be recognised, and when?

" I think that the fellow ought to have his chance," said the Squire. " There are all sorts of stories going about as to what he's going to do, but nothing is known for certain yet, and if people like ourselves show him that we're quite ready to be friendly, if he behaves himself, it may keep him from making mistakes that will set the whole place against him."

" Kemsale won't have anything to do with them," said Dick. , Kemsale, it will be remembered, was the name by which Lord Meadshire was best known to his relations.

" Oh, Kemsale! " said the Squire. " I've no patience with Kemsale. He's thrown away everything, and now he wants to begin to rule the roost. He's never been any good to anybody. He hasn't even hunted, or shot, for years. He'll find that nobody cares a bit what he says or does. Besides, he's sold the place to these people, and got their money. It isn't fair to go and plant himself down on their doorstep and lay himself out to annoy them. That's what he's doing, as far as I can make out, and I say it isn't playing the game."

" I think you're right," said Dick.

" There's that dozen acres or so carved out of the very middle of the property," said Jim Graham. " That's a serious matter for a landowner."

" I don't suppose it would worry a man like that," said the Squire. " He wouldn't understand it."

" It might worry him rather if the people who lived there made up their minds to be disagreeable to him," said Joan.

Frank looked at her, and laughed with considerable enjoyment.

Joan laughed too. " Oh, I join in the conversation occasionally now," she said. " You must get used to hearing me air my views."

The Squire remained grave. Joan's incursions into conversations were permitted, as coming from the Countess of Inverell, but not considered of intrinsic importance. " You have met these people, Dick," he said. " What are they like? "

The question had been asked and answered a dozen times. It was the way at Kencote. Virginia answered it this time. " They are on the whole what you would call in this delightful country ' all right,' " she said. " In fact, Mr. Armitage Brown has the appearance of an American millionaire—some of the manners, too—which endears him to me. I shall call on them at once, and bathe myself once more in a sea of dollars. It will be like home."

" Are they—are they—vulgar with their money? " inquired the Squire, who adored Virginia, but was far too British in his prejudices to extend his approval to her countrymen at large. The American aristocratic invasion had risen to prominence after he had retired to the seclu-

sion of Kencote. He may have had speech with half a
dozen Americans in his life, probably with less. But he
thought he knew them as a nation through and through,
and in his eyes they suffered from the serious taint of
resembling the English lower middle-class in many of their
ways and ideas. He was polite to such people, but did not
treat them as on an equality. Virginia was everything that
she should be, of course, but then she had adapted herself;
one would hardly have taken her to be an American at all.
He had once told her so, and she had been so angry with
him that he had almost noticed it. Sometimes she pretended to be more American than she really was, after so
many years of English life. She seemed to be in that
mood now, and it was in implied disapproval of her attitude that he asked: " Are they—are they—*vulgar* with their
money ? "

" They spend it," said Virginia. " Mrs. Brown's clothes
made me want to go and buy a shopful. And her luncheons
and dinners at Cap Martin were too expensively perfect for
words. She must pay her *chef* a fortune."

" She's dull enough," said Dick. " Hardly a word to
say for herself. But they do you well. I will say that for
them."

The Squire privately thought that this *was* rather vulgar,
or at least ostentatious. " People like that " had no right
to pay their *chefs* a fortune. Or if there was not much
objection to their doing it in foreign parts, they would
find that that sort of thing wouldn't go down in the English country. " They won't get on here by aping extravagant French ways," he said.

" Do they want to cut a dash ? " asked Joan.

" If so, you might give them a leg up," said Frank, with
a grin.

" Oh, I could if I liked," she said.

"Is the man a sportsman at all?" asked the Squire. "I suppose not, if he's spent all his life grubbing after money."

The Squire had a deep respect for money, but preferred that it should come of itself rather than be made. At the same time, if enough had been made to put its maker into the position of owning a place like Kemsale, its source might be forgiven, other things being equal.

"I doubt it," said Dick. "But he's not going to let the shooting again to Irving."

"Jim met Mr. Brown's son when he shot with Captain Irving at Kemsale," said Cicely.

"And what's *he* like?" asked the Squire. "You never told us that, Jim."

Jim Graham paused for a moment, as he always did before he replied to a question. "He seemed all right," he said.

"What a thoroughly British answer," said Virginia. "But I know exactly what it means. He wore the right sort of clothes, and didn't trouble to make himself agreeable."

Jim smiled his slow smile. "I didn't notice his clothes," he said. "But he did make himself rather agreeable. He enjoyed himself. Irving and his friends liked him."

"Then he must be 'all right,' as you say," said Virginia. "They could never like anybody who only made himself agreeable and enjoyed himself."

"How did he shoot?" asked Dick.

"He didn't shoot. He said he never had, but Irving was going to put him in the way of it. He seemed rather keen. I think he's an artist, or something of that sort. He said something about the trunks of the trees being a jolly sort of grey as we were going through Beeching Wood."

Every one laughed at this, even the Squire, who said that tree trunks were only grey on the north side.

" I think he must be a nice young man," said Virginia. " Do you mean to say he wasn't ashamed of not being able to shoot? "

" I don't think so," said Jim. " There's nothing to be ashamed of."

" There's a daughter, too," said Virginia. " Quite bright and nice. I hardly spoke to her, but I liked the look of her very much."

" She'll be a nice companion for you, Joan," said Frank.

A slight diversion was caused here by the appearance of the Rector of Kencote, whom every one but the Squire rose to greet. He was the Squire's half-brother, some years younger than he, but looking older. He was a big mild gentle creature, and everybody at Kencote loved him. His wife had died about a year before, and he still seemed lost without her. That was why everybody rose to greet him and to bring him into the circle.

" James Compton has just been over to see me from Kemsale," he said, when they had all settled themselves again.

" Oh, why didn't you bring him on here, Tom? " said the Squire. " He hasn't been near us for months."

" Well—er—he wanted to get back. He is leaving Kemsale."

" Leaving Kemsale! " This was news indeed. The inquiries that followed elicited from the Rector, who gave the information with some reluctance, and left a good deal of it to be inferred, that Compton had taken the late happenings at Kemsale very seriously. It had been the breakup of everything there, as far as he was concerned. He was not going to stay in a place dominated by a London money-grubber who had risen from the gutter.

The old man brought himself to repeat these words.
" I didn't think it was a nice way of putting it," he complained, " and I took the liberty of telling him so. He
admitted that he had kept out of the way of this Mr.
Armitage Brown, and couldn't really tell me anything
against him, except that he had given all the tenants at
Kemsale notice to quit."

" Well, that's a pretty strong step in itself," said the
Squire.

" It was only meant to be a formal notice," said Dick.
" Fuller told me so."

" He said he had always lived amongst gentlefolks,"
pursued the Rector. " He wouldn't be comfortable with
these new people there."

" Well, do you know, I think that's rather fine," said
the Squire. " Compton sticks by the old order. So do
we all, but I don't know that we should all be prepared
to make sacrifices for it in that way. Kemsale is a good
living, as these things go nowadays, and he's prepared to
give it up for the sake of his principles. Yes, I call it
rather fine."

Nobody else seemed to think it was particularly fine,
or if they did they didn't say so. " Is he going to take
another living? " asked Dick.

" I didn't gather so. He said something about buying a
house in Northamptonshire."

" Of course, he's well enough off not to have to work if
he doesn't want to," said the Squire. He must have
been at Kemsale ten or fifteen years now. He was quite
a young fellow when he came there. He's done his
work."

" Been pretty well paid for it, too," said Jim Graham,
who disliked Compton thoroughly, otherwise he would
hardly have brought criticism to bear upon such an old-

established institution as the private patronage of the Church of England.

"He's had what the living is worth, and nobody has ever said he hasn't done his work," said the Squire, who saw nothing to criticise in a system by which in this instance a young man of five-and-twenty had been put into possession, for life if he chose to remain there, of a large house, several acres of ground, and an income of between five and six hundred a year for doing just as much work as he pleased. "Besides, the patronage of the living is his own now," he added. "He bought it from Kemsale. I wonder why he did that."

"He only bought the next presentation, as I understand," said the Rector.

"Oh, well, I suppose it was just to put a little money into Kemsale's pocket. By the by, he'll have to find a new incumbent."

"He has done that already. He has been occupied with it for the last few months. He made up his mind to go when Kemsale was sold, and has only waited till he could find somebody to take his place."

"Well, he ought not to have much difficulty about that. It's a place any parson might be pleased to take. Nice house and a decent income for a man with something of his own, a small parish, and a fair all-round sporting country. I hope he has found the right sort of man."

The Rector hesitated. "It is hardly the sort of choice I should have expected him to make," he said. "It is a Mr. Sheard."

This did not tell them much, though his tone told them something. He was pressed for further information.

"Well, he has been for some years a curate at Melbury Park."

"Melbury Park!" exclaimed the Squire, and every one

went off into peals of laughter, in which he joined himself when he had got over the first shock of surprise.

Melbury Park, an over-built suburb of London, had been the scene of Walter's first exploits as a medical practitioner. The story has been told elsewhere of how strongly the Squire had objected, first of all to his being a doctor at all, and then to his settling himself in a place so far removed in quality if not in space from the world a Clinton should inhabit. It had even been a cause of disquiet to him that Walter's eldest son, who, in default of children of Dick's or Humphrey's, would some day succeed to Kencote, might have been born in Melbury Park. But that disgrace had happily been averted; only daughters had been born there, and they didn't matter. Walter had left the place two years before, and its ghost seemed finally to have been laid. And now here it was cropping up again.

"Can any good thing come out of Melbury Park?" asked Virginia.

"A curate, you say?" said the Squire. "Well, young fellows who are in earnest do go and work in the slums nowadays. Still, it's odd that he should come from that particular place."

"Mr. Sheard isn't young," said the Rector. "He is a married man with a large family. He took orders comparatively late in life. He was, in fact, a—a sailor."

"Oh, was he?" said Frank. "That's interesting."

"He was not in the—er—Royal Navy," said the Rector. "The mate of a merchant vessel, I understood James to say. But a good earnest man; I asked particularly about that."

There was a pause of consternation. "What on earth can have induced Compton to put in a man like that!" exclaimed the Squire. "He must have gone out of his senses."

CHAPTER XIV

SUNDAY MORNING

"The first day in the new home," said Alfred. "Father ought to be nailing up a picture almanac, with Kate and me holding the hammer and tacks, and mother smiling at us over the teapot."

It was the Sunday before Whitsuntide. They had met in the "summer breakfast-parlour"—the Brown family and Uncle James and Aunt Millie. The large room—there were no small rooms at Kemsale—faced on to a garden at the back of the house, and had access by French windows to a broad flagged walk that ran the length of the west wing. The famous upholsterer had done well with this room, and the soaking heat, which had already set in at nine o'clock in the morning, was exactly what he had worked upon, though he could scarcely have expected that it would justify him so early in the year. The room was both bright and cool; brightness he had considered to be the one salient Victorian note never to be lost sight of, but in this case he had permitted himself to soften it by the judicious addition of more ancient touches in furniture and ornament. He had wished to preserve the tradition of a morning "parlour," which the Victorians had carried on from an earlier date, and the only difficulty he had foreseen was in the large number of ground-floor rooms at Kemsale, which would prevent any one of them being used for more than a single purpose.

He would have been pleased with Aunt Millie's expression of appreciation. "Really, this is a charming room," she

175

said. " Just the place to spend a quiet and happy morning in."

" Oh, my dear, you can't do that," said Alfred. " What's to become of the magenta morning-room and the puce boudoir? You've got to use them. You're allowed to have your breakfast here, and then you must go somewhere else."

Mrs. Brown disliked this kind of chaff, but had no weapons with which to meet it. She sat stiff and stately behind the massive silver of her tea and coffee equipage, full of doubts and hesitations, of which she allowed no trace to appear. For the first time in a stage of her progress, she found herself at sea. She did not know how life ought to be lived in a house like this, so as to occupy it fully. Alfred's pleasantry was hardly a caricature of her own feeling as to what was due to the overpowering choice of rooms. Nor did she know how the great tribe of servants should be made use of; her difficulties had even stretched to such points of detail as the question of powder and plush for the footmen.

She had advanced her knowledge during the winter and spring tenancy of the house in Berkeley Square. Her progress had been almost triumphal there. She had given many dinners, and a musical party, at which performers of such eminence had appeared that invitations had been indirectly pressed for from the most gratifying quarters. The house in Berkeley Square had now been bought, and was undergoing the same reconstruction as had befallen Kemsale, which was the reason, or part of the reason, for this early move to the country. The capture of London was easy enough, with limitless wealth at command, and a willingness to use it to provide entertainment; and if the capture was not yet complete, the affair was all the more interesting on that account. It was the fight for recognition and social eminence that gave the zest, just as the

fight for money was more to her husband than its possession. And the means had been adapted to the end. The
large London house had presented no difficulties, nor the
marshalling of its attendant hosts. The rooms of state had
had their appointed place, the private rooms had not
been too many even for a life that was seldom private.

But here it was all different. The rooms of state were
here too, but there were no people to furnish them, nor
to employ the mobilised army. A houseful of guests!
She shrank from it. Part of her success in London and
on the Riviera had arisen from the fact that she had received her guests and lavished her gifts upon them with
a sort of aloof pride. She had run after nobody, and
become intimate with nobody. It had been enough for her
that the people had been there, just as the elaborate food
and the priceless wines, the gold and silver and glass, the
rare flowers, the tribe of silken powdered servants, the
famous musicians, had been there. Entertaining was her
occupation, to which the entertained were essential; otherwise she would have preferred to do without them. They
came at the appointed hours, to the set piece, played their
parts in the carefully organised scheme, and went away
again, leaving her to her cold triumph. It was all that
she wanted of them.

But what to do with a houseful of guests all day long!
It would be an intolerable burden.

The mistake, she was beginning to think, was in having
bought a house of the size of Kemsale. She was not at
all without her restful moments. A country house no bigger than " The Towers " would have been a pleasant place
to come to, as a relief from the arduous but exciting career
to which she had committed herself. With Millie, or some
of her own relations to keep her company, with the garden,
the house in which she could take a pride, Katie and some

of her friends, and Alfred sometimes, to provide the youthful stir, time would have passed pleasantly, in a country house of ordinary size. The family side of life, in appreciation of which she was not deficient, would have been represented there, and would have provided a welcome set-off to the public side, which could have been left for London and the French villa. Her small gift for genuine hospitality would have been satisfied by having with her as often as possible the mere handful of friends she possessed out of the large and always-increasing number of her acquaintances, and in giving Katie's friends, and Alfred's, if he liked to bring them, all facilities for amusing themselves. A " house-party " drawn from other sources would simply spoil her holiday. She would never be at ease with her guests, even if she were successful in providing them with something to do. Her own very rare visits to country houses had shown her, always on the look-out for such lessons, that the " note " of life in them was intimacy. Ordinary family life might be decked out to some extent, expanded to arranged pleasures, for the sake of guests, but in essence the pleasure to be derived was from sharing ordinary pursuits with congenial people. If a woman— men, with their sports, were different—but if a woman could not find her enjoyment in that, she would gain little pleasure from country-house visiting; and indeed Mrs. Brown had gained no pleasure from her small experience of it. The people she met were not her people, and she could not make herself at home with them. In spite of her social developments she remained as to her private tastes exactly what she had been before her rise to fortune. She warmed only to those of the class from which she had sprung; towards the others she must always be playing a part. This was why she had gone near to making a friend of Mrs. Fuller, whose assumptions of superior birth, even

if she had allowed them to deceive her, had not destroyed
the sense of their being of the same clay.

She had allowed that vision of the country house as a
place of rest and retreat to play about Kemsale, and she
knew that her husband regarded the place chiefly in that
light. He would want to live his own life in it, according
as he might adjust it to new pursuits, and would not
permit her to use it in the main as a great palace of entertainment. And if she could have been satisfied to allow
its decorated vastness to lie idle, she would have been as
simply content at the present moment, with all those whom
she loved best around her, as she had ever been in her
life. But the empty saloons, the long succession of furnished rooms, the host of servants, oppressed her. She
could " settle to nothing."

As for the rest, they were each in their own way pleasantly excited by the new beginnings. Armitage Brown
regarded the large estate, which had supported the dignity
and circumstances of a great family for so many generations, as a toy to play with—one of the first he had permitted himself. He wanted nothing from it but a new
interest. It had been bought and paid for, and " written
off." Its purchase had satisfactorily accounted for some
of his superfluous thousands, which he would miss no more
than he had missed the purchase price of his first semi-
detached villa, or, later, of " The Towers." He would
make it pay, not because he wanted its returns, but because
his amusement in it would be enhanced by doing so. The
stakes, though not essential, were high enough; and he
would be dealing with actualities, where previously he had
dealt only with the paper that represented them. He was
eager to get to work, with Fuller, over the schemes he
had foreshadowed; and in the meantime he felt arising in
him a faint pleasure in the details of his ownership that

was a new experience to him. He had already inspected Alfred's formal garden, now finished, except for the maturing hand of time. He had been interested. He did not suppose he would ever " take to gardening," but a vision had crossed his mind of large " improvements " of the same sort. There was something to base them on now. Kemsale was his in a way that " The Towers " had never been. " Improvements," there, had been dictated either by the desire of the moment or by the prospect of ultimate return. " The Towers " had been his as long as he had chosen to live in it. Then it had been sold without a qualm. Kemsale was his in perpetuity, his for much longer than his own life should endure. It was part of him, endued him with something that he had not had before, something that counted in his character and in his presentation of himself to the world. It was curious that Alfred's garden should have brought this home to him, but it was so, and not entirely because it was Alfred's who would succeed him; although that pleased him too, because Alfred for the first time had done something that showed a tendency in him to anchor himself.

Alfred had suddenly left Kemsale when the work in the formal garden had been satisfactorily inaugurated under Douglas Irving's directions. He had grown tired of it, as he had generally grown tired of a place in which he had lived for a month. But after a winter and spring spent chiefly abroad, he had returned with some eagerness. Kemsale had taken hold of him, and on that Sunday morning, getting up at five o'clock and wandering all over the gardens and up into the beechwoods at the back of the house, he had thought he had never been so pleased to find himself anywhere.

Katie—bright little simple soul that she was—rejoiced in her two " own " rooms and the lovely prospect from them, in the quiet of the country after London, in the holiday feeling of her father and Uncle James being in the house and not having to leave it immediately after breakfast, and in fact in everything that marked the freshness and newness of the change. She had made many plans for life at Kemsale, based chiefly upon what she had read of country-house life in novels; for she had had no experience of it on her own account. She was to make friends with all the comfortable farmers' wives and their families, and " visit " all the cottagers, making friends with them too. She was to be made free of the village school, and help to decorate the church in festal seasons. She was to find girls of her own age and tastes in the houses around, and especially in the various rectories and vicarages; and when she should have made herself at home with them all they were to have splendid times together in the great new house, which would afford such opportunities for games and dancing and all sorts of merriment. She would ask her old friends there too. It would be no burden to her to look after a party as big as the house could hold, and for as long as she could keep it together. The only shadow in her future was cast by her mother's great formal parties, which, if they were to be anything like the parties at Cap Martin or in Berkeley Square, would consist of scores of people whom she did not care for, and who, judging by the way they ignored her, did not care for her. The thought of a house-party of that sort oppressed her as much as it did her mother. But in the meantime here they were all together, with dear Uncle James and Aunt Millie added, and nothing to do but enjoy themselves in the lovely weather and the lovely new place.

Armitage Brown sat at the breakfast-table in a black morning coat, and would presently endue himself with a tall hat to go to church in. He always went to church on

Sunday morning, and this was the costume that he had been accustomed to go in. His wife was very elaborately dressed, for the same purpose.

"By the by," he said, "is there a pew that goes with the house? I didn't ask Fuller."

Alfred was reminded of events that he had almost forgotten. "I'm afraid you'll have a little trouble there," he said. "There is a pew, in the chancel, and as far as I could make out from Fuller, it does go with the house; you've got a legal right to it; at least he thinks so, and Mrs. Fuller is sure of it, though how she knows I can't say. But Lord Meadshire intends to make a fight for it, apparently. He gets there early and occupies it, and unless you want to turn him out by violence, you will have to sit elsewhere."

Everybody looked at the head of the house, most of them with some consternation. Meadshire's hostility had no yet become known to them, and this example of it was disconcerting. What would be done?

Armitage Brown's face was dark. If there was a legal right, it was in his character to fight for it to the bitter end. Unless Meadshire was prepared to pay heavily for an empty privilege, he had been ill-advised to invite litigation that would be taken up to the highest court if it was entered upon at all.

"We had better find another seat for the present," said Armitage Brown shortly.

Mrs. Brown was loath to give up any seat of honour. "For the present, yes," she said. "But if it really belongs to us, Lord Meadshire ought not to be allowed to take possession of it."

Armitage Brown was still frowning. Now he raised his eyes. "I'm not going to enter into a struggle about a seat in the House of God," he said.

It was the ingrained Puritanism in which he had been brought up coming out in him. His religion, ever since his youth, had begun and ended with his Sunday morning attendance at church; no one in the room had ever heard him mention it. But, apparently, it was strong enough as a sentiment to prevent his stirring to claim his just rights.

"That's the way to take it," said Uncle James, who had relinquished regular church-going years ago in favour of golf. "If he sees you don't care, he'll be ashamed of himself. At least he ought to be. I should."

Meadshire did look rather uncomfortable, although he carried it off with an air of being much at his ease, when the Brown family took the places to which Fuller conducted them in the front pew of the nave. He was accompanied by two elderly ladies and a young one. Grace was not there. He stared at all our friends in turn, but removed his eyes when he met those of Armitage Brown, which were slightly narrowed. It was the first time that he had seen the man from whom he had bought Kemsale.

There was some stir in the church when there entered, instead of Compton, a short sturdy bearded man in surplice and stole, but with no academic hood, who, at the appointed time in the service, read himself in as the new Rector of Kemsale. The rumour had got about that Compton was going to leave, but nobody had known, until a few days before, that he had long since made his arrangements to do so, and had already appointed his successor. Fuller had whispered the news to Alfred as they had entered the church: "The new Rector reads himself in to-day—man of the name of Sheard." That was all the information that anybody had, and the whisperings and buzzings that spread over the church marked the degree of surprise that was felt at the sudden occurrence.

Meadshire seemed more surprised than anybody. He

tugged at his moustache, frowned and stared at the new-comer, looked all about him for enlightenment, and apparently found none. It would have seemed that in vacating his living and appointing as his successor a man as unlike what the Rector of Kemsale had always been as it was possible to find, and keeping it all secret till the last moment, Compton had meant to mark his contemptuous forsaking of a place that was no longer fit for him, and to do it in such a way that his cousin, who had brought about the catastrophe, should feel his displeasure. Had that idea been at the root of his curious behaviour? Nobody ever knew. He had advertised for an incumbent for a country living. Mr. Sheard had answered the advertisement, had seen his patron, and been informed later that his application was accepted. Compton had already left the rectory, and was not seen at Kemsale again.

But it's an ill wind that blows nobody good. Here was a man of small education, but a strong inclination towards the ways of the Church, who had arrived after many years and great difficulties at his goal, but could hardly have expected to have come in for one of the " plums " of his new profession, as he had now so surprisingly done. The house and glebe, the five or six hundred a year of income, might have been only something in the way of a rich " extra " to a man of Compton's resources; to this man they meant everything he could desire in life, for himself and his family. It is to be hoped that in presenting Mr. Sheard to the living of Kemsale, its patron had not been unmoved by the consideration that he was bestowing his favour where it would bring the greatest benefit.

The service was read slowly and quietly, in a voice not without the suspicion of a " burr." The sermon was short, and what in Armitage Brown's youthful days he had been accustomed to hear spoken of as " earnest." He listened to it with appreciation, though he was, in fact, in a state of some bewilderment about the whole affair. He was not quite satisfied that the advent of this new Rector on the first Sunday that he himself had come to church at Kemsale did not represent a move against him, of the same nature as Meadshire's occupation of the chancel pew. He was dimly aware of the fact of private patronage in the Church of England, and thought that if the patronage of Kemsale had been vested in the family of Meadshire, it was quite likely that he had bought it with all the rest. He meant to look into the matter later, but in the meantime he was inclined to like this honest, rather rough-looking man in the pulpit.

His mind was set at rest upon the subject of the patronage by Fuller, who came to luncheon with his wife and daughter. " The presentation to the living is a separate affair," he said. " I think you might have been consulted on the matter, as you'll be the chief man concerned; but Compton was a queer fellow. To tell you the truth, I don't think you'll find him much loss."

" I don't suppose I shall," said Armitage Brown, who had heard something about Compton from Alfred. " And Mr. Sheard will suit me very well, as far as I've got anything to do with it. Has he moved in yet? Is he a family man? Oughtn't we to do something to show him that he's welcome? "

Kind little Herbert brightened. " It would make things comfortable all round," he said. " It's a bit of a surprise to us all, having a man like that put in here, but there's nothing against him, as far as I know, except that he's poor."

" That's nothing against a clergyman," said the millionaire.

" Oh, no. And I dare say there will be opportunities

of lending him a helping hand. Yes, I believe he has a considerable family. They all move in at the end of this week. Compton's things are to be taken away to-morrow. Compton has already gone. Sheard is in the rectory to-day. I don't know whether he is going back to London, or whether he'll stay on here."

"What about this chancel pew?" asked Armitage Brown. "Is it mine or Lord Meadshire's?"

Fuller's face fell. This was an unpleasant topic, and foreboded strife. "I believe it to be yours," he said, "though Lord Meadshire says it's his. The lawyers will know."

"He can keep it," said Armitage Brown, "though I shall be obliged if you will get a legal opinion on the point. And you can tell his lordship, if you get an opportunity, that he needn't come to church early to take possession of it. You can tell him, too "—he raised his voice here—" that if he wants to go to law with me, and will find a decent excuse, I shall be quite ready to oblige him. He can have his bellyful of law, if that's the line he's going to take up."

This conversation took place on the way from church. Over the luncheon-table Mrs. Fuller made the mistake of criticising the appearance and speech of the new Rector. "It has been the most extraordinary affair altogether," she said. "Mr. Compton was not a very amiable person, it's true, but he was a gentleman. What on earth can have induced him to put a man like this into the living beats me altogether. It looks very much as if he had wanted to score off us all."

Armitage Brown bent his brows upon her with a look of inquiry and dawning dislike. Then he said: "Alfred, you and I will go down and see Mr. Sheard this afternoon; and I shall ask him to stay here, my dear, till he moves in, if it's any convenience to him."

Mrs. Fuller hastened to amend her error, if by any adroitness she could do so. " Now I call that really kind, Mr. Brown," she said. " I was going to ask Herbert to do the same, but of course Mr. Sheard would far rather come here than to our little place. I thought he seemed a particularly nice man, from his sermon this morning. I only thought it odd that, being what he was, Mr. Compton should not have chosen to put one of his own sort into so good a living as this. If you had known him, that is what you would have expected of him."

." We'll go round the place this afternoon, and see where those golf links are to be laid out," said Armitage Brown to his brother.

CHAPTER XV

SUNDAY AFTERNOON

It was a good mile from the house to the church, and Mrs. Brown had wanted to drive there and back. It was partly for this purpose that horses and carriages had been added to the stud of motor-cars. There were progresses that she wished to make in the more stately fashion, and her husband had had no objection to the acquirement of the necessary means. He had objected, however, to the taking out of horses and carriages on Sunday. Motor-cars were different; or so he said, and thought. So Mrs. Brown and Aunt Millie had motored to church, but walked back, and it had been possible for Alfred to introduce his friends from Little Kemsale to his family, before their respective ways diverged.

The Irvings would not come round by Kemsale, as they were invited to do, because of the heat for Woozle and Jimbo, but engaged themselves to come up in the afternoon and talk about the garden. The arrangement rather displeased Mrs. Brown, who thought that Beatrix, at least, ought to have "called" before being made free of the house; but she hid her slight displeasure and intimated a welcome. Alfred and Katie were always doing that sort of thing—making friends and throwing all proper ceremony with them to the winds. But as they also took the burden of privately "entertaining" them off her shoulders, there were compensations. She intimated to Katie that that must be done in this instance. "They're your friends," she said; "yours and Alfred's. They seem to be quite nice people, but I mustn't be left to make conversation to them."

They were not yet Katie's friends, but she hoped they would be; and conversation had already flowed so freely that there would be no need for anybody to "make" it. She already adored the children, and admired and liked Beatrix.

She managed to get Beatrix to herself when the Irvings came up early in the afternoon, and took her up to her "own" rooms for a talk. "I suppose you have been here before," she said. "These were Lady Grace's rooms, weren't they? Why wasn't she in church this morning? Alfred said that neither of those ladies was she. Has she gone away?"

Beatrix selected the question easiest to answer. "She hasn't gone away," she said. "She is coming to tea with me this afternoon. She generally does on Sundays."

"Oh, then you won't be able to stay here. I'm so sorry. Isn't this room nice? I've left it almost entirely as it was. I do so admire her taste. I could never have made the room anything like this. I am sure she must be nice. Why didn't she take her things with her to her new home?"

Beatrix looked at her. She was such a cheerful simple little soul that she felt like loving her already. Should she tell her? That Grace had not taken her "things" with her was the main reason why the enmity, of which this little person seemed as yet to be unconscious, was to be kept up, from the Herons' Nest. She decided that she would not tell her. It would spoil her pleasure in her "things." And Beatrix was not without hope that the enmity would dissolve before it became too apparent. She had made light advances to Grace on the subject, and Grace had avoided them, but had showed, Beatrix thought, that it distressed her. She, at least, with her kind heart and gentle ways, could not feel enmity against Katie Brown. Nobody could, if they knew her ever so slightly.

"She *is* nice," she said. "You will be sure to like her. Come down to tea with me this afternoon and get to know her."

Katie's face lit up, but subsided again. She had learnt her mother's views with regard to conventional methods of approach.

"I should love to," she said. "But I don't know. Wouldn't she call on mother first, if she wanted to know us?"

Beatrix stiffened. She had not expected this sort of "nonsense" from Katie. "As you like," she said. "But if you are coming to my house often, as I hope you will, you can't always expect to avoid her."

Katie looked puzzled. Her simple heart went along with a clever brain. "That means that she won't call on mother," she said. "She doesn't want to know us." Then, as Beatrix made no reply, she said: "What is it all about? They talked about Lord Meadshire fighting father this morning. There's a sort of feeling in the air that they want to quarrel with us. Why should they? Does Lady Grace want to quarrel?"

"No, I'm quite sure she doesn't. But——"

"But what? She doesn't want to know us? Does she think we're too common for her?"

"Common" had been a word much in use at Katie's school. Her own happy nature, as well as the riches by which she was known to be surrounded, had prevented the word being applied to her; but she kept her eyes open, at Cap Martin and at Berkeley Square.

"She certainly wouldn't think that if she saw you," said Beatrix. "That's why I asked you to come to tea with me. There's really no reason why you shouldn't."

"I should like to come," said Katie. "I want to see your house, for one thing. And I should like to see her too. I feel that I know her a little, living in these rooms that were hers, and I feel that I should love her too, if she'd let me. Alfred has told me about her. It is mother who thinks calling is so important. I don't, especially if you don't. But I want to know how we all stand first. You haven't told me. You shirk my questions."

Beatrix laughed. "I won't shirk them any longer," she said. "I'll be as straightforward as possible. Lord Meadshire *is* up against your father, as they say. He doesn't like to be turned out of Kemsale, and see him taking his place."

"Turned out of Kemsale!" exclaimed Katie. "But he *sold* Kemsale to father. Surely——"

"Oh, my dear, I know all that. His feeling is unreasonable—on the whole. But you can make allowances, can't you? And Lord Meadshire isn't a very wise man. He's a kind one, though. I think his feeling will die down, when you all come to know one another."

Katie considered this. "It does seem to me unreasonable," she said. "But I suppose one can make allowances for him, as you say. Does *she* feel as he does—Lady Grace, I mean?"

"No, I don't think she does. She's sensible, if he isn't. I should say that she minds leaving Kemsale very little. She loves her Herons' Nest."

"But she takes her line from him?"

"I don't know that she even does that. Come and see for yourself."

"Well, perhaps I will. I shouldn't like to make her uncomfortable, though. I don't want to be made uncomfortable myself."

"You won't be. There'll be the children—and me."

" Yes; she couldn't be really rude to me, could she? "

" You wouldn't ask that if you knew her."

" You like her very much, don't you? "

" Yes, very much. So will you. Now say you will come."

Katie said that she would.

The five men smoked and drank their coffee in the garden behind the house, where there were cushiony lawns and cedars and peacocks, dividing walls of mellow red brick with arched openings into other divisions of the garden, and beyond it, and on one side, balustraded stone stairs leading to higher and lower levels. There were at least a dozen separate gardens at Kemsale. To Douglas Irving, looking round him at this one, which was not the least beautiful of them, there came a sense of the futility of such an overwhelming aggregation of possessions as was indicated everywhere at Kemsale. This garden would have been a delight to any one, if it had stood alone, with the necessary *addendum* of ground for use somewhere behind its boundary walls. It would have been more than big enough to do anything that one wanted to do with a garden, would have provided endless resources for its owner. But as it was, it was just there, a charming place to look at, to walk about in, to sit in, but providing no interest of scheme or anticipation, except in its yearly flower-furnishing, which was attended to by gardeners. With a garden that was finished and matured, as far as design and planting of trees and shrubs was concerned, the arrangement of flowers would provide the necessary interest if one were to feel it as a living, moving part of one's experience. To allow it to be done by others as part of a routine, however well it might be done, was almost to lose possession of it.

He looked at its owner with a sort of baffled curiosity.

Armitage Brown was at full ease, smoking his cigar, not
troubling himself to talk much. Probably he experienced
some pleasure in this quiet gracious place, possibly some
mild proprietary gratification over it. And, as it was, it
called for no other feeling from him. It was too finished,
too perfect; and he had had nothing to do with making
it so. Was that, then, all that his wealth could procure
him—the expensive finished article? If so, Douglas himself, every inch of whose garden was alive to him, was
better off in that respect than he was, with his acres upon
acres of ground, most of which he had not yet seen, and
was in no hurry to see.

Was this great wealth, which in so many cases seemed
to belittle all simple satisfactions, really to be desired?
Not if one made no more of it than an Armitage Brown.
But then, one would. One would use it to the full, revel
in it, get the last ounce of gratification out of the opportunities it afforded. Why was it that the people who
had it never seemed to know how to make use of it?
Its very proximity, in the person of this millionaire, excited Douglas. He saw for a moment quite clearly for
how little the wealth might count, but could not see that
it might count for little with himself. His own satisfactions seemed to have shrunk, in comparison with what
they might have been if he had had limitless money at
command. He no longer felt that he had everything in
the world that he could possibly want, when this man had
so much more, although he seemed unfitted to make use
of it. He had a feeling towards him that he could not
have justified. His wealth was so great that it loomed
much larger than his personality. If he had been without it Douglas would have found him quite uninteresting,
their lives and their habits lying so far apart. With it,
he was a man to cultivate, if possible to be liked, and

by all means short of a loss of self-respect to be encouraged to liking.

They all walked about the park together, and discussed the laying out of the golf links. Douglas and Uncle James, who were the only golfers amongst them, quickly agreed upon the general lie of the course, and discussed details with energy. Alfred scoffed at the whole scheme; Fuller made suggestions of little value. Armitage Brown was grimly humorous about it, and encouraged his brother and Douglas to differ on the points where they were inclined to do so.

"Well, Captain Irving," he said at last, "you seem to know all about it. I think you'd better lay out the ground. If you do it half as well as you did Alfred's garden, we shall have something to be proud of."

Douglas was immensely pleased. He had forgotten the millionaire in his host for a time. Now he remembered it. Armitage Brown was inclined to be friendly with him.

Uncle James, who could never have enough exercise, persuaded Fuller to go off for a walk with him. Douglas Irving went with the other two to call on the new Rector.

They found him just returned from the school. He was in the big room, intended for a drawing-room, which Compton had used for his books. It was lined with them; nothing had as yet been removed from the house. It was as attractive a room for a bookish man as could have been imagined, luxuriously but soberly furnished, and looking out on to a quiet shady garden.

Mr. Sheard seemed at first to be somewhat disconcerted by the visit. In this house, so different from any he had ever expected to inhabit, so unlike what it would be when he did come to inhabit it, and in surroundings so much in contrast with those in which his clerical life had been spent, it was not surprising that he still felt astray. When

he understood that the visit was one of welcome, he
showed himself gratified, and talked with more freedom;
but it was not until Armitage Brown, finding himself
hampered in saying various things that he wanted to say
by the presence of Douglas and Alfred, suggested that
they should go away, that the ice was broken between
the two elder men.

They were not unlike in their rugged directness, to
which the one had attained in his fight for wealth, the
other in his long struggle against poverty. It had, in
essence, been the same struggle, though with very different
aims and issues, and each in his own way was sure of the
ground on which he stood.

" You'll find it rather an expensive business, moving
here from London, Mr. Sheard."

" Oh, not so very, sir. I've not much to move; nothing,
I'm afraid, that won't look very poor in a house like this.
But we'll make the best of it. We shall have the fine
rooms, and the garden, and all the rest of it. It'll be a
great change for us."

" May I ask if you have a large family? "

" Four boys and two girls. Large enough, but I wouldn't
have it smaller; and they're all doing well for themselves,
those that are old enough."

" Grown up, then, most of them? "

" Oh, yes. The youngest is eighteen. That's William.
He's at school still; but I think he'll have to come and
study at home now. He won't mind that; he's a good
hard-working boy. So are they all. Oh, they've done
well for themselves."

" Tell me about the rest, Mr. Sheard."

" Well, sir, I'm proud of them. There hasn't been
much money, but we've been lucky in education. We've
had good schools within reach; we've always lived in

London, even when I was at sea; and with scholarships, and so on, they've hardly cost me a penny. There's John, my eldest, he's a Fellow of his College at Cambridge, and in Orders, married, and doing well. Henry's a doctor, doing well, too; he cost me something, but not much. Charles is in the Navy; his godfather helped him; one of 'em had to follow the sea; it's in the blood. That's all the boys. Mary is mistress in a high school; and little Anne—well, she's nineteen, but we call her little Anne—she's been at home so far."

"And you've really been able to do all that for your children, Mr. Sheard! Well, I think it does you credit, and them too. Now you've got to take it easy a bit, and we've got to help you. I'm glad you've come here just at the time we have. We shall be new brooms together. One of the things I want to say to you is that where money is wanted for your work here, you can always come to me. I want to do what's right by the place, and I look to you to help me there."

"Thank you, Mr. Brown. I shan't forget what you've said."

"Now can I do anything for you personally?" He spoke quickly, to get out what he had to say against possible protest. "I should consider it a privilege, and nobody need know of it but ourselves. I've a great respect for the clergy—those who do their work without getting much pay for it, and I don't think they need feel ashamed of letting other people give them a helping hand. I should like to pay for your move down here, if you'll let me. I should like to make you a present to help you fill this house a bit, if you haven't got much furniture. Let's shake hands on it as friends, and let me send you down a cheque."

Mr. Sheard had looked at him closely as he spoke, and now their eyes met. "I shall be proud to shake hands

with you as a friend, Mr. Brown," he said. "I shall value
your friendship, and you've made your offer in such a
way that I shouldn't feel any shame in accepting it if I
had any need of that sort of help. But I'm glad to say
I haven't. I had a good command in the Merchant Se.vice
for a number of years, and I was able to put something
by nearly every year. I've got money in hand for the
move, and the income I shall have now will enable me to
get what's wanted extra for this fine house by degrees.
My wife will prefer to do it in that way, I know;
but she'll feel grateful for your kind offer, when I tell
her of it, and I needn't say that I feel the same."

"Well, I should have liked to make you a present,"
said the millionaire, "but if you won't take it, you won't.
But there's one thing I hope you won't refuse me. Bring
your wife, and your son and daughter too, to stay with
us while you're moving in. That will put us all right
together. We shall be all alone, except for my brother
and his wife, and you can take us without any ceremony.
We've only just moved in ourselves."

Mr. Sheard provisionally accepted this invitation, and
after some further conversation the two men parted, liking
each other very well.

CHAPTER XVI

THE ICE BROKEN

DOUGLAS IRVING was slightly disconcerted by the unceremonious way in which Armitage Brown had intimated that he wished to be left alone to talk to Mr. Sheard. Alfred took it as a matter of course, but was interested in what the request betokened. " The parson has fallen on his feet," he said, as they walked away from the rectory together. " When my father has taken a fancy to a fellow, there's nothing he's not ready to do for him."

" Do you think he's taken a fancy to Sheard? " asked Douglas.

" Oh, yes, it's clear enough. And he's the sort of man he likes—plain and straightforward and rather rough. He won't try to ingratiate himself. Father hates to think that people are trying to get something out of him. They never do get much if they try, though they can get anything they want if he likes them, and they leave him alone."

Douglas would have found it difficult to say what he wanted to get out of Armitage Brown, but he felt that he had received valuable information as to the course of conduct to be pursued with him. He thought that he himself was at least as likable as the new Rector, and as for being straightforward, wasn't he always that, even if he had no natural quality of roughness? "

" Sheard is certainly plain enough," he said. " He's an odd change here from Compton."

" He's quite a satisfactory one," said Alfred. " He won't try to treat the important family of Brown like dirt beneath his feet. I suppose Compton put him here because he thought he'd suit us. Well, he'll suit us very nicely."

"Oh, he'll suit us too," Douglas made haste to reply. "I wonder whether he'll suit Meadshire."

"I don't suppose Meadshire bothers himself much about the clergy, does he? It's more a question, I should think, how he'll suit Lady Grace."

Alfred had not thought much about Lady Grace since he had been at Kemsale last, but now that he was back there again her personality was constantly present to him. It was a fragrant gentle influence that hung about the whole place, that made itself felt even through the glaring opulence that was the new note of Kemsale, now that it had once more a living note of its own. He had talked to Katie, and found that Katie had much the same feeling about her, which pleased him, and justified his sentiment for a woman some years older than himself. He had now brought in her name, when mention of it was scarcely called for, for the pleasure of hearing something more about her.

"Oh, any parson would suit Lady Grace," said Douglas, "if he went about his parish and the people liked him. But we shall see what she says about it. You're coming to tea, aren't you?"

After a moment's hesitation, Alfred said that he would. He could not forever avoid meeting Lady Grace, and he wanted at least to see whether she wished to avoid meeting him.

She was in Beatrix's drawing-room when the two men entered it, and so was Katie, who was flushed, and not altogether from the heat. Alfred saw at once, from the appearance of all three ladies, that the meeting so far had not been a brilliant success.

He was introduced to Grace, who bowed to him coldly, and immediately turned to talk to Douglas, explaining with unnecessary particularity that she had not been able to induce her aunt and cousins, who were staying with her, to come out, because of the heat.

But it was obviously impossible that conversation could be carried on on these lines for any length of time, and she must have seen it, for she next, not without a plain effort, addressed a word to Alfred. It was about the weather. There seemed to be absolutely no other topic possible, if she were to keep him and his sister at arm's length, as she seemed to wish to do, and yet not make her host and hostess too uncomfortable.

They were uncomfortable enough as it was, Beatrix talking to Katie, constrainedly, on the sofa, and Douglas fingering his clipped moustache, with a bewildered frown.

But Alfred had the valuable gift of retaining a bright calm in face of an awkward situation. He smiled ingenuously. "I can't talk about the heat to you, Lady Grace," he said. "There are so many other things I want to say."

She blushed and showed her confusion, while the others held their breath for what should follow. Then she looked up, and smiled faintly in her turn, but immediately became as serious as before. "Yes, it is foolish," she said, looking at him and Katie in turn, "that now we have met, we should not say something of what is in our minds. You know, perhaps, that Kemsale has been my home all my life, and Mrs. Irving will tell you how much I have at heart the happiness of all the people who live on the place. Cannot either, or both, of you persuade your father to treat those of them who have been here for so long less harshly? Oh, I know I have nothing to do with it all now, except that I am so fond of the dear people who are going to be turned out, that I feel I must speak for them."

She turned particularly to Katie. " You are in the position here that I used to be in," she said. " Surely you can do something, if you try. I would have tried, when I was your age, and I think my grandfather would have listened to me. He always did, though he would never have done what is going to be done now."

Poor little Katie was almost in tears. She had very little idea as to what it was all about, but was greatly affected by Grace's emotion, and would have promised her anything if she had had time to speak.

But it was Alfred who replied, immediately. " I am quite sure my father would be unwilling to act harshly in any way," he said. " Who is going to be turned out, Lady Grace? "

" Why, everybody," she said, not without indignation. " Even the cottagers have had notice, those of them who pay rent directly to the estate."

" Yes, they have had notice, but Fuller was authorized to say that the notice was only a matter of form, in the great majority of cases. He told me so himself."

" That's not unusual when a property changes hands," Douglas put in.

" Perhaps not," she said, speaking more quietly; " but if it was only a matter of form, surely one would expect that everything would be settled as soon as possible, so that people who had a right to expect to stay on would not be kept in anxiety. But it is six months now since the notice was given, and not a word has been said to them since as to what is going to happen. Can you wonder that they are crying out, and expecting the worst to happen? "

" I don't quite know what to say," said Alfred. " I know nothing about my father's plans. I have not seen him for six months until a few days ago, and he has been abroad most of the time himself. He has been in America; he stayed on there much longer than he intended, or perhaps he would have settled matters here before this. We only came down last night, you know. I think he won't lose much time in taking things in hand now he *is* here."

"And I'm *sure* he won't do anything unkind," added Katie. "If you knew him, you would know he wouldn't."

Lady Grace looked at her more kindly than she had done before. "I don't think *you* would," she said. "Perhaps I ought not to have said what I have. I suppose we must just wait and see what *is* going to be done, and hope for the best."

"A lot of people are upset," said Beatrix. "Douglas and I have talked about it sometimes and thought that it might be as well to tell you of it"—she spoke to Alfred— "so that Mr. Brown might know."

Douglas roused himself. "It's like this," he said. "We have made friends, you and we, and we've thought it wouldn't be friendly not to give you the tip. From what you have told me yourself, your father doesn't know the ways of a country landlord, and he might quite well make mistakes that he'd be sorry for afterwards. It has seemed to be up to us to give you a friendly warning, if we see anything going wrong."

"But what *is* going wrong?" asked Alfred. "You said yourself just now that what has been done isn't unusual. Fuller told me that he'd given just such a warning as you talk about, and my father had taken it much better than he had expected, and practically given him a free hand to keep the tenants from worrying. If they are upset, as you say—well, Fuller can't have been very successful with them; I don't see what blame lies with my father."

"Oh, well—Fuller!" said Douglas. "But there's Mrs. Fuller.

"We know how kind Captain Fuller is," said Grace.
"But what he says is very likely to be upset—afterwards."

"By Mrs. Fuller?" said Alfred. "What on earth has
she to do with it?"

"She is determined to move into 'The Limes,'" said
Beatrix, "and has made no secret of it. She doesn't
mind in the least what becomes of Miss Merriman."

"Dear Miss Merriman, who has lived here for more
than ten years," Grace took it up, "and has spent her life
in being good and kind to everybody about her. There is
nowhere else she could go to in Kemsale. Barton's Farm
is too far from the village and the church, and there would
not be room enough for her to have the people staying
with her that she likes to have. If the Fullers go to 'The
Limes' she will have to leave Kemsale altogether."

"But Fuller is determined not to move from Barton's
Farm," said Alfred. "He said so quite decisively when
his wife mentioned it, the first time I saw them together."

There was a slight pause. "What Fuller says quite
decisively," said Douglas, "isn't always what happens in
that amiable family."

"Oh, well," Alfred said. "I'll certainly tell my father
what you say about Miss Merriman. If Fuller doesn't
want to move, and only wants stiffening against the lady,
I should think we might be able to manage as much as
that. But, surely, that's a case that stands by itself, isn't
it? It isn't like the farming tenants? Isn't it a little
unfair to make my father responsible for Mrs. Fuller's
little games?"

He looked straight at Grace. It was she who had to
answer the question, or evade it.

She dropped her eyes. "No one has been inclined to
blame Mr. Brown for anything that might happen there,"
she said. There had been a slight emphasis on the "Mr.,"

but she went on quickly, as if she had had something more in her mind that she was unwilling to express. " I think you got to know some of the farming tenants when you were down here last. There are the Davises at Points Farm. They have been there for nearly two hundred years; they look upon it as their home, just in the way that people like us look upon the houses we live in."

" I should hope they wouldn't have to go," said Alfred. " I don't see why they should, if they are the right sort of tenant, and I suppose they are, or they wouldn't have been there so long."

When Alfred had been at Kemsale during the previous autumn he had once or twice motored Fuller about the estate, on his agent's business. He had been made very welcome in snug farmhouses by comfortable friendly farmers' wives, and had carried away with him the pleasantest recollections of their hospitality, and the general atmosphere that surrounded them. He had not known, and did not know now, what hopes had been founded upon his own cheerful friendliness in some quarters, nor of the jealousies and fears aroused in the minds of those whom he had not been taken to see. The impression that had remained with him had been far from that of a whole community disturbed and alarmed, as this at Kemsale was now represented to be. He thought there must have been influences at work since, and that the delay in settling matters, owing to his father having been abroad longer than he had anticipated, would not entirely account for it. He was also inclined to resent, on his father's behalf, the implication that because under the previous ownership an informal fixity of tenure had been the tradition in certain cases, the new owner was to be considered bound by it. After all, the previous owner had played havoc with his own fixity of tenure, and it was on that that the right of others to con-

sider their's permanent could only rest. He did not resent
it as it had been expressed by Grace. He liked her for
feeling as she did about the humbler friends amongst whom
she had been brought up, and for being willing to fight
their battles. It was elsewhere that the source of the
mischief that seemed to be in the air was to be sought.

"If there is anxiety amongst the tenants," he said, "I
think that trouble must have been made about us—about
my father—that isn't justified; certainly by nothing that
he has done yet, or as far as I know is likely to do. I
feel quite safe, Lady Grace, in asking you to hold over
your opinion for the present—about him, I mean. Everything will be settled pretty quickly now. And of course
I shall tell him what we have heard just now."

Grace was not inclined to hold over her opinion about
Armitage Brown. His high-handed proceeding in the matter that had touched her personally had given her an impression of him that was not altered by the loyalty of his
son and daughter. She simply thought them mistaken.
He might be kind enough to them, and still harsh and
overbearing in his business dealings, as he had already
shown himself; and the whole point of the difficulty was
that the business of a landed estate could not be carried
on in the impersonal way of other businesses, and that he
could not be expected to know that. But she could do
no more at present. She might have done something useful
in speaking to these young people about it, or she might
have done something that would only put his back up.
Time would show. It was something that they seemed to
be "nice"—much nicer than she had thought possible
with such parentage; for their father was what he had
shown himself, and their mother seemed already to have
made a close friend of Mrs. Fuller, and was very likely
at the bottom of the disturbance caused in the life of dear

Miss Merriman, whom she could hardly be expected to appreciate.

Beatrix sent for Woozle and Jimbo, as a relief to the situation, and they effected their purpose until tea was finished, when an adjournment was made to the garden.

Douglas and Alfred detached themselves from the ladies and children. " I suppose the fact of the matter is," said Alfred, when they were out of hearing, "that Meadshire has been stirring up discontent. It's what he seems to be out for. I think, as he's sold the place and got his money for it, he might leave us alone. I wish he'd go away somewhere else and spend it."

"Oh, he's spent most of it long ago," said Douglas. " Still, I'm bound to say that I've never known him stay here for so long together before. Poor Grace is doing her best to keep him in order. She seems to be succeeding too. He hasn't had what we've been accustomed to call one of his bursts for nearly a year. When he does have one, as I suppose he will sooner or later, he'll clear out, and very likely he won't come back again, for some time at least."

" Here he is, by Jove! " added Douglas, as Alfred was just about to speak. Meadshire's car had slid up to the gate near which they were strolling. The three ladies who had been in church that morning alighted from it, and Meadshire, after a word of greeting, went to the front of the car to make some examination of the machinery.

The ladies went up the drive with Douglas. Alfred stayed behind. He would have it out with the mischief-maker.

Meadshire's examination was almost immediately over. He shut the bonnet of the car and came through the gate. His face wore its customary expression of careless good-nature, and did not change when he saw Alfred standing

as if to await him. "Hullo, here's the enemy!" he said
lightly. "Well, I hear you've begun to knock the place
about already."

Alfred was stung by his manner. "We've done away
with the beastly carpet garden, if that's what you mean,"
he said.

"It ain't much loss. I wish I'd done it myself." He
had begun to walk quickly up the drive, as if what he had
said already was all he wanted or meant to say.

Alfred did not feel disposed to run after him. "I'd
like to have a word with you, Lord Meadshire, if you can
spare me a minute," he said, standing where he was.

Meadshire stopped suddenly, and turned round. "Why,
certainly," he said, and waited for him to speak.

Alfred found some difficulty in beginning, but made a
plunge at it. "I hear there's some uneasiness amongst
the farmers and people as to what my father is going to
do here," he said.

"I hear the same," said Meadshire.

"I think it's a pity that they should be upset when
there's no need for it."

"So do I."

Alfred stiffened himself. "Well, isn't it you who's
upsetting them?" he asked.

Meadshire's eyebrows went up. "I?" he exclaimed.
"What on earth have I got to do with it?"

"Well, that's what I'd like to know. My father has
been abroad for nearly six months. Now he has come
down here for some weeks, and will be hard at work getting affairs into order. I think he might be allowed to
have his chance, without having people prejudiced against
him."

Meadshire retained his expression of innocent goodwill.
"So do I," he agreed heartily, "and if he succeeds in

removing the general impression that he's a precious hard nut to crack, he'll be doing a good work."

Alfred was angry, but he did not show it. "Who has given people that impression?" he asked.

"Well, I should say he had given it himself. He's given it to me, anyhow."

"And you have passed it on, I believe. It's quite an unfair impression. I know he's anxious to do well by the estate, and the people on it."

"Well, now, I'm very glad to hear you say that; and as you've spoken to me first, and not me to you, I'll make a clean breast of it to you. We've always done well by the tenants on this place. I believe they'll tell you that even I have done well by them, though I've done devilish badly by myself. But we needn't go into that. Now your father knows nothing whatever about the land, or what's due to the people on it. You'll agree to that, I suppose?"

"I don't agree to anything of the sort. He knows something about every sort of business, and what he doesn't know he'll pretty soon pick up."

"I dare say; but he hasn't picked it up yet. And the very word 'business' that you use shows how little you know about land yourself."

"I didn't say that I knew anything about it myself."

"Well, it's the word *he* would use, isn't it? He's going to make all sorts of experiments here, and——"

"I don't know that. He's never said so to me. Has he to you?"

"Of course he hasn't, my young friend. We've never spoken to one another. But every one knows it. Besides, it's exactly what he *would* do. He's a business man, and they always make experiments when they buy land—that sort; generally lose by them too."

"Let me ask you plainly whether you have heard

anything whatever about his intending to make experiments."

"I tell you plainly that I've heard nothing else."

"I don't mean rumours, from people who know nothing about it. I ask you if you have definite information."

"Where could I get definite information about your father's plans? There's no smoke without some fire; and what has little Fuller been about, making all sorts of inquiries everywhere?"

"What about?"

"Why, about everything in connection with farming that he never worried about before. It isn't his job."

"I should have thought it was his job. Then you've nothing to go on at all except rumour, and yet you've been setting all the tenants against my father."

"I haven't. I say I haven't. I've nothing to do with the tenants now, except that a lot of them are childhood's friends and all that sort of thing. They've always been pleased to see me, and they're pleased to see me now, and talk things over. Do you mean to say that I can't go and see my friends in their own houses, because your father has bought them over their heads? Why, you might as well say I couldn't go and call on my aunt in Portland Place if I didn't know the Duke of Portland."

"Well, I see there's no satisfaction to be got out of you," said Alfred. "You've made it plain, though, that you *are* trying to creat prejudice against my father, and I think it's a damnably unfair thing to do. I'm glad I've had the opportunity of saying so."

He moved away up the drive. Meadshire accompanied him, still apparently in high good humour. "I'm rather inclined to like you, young Mr. Brown," he said, "and I don't in the least mind you're speaking rather sharply. I'll tell you what, now. If your father *doesn't* turn out the nice old people who have held their farms under us for generation after generation, I'll tell all of 'em that I was mistaken in him."

Alfred stopped again and faced him. "That's very generous of you," he said. "You throw them all over yourself, you expect the people who come after you to take on all your responsibilities towards them, and yet you can't wait to see whether they're going to do it or not. You make all the mischief you can, and then, if everything goes right after all, you're going to say you've been mistaken. Thank you for nothing."

"Ah, now you seem to me to be speaking rather rudely," said Meadshire. "Well, I think we understand each other on the whole, don't we? We'll talk of it all again some day or other. I want to have a word with Beatrix Irving now."

Alfred took Katie away as soon as he could. The space at hand was too limited for him and Meadshire to occupy it at the same time. He said nothing to his sister concerning the late passage-at-arms. He had considerable control over himself, this young man, and a broad reservoir of wisdom on which to draw. If trouble were to arise it would affect her more than it would him, who need not be at Kemsale oftener than he wished. He was not going to make trouble for her.

He was instantly rewarded for his omission, for she said to him, as they went down the drive together: "Alfred, Lady Grace is such a dear. She was as nice as possible to me when you had gone away with Captain Irving."

He laughed at her. "Do you think it was because I was there, then, that she wasn't particularly nice before?"

"Oh, no, I didn't mean that. I think it was what you said that cleared up her doubts about us. Besides, she likes you."

" How do you know that? "

" Well, she said that now she had seen you and me she should feel much happier about the people who think they are going to be turned out. Of course, they won't be turned out, will they? It was all a mistake of hers? "

" I think most of it was. Did she seem as if she wanted to make friends with us? "

Katie was a little doubtful about this. " I don't believe she means to call upon mother," she said. " She didn't say anything about it."

" Well, you see, that's rather a slap in the face for us in itself."

" Is it? Of course, I know we're awfully rich, and all that, but we're nothing much beside people like her, are we? "

" I suppose she thinks so," said Alfred, " or her brother does. No; I don't believe she would. Well, if you like her, Kate, and she likes you, I hope you'll be friends together some day. At any rate, the ice is broken now."

CHAPTER XVII

EXPERIMENTS

"Before we begin, Captain Fuller, there's just one little personal matter I want to clear up."

It was nine o'clock on Monday morning. Armitage Brown and Fuller were closeted together in the room that the new owner of Kemsale had chosen for his business room. He had breakfasted at eight o'clock, an hour which as far as he was concerned he did not propose to give up for anybody, though the rest of the household were at liberty to breakfast at any later time that suited them. When the day came he wanted to begin the day's work, and it was with genuine relief that he had awoke on that Monday morning to the knowledge that there was work to be done here at Kemsale, and not a day to be got through in idleness, as was too often the case when he was at Cap Martin.

Fuller had brought up his bag of papers. He was rather excited as to what was to come. He had worked hard during the winter at the task that had been assigned him, and was in the mood of a well-prepared schoolboy who expects to do well in an examination.

But a personal matter! What could that be? His half-guilty feeling of having concealed his actual age rose within him. He wished he could have demonstrated how competent he was before any personal matter was touched upon.

"This house in the village—' The Limes '; it has always been understood to be the regular agent's house, I'm told."

Oh, that was it. Nothing very dreadful there!

" It was, before I came here," said Fuller. " The agent who preceded me was only here a short time. He was a bachelor and preferred to live at Barton's Farm, where I live now. When I came, ' The Limes ' had been lent for a year to an old lady who was a relation of Lord Meadshire's, and I went to Barton's Farm, where I've been ever since."

" And now you want to get into ' The Limes,' I understand."

" No, Mr. Brown, I don't. It's too big for me. I'm quite contented where I am."

A faint smile came over Armitage Brown's face. " Mrs. Fuller doesn't seem contented," he said.

"You must leave me to deal with my wife, sir. I've no intention of moving, unless you make a point of it yourself, which I hope you won't do."

His employer looked at him, still with the shadow of his amused smile. " It's a good deal nearer here than the house you're in now, isn't it? " he asked.

" Yes, it's half a mile nearer, perhaps. But I'm in the estate office all day, except when I'm out and about. And there's the telephone between this and Barton's Farm, if you want me out of office hours. I really don't think you'd find it any greater convenience to have me at ' The Limes.' "

" My wife seems to think it might be more convenient to have Mrs. Fuller there. The ladies have struck up a friendship. And Mrs. Fuller particularly wants to get into a more convenient house than the one she's in now, it appears."

Poor little Herbert's face fell. He had held out against never-relaxed pressure for six months, and had not expected the attack to come from this quarter. But he might have known that his wife would leave no stone unturned to get her own way.

"I think it would arouse a good deal of feeling in the place if Miss Merriman were to be turned out," he said. "She's been there for ten years or more; she's a very charitable woman, and does a deal of good work in the place. Pays a good rent too. It's practically so much extra. I doubt if I could let Barton's Farm for more than forty pounds a year, as it stands, without the land. Miss Merriman pays a hundred and ten for 'The Limes.'"

"The agents who occupied it didn't pay rent, I suppose?"

"Oh, no. It would be seventy or eighty pounds a year loss to the estate."

"That practically comes out of your pocket, then?"

"I don't look on it in that way at all. It suits me much better to live in a smaller house. 'The Limes' would cost me a lot more to keep up."

"Well, I suppose we've got to consider the ladies in these matters, eh? You've taken on more work, and are getting a higher income for it. Mrs. Fuller thinks she ought to benefit by that, I take it. That's the idea, isn't it?"

This was really beyond everything. If his wife had made that plea to Mrs. Brown, then it absolved him from the ungrateful task of shielding her. "The fact of the matter is," he snapped out, "my wife, unfortunately, is a bad hand at managing an income. Living in the way we do, I've had my work cut out ever since I've been here to keep straight; and I haven't been able to put by a penny. I *ought* to save money; it's for her sake I ought to do it, and my daughter's; and your keeping me on here, which I wasn't sure you'd do, and giving me another hundred a year into the bargain—it's a chance that I'm not going to let slip. I tell you, I'm ashamed of myself, Mr. Brown, at my age and with the luck I've had to be in constant work up to a time of life when most men are laid on the shelf—I was sixty at the beginning of this year—I'm ashamed of myself at having done nothing to make provision for the future. I can do it if I'm left where I am. I can't do it if I've got to waste money in keeping up a house bigger than I want."

He had plumped out the devastating fact of his age, but it did not seem to have given Armitage Brown any great shock of surprise. "I'm glad you've told me how matters stand," he said. " It shan't go any further. And I think you're quite right to stay where you are, under the circumstances. I'll put that right too. I'll say it's my wish. But I'll tell you what, Fuller; we must humour the ladies in their fancies, you know; is there any way in which we could make Barton's Farm a bit smarter—a bigger drawing-room, or a few bow-windows, or something of that sort? It might ease matters, eh? By your own showing you're saving the estate seventy or eighty pounds a year by living there. I'm quite ready to spend a few hundreds on it, to make it more like a gentleman's residence, which I understand is what's chiefly wanted."

Poor little Herbert could only stammer out his thanks for this generous and unexpected alleviation of the troubles he was bringing upon himself. It was another piece of kindness from a man who had the reputation of being hard and inconsiderate in his methods. There was growing up in him a strong feeling of gratitude and liking towards his employer. " It certainly would do a lot to make up for the disappointment," he said, " though as far as I'm concerned the house suits me very well as it is, and nothing is really wanted."

" Well, you talk it over with your good lady, Fuller.

Tell her I'm sorry I can't see my way to turning out Miss
—what's her name?—Miss Merriman, but I'm anxious to
do what I can to make your house more what it should be.
I'll go up to three hundred pounds. You can use it as
you like. I've no doubt you'll get the best results out of
it, and improve the place for later on."

" Oh, I shouldn't want to spend anything like as much
as three hundred. If I were to make the place bigger, I
should be doing just what I want to avoid. A bow-window
to two of the rooms, and a good bathroom, and one or
two little conveniences—a hundred pounds would cover
it all."

" Well, spend what you like up to three hundred. I
should give her a conservatory, if you haven't got one.
Ladies like that. Spend something on decoration; they
like that too. You might get in some labour-saving appli-
ances—kill two birds with one stone, eh? Do it as well
as you can; don't bother about saving money within the
limit; I'd rather you spent more than less. I mean that,
so don't go against my wishes. Well, now then, what about
this dairying business? Let's get to work on that, and
see if there's anything in it."

His complete change of tone, and hitching of his chair
round to his desk, shut off the previous subject entirely.
But the sense of gratitude and pleasure remained with
Fuller throughout the long affair that followed. He loved
pottering about with " improvements." There were many
that he would always have liked to make at Barton's Farm,
if he had had the money, or the authorization, to do it.
He could make them all now, even the most extravagant
of them; and he knew that by making them he could add
at least another twenty pounds to the letable value of the
house. And surely the news that he would have to take
home would bring him peace at last, and he could go about

his work, which would be much more interesting now than it had ever been, relieved of a constant burden.

For the next hour the two men stuck closely to the work in hand. Armitage Brown showed an extraordinary aptitude for assimilating the facts that were put before him so abundantly. Fuller had collected and collated every sort of fact from the material that had been given him, relevant and, as it sometimes seemed, irrelevant. And he had done what he had not been told to do—made journeys to see things for himself, from which he had collected other facts, perhaps more important still, as to practical working. Very slowly, during his six months' work, he had attained to a grasp of his subject. But it was nothing to the grasp that Armitage Brown attained during the hour in which he attacked the great mass of figures and details that were put before him. His eye for their significance was wonderful. Several times, as he stood up to his flood of quick questions, Fuller blessed his own thorough habit of going into everything that had the slightest bearing on his subject, whether important or not. Facts that he had not thought to be important were proved to be so, to the quick and solid building up of Armitage Brown's knowledge. He had thought he had left out nothing. He had gone over his lesson again and again, trying to find gaps in his knowledge, and when he had found them filling them up with the same painstaking care, whether they were noticeable or almost invisible. But Armitage Brown found a few further gaps—not big ones—and gave him a little more research to do, seeing that he made careful notes of what was wanted. His own grasp of exactly what was wanted was masterly. Fuller thought that if his employer had had to do all by himself what had taken him six months of careful work to accomplish, he would have done it in a week. It seemed to him that there was no complication through which he could not cut his way at a stroke, no balancing of doubts that caused him a moment's hesitation; and, in sum, that such a man could master any operation that he put his mind to, teach every expert whom he might employ how to do his work to the best advantage, and run any business in the world, from land agency downwards.

But if the business that he chose to run happened actually to have connection with land agency, it might be run most efficiently to pay, but other considerations bearing upon it were not likely to be dealt with tenderly. Armitage Brown still had something to learn with regard to that particular business. The question was whether he would judge the lesson of enough importance to be willing to learn it.

"Well," he said, leaning back in his chair, " I think I've got everything at my fingers' ends now, except those few little points which you've made notes of, and they needn't delay us in setting to work."

Fuller experienced a momentary tightening of the brain. He had been at full stretch for a long hour. The work seemed to have been finished for the time being. But apparently it was only just about to begin.

"What we have to do is to built our factory as soon as possible, and I think we know where to build it. We'll go over there this afternoon and have a look at the place. To-morrow or the next day we'll take a run over to Denmark and get the latest information we can. It may save time to bring a man over from there to make our plans. We shall have to find one. We must have the most up-to-date building and machinery we can get hold of. We shall want a manager too. There's a great deal to do, but I've nothing else important in hand now, and I shall work at it myself for the next few months, here on the spot chiefly.

You've got the subject up remarkably well, Fuller. I
don't think I've ever been so well primed about anything,
or wasted less time in getting at what I wanted to know.
You shall have an interest in the concern; that's only fair.
You'll have a good deal to do with the working of it.
But it's going to be a bigger thing than I thought it would.
I think I see my way now. The factory will have to be
under separate management altogether. You won't have
anything to do with that, except that you'll know all about
it, of course, so as not to make mistakes at your end.
Now we'll go into the question of the farms that are to
feed it. You've got a map of the estate?"

"I've brought up a little one. The 25-inch survey is
down at the office."

"A little one will do. You'd better get me one to hang
up here, by the by. I shan't be in the office much; I like
working in my own room. Now then, here's Oldmeadow
Farm. Yes, it's even better than I thought. Here's the
spot for the factory—roads from every quarter, and within
a mile of Ganton Station. Pretty clear land too; the town
seems to have spread the other way; we might put down
a line by and by. Whom does the land belong to between
this and the station?" .

"It has changed hands lately. I think Mr. Clinton, of
Kencote, has bought it. He runs up to here, and here, I
know; a good part of the building in Ganton lately has
been done on his land."

"Is he a go-ahead landlord? He owns a large property,
doesn't he?"

"Yes; he's one of the biggest landowners in South
Meadshire. They say that Kencote has been in his family
for over five hundred years; but I fancy most of this land
about Ganton has been bought or come in to his estate in
his lifetime. He's a rich man, I believe. His son, Captain

Clinton, looks after the property now; looks after it very well, I believe. But I don't know whether you'd call him go-ahead exactly."

" I see. Well, we'll bear in mind the question of a line of rail, and see about it before the land gets built over. It looks to me as if we were just in time. I don't think we could hit on a better spot than this for the factory. It seems to answer all requirements. What do you think? "

" It's right on the edge of the estate. Half the roads go off on to other properties, as you see."

" Oh, but that doesn't matter. We shan't want to keep the factory only for our own farms. You'll see how the rest will come in when we've shown them the way. We shall tap miles of country by cart and motor-traffic, and I dare say the rail will feed us later on. Three lines running from Ganton, look. We're very lucky to run up so close to a terminus. I had a sort of idea it would come in useful when I bought this place. I wish I'd known about that strip of land, though, in time. I wonder whether Mr. Clinton would sell."

" I should think it's quite possible he might, at a profit. He has never cared much about town property. I fancy he only bought this to save some of it from being built over. He has a very good house—here; Chequers it's called. It's let now, but the idea is that he'll leave it to one of his sons."

Armitage Brown laughed. " Bought it to stop its being built over! " he echoed. " That doesn't look like being up-to-date. However, the bit I should want lies at the other end. We'll see about it when the time comes. Well, then, there's Oldmeadow. That's practically a dairy farm already, I understand. Supplies Ganton, I suppose. What sort of a man is the tenant? "

After some discussion it was accepted that he was the

right sort of man on the whole, not likely to be averse to developing his dairying on lines that would be explained to him, or holding his land with some alterations and compensations then and there arranged and noted.

" These are the farms we'll start on," said Armitage Brown, drawing the butt of his pencil round half a dozen holdings, mostly of respectable size, on that part of the map towards the town of Ganton. " They have the most pasturage, and they are nearest to where the factory will be."

He seemed to Fuller to be going very fast. " Isn't that a big acreage to start with? " he asked, " with all the alterations to farm buildings that we've discussed, and——"

" I believe in starting things in a big way when you've made sure of your ground, and know exactly what you want to do, and how you are going to do it. It's the only way to make them pay. And I don't call this a big way. It's only because I don't yet know enough about the difficulty or otherwise of making the changes in the farms that I'm taking only these to start with. Here's Points Farm now. Let's go into that, as an instance. How much of this arable land can be profitably laid down in pasture? When we've settled that we'll talk about whether the present tenant is the right man to take up a new idea. We must treat each holding in the same way, but of course I must go and see all the country for myself before I can get a real hold of the question. One of these farms I shall certainly cut up, so as to give the small men a chance. We shall have to settle which. But take Points Farm first."

Points Farm was the one about which Grace had specially spoken to Kate and Alfred. Armitage Brown had had the conversation and that of Alfred with Meadshire repeated to him. Did he remember the half-hereditary basis upon which Points was held, or was it just chance that had led him to hit upon it for examination now? Fuller collected himself to present his report. Out of these half-dozen farms that were to be subject to the experiments, Points would be the one upon which the difficulties that had so far been ignored would concentrate themselves.

"Points Farm has been held by the family of Davis from father to son since the year 1746," said Fuller. "I've looked up its history in old estate books and papers. The house, which is called Points Manor, was built for the first Davis who took the farm. It's a fine one, and in the best days of farming they seem to have lived there like gentlefolk. Well, they're that now, though they don't grow rich on it any more, and their way of living isn't much different from that of the other farmers."

"You're rather putting the cart before the horse," Armitage Brown interrupted him. "I want to know about the proportion of pasture and arable land first."

"Well, it rather hangs on the history of the tenants. When wheat was at its highest a good deal of pasture was cut up. It seems actually to have been a dairy farm, chiefly, before that, and as you can see by the map it lies in the middle of the largest stretch of grass country that there is on the estate. There's no doubt, leaving the tenants out of account for the moment, that very nearly the whole of Points could be profitably laid down in pasture again. The land is mostly flat, and well watered. I'm bound to say that for your scheme Points is the best of the holdings you could take—I mean of the larger ones where a great many changes will have to be made."

"Well, that's satisfactory. Perhaps it would be a good farm to break up. But let's hear about the tenants first. Why did you say that breaking up the pasture had to do with them particularly? Wasn't it done all over the place at the time you mention?"

"Yes, it was done a great deal. But the Davises did it on a big scale, and grew rich on it. They're not rich any longer, as I say, but they've kept up a tradition about it. There's always been more wheat grown at Points than anywhere else on the property—anywhere else in Meadshire, I believe. There's a Davis a corn factor in Ganton, from the same family—a very old business it is, and used to be a very big one."

"What's that got to do with the farm?"

"Nothing at all. But it's the tradition in the family, you see. They've kept it up."

Armitage Brown considered for a moment, his face showing some vexation. "What age is the present man?" he asked shortly. "And has he any sons?"

"George Davis is getting on for seventy, I should say. Yes, he has sons. The eldest works the farm with him, as their eldest sons always do. Another's a clergyman. Two more are in business in London."

"Well, I see what all this comes to," said Armitage Brown after another short pause. "It means that with land that belongs to me, land that I've bought as an investment, and have as much right to use in the way that will bring me in the best return as if it were any other commodity, I'm to be prevented from doing what I please by considerations that wouldn't arise in any other form of property in the world. What tenure have these people held their farm on?"

"Always on a yearly tenancy. There has been a pride on both sides that they have never had more hold on it than that."

"Yes, very creditable, I dare say, when land ownership has been carried on as a sort of game, as it seems to have

been here. I'm not going to carry it on in that way, and
I don't care if it brings me up against every old-fashioned
landowner in the district. How long has Lord Meadshire
been going about trying to make mischief amongst the tenants against me?"

The sharp questions at the end of speeches of comment
were beginning. Fuller roused himself to meet them as
they came.

"I'm afraid he *has* been making mischief," he said. "I
hope you'll believe me when I say that I've been uncom-
monly careful not to let out anything that we've been talking about. I've worked at the statistics I've got together
for you in my room at the office, and sometimes at home,
in my den, at night, and I've always locked the books and
papers away, so that nobody should get wind of anything."

"Oh, yes, Fuller, I don't think anything has got about
through you. I satisfied myself of that. My boy, Alfred,
tackled his lordship yesterday about making mischief, and
he couldn't give any grounds for it, except that these
notices had been hanging about longer than I intended.
I'm going to make experiments because it's what I *should*
do, being what I am; I'm going to turn out everybody,
it seems, and they're all up in arms against me. Is that
true?"

"Well, there's a good deal of unrest. I've tried to keep
it down, but Lord Meadshire has tried to keep it up. I've
no hesitation in saying so, and I've spoken to him about
it, but you might as well speak to a weather-cock. Of
course the people like him. They've known him since he
was a boy, and he has a pleasant way with him. And
they've never suffered from his spending money as he
has. The estate has been the one thing he hasn't bled.
When his difficulties got too big for him he sold it."

"Yes, and he sold it to me, and I paid him a higher

price than I need have done, because I never bargain
beyond a certain point. What right has he, I should like
to know, to behave as if he were still master here, after
taking my money? "

" I shouldn't say he behaved as if he was master. But
he's making trouble with the tenants, and if you hadn't
heard about it already, I should have told you. I served
him loyally when he owned Kemsale, but I'm not going
to stand by and see him making mischief when he ought
to keep clear of the place altogether."

" Well, we won't waste time in discussing him. If he
goes too far, he'll find that I'm a pretty good fighter, and
he may come to feel sorry for interfering. In the meantime you can tell him this, Fuller. I've every disposition
to treat the old tenants on the place well, but I've no intention of binding myself by his rules. If he likes to stir
them up against me he'll be doing them the worst disservice.
It ought not to be difficult to see that. I shouldn't have
any qualms about getting rid of anybody who was really
set against me, if it suited me to do so otherwise. If they
are well-disposed I should think twice about it. Now as
to this man, Davis, at Points. It's a difficult question, and
if Lord Meadshire has been interfering there it won't
have made it any easier. And yet it's not so difficult if it's
looked at squarely. All that you've told me about the
family growing wheat as a tradition strikes me as simply
childish, and no man in his senses would expect a new
owner to consider that for a moment. But I'm ready to
consider their long tenancy, and in my view that's a big
concession, because Points is the farm that I should prefer
to cut up, for one thing, and if I didn't I'd rather have a
younger man there, and one who was less likely to be
prejudiced against a new departure. I'll stand a certain
amount of gambling and difficulty from this Mr. Davis, but

I won't stand more than a certain amount. If he wants to keep on where he and his family have always lived he'll have the chance to do so, and I shan't expect too much from an old man. But he'll have to give up his wheat and take to dairying, which, after all, as you've told me, his own forbears used to carry on. That's the long and the short of it. If he likes to do that he'll have all the help we can give him, and he can stay on at Points as long as he lives, and his son can stay on after him. If he's fool enough to stand out against the challenge, he can go. It will be his choice and not mine."

"That's fair enough," said Fuller. "And if you're ready to make allowances for the old fellow's grumbling a bit at the change, I dare say Points will settle itself quite comfortably. The son is sensible, and well-educated too. He may take to the idea quite kindly. Do you want me to talk to them about it now, and to the other tenants? We shall have to tackle them all separately."

"I want you to come round with me and introduce me to them. I'll talk to them all myself. We'll go to Points this afternoon."

CHAPTER XVIII

PERSUASION

THE two men set out early in the afternoon on their tour of inspection. The road to Ganton kept for two or three miles upon the level on which Kemsale was situated, and showed wide views of the country beneath it. Then it wound round in a northward curve, always dropping a little until the hill died away gently down to the wide gap where Ganton was situated, upon the other side of which the hills rose again. Through this gap flowed a respectable river; broad high roads from the three valleys centred in the town, and along each of the valleys ran a line of rail.

Several times the car was stopped at a vantage point from which wide stretches of country could be seen, and the owner of a great part of it studied it eagerly, his mind now firmly set upon his scheme, in which his agent was also becoming more and more interested. It was inspiring to go into an affair with such a man as this, for whom difficulties existed only to be overcome, and who impressed one with the conviction that anything he undertook he would carry on to success. It was gratifying too to feel that there was money behind it all, as much money as would be needed to start everything on a handsome scale; so much of this particular agent's work, as of many others, having been directed towards husbanding money everywhere. Armitage Brown had made it quite clear that his way would be not to spare money on the first outlay. The profusion with which it would be supplied was expected, as it seemed, to mark the measure by which it would be returned later on.

There was a largeness about his ideas that gave confidence, which was increased by the conviction that he knew very well what he was about, and that his agent need have no fears in suggesting expenditure.

Where the road began to bend round the spur of the hill, and the land upon which the experiment was first to be tried came into view, they got out of the car, and stood for some time leaning over a gate by the side of the road. Armitage Brown had never leaned over a gate in his life before. It was an initiation.

"I haven't an eye for land," he said—"not yet, though I think I shall get it; but it does look to me as if this was a natural grass country. The grass that is there seems to be the right thing, somehow, with all those brooks and willows, and I don't see that any of those big ploughed fields that cut into it have any particular reason to be there."

"There's a great deal more grassland on the other side of the hill, all round Kencote," said Fuller. "We might go round that way if there's time when we come back; I should like you to see it. It's just the same sort of country as this, but it hasn't been cut up nearly so much."

"Kencote! That's Mr. Clinton's land, isn't it? Does he go in for dairying?"

"No; more for stock, I think. He has a fine herd of Herefords on his home farm. They've only been going in for them for a few years, but they've won a lot of prizes. It has been Captain Clinton's hobby, I fancy."

"Well, that sounds as if they aren't altogether asleep. Are Herefords good milking cattle?"

"No; they're more for fattening."

"I shall learn all about these things by and by. It seems to me there's a great deal to learn, Fuller, and a great deal to interest one. I must get hold of books, and

I must talk to people. Well, we had better be getting
on."

He still lingered a moment, leaning over the top bar of
the gate. " I shall come and look at this again from here,
when most of it's laid down in grass," he said as he
moved away.

" There's one thing," said Fuller, as they were getting
into the car, " Kemsale will be popular with the hunting
people, if it gives them several more miles of grass instead
of plough."

Armitage Brown settled himself in his seat. " You don't
suppose I'm going to have the hunting people galloping
about amongst my dairy cows, do you? " he asked.

It was a dreadful question. Fuller made no attempt to
answer it, but remained very quiet until they came to the
proposed site of the factory.

Later in the afternoon they arrived at Points Manor.
It was a sweet mellowed old house, with few signs of the
farm about it. It stood near the road; a gate of wrought
iron between high pillars of red brick led through a garden-
court to the front porch, and another gate, at the side, to
the stable-yard. Beyond that there was a walled kitchen
garden, and then an orchard, and the farm buildings were
separated from the house by the width of those amenities.
It was, as Fuller had indicated, a gentleman's house, but
the iron gate was padlocked, and the bricks of the garden
paths wanted weeding. They entered by a side door leading
into the yard.

They were shown into a charming faded old-fashioned
drawing-room, which looked as if it were little used, and
smelt a little damp, the front of the house facing north.
Here they were joined by Mrs. Davis, who showed some
nervousness on her introduction to her husband's new landlord. She was a thin elderly lady, with a refined face;

she wore a cap on her grey hair and a collar of old lace over her black gown. She had already sent for her husband and her eldest son, she told them.

"You have a very nice house here, Mrs. Davis," said Armitage Brown, as she begged them to be seated, and took a chair herself.

"Yes," she said. "We are the fifth generation of Davises to live in it. We did hope, my husband and I, that we should end our days here."

"Well, I hope you will, Mrs. Davis; I hope you will. I have come here to talk over matters with your husband. I've left it a good deal longer than I intended to, but I only came down on Saturday afternoon, so I've lost no time now I *am* here, you see."

Fuller thought that his kindly encouraging tone was admirable. No country landholder, born and bred to the game, could have bettered it. He was beginning to think that he need have worried himself much less than he had done about his employer's willingness to take the personal factors of landowning into account. The thought crossed his mind, as he saw Mrs. Davis's rather melancholy face brighten at this speech, that personal factors existed in every kind of business, and that Armitage Brown would not have had the success that was his unless he had known how to deal with men. He felt some interest in sitting by and seeing how he would deal by himself with the situation here.

He seemed, at any rate, to know exactly how to deal with Mrs. Davis, who talked to him quite freely during the ten minutes or so that elapsed before her husband and son came into the room. Nothing more was said about the future, which was somewhat of a triumph in itself; for it had seemed as if the poor quiet lady had girded herself to talk about nothing else, and to exercise whatever small power she might possess to avert the stroke that was hanging over her home. She could not, perhaps, have been directed from her intention by an obvious avoidance of the subject; but she was encouraged to talk about the Davis forbears, and their connection with Points, which had so important a bearing upon the question that she probably never realised that its application was avoided altogether.

Mr. Davis and his son came in together. They were a striking-looking pair. The old man—very tall and very upright, white-haired, clean-shaven except for a clipped moustache, dressed in well-cut homespun, gaitered—would have been a king of the soil in any new country, where men who work the land own it. This idea came to Armitage Brown, who had lately been in Canada as well as the States, as he shook hands with him. And his son, who was past his first youth, was like him, with the same strong well-knit frame, and the same quiet air of dignity. Their greeting was courteous, but unsmiling. It showed watchfulness, perhaps to the extent of suspicion, if not hostility.

" I have been telling Mr. Brown all about the long line of Davises that have lived in this house ever since it was built, and he has very kindly said that we are mistaken in having supposed that it was his wish to bring it to an end."

It was an attempt, not without pathos in the way in which the statement was delivered, to gain an advantage at the start, or to show that the advantage had already been gained. Fuller, somewhat taken aback by its hardly justified terms, wondered whether they would be corrected.

But they seemed to be accepted without question. " I should be very sorry to bring such a line to an end," Armitage Brown said at once, " especially now I have seen the promise it shows of going on." He looked towards the younger man, who dropped his eyes, and did not smile. The watchfulness was not to be allayed by a graceful word, although if he had known how little graceful words were in the speaker's way, when he was intent upon negotiations, he might have wondered what this one betokened.

The old man, slow of speech, and perhaps, in some respects, of understanding, met the advance more readily. "I am very glad to hear that," he said. "It would be a sad thing to be turned out of this, after so many years, and for no fault committed."

It would not have been easy to embark upon the necessary discussion without first destroying the large assumptions that lay under this simple speech. But Mrs. Davis put in a word.

"I told Mr. Brown," she said, "how very anxious we have been for the past six months. But he has very kindly explained that he was unable to avoid the delay, and has come to us at the first possible moment to settle everything."

"Yes," said Armitage Brown, "there is a great deal to be settled when a property as large as this changes hands. A new owner isn't to be expected, naturally, to carry on everything in the same way as the old owners, but that isn't to say that he wants to upset things for the sake of upsetting them. I certainly don't want to do that. I want to carry the people who have been settled on the land here with me, as far as they are ready to go, and that's why I have left the re-arrangements that I am going to make until I could come and talk them over with them myself."

The old man spoke, after a pause that made speech from the other side necessary. "A great deal has been said lately about experiments on the land that has upset people," he said slowly. "I should be glad to know that there's no fear of that."

"Who has it been said by, Mr. Davis?"

"It has been the general talk all over the estate."

"But who started it? I didn't, you know, and I'm the only person who knows what is in my own mind about the estate, unless it is Captain Fuller, and I don't think he started it, did he?"

"No; Captain Fuller has always said that if we would wait till you came back from abroad we should find we had been worrying ourselves about nothing."

"Well, you haven't chosen to believe him, apparently. And yet he's my agent, and the only man who could speak with any authority about me. Who have you chosen to believe instead?"

"It has been said constantly all over the estate that there would be experiments tried that wouldn't do us any good, and that if we didn't choose to fall in with them, and give up all that our experience has taught us, we should be turned out neck and crop."

Fuller noticed the flash of annoyance that passed over Armitage Brown's face. John Davis, the younger, probably noticed it too, although it was gone in a moment. He spoke for the first time. "It wouldn't be fair to go by rumour, not based upon anything," he said. "It was his lordship who told us we must look out for trouble."

Armitage Brown turned to him quickly. "So I understand," he said. "And I should like to ask you whether you think it is likely that I should have spoken about my plans to his lordship?"

"I don't know that he ever said more than that it was likely to happen, sir."

"Why should he have said as much as that? He knows nothing about it. I've never spoken to him. Until yesterday in church I never set eyes on him. The fact is, his lordship has been trying to raise up prejudice against me, and if you talk about fairness, I should like to ask you whether you think *that* is fair. I've bought Kemsale from him, you know, and paid him a very big price for it. He's had his money, and has got rid of all his responsibilities. I've taken them on. Don't you think he ought to have been careful not to make difficulties for me over them?"

"If it's not true that experiments are going to be tried on the land, I don't think he ought to have said so," said John Davis unwillingly.

But even this admission was too much for his father. "His lordship, you might say, is a friend of ours," he said. "We've lived in the place so long that I think he would let us call him that, and he has always behaved as such. He is very much blamed for what he has done since he succeeded, but whatever he has done it is himself that he has hurt, and not us. It is not for us to blame him. I think we had better leave his name out."

"Very well, Mr. Davis," said Armitage Brown, and now his tone was harder. "As I understand your attitude, Lord Meadshire is your friend, and I am not to be allowed to complain of his trying to persuade you that I am your enemy, although I take the trouble to assure you that he knows nothing whatever about me. But it doesn't give us very encouraging ground to stand on as landlord and tenant, does it?"

Poor Mrs. Davis did not understand it all very well, but she saw with dismay that the favourable atmosphere she had created seemed to be changing. "I'm sure, if Mr. Brown assures us that Lord Meadshire has been mistaken," she said, "we are ready to accept that, kind as Mr. Brown has shown himself to be."

"We had better hear what Mr. Brown wants of us, my dear," said her husband, not yielding an inch.

But his son saw more clearly than he did, and put in his word too. "Mr. Brown can have no objection to our keeping on friendly terms with Lord Meadshire. But he

is not our landlord any longer, and we ought not to let
what he says come between us and Mr. Brown."

" I'm glad you've said that," said Armitage Brown,
" for it was beginning to look as if I was going to waste
my time talking at all, and I'm not a man who likes to
waste time. I said what I did about Lord Meadshire not
in the least because I care for what he says about me, but
because I wanted you to understand quite plainly that he
has done nothing—nothing whatever—to dispose me well
towards his old tenants. Whatever he has done has been
with the object of setting us against one another. You
may reconcile that with his friendship for you just as you
please. That's your business. But it is me you have to
deal with, and if I am ready to give you as much consideration as one man can give to another, as indeed I am "—
he was addressing the old man now—" well, it's a matter
between me and you, and, as your son says, Lord Meadshire and his way of doing things don't come into it."

His direct dominant speech was beginning to tell. The
old farmer was influenced little enough by his world-wide
reputation as a great figure in finance; to him he was only
a new rich man likely to make great mistakes in the business of landholding, and a very inferior substitute in every
way for those whom he had dispossessed. But he recognised unwillingly his quality of mastership, and he had
been bred through long generations to accept mastership
from the men who held just the one position towards him
that this man held, though without loss of dignity on his
own part.

" It is my duty," said the old man with grave courtesy,
" and I shall hope to make it my pleasure, to stand well
with my landlord, as I have always done. And I thank
you, sir, for your statement that you wish to stand well
with me."

"I do wish that," said Armitage Brown. "I have come here to you, first, as the oldest tenants on the estate, at the earliest possible moment to tell you so. And also to tell you what my plans with regard to this part of the property are. They are such that I look to you particularly to help me in, and such that I think I can hold out to you the prospect of larger returns than you can have had from your farm for a good many years back."

"Wheat is not what it was in my father's or my grandfather's time," said the old man, "but it is looking up again, and I think it is likely to look up still further."

"I don't want you to go on growing wheat. I am going in for dairying on a large scale. I am prepared to spend a large sum of money on it, and I want the men who hold land from me hereabouts to go in for it with me. They will have no initial expenditure of their own, and they will be compensated—those who choose to stay on—for any temporary loss that they may be put to, just as if they had previously held their farms under me, and I were not beginning here entirely afresh. Now I understand very well—I have gone into it thoroughly with Captain Fuller —that to change Points Farm from one where wheat is chiefly grown to a dairy farm goes against the traditions you have carried on for some generations; but I also understand, Mr. Davis, that before your family took their lead in wheat-growing they were big dairy-farmers, here at Points: so I think that any natural disappointment you may feel at changing your ways to that extent may be fairly balanced by knowing that you're only going back to a still older tradition of your family."

The old man sighed deeply; the young one frowned. What was all this but one of the wild ignorant experiments that they had been warned against, that they had yet begun to hope would not be tried after all?

" I understood you to say, sir, that Lord Meadshire was mistaken in saying that you would want to change everything round here," said John Davis.

" I said that Lord Meadshire knew nothing whatever about what I wanted to do. But what do you call changing everything round? How much am I wanting to change, here at Points, and how much am I desirous of leaving as it is? There are two things, I take it, that count with you. One is staying on in the house that has been yours for nearly two hundred years, the other is carrying on your farming as you've carried it on for about a hundred. Which counts for most?"

Again he began with the younger man and ended with the older, and the old man answered him with proud resignation. " If I've got to change all my ways, sir, at the end of fifty years of work, and my experience is to go for nothing, I may as well leave the old house at once. I'm too old to begin again."

" Is wheat the only thing that you have learnt to grow in fifty years, Mr. Davis? We have just come through your land, and I noticed that a good deal of it was pasture, and we stopped for a moment to look at a herd of cows. Do you know nothing about dairying at all?"

" Oh, indeed," said Mrs. Davis, " we have been very proud of our dairy. Next to the wheat it has been the chief thing with us. When I was younger and could do more myself, I looked after it entirely, and it is still a model dairy for its size."

" There you are!" said Armitage Brown in good-humoured triumph. " I thought I had come to the right place to get advice upon details. Mr. Davis, I expect you know just as much about dairying as about wheat-growing, and I think when I've told you a little more about the scheme I have worked out, you won't, after all, find it such a terrible thing to make one rather than the other your chief interest. I don't want you to give up wheat-growing altogether, you know."

The old man gathered himself together. " I hope you won't take amiss what I am going to say, sir. I mean no disrespect to you, but you are a man many years younger that I am. As I understand, you have been engaged in business in the City of London all your life, and have grown rich on it. And now you come into the country in middle-life and want to teach their business to men who learnt it long before you were born, and had it in their blood and bones before *they* were born. I ask you fairly, now, which is likely to know more about farming—you or I? "

" I'll answer your question, Mr. Davis, and then I'll ask you one. If you were to put me down in the smallest possible farm you could find, I shouldn't begin to know how to work it. Now is that a straight answer to your question? "

" Yes, sir. I think you've answered everything. If you admit that, then you had better let me go on doing the best I can for you, as I did the best I could for those who came before you. For I *do* know how to work a farm, and so does my son."

" But wait a minute. I've got a question to ask you first. You said just now that I had been working all my life in the City of London, and had grown rich on it. That's true; and I began without a penny, and, as you say, I'm not old yet. And how do you suppose I made my money? I'll answer that question for you myself. No money is made, Mr. Davis, in the City of London, or anywhere else, that does not come, if you trace it back far enough, either from exploiting land or from exploiting labour. A few years ago I made a great deal of money out of rubber. What do I know about rubber-growing? I have never seen a rubber-tree. But I made it my business, and worked very hard at it, to know exactly what a given rubber plantation was worth. That's why I not only made money when other people were making it, but went on making it after other people had begun to lose. A month or two ago, when I was in America, I heard something about timber in Canada, and I went out to the west of Canada to see for myself. What do I know about timber? I doubt if I could tell you the names of a dozen English trees if you were to show them to me. But I stand to make a great deal of money out of what I found out about timber. Have you ever heard about the Wheat-Pit in Chicago, Mr. Davis? Wheat is your family tradition. Some of your forbears grew rich on growing wheat in the good times. Did any of them ever make three thousand pounds in ten minutes out of selling wheat? Because that's what I did the other day in Chicago. I had had a little piece of information given me, and I turned it into money. All the work I did in connection with it didn't take me more than ten minutes, and I ran no greater risk than you would run from a bad harvest—not so much, because as far as I had to know something I knew it exactly. And now I come to my question. When it's a matter of making money, out of rubber or timber or wheat, or anything else you like to mention, which is likely to know most about it—the man who studies their growth, or the man who studies their value? "

There was silence. Fuller broke it, speaking for the first time. " I've never heard a subject dealt with in a better way than that," he said. " It's as clear as daylight, Mr. Davis, and if Mr. Brown won't mind my saying so, it's a great compliment on his part to tell us these things. What he has told us is exactly how he has made his great fortune. It's by taking a lot of pains to find out where opportunities lie, and then taking them. Well, he's found an opportunity here, and I can tell you this, that he's already taken such a lot of pains about it, that there's no room for mistake. And what he's offering you is to go in with him, and to go on living here at Points into the bargain. I should take the chance if I were you. There aren't many who wouldn't be glad of it."

The old man still looked troubled, and the old lady bewildered, but the young man, who had listened with increasing interest, now spoke, in a more alert voice than he had used before. "If Mr. Brown has a well-worked-out scheme by which money can be made out of dairying —I suppose it would be on a large scale from the way he has spoken—and we are invited to come into it, then I for my part do take it as a compliment that he has come to us in the spirit that he has. For I suppose, as far as he is concerned, he would just as soon have new people here to work with him as not."

Armitage Brown turned round to him sharply. "Ah, now you see it," he said. "Well, you may judge how much of a compliment I've paid you, when I tell you that I've never in my life taken as much trouble to interest anybody in anything I've taken in hand. It's a great many years since I've taken that sort of trouble at all. I've had to keep off the people who wanted to come in with me instead of persuading them. I've taken trouble with you " —and now he had turned to the old man once more— "because I don't want you to leave this house, where you have been so long. It's not a matter of business at all; it's a matter of sentiment. If it were a matter of business I would start everything afresh, as your son quite rightly judges. I should make a great deal more money for myself if I took over all the farms I want to bring into the scheme, and put in men to work them under a manager. But I don't look for more than a fair return on my capital

out of this particular scheme. I want others to benefit by
it—the people on the land, and the more of them the better.
They will use their knowledge, and I shall use mine; we
shall work in together. Now, Mr. Davis, I've put it fairly
before you; it's for you to choose. Are you going in with
me? "

The old man hesitated for a moment, and then said
quietly: " I'm ready, sir, to hear about the scheme you have
spoken of."

CHAPTER XIX

KEMSALE RECTORY

ALL sailors are said to love a horse. Frank Clinton, who had been brought up to look upon horses as affording the chief pleasures open to mankind, was no exception. When his periods of leave had coincided with the hunting season, he had reckoned it an unsatisfactory week in which at least five days had not been spent in the saddle; and even in this hot premature summer he found some excuse nearly every day for betaking himself somewhere on horseback. He had learned lately that a shipmate, also on leave, was to be found at Kemsale Rectory, and set out one morning to visit him there.

It was a ten-mile ride, and he enjoyed every moment of it. He was a young man cut out for the enjoyment of the moment. Whatever he had to do he did as well as he could and interested himself in it; he was a capable and thoroughly reliable officer, though not a brilliant one. His days were contented, wherever he spent them, because he was not always looking forward to better ones. So when the better days came he was more than contented; they were not spoilt by regret, nor by the hampering sense of their coming to an end. He had no debts, no personal worries, no ambition except to rise steadily in the service, which he was doing, and no keen desires unlikely to be fulfilled. As he trotted along the country roads and lanes, and occasionally cantered upon grass, whistling to himself, and cracking the long lash of his hunting crop at the dogs that accompanied him, he was the entirely free and happy man.

He stayed to luncheon, or rather early dinner, at Kemsale Rectory, and was treated as an honoured guest. Charles Sheard, who had lately served on the same ship as himself in the Pacific Station and come home at the same time, was a junior lieutenant, while he was a senior one, and visitors of Frank Clinton's particular quality were a new experience in this family.

It may also be said that this family was a new experience to Frank Clinton. Those who belong of old-established right to the world of big country houses are liable to gaps in their social knowledge. They are familiar with the lives of the poor, but not with the lives of those who come between the labouring and the professional classes. Rectories and vicarages they know, where there is apt to be genteel poverty; but the rectories and vicarages of South Meadshire were filled for the most part with families whose ways differed little, except sometimes in respect of money at command, from those of the country-house families. The Sheards came from different surroundings altogether. Neither Mr. Sheard nor his wife were by birth what the Clintons of the world would have called gentlefolk; Mr. Sheard's profession had raised him a social step, although that had been very far from his object in embracing it, and the step had not been marked in the place in which his clerical life had hitherto been spent, except by the success of his sons, who had also entered the professional classes one after the other. The good man wanted this kind of success for his children, made sacrifices for it, and was proud of it when it came. For himself he wanted nothing of it, and, other things being equal, would have preferred to do the work on which his mind was set amongst the people from whom he had sprung. It was a calm joy to him to be put into possession of this large house and its beautiful surroundings, and the comfortable income of which he would never waste a penny. But he had no idea of presenting himself before the world as anything other than what he was. The large house made no demands upon him to live up to its standard; it was made to adapt itself to his. His parish was his sole social unit; no concessions were made to outside claims. He had not considered it necessary to have anything, however modest, in the elaborate stables, " to get about in "; he did not wish to get about. He did not claim an equality with neighbouring squires, or socially even with neighbouring parsons; their ways were not altogether his ways, and his ways were sufficient for him. It followed, therefore, that he was invulnerable to the snobbery that attaches itself to so many country parsonages. The kind of criticism that is brought to bear upon a man born below a certain stratum, and lacking the conventional education that may hide it, did not touch him, because he accepted those facts about himself and was not ashamed of them. His manhood was revealed; it was his only standing-ground—that and his religion.

Charles Sheard was in the garden when Frank rode up. His sister was with him, but she had disappeared before Frank dismounted, being at the age of sudden disappearance before the unfamiliar. Charles Sheard was the typical sailor, short and stubby like his father, with a pleasant open face—more typical than Frank, who was tall and fair, and except that he was clean-shaven, wore an air more military than naval, especially in his smart riding-clothes. They went round to the empty stables together, but when Charles Sheard insisted that Frank should stay to lunch, they went down to the village inn, so that the horse could also have refreshment, of which the rectory

stables were now denuded. Frank had intended to go on
to the Herons' Nest for lunch, but he had caught sight
of Charles's sister, before her disappearance, and had the
sailor's interest in a pretty girl. Anne was pretty enough
to make him quite willing to change his plan.

" I haven't been to this house since I was a boy," said
Frank, as they walked up the rectory drive again. " A
sort of cousin of mine was rector here then, but he died
when I was on the *Britannia*."

" I expect you'll find it a good deal altered," said
Charles. " We lived in a very small house before we came
here, and our gear doesn't make much of a show. I'll
just take you to see my father, and then we might go
out in the garden till dinner's ready."

The square hall, which in Compton's time had been
furnished luxuriously as an extra sitting-room, was almost
entirely bare. There was a square of oilcloth in the middle
of it, and a stand for coats, hats, and umbrellas against
one of the walls, and that was all, except a large almanac
pinned to another wall. The door leading into what had
been Compton's large book-room was open, and revealed
a still more complete desolation, for the shelves that surrounded it were all empty, and it contained nothing but
some packing-cases and a few odds and ends of furnishings
that had not yet found their place.

" This is a jolly room," said Charles, pausing at the
door. " It will be the drawing-room some day, but it
would have to be repapered and the shelves taken down;
and there isn't enough furniture for it at present."

" Yes, it's a fine room," said Frank, somewhat taken
aback by the poverty that his friend accepted as so natural
a state of things. He followed him down a passage and
into a small room looking out on to the garden, in which
Mr. Sheard sat at his desk, surrounded conveniently enough,

if somewhat austerely, by the books and other accessories
of his calling. A large picture of a four-masted ship with
all her sails set formed a somewhat incongruous ornament
above the mantelpiece, and Mr. Sheard referred to it after
the introductions had been made.

"I see you're looking at the old *Orion*, Mr. Clinton,"
he said. "I made just twenty voyages in her, out by the
Cape to Australia and back round Cape Horn. She was
one of the fastest wool clippers afloat; we only missed doing
the record passage home by fourteen hours. I like to
think sometimes that I was a sailor once; a real sailor,
you know. I was never in steam during all the thirty-two
years I followed the sea."

"I suppose no seaman could say that now, could he?"

"Very few, I should think. When I first went to sea,
a great many battleships only had auxiliary screws, and
I rather think there were some of the old wooden ships
still on duty here and there without any steam at all."

"They don't make sailors of us now," said Frank;
"we're all mechanicians." He was inclined to like this
rather unusual kind of rector, with his simple speech and
his years of hard seafaring life behind him. "I'd like to
hear about some of your voyages, Mr. Sheard," he said.
"You get a bit of a draught round the Horn sometimes,
don't you?"

"If you start father on that subject he'll never have
done," said Charles.

"But we'll have some yarns, all the same, later on,"
said Mr. Sheard. "You're going to keep Mr. Clinton to
dinner, aren't you, Charles? If you take him into the
garden now, I'll come out to you when I've finished what
I have to do. I shan't be long."

Neither of them was interested enough in a garden to
care to inspect this one. They sat under a tree and

smoked. Each of them was readjusting his view of the other. They had hitherto been equals, except for Frank's seniority, living the same life and interested in the same pursuits. Charles had known that Frank, who had a larger allowance than most of his shipmates, came from a big country house somewhere; Frank had known that Charles was the son of a clergyman. Photographs and cabin adornments indicate these things, as well as talk about sport and other doings ashore. But it had made no difference. Now the difference of origin seemed very marked, and perhaps both of them were looking for signs that it was noted in the other. It could not help being noted, and there was a slight awkwardness between them during the twenty minutes or so during which they were alone together. But at the end of that time each liked the other better than he had done before. There was a broad simplicity of mind in both of them that based itself upon essentials, but shirked nothing. Their previous intimacy, which had been fed by their long and close proximity in a life in which their interests were the same, stood the test where the influences that affected them were widely different. The accidents of environment were seen to be nothing; the friendship dug deeper than the accidents.

William, the youngest son, came out to them. He was something like Charles in appearance, already settling to the stocky Sheard breed, although he was not quite eighteen years of age. He was something of a problem in the family. He had been educated at the big London school at which his two elder brothers had done so well, taking it as a spring-board from which to get the scholarships and prizes that had made their after education possible to them. But William was not a winner of prizes and scholarships, though he had worked steadily up to his full ability. He was great at games, and a personage in the little world of his school; but that kind of eminence, while it may earn results at a later educational stage, has to be supported at his age, and the support was not available here. He would have been allowed to stay at school for another year if his father had not moved away from London, but there was not enough money to keep him there as a boarder, unless it had been worth while for the sake of rewards that would carry him on a stage further. He was at present "resting" at home, until a career should be decided for him, and enormously enjoying the change to a country life.

He was shy and awkward, and badly dressed, in a much-worn black jacket, trousers too short for him and bagging at the knees, and his school cap on the back of his head; just the figure that might test Frank Clinton's ability to pierce beneath the surface; for his own brothers, as school-boys of mature age, two at Eton and one at Winchester, had presented a very different appearance, and acquired a very different manner. He passed the test. Young William found no difficulty in talking to him—village cricket was the subject for the moment—and as he followed him indoors later threw a look almost of hero-worship at him, so easy is it for an older man by a little kindness and attention to arouse the admiration of youth.

Mrs. Sheard and Anne were in the dining-room, to which the furniture that had been transferred from the thirteen-by-twelve apartment at Melbury Park gave the appearance of a large stage inadequately set. Mrs. Sheard still bore the appearance of a sea-captain's wife; Anne was much prettier than Frank had taken her to be on his first glimpse of her. She was as tall as her brothers and her father, which with her youthful slimness gave her the appearance of height in which they were conspicuously lacking. Her face was demure and merry at the same

time; her eyes were on the look-out for laughter, and her
lips ready to follow suit upon the slightest provocation;
but she could look very grave. There was something
kittenish about her soft roundness, but she had the natural
grace of her growth besides. A severe critic might have
denied to her beauty of a high type, but must have been
visited by grave doubts as he did so, wondering whether,
after all, so sweet a face could have been improved upon
by features or profile.

The maid, who with a man for the garden and for odd
jobs took the place of Compton's indoor and outdoor
staff of nine, brought in an Irish stew, and after it an
apple tart. There was beer to drink for the men, and at
dessert, which included one or two rare edibles from distant climes, Mr. Sheard brought out some very ancient rum.
There were flowers on the table, massed chiefly in a heavy
piece of presentation plate in the centre. The slight air
of festivity afforded by these arrangements was no doubt
due to Frank's appearance as a guest. There was a little
ice to be broken at first with Mrs. Sheard, but it soon
thawed under his natural geniality, and he had her laughing and enjoying herself long before the remains of the
Irish stew were exchanged for the apple tart. Her pretty
daughter had inherited her dimpled merriment from her,
and it was a relief to the good lady to give vent to it in
these broader surroundings, for of late years she had had to
play a part to which she was not altogether suited.

Anne was, of course, brought into the conversation.
Frank turned to her more than was absolutely necessary
for the sake of seeing her pretty face break into smiles,
her lips apart, and the white teeth show themselves, while
the sweet little trill of laughter came, with the head
slightly thrown back, and the dimples showed themselves
on rounded chin and cheek in the most entrancing fashion.

If Frank exerted himself to produce these attractive exhibitions, and took more and more pleasure in them each
time, he was not only gratifying himself, as it appeared.
There was an admiring tenderness shown towards this
pretty child by her father and mother and brothers alike.
She was the flower of the family, greatly loved and cherished. Her father's rugged face grew wonderfully soft
when he looked at her; she was sitting next to him, and
once or twice he put out his hand on to hers as it rested
on the table. Her mother once rebuked her for talking too
much, but the last thing that her tone and her smile demanded was that her rebuke should be acted upon. Charles
encouraged her by an occasional dry word of chaff. William was the only one who looked at Frank more than he
looked at her, and Frank's undisguised admiration of
her seemed to gratify him exceedingly, so that when
he did look at Anne it was with new admiration of his
own.

The talk that brought them all in in this happy way
was founded upon the experiences of distant seas and
countries that the three men had enjoyed, and that had
always held open for this family a window towards a larger
brighter world than the one they inhabited. When it drifted
nearer home, Anne took little part in it, but her eyes were
upon Frank almost as much as William's, who sat next
to her.

William was in the seventh heaven of delight. There
had been mention of a trout-fishing expedition that Frank
and Charles had made in New Zealand. Frank had asked
Charles to come over for a day's fishing at Kencote, and had
extended the invitation to William. The happy boy, cut out
by nature for every country pursuit, but condemned hitherto
to the uncongenial restraints of the town, saw a glamourous
new life opening up before him, and his feelings towards

Frank had flowered into something like adoration already.
" Oh, we'll put you into the way of it," Frank said, " and
there are plenty of rods at Kencote. Plenty of trout, too,
though they're not the monsters that Charles and I caught
in New Zealand. Who fishes here, by the by? There's
some good water at Kemsale."

" I don't believe anybody does," said Charles. " William
and I were looking at the fish the other day. We'd half
made up our minds to ask Mr. Brown if we might have
a try some evening."

" I don't know about that," said his father. " Mr.
Brown is so kind that I shouldn't care to ask him for
anything that he didn't offer himself."

The attribution of this particular quality to the arch-
millionaire, of whom he had formed quite a different idea,
was a surprise to Frank. " Is he behaving well—Armitage
Brown? " he asked. " There are all sorts of stories flying
about the country."

" He has shown the utmost kindness to us," said Mr.
Sheard gravely. " The difficulty has been to prevent him
doing more than a man of independence wants another man
to do for him."

" I'm glad to hear he is like that," said Frank. " Kemsale coming into new hands is a great change for us in these
parts."

" Kemsale is a very fine house," said Mrs. Sheard. " We
all stayed there for a week while we were moving in, except
Charles, who was with his godfather."

The good lady had been enormously impressed by Kemsale, which was quite different from anything she had ever
known before, or dreamt of as likely to come into her
experience. She had not been altogether comfortable there,
although Mrs. Brown and Aunt Millie had taken to her,
and done their best to make her so. It had been too great a

change. But she liked to think about it all, and had written many letters to relations and intimate friends on the subject.

"It's the largest house in these parts," said Frank. "It was quite a shock to me when they wrote and told me it had been sold."

"I suppose you knew it, Mr. Clinton, when Lord Meadshire lived there."

"Oh, yes. He's my cousin, you know. I knew it best when I was a boy, and his grandfather was alive. He was a dear old boy, and was always getting us over here and doing things for us. He was the great man in these parts too, and one would never have thought it possible that Kemsale should ever come to an end as it did. I couldn't believe it when I heard it."

This was an entirely new point of view, except possibly to Mr. Sheard, who had been diligently going about his parish. Mrs. Sheard, certainly, had never thought of Kemsale as having come to an end, in any way. To her it was in the full flood of its opulent progression, and she couldn't imagine anything more splendid than the figure it cut. "It's a very beautiful house," she said again, rather weakly.

"I suppose you know my cousin Grace," said Frank to Anne. "She is a dear thing. She and I were born on the same day."

"She has been to see mother, but I wasn't here," said Anne. "I have only seen her in church, but I thought she looked very sweet. And she was very kind when she came, wasn't she, mother?"

"Yes, she was," said Mrs. Sheard. "She made us welcome to Kemsale. Everybody has done that. Everybody has been very kind."

"Do she and Meadshire get on with the new people?" asked Frank.

"Katie Brown and Mr. Alfred—that's Mr. Brown's son —know Lady Grace, and they like her tremendously," said Anne.

"I think the two houses have not come together yet," said Mr. Sheard. "There are certain things upon which there has been disagreement; but whatever feeling there may be, I am sure that it will die down very soon. Lady Grace is so gentle and so kind, and our friends at the big house are so anxious to treat everybody in the place well, that they really want the same things, and can't keep apart for long. We shall see them good friends, no doubt, very soon, and as Anne says, the young people up at the big house have already a great admiration for Lady Grace."

"Grace isn't capable of bearing enmity to anybody," said Frank. "If there is any, it must be Meadshire who is keeping it up. But he never keeps up anything for long. Tell me what the young Browns are like. Are they both here now?"

He had turned to Anne again. It seemed rather important to know on what terms she stood with the young Browns—or at least with one of them.

"Oh, they're very nice," she said, "and very lively. We had great fun when we were staying there, and we often go up now to play games with them."

"Yes, they're a godsend," said Charles. "Father, I really don't think there would be any harm in asking Alfred about the fishing. I expect he would like to fish himself, if it were suggested to him."

"He loves the country, and doing everything that people do who live in it," said Anne. "And so do we. I adore everything to do with the country."

As Frank rode on to the Herons' Nest later in the afternoon he found himself wondering how far the intimacy between Alfred Brown and the young people at the

rectory had extended.   He had not been able, in subsequent conversation with Charles, to gather whether Alfred
showed himself at all enamoured of Anne, as might possibly
have been expected of him under the circumstances.   He
could have seen few prettier girls anywhere, and whether
enamoured or not he was undoubtedly on terms of bright
companionship with her as well as with her brothers.
And she liked him; she had said as much herself, with a
smile of reminiscence at the " fun " they had all had
together that had struck Frank as possibly significant.
Alfred Brown seemed to be a nice sort of fellow, by all
accounts; there was no sense in denying that; and the
enormous wealth at his back was certainly no drawback to
him, even if these honest simple Sheards were as little
affected by wealth as people in their position very well
could be.   Frank came to the conclusion, as he rode up
the steep road to the Herons' Nest, that it was no business
of his, but that it would be rather a pity if Alfred Brown
fell in love with Anne Sheard and she with him.   But he
had no time to explain to himself why it seemed to him that
it would be rather a pity.

CHAPTER XX

THE HERONS' NEST

GRACE was at home, and she was alone. She gave Frank
the warmest greeting. The terms they were on were more
those of brother and sister than is usual between cousins
of different sexes. Their cousinship only derived from
Grace's great-grandfather having married a Clinton from
Kencote; but the proximity of the two houses, and other
accidents, had kept the families intimately connected
through three generations, and the relationship was closer
than it had ever been.

" I am so glad you have come over, Frank," Grace said.
" I hardly saw anything of you the other day at Kencote,
and I want to show you our new house. But why didn't
you come to lunch? Kem has gone off somewhere, and I
have been by myself all day."

Frank told her where he had lunched, and why.

" I had no idea Mr. Sheard had a son in the Navy,"
she said in some surprise.

" Charles Sheard told me that his godfather had seen
him through. They're awfully nice people, Grace."

" I like Mr. Sheard," she said. " I am sure he is a
good man. But Kem is furious with James Compton for
putting him in here."

" Why ? "

" Well, he did everything in such an extraordinary way.
He would hardly speak to Kem after the sale was decided
upon. I absolutely refused to quarrel with him myself,
but he never came near us here, and if I hadn't gone down

to the rectory when I heard he was going, he wouldn't even have said good-bye. He didn't say good-bye to Kem."

" But why is Kem annoyed with him for putting Sheard in ? "

" He thinks he did it out of spite. I don't think that myself, but I think he did go out of his way to find a man as unlike himself as possible. I suppose he wanted to show us what we had brought upon ourselves."

She laughed, but Frank took the information seriously. " Well, I don't want to say anything against a relation of yours," he said, " and I hardly knew Compton; but I'd a great deal rather have the Sheards here than I'd have him."

" I think they will do very well," she said. " Now I must show you all over the house and the garden."

It was as charming a house as anybody could have wished to live in. It was built upon two floors only, and covered a lot of ground. There were spacious rooms in it, as well as a great many of moderate size, and the beautiful things that had been brought from Kemsale to furnish it had been arranged to such an effect as to give it an air more settled than the newness of the greater part of it would have seemed to allow. Kemsale had contained such abundant riches that nothing had come out of it that was not good to see in these new surroundings. The things that Grace had not been able to buy back were not intrinsically better than those she and her brother had kept. If she still missed them she said nothing about it to Frank, who told her that he knew little about these things, but to him the Herons' Nest seemed more beautifully furnished than Kemsale had been.

" There is nothing of very great value here, as there was at Kemsale," she said, " but we picked out what we liked best, and of course it is more concentrated. I am so glad you like it, Frank; I think we have made a success of it. Kem has been very interested. He says he wishes he had let Kemsale and come to live here when he first succeeded. He likes it ever so much better."

" How *is* Kem in these days? " asked Frank.

The way in which he put his question made it plain to what he referred. He could talk to Grace about it; they had talked together about it before.

" Oh, he has been quite all right since we came here, more than six months ago now," she said eagerly. " I am so deeply thankful, Frank. Dear Kem! He has had such a lot to fight against, and he is so kind and good when he is entirely himself. I would never have thought that he would have been happy and contented living quietly here with me for as long as he has. Do you know that he has only slept out of the house once since we came? He went up to London just after Christmas, and I was so afraid of what might happen. But he came back the next day, and said he liked being here better than anywhere. I could have cried for joy. And every month that passes makes me hope still more that he is getting over his temptations at last. Poor Kem! "

" That's very good hearing, Grace. What does he do with himself? "

" He is immensely interested in making the garden. I should never have thought he would have taken to that, but he works at it with his own hands. And he is out in his car a great deal. He reads too, which he never did before. He seems to enjoy the quietest sort of life. He doesn't even want to have people stay here. And he looks ever so much better. Now you must come and see the garden, Frank."

The house was built on a plateau, part natural, part excavated from the rock. It faced west, but its chief living-rooms were at the back, and opened on to a broad terrace, which hung over the gorge. It provided a view of the chief fall of water, as well as a glimpse of the blue country to the south through the gap. It was a surprising scene to come upon in this country. Nothing could be seen close at hand from the terrace but rocks and pines, and the miniature mountain terrace. It was difficult to imagine one's self in the heart of such a county as Meadshire.

Frank exclaimed in admiration. " I didn't remember that it was half as jolly as this," he said. " You might be in the Rockies. But where's the garden, Grace? "

" Look over," she said.

The greater part of the terrace was cut out of the living rock. It was bounded by a rough stone wall, and beneath this wall paths and steps had been cut out of the rock, running here and there along its face and leading down to the water at the bottom of the gorge. Here was a natural rock-garden, already gay with drifts and patches of colour.

" You must remember that it has only just been planted," she said. " Next year the things will have spread tremendously, and it will be a lovely sight. I don't think there will be many rock-gardens in England to beat it; it is all so natural, and we can go on with it to any extent. Now you must come and look at the flowers. We have all sorts of rarities, and are both getting very learned upon how to grow them."

Frank showed as much interest in the flowers as his state of ignorance upon such matters allowed, and they went up and down the rocky paths and stairs, and then to the upper parts of the gorge, where the more ordinary parts of the garden lay, or were in the making. " I believe I should take to this game myself if I ever settled down ashore," was Frank's gratifying comment on what he had been shown, when the inspection was over and they returned to

seats on the terrace. " I think you've done it awfully
well. On the whole I should say it was more fun living
here than at Kemsale."

Grace sighed. " I shouldn't feel leaving Kemsale a bit,
if the Herons' Nest had been in quite a different part of
the country," she said.

" I'm glad it isn't, for our sake. But of course it must
be a bore having those new rich people there, and not being
able to get away from them. What are they really like,
Grace? The Sheards can't speak too highly of them."

She did not answer immediately, and then said, with a
shade of unwillingness: " I think Mr. Sheard is a good
honest hard-working man, and will do well as Rector of
Kemsale; but being what they are they are likely to be
over-impressed by people like the Browns, who are enormously rich and rather ostentatious; and it is perhaps
natural that they should wish to keep in well with them."

Frank looked at her in surprise. " My dear girl," he said,
" that's the first time I have ever heard you say anything
uncharitable about anybody. They speak in a very different way about you."

She blushed and looked deeply distressed. " Oh, I
don't want to be uncharitable," she said, " but one can't
help feeling a little sore about certain things. I don't
really know them. I have met the son and daughter, and
I think they are nice; but——"

" Oh, I don't mean the Browns; I mean the Sheards.
You have quite misunderstood them, Grace. I don't believe
they'd go an inch out of their way to keep in with rich
people, as you say. I should think Sheard was quite as
independent as Compton, and with very much less to support his independence on."

" Well, I don't want to be uncharitable towards the
Sheards either, dear Frank. I don't think I am. But one

must look facts in the face. I did find Mrs. Sheard very much inclined to talk about the Browns and their grandeur. Of her class she is a thoroughly nice woman, I am sure, and it is because of her class that one needn't think much of her talking in a way that would mean something quite different if she were of ours."

It was unpleasant to Frank to have Mrs. Sheard's class thus assigned to her; it reflected on the delightful Anne, who would have adorned any class. Nevertheless, Grace's logic was unassailable. Mrs. Sheard's innocent wonderment at the revelations of wealth that had been made to her was only innocuous if she placed herself quite below the level on which admiration of wealth would be an ugly quality to display. And if she did so place herself, as undoubtedly she did, there could be no offence in accepting her own view of herself.

"I'm quite sure you're wrong in thinking that Mrs. Sheard, or any of them, would run after people because they are rich," Frank said. "They are very simple people in their ways, of course; they can't ever have had much money, and they're are not ashamed of it. I admire them for the way they've settled down here exactly as it suits them to live. As for these rich Browns, they seem to have behaved very well to them, putting them up while they were moving, and wanting to do more for them than they would accept. Charles, my friend, told me that. They're very careful about keeping their independence."

"Well, then, I think I must have been mistaken about them, Frank, and I'm sorry I said what I did. They have a very pretty daughter. Did you see her?"

"Yes, she was there. I think she's one of the prettiest girls I have ever seen. And she admires you tremendously, Grace. She has seen you in church."

"I must go and see them again and make friends with

her. I love young things, and I'm glad there's a family at
the rectory. I did like Mrs. Sheard. I don't think I
should have thought anything of her speaking in the way
she did about the Browns if I hadn't wanted not to hear
about them at all. But I'm beginning to think that one
won't be able to keep away from them, and one might as
well make up one's mind to make the best of them."

" You've met the son and daughter, haven't you? You
seem to have made as deep an impression upon them as you
have on little Miss Sheard. She told me so. They had told
her. It's no use your trying to stand out against people,
Grace. They won't let you."

" It is very nice to be liked," she said with a smile.
" I'm afraid I didn't take much pains to make young Mr.
Brown and his sister like me. I was rather struck with
both of them, really. The girl is a happy warm-hearted
little thing, and the young man is straightforward and
amiable. No; I should be quite ready to make friends with
them. I don't think it would be so easy with the father
and mother, and Kem is so up in arms against them about
everything, that I think he would throw me over if I
were to try to."

At this point Meadshire himself arrived upon the scene.
His welcome of Frank was almost vociferous. He seemed
full of life and energy. The unpleasant appearance of
over-indulgence had departed from his face; his eye was
clear, and his skin only red from the sun.

" Well, what do you think of the rock-garden, Frank? "
he asked at once. " You've never seen anything like it
before, I know. It was Grace's idea to begin with, but
I've carried most of it out. Now we're beginning to get
our reward. I tell you, I wouldn't be away from it in the
spring, for long, for any fun you could offer me. I've become a country potterer, my boy. I go to bed early; I

get up early; and all through the winter I was slinging rocks about, and working like a navvy."

" It seems to have done you a world of good, Kem. You're looking ten years younger than when I saw you last."

" Oh, I'm a reformed character. But I'm doing a little mischief too. I'm putting spokes in the wheel of Mr. Banknotes Brown, who has come down here to upset every mortal thing in the place. I tell you, it's quite pathetic the way the people cling to me and Grace. I can't do much for them now, worse luck, but it makes me feel a good boy to go and sit with them and hold their hands, and listen to all their dismal tales. What do you think the fool's doing now? Turning all the tenants out of their farms at the Ganton end, and making plans for a great butter factory to which they've got to send their milk."

" Yes, we've heard something about that at Kencote. But I don't quite see how they're going to send their milk to his factory if he turns them out."

" Oh, well; he's going to put his own people in. They've got to work their farms according to his ideas. A fat lot he's likely to know about dairying! When he's made a mess of it, and lost a pot of money, you'll see, he'll turn out the people he's put in just as sharp as he's turned out the others; and he'll want to get the right sort of people back; and he won't get 'em, unless they're bigger fools than he is."

" He hasn't turned everybody out, Kem," said Grace. " The Davises are staying on; and the Blakes; and I think the Pettifers."

" The Pettifers aren't. I've just been there. They asked me what I thought about it all, and I told them. ' I wish I'd got a farm of my own to put you in,' I said. ' But there are plenty of farms to be taken under landlords who

know their business, and don't want to play old Harry
with their land. If you do stay,' I said, ' you employ a
jolly sharp lawyer and fix the gentleman down in black-
and-white, so that when his precious scheme comes to an end
you won't get left.' However, they're not going to risk
it. They're leaving. A beastly shame I call it. The
Pettifers have been there ever since I was a boy. So have
the Davises, of course, but he seems to have talked them
round. John Davis is all for it, and had the cheek to
tell me that they expected to do better under Mr. Banknotes Brown than they did under us. That's human nature,
I suppose. They've been at Kemsale almost as long as we
have, made pots of money out of their farm in good times,
and never had their rent raised a halfpenny. Now we're
down and no good to them any longer, they go over bag and
baggage to the new fellow. I don't want to hear any more
about the Davises. I've done with them."

"Dear Kem, I don't think you ought to go about stirring
up people against Mr. Brown," said Grace. "It isn't true
that he is turning everybody out. On other parts of the
estate most of the farming tenants are being allowed to
renew their agreements if they wish to, and there has been
scarcely any change made in the cottages. Miss Merriman
is staying on at ' The Limes,' and Captain Fuller told her
that it was by Mr. Brown's wish. So we certainly did him
an injustice there. The people are settling down, and are
prepared to see how things will work out. It ought not
to be we who upset them."

But Meadshire would not take this view. "They'll settle down for a year, perhaps, and then all the trouble will
come over again," he said. "This is only the beginning
of his ridiculous experiments. He'll be trying for coal
somewhere, next. Besides, I'm not upsetting anybody.
The people all know me, and they're only too pleased to

talk. If they ask my advice, I give it to 'em. I can't be blamed for that."

"If you're not careful you'll have Mr. Brown suing you for libel, or scandal, or whatever it is," said Frank. "I should leave him alone if I were you, Kem."

CHAPTER XXI

RECOGNITION

" Now, Mr. Brown, I want to hear all about this dairying scheme of yours. We needn't go in to the ladies just yet. We'll have it all out. Let me fill your glass."

The Squire had moved down to the other end of the table, decanters in hand. The Browns had come over to Kencote to dine, all four of them. Dick and Virginia, and Jim Graham and Cicely, had been asked to meet them. It was a party of recognition, and had so far passed off fairly well. The Squire had seen Mrs. Brown's well-decked back pass through the door with a sense of relief, for he had found her very heavy in hand, and Mrs. Clinton had not succeeded in establishing relations of any cordiality with Armitage Brown. But the younger generation had talked and laughed freely enough during dinner. Alfred and Katie had justified their inclusion in the party.

Armitage Brown passed his hand over his heavy moustache. He was struck with sudden amusement at being told to stand and deliver by this old country squire, who had treated him with hearty hospitality, but not without a hint of condescension. He had become used to being approached about his schemes, but in a very different manner. However, as he wanted to talk to Mr. Clinton about this one, one method of approach was as good as another.

It may be supposed that, with his record, he was not unversed in presenting a statement in such a way as to attract those who were already interested in its subject. On the financial side of any scheme he could speak with a clearness and authority that was bound to carry weight. At the end of his preliminary exposition, which had been listened to without interruption, he stood before his hearers no longer as the rich Londoner who had been tentatively received as a country neighbour, to be politely dropped if he failed to come up to their mark, but as the man who made money as if by magic, which was the way in which he was generally regarded by the world outside.

The Squire was particularly struck by his speech, and the qualities in him which it revealed. He so seldom came into contact with power based upon anything but the accidents that brought the kind which he enjoyed himself; but he recognised it here. He no longer felt any inclination to patronise his guest. He remembered what a reputation this man bore, and had been brought by the cold mastery of phrase he had used to recognise it as effective. At the beginning of the exposition he had been ready to criticise it from every point of view; at the end he was feeling rather flattered at being taken into the confidence of a great financier, and was searching in his mind for points which would display any knowledge that he might have of his own.

Dick and Jim Graham were also impressed. They had already talked the matter over between themselves and agreed that whatever the scheme might be it was not likely, originated by such a man as this, to fail at its business end; which was a considerable admission for men of their prejudices to make. If Armitage Brown was prepared to spend a large sum of money in building and equipping a butter factory on the outskirts of Ganton, he had probably satisfied himself that that was a suitable place for it; and, assuming that he could obtain his supplies, he was probably capable of making it pay. They were helped to this opinion by the fact that they also thought the place suitable and the supplies quite possible to get. What they had both of them doubted was the financier's ability to organise the supplies. Very many considerations came in there of which he must be entirely ignorant. They were both prepared to watch closely for signs of that ignorance, and to concentrate their criticism on it. The criticism would not be destructive; they were inclined to encourage the scheme, if it were put on a sound footing, for they saw profit in it both for Kencote and Mountfield. But it would be searching. In the talk that was going about, there was more than a hint of the faddy experiments that a new rich man who knew nothing about the land would be likely to try when he had turned himself into a landowner. This new rich man was to be shown that he had everything to learn upon that side of his scheme.

But apparently he hadn't. The explanation was only in outline, and dealt more with the handling of supplies than with their source; but it was quite as well-informed on the points which their special knowledge enabled them to test as upon the others. As Dick said to Jim afterwards: "You'd have thought the fellow had milked cows all his life."

The statement came to an end suddenly. Not a word had been said to invite co-operation or even approval. The facts were left to talk for themselves. "That's how I see it," said Armitage Brown; but added, as he raised his cigar to his lips: "But naturally I'm liable to error when it comes to dealing with the land. That's where I look to you for expert opinion."

These words did almost as much for him as all his previous ones. They put him absolutely right with his hearers. He had shown his mastery over detail, but was still willing to learn from them.

"It doesn't seem to me as if you are liable to much

error," said the Squire handsomely. "You must have taken a lot of trouble to get at your facts, and as far as I'm able to judge, you've got at them remarkably well. What do you think, Dick?"

"I like the idea," said Dick. "It has been closely worked out; of course one would expect that from Mr. Brown; and he has given us something definite to go upon. As a matter of fact I think we are more ready for it here than he is at Kemsale. It's a question of getting the farmers to go in at first."

"You have more grass here, I know," said Armitage Brown. "I've seen that. But I don't see why we shouldn't get as much grass on our side."

A long discussion followed, in which the Squire and Dick took the greater part, the Squire displaying considerable knowledge, but apt to go off into irrelevancies, Dick bringing him back to the point, and working things out by degrees in a way that showed him clear-headed and with a grasp of his subject, if rather slow at coming to conclusions. After a time, Armitage Brown paid no more than perfunctory attention to the Squire, but had his eye on Dick all the time, sizing him up, testing him by little speeches and questions thrown in, and gaining as it seemed a respect for him which he had hardly thought would be called for.

"Well, you can teach me a lot," he said. "You have taught me a good deal already. A scheme like this may look all right on paper, but unless it takes in all the factors that you know about and I don't, it may be all wrong."

It was doubtful whether Dick had taught him very much that was of importance. He had been racking all available brains for a fortnight, including John Davis's, whose intelligence was as great as Dick's and his practical experience greater. John Davis had become his enthusiastic lieutenant, and had even brought his own father to the belief that Points Manor was about to recover some of its ancient glories. But perhaps he had been won over by some such judicious sops to his self-esteem as were now being offered to Dick. Armitage Brown knew very well how to administer them where it was worth his while to do so.

"Are you going to try the share system?" asked Jim Graham. It was the first time he had spoken.

"What do you know about the share system?" asked Armitage Brown in some surprise. He had taken no notice of Jim whatever, putting him down as of no importance in the discussion.

"Oh, I've been in Australia. It works well there. If you start your factory, I shall probably cut up one of my farms, if I can find the capital to do it. It will bring people back to the land."

"Have you got land near here, sir?"

"I shall be within your radius, with a co-operative motor-lorry."

Armitage Brown laughed. "Here's another gentleman that can teach me something," he said. "Don't you worry about capital, Mr. Graham. If you've got the land and are prepared to use it in that way, you can have all the capital you want. Yes; I've gone into the share system; only on paper, of course. If you've seen it in practice, I should like to go into it with you. I'm going to try it on one of my own farms."

"What is the share system?" asked the Squire, who was inclined to be suspicious of this talk of cutting up farms. Jim, for all his steadiness and slowness, had a few Radical crotchets in his head, and it was not to be supposed that Mr. Armitage Brown would be without them, in spite of the unexpected soundness he had hitherto displayed.

"As it is worked in Australia," said Jim, "it means that the landlord provides everything—land, buildings, herd, and so on—and takes his proportion of the profits. The holdings are mostly small, because there's a difficulty about regular labour there; but a man with a family can make a handsome living out of a few acres."

"That means cottage-building," said the Squire. "If you once start that on any scale your done. What farm were you thinking of cutting up at Kemsale, Mr. Brown?"

Armitage Brown probably had his own reasons for answering this question directly. "Warren's Farm," he said.

"Warren's? That's Pettifer's farm. He has been there a great many years. Is Pettifer going?"

"I don't know yet. I gave him the chance of coming in."

"I don't think he would be much use," said Dick. "Old Cousin Humphrey only let him stay on, father, because he had a large family."

"I believe so," said the Squire rather unwillingly. "Still, one doesn't like to think of old tenants being shown the door."

"I felt the same," said Armitage Brown. "I've given all those on the six farms I mentioned to you the chance of staying on, of course on condition that they would work in with me. I should do all I could to help them. But I rather fancy Lord Meadshire has persuaded Mr. Pettifer that he'll do better for himself if he clears out. He'll certainly do better for me; but I was careful not to say that."

There was a silence, and then Frank laughed. It was only a few days since he had paid his visit to the Herons' Nest.

"The sooner Meadshire learns to mind his own business the better," growled the Squire. "I'll take the liberty of telling him so the next time I see him."

The Browns left punctually at half-past ten. Cicely's

carriage had not been ordered until eleven. On such occasions as this the Squire liked a final conversation with the men of his family over a cigar. But he did not suggest an immediate adjournment to his room when he had hospitably seen his guests off at the door; he went back into the drawing-room.

"Well, I think these people will do," he said largely, looking round upon his womenfolk there assembled.

"Alfred and Katie will," said Joan. "Alfred and Katie are treasures."

It might have been supposed that an opinion upon Alfred and Katie was not exactly what he had asked for. They and Joan and Cicely and Frank had spent most of the evening at a table apart from the groups made by the rest, playing games, and the talk and laughter that had come from it had only not disturbed conversation because the room was so large. The Squire had once or twice gone over and stood by them, and had seemed by his reception of Joan's remark to have given more attention to his younger guests than might have been expected of him.

"The girl struck me as a very nice girl," he said. "Not pretty exactly, but bright and sensible. We shall always be glad to see her here when she likes to come."

"Oh, and Alfred too," said Joan. "I adore Alfred. He is full of character. He hates being rich."

"Did he tell you that?" asked Frank.

"No, I found it out for myself. I found out a lot about him. Mother darling, did you tell Mrs. Brown we were expecting Royalty? She was a diamond shop."

But the Squire, apparently, did not wish to hear Mrs. Brown discussed. "I like that girl very much," he said again. "*You* seemed to find no difficulty in making friends with her, Frank—what?"

"We'll make up a match between Frank and Katie," said Joan. "Then I shall have Alfred as a sort of brother-in-law."

"You're letting your tongue run away with you, Miss Joan," said the Squire, quite in his old-time style of rebuke. "Well, we'll go and have a cigar in my room. You don't want to go off just yet, Cicely? That's right."

Talk over the cigars was not entirely on the subject of the dairying scheme, although that was the point from which it started. Armitage Brown, without apparent effort on his part, had succeeded in impressing his personality upon the three elder men, who were each a little excited at having come into contact with him. Jim Graham was the only one of the three whose command of money was less than was convenient for the way in which he lived, and the things he wanted to do. The excitement he felt was at the prospect of carrying out an idea of the kind that he had often considered in connection with his estate, but had been too cautious to try at the expense of burdening it with mortgages. Now these difficulties were to disappear. The millionaire had swept them away, with a laugh. And he was backing the scheme himself, with his genius as well as his wealth, on the side on which Jim would have been powerless. His imagination went no further than the idea by which he knew he would profit, on the lines on which all his quiet steady work were set. But Armitage Brown's advent into his life was a stirring event viewed from that standpoint alone.

Neither the Squire nor Dick had any need of more money than they possessed already. Each of them lived exactly the life that suited him, and spent less than his income. But the Squire liked the "feel" of money, not in elaborate expenditure, which he was inclined to deprecate, unless it was in support of legitimate state, but for the sense of power that it brought. The almost unlimited wealth with which Armitage Brown was generally credited made a personage of him. The Squire had not quite realised how much of a personage he was, hitherto; but now he did. He had recognised some of his quality. He was a man to cultivate.

Dick was very much like his father in essentials, but with a clearer head and a wider knowledge of the world. He was the least moved of the three by contact with the millionaire, but he was not unmoved. He had had a glimpse of the workings of a mind that coins money out of every combination of facts that it takes in, where other minds only use them for idle amusement. It had stimulated his own mind. The activities in which he contentedly spent his days seemed rather poor and dull beside the workings that brought such royal harvests.

" It seems to me," he said, " that this fellow can teach us something about the land after all."

" Well, I don't know about that," said the Squire. " He seems pretty sharp at picking up information, but what he said was that we should have to teach *him*. I rather liked that in him. I hadn't expected it. These new rich fellows generally think that if they've read a few newspaper articles they can start straight off and teach people who've been connected with the land all their lives."

" We'd better get it out of our minds that he's a new rich fellow," said Dick. " He isn't particularly new as far as his riches go, and that's what matters to us if we're going to take advantage of his ideas. As for his not being what we've been used to having at Kemsale, that's all done with now, and we needn't worry about it any longer. They're not bad sort of people to have there; we might have been much worse off."

" Oh, yes," said the Squire. " They'll do very well. I

don't care for the lady much, but there's no fault to find with the young people. I thought the girl was a particularly nice girl."

" The way I look at it," said Dick, who was not interested in the girl, " is that what we know about the land and he doesn't is the least important part of the business. It wouldn't be if he left it out of account; but he doesn't. He'll use all we can tell him. We're the experts, and I suppose men in his line of life are always using experts, and know how to use them. But they manage their businesses themselves."

The Squire did not quite follow this. " I haven't got as far as seeing him manage mine," he said.

" No, but he'll bring us in new ideas. Probably what he thinks of us is that we hate new ideas. We don't. We're always ready for them, if they fit in with what we know."

" There isn't much wrong with this dairying idea of his."

" Well, see how he's worked that out. Left no stone unturned to get every bit of information available. Went over to Denmark and looked into everything, just as we should go and have a look at something new in a farm next door."

" I should be inclined to be careful about introducing foreign ideas into this country. I was a little doubtful about all that."

" It's all material. That's what struck me more than anything about him, the pains he takes to collect material, and the way he uses it. Didn't you notice that, Jim? "

" Fuller has been grinding at statistics for him for the last six months," said Jim. " He told me there was nothing he didn't want to know, and nothing he couldn't take in."

" Well, there it is. I'm quite willing to follow his lead if he works things out as carefully as that, and is willing

to make the use he does of all one can tell him. It seems
to me that he brings us something we haven't got, and we
can give him something that he hasn't got. I'm not sorry
that he's come here."

While this conversation was going on, the Browns were
flying homewards in their luxuriously appointed car. Alfred
and Katie were doing most of the talking. They had
enjoyed themselves, and liked all the people they had
met, as they usually did. Mrs. Brown paid little attention
to their chatter. She was seriously exercised in her mind
as to the diamonds she had worn in such profusion. Lady
Inverell had worn but few jewels, but Mrs. Brown had
seen her at a party in London with diamonds finer than
her own. Had she made a mistake? The thought kept
her silent and depressed during the ten-mile drive.

Armitage Brown had also kept silence during the first
half of it. Then he roused himself. "Well, I've corrected
some of my ideas," he said. "There's not much to be
done with old Mr. Clinton, but that son of his has some
brains in his head, and so has Mr. Graham, though he's
one of the quiet sort. If I'm not mistaken, we shall make
this bit of country hum between us."

But he had said nothing about warning the hounds off
his land.

CHAPTER XXII

HAVING IT OUT

KATIE stood under a tree by the side of the road, while the rain came down as if it wanted to make up in a few minutes for holding off for the best part of two months. She had walked out three miles to a lonely cottage, where there was a sick woman with a young baby, and when she had started the sky had shown no threat of rain, though if she had thought of looking at a barometer she would not have gone without protection. She had set out for home again under black thunder-clouds, and was now rapidly getting wet, as the leaves over her head were yielding to the terrific downpour.

A motor-car came slushing along in the mud. She knew it for Lord Meadshire's, and felt a sudden alarm lest he, who was in it alone, should offer her assistance. She would rather have got wet through.

He had his hood up, and was peering straight ahead through the blurred glass screen, but just as he passed Katie's tree he caught a glimpse of her, and had not gone many yards further before he stopped and then backed towards her.

"Hullo! want a lift?" he called out, and then recognised her. "Oh, it's you, Miss Brown," he said, as if they had been on the most friendly terms. "I say, I think you'd better hop in. You'll get soaked through in a few minutes."

"Oh, thank you very much," she said hurriedly. "I'm all right. I expect it will leave off soon."

He laughed and opened the door for her. "Come in quick," he said. "I'm going to stop here till the worst is over. It gets in through the chinks."

She got in, feeling like a child whose will has been over-ridden by one in authority, and sat down next to him.

"That's right," he said, grinning affably at her. "I'll drive you home when it eases up a bit. I'm going up to see your father."

"You are going to see father!" she exclaimed.

"Yes. Do you think he'll want to bite me?"

She had recovered her wits. She was not going to let him treat her as a child. "I think you would deserve it if he did," she said.

He roared with laughter. "That's right; you stick up for your father," he said. "He wrote and asked me to come, you know. Either he would come and see me, or I could come and see him, or he'd put his lawyers on to me. That's the sort of man *he* is. I thought I'd go and beard him in his own lair. I rather want to see what you've done with Kemsale. I'm glad I met you. Perhaps, if I take you home dry, he'll let me off easy, eh? I'm in an awful funk, you know."

She could not help laughing, but immediately became serious again. "Why do you dislike father so much?" she said. "He has done nothing to you, and yet you do all you can to set people against him. You go about everywhere making mischief. I think it's very mean."

"Oh, but you mustn't say that, Miss Brown. I've got my feelings, you know. I'm sure you wouldn't like to hurt them."

"If you are going to talk to me like that," she said, "I shall get out. I don't mind if I do get wet. I'm not a child to be laughed at and held of no account."

She was already fumbling at the catch on the door.

His face changed. "All right," he said, " I'll tell you why I'm up against your father. Anybody in my position would be. He comes down here and rides roughshod over everything and everybody. He uses his beastly money as a sort of steam roller. You're expected to get out of the way of it, and if you don't he thinks he can crush you with it. He's not going to crush me. I've got my little place in the world, and I'm going to keep it. Money isn't everything, and I'm going to be the person that will show him that."

"I don't in the least know what you mean," she said. " I suppose I've no right to be offended by the things you say, as I asked you a question, but there is nothing in them at all like my father. You must have made some mistake."

"I've made no mistake. I had a taste of his quality before ever he bought the place, and I'm not likely to forget it, or forgive it either. However, that's no reason why you and I should quarrel. My sister likes you, you know, and we've both come to the conclusion that there's nothing in the way of our being friends, as we shall have to meet each other now and then, living next door as we do. Your father! Well, that's a different matter."

"We can't be friends," she said uncompromisingly, " if you treat my father as you do; I mean that she and I can't be, if she looks on him like that. But perhaps she doesn't. Perhaps it's only you who are so unfair about him."

"She looks on him in exactly the same way as I do. She's reason to, after what he did."

"What did he do?"

She asked the question boldly, but not without inward tremors. If it was "business," she thought her father might have been hard, and that in any case she might not know enough to be able to defend him.

He looked at her sharply. " I don't know that I want to go into it with you," he said. " From what I've heard, you're concerned in it yourself, though it's quite possible that you haven't known."

" *I* concerned in it! " She was utterly at a loss.

" Well, I will tell you, then. You have my sister's two rooms up at Kemsale, haven't you? Yes, Beatrix Irving told me so. And every mortal thing in them—or very nearly everything—that she'd always had. How would you like it if somebody took advantage of a little mistake you had made, and did you out of all the special things you'd had round you all your life, as your father did her? "

" What do you mean? " asked poor Katie, bewildered and distressed.

" Well, I suppose you don't know anything about it. You'd better ask your father what he paid for the contents of those two rooms."

" He did tell me that they cost a great deal. But do please explain. You can see that I don't understand."

" Grace's things ought never to have gone into the sale. But we didn't take them out because we thought it would be just as easy to buy them back. Well, your father wouldn't let us. He had them bid up to preposterous prices. We just managed to get two family portraits—our grandfather and grandmother—by frightening the man who was bidding, and paying ten or twenty times their value. After that they wouldn't let us have a thing. We'd had two rooms built at our house almost exactly like my sister's old ones, so that she should feel at home in them. They're empty. She didn't want to furnish them afresh. That's what we have to thank your father for; and if Grace can forgive it, I can't."

The tears were in her eyes, half of indignation, half of deep distress. " Oh, how can you think we knew that? "

she cried. "Father had no idea that the things we bought were wanted for her. How could he have? He wasn't there himself. They were bought with all the rest at the sale."

"I tell you he did know. They telephoned to tell him in the middle of the sale. I sent the message myself, and he took no notice of it whatever. They were to buy them in, whatever it cost."

"I tell you he didn't know; he couldn't have known. Yes, I remember now he did say something about a message, afterwards. He thought it was about the pictures only. If it was what you say, he didn't understand it. And as if *I* should want to have things that Lady Grace wanted for herself. She shall have them all back, every one. I know father will let me give them to her if I ask him."

She was in actual tears now. He looked at her curiously and kindly. "Well, don't upset yourself about it," he said. "*You* are kind and nice enough, anyhow. Of course it was a jar for my sister, losing all her little private treasures; but she's got used to it now. If *you've* got them, and like them, we'll leave it at that."

"I liked them because they were hers," she said. "I haven't changed anything in the rooms. Nearly everything else in the house is altered, but her two rooms are just the same. I hoped she would see them some day, and be pleased."

"I think that's very sweet of you. I'll tell her. Perhaps she will see them some day."

"Oh, but she must have them back. Now we know that there was a mistake we can put it right. I shouldn't have a happy moment using her things now."

"Well, you see, we couldn't very well take them as a present, though it's kind enough of you to think of it.

Don't worry about it any more. We can be getting on now, I think."

It took them only a short time to cover the four miles to Kemsale. Katie dried her eyes and sat very thoughtful, only answering by monosyllables what Meadshire said to her, and hardly hearing it. He had a fund of easy talk that required little attention, and used it so as to put her at her ease. When they drew up before the great porch at Kemsale he said to her: "Now don't you think anything more about those rooms. I shan't, and Grace won't either. I dare say there was a mistake, and your father didn't understand."

"Oh, I shall talk to him about it," she said. "Thank you for saving me from getting wet. Good-bye."

The rain had ceased and she went round to another entrance, leaving him to make his way into the house.

He was shown straight into Armitage Brown's business room. The millionaire was sitting at his desk, awaiting him.

"Good-morning, Mr. Brown," said Meadshire affably. "I've just brought your daughter home to you. I found her getting wet under a tree."

Armitage Brown was not often at a loss, but he was so now at this unexpected opening. He mumbled a word of thanks and asked his visitor to sit down.

"Thanks," said Meadshire, and took a chair, in which he leaned back, crossing his legs and looking with amiable expectancy into his adversary's face.

Armitage Brown recovered his equanimity. "I wish to put a few facts to you," he said, "before I instruct my solicitor to take proceedings."

"Oh, yes. It's just as well to have a little talk. Perhaps when we've finished we shall find it unnecessary to bring our solicitors in at all."

Armitage Brown thought that he was going to be treated with the bland impertinence that had been used towards Alfred, and perhaps invited to lose his temper. He was not going to do that. He was going to say what he had to say in the most direct fashion possible, and if complete satisfaction were denied him cut the interview short and take his proceedings. He was going to take no notice of the impertinence.

"What I shall take action on," he said, "is your having told Mr. Blake of Stubbington Farm, on a certain date, and before witnesses, that I was not in a position to carry out engagements I had entered upon with him, and that if he didn't wish to be ruined he had better find a farm under another landlord."

Meadshire appeared to give this statement full consideration. "Well, it does seem rather strong if it's put like that, doesn't it?" he said.

"That will be the chief ground of the action. I shall bring up other witnesses to prove that ever since I bought this property from you you have persistently gone about amongst people who were your tenants and are now mine, raising prejudice against me. It will be shown that you have kept a footing here in the middle of the estate, that you took very little interest in the tenantry on it when it was yours, and were not often here, but that since selling it to me you have been constantly here, and constantly in communication with the tenants; and that this has been happening while I was abroad and was unable to take steps to counteract your influence."

"It begins to look worse and worse, doesn't it? As I understand it, all this will be brought up to create prejudice against me in the eyes of a British jury."

"It will be brought up to prove that you have been chiefly engaged during the past six months in spreading

scandal against me. But it isn't by any means all that
will be brought up. It will be proved that in the negotiations that took place leading up to the sale of this property
I gave way upon many points that I might have held out
on, that, in fact, you received the full price for everything
that you sold me, that you were difficult and inconsequent,
while I made one concession after the other, that we never
even met personally, and that I gave you no cause whatever
for feeling any rancour against me. It will also be proved
that you sold with the rest the chancel pew in Kemsale
Church, and that you have taken steps to prevent my occupying it, which will probably bring some light relief into
the proceedings when they come to be recounted, and your
attendances at church previously to my coming here are
touched upon. It will be shown that I gave way to you
there, and I shall state the reason why I did so—that I
was not going to enter upon any litigation in respect to a
seat in a church. So it will come out gradually that you
have been the aggressor throughout, and that I have not
been able, even by giving way to you, to soften your
rancour."

Meadshire's face had changed somewhat during this
speech. It might have been supposed that ridicule was
the one weapon that he was unable to stand up against.
But he must have been aware that he would cut a poor
figure before this strong self-possessed man, and deliver
himself into his hands if it was to be his own temper that
should be lost. "Well, it's beginning to look like a good
case," he said, in the same tone as before, but not with
quite the same easy smile. "It will rest upon my actually
having no complaint against you and your methods; but
we'll leave that aside for the moment. Supposing you're
going to have everything your own way, what will be the
reason to be fixed upon me for my attitude towards you?"

" Oh, that's very easily answered. Jealousy. Jealousy
of a particularly contemptible sort. All the world knows
what you are; all the world knows what I am. You're a
peer, the head of an old family, who have acted in such a
way as to have to sell everything you had, and bring your
family to an end. I'm a rich man, who have made enough
money to step into your shoes. And you don't like it. You'll
take my money, but you'll do all you can to prevent my enjoying what you've sold to me. You'll sit down here next
door to me, and see that you mop up all the bowings and
scrapings that are due to you; you think I want them as
much as you do, and you'll prevent me getting them if you
can. You'll scuttle into church half an hour before the service, when you hardly went at all before, so that I shall be
prevented from sitting in a seat that belongs to me a couple
of steps higher than the rest of the congregation. You've
thrown over the people that have lived on your land for generations; you encourage them to think that I shall turn them
out. When you find I mean to take over the responsibilities
that you've chucked away and keep them on, though there's
no obligation on me to do it, you can't bear that either.
You don't care what becomes of them; you set yourself
to persuade them to go, because you think you can harm
me by it."

" Oh, that's enough," said Meadshire. He was red and
scowling; the indictment had been too wounding. It had
been impossible to keep up the air of jaunty indifference
with which he had listened to its opening. " If you want
to bring an action against me, bring it and be damned to
you. You won't get it all your own way."

He rose from his seat, and prepared to leave the room.
Armitage Brown did not shift his position, nor look up at
him. " Well, that's how it will show up if I go to law,"
he said in the same even voice. " The question is whether

what you can bring up in defence—and I've no doubt you'll
bring up something—is going to harm me as much as what
I shall bring up will harm you. If not, I don't see why
money should be wasted in litigation when matters can
quite easily be settled between ourselves."

He looked up now, inquiringly. There was no passion
in his hard gaze, no annoyance, no contempt even. He was
proposing a business negotiation. Meadshire was being invited to ignore his outbreak, as completely as his adversary
had ignored it.

He decided to do so. The stronger character had won.
He could only lose more and yet more by keeping up the
struggle.

He glared down at him for a moment and then threw
himself into his chair again with a laugh. "I told somebody the other day that you were a hard nut to crack," he
said, "and, by Jove, you've cracked me. I don't wonder
that you've got on in the world."

Armitage Brown was ready to allow him to recover his
equanimity, but was not yet ready to relinquish his impersonal attitude. "What I should expect to gain by litigation," he said, "would be to put a stop to the annoyance
I'm subjected to now by finding you continually in my
way. I've stood it up to the point at which I'll stand it
no longer; but if you can satisfy me now that the annoyance will cease I shall get all I want. I'm not anxious
to waste my time in the law courts. I can find better use
for it."

Having once got rid of his fit of temper, Meadshire was
now himself again, and proof against showing temper
again. "You'll give up the idea of scoring against me,"
he suggested.

"Scoring against you! I shouldn't waste five minutes of
my time or a shilling of my money for the sake of scoring

against you. I don't care anything about you, if you'll keep out of my way. That's all I want."

The temper showed itself for a moment, but was under control. "Well now, that's just the attitude that has riled me, you know,' and led to my doing things that perhaps I shouldn't have done if you had shown yourself a little more agreeable. Keep out of your way! It's what I call riding roughshod and you can only do it because you're rich."

"What chances have I had of making myself agreeable, as you call it? Did you expect me to come hat in hand to you for leave to live peaceably in the place I've bought from you? What *did* you expect? I'm hanged if I know. If you've made up your mind to avoid having an action brought against you, by giving me the undertaking I want, you might tell me how I've succeeded in offending your lordship—what I've left undone, that a marquis might expect from a man in the City. I'm not above learning."

"You've got a damned rough tongue in your head, Mr. Brown. If I hadn't happened to have had a little conversation with your daughter just now, which has thrown rather a new light upon a certain subject, I shouldn't sit here taking all this from you. You're showing yourself all the time exactly what I thought you. I don't stand on what I happen to be by accident. I've stood on it a great deal too little, according to the general opinion. But you do stand on your money. It's what has given you your position here. I dare say I've played the fool and given you a handle against me. I generally do play the fool somehow; it's what I'm noted for. But there's been something behind it. I thought if I didn't show that I wasn't going to be snowed under by you and your money, here in the place where I live, and have a right to live, you would—well, you would behave exactly as you're doing now."

" I'm behaving now as you've invited me to behave. If you had shown yourself disposed to be friendly when I came down here, you wouldn't have had anything to complain of in my behaviour. Nobody else about here has, as far as I know. At the same time I should like to make it quite plain that I'm not grumbling at your holding off from me. You'd a perfect right to do that if you didn't think I was good enough for you. But I suppose I've as good a right to show myself independent as you have, and you've no cause to complain, after what has happened, at my wanting to have it understood that I'm not the sort of man to care a snap of the fingers whether you had thought me good enough or not. What were you referring to when you mentioned my daughter just now? "

" Well, it's at the bottom of the whole thing. You used your money in what I call a brutal way, to prevent us getting some things we wanted out of this house."

" You must speak more plainly, please. I don't know what you're referring to."

" I made the mistake of leaving things in the sale that ought to have been taken out beforehand. I thought we should be able to buy in what we wanted. Well, you wouldn't let us. The contents of my sister's two special rooms were bid up to extravagant prices, and she lost them. I suppose you'll say I got twenty times their value in money, and so I did, and more; but I didn't want the money, I wanted the things, for her."

" It's rather an absurd charge to make, if you mean by it that I should deliberately pay twenty times the value of things, and pay it to you, in order to prevent your having them. Why should I do a thing like that? "

" That's what I want to know. You did do it."

" What happened exactly was that I gave instructions

that certain things were to be bought. How was I to know that some of them weren't meant to be sold?"

"They telephoned to you in the middle of the sale, and I sent a message myself."

"Well then, they muddled it. I do remember being rung up. I was very busy at the time and I'd given them my instructions, so I didn't waste much time over them. They certainly didn't put it on the ground you mention, or I should have listened. I don't remember anything being said about that at all. It was on the ground of things fetching a higher price than they had expected that they telephoned."

Meadshire remembered how little trouble he had taken to get the right message through, intent on his " fun " as he had been. " Well, it's all over and done with now," he said. " I dare say I did you some injustice, but surely you must have found out how things stood afterwards. You paid something like a couple of thousand pounds for those two rooms, and they were worth a couple of hundred at the very outside."

" I was surprised; but I don't worry about that sort of thing when it's over. I thought I had myself to thank for it. It was foolish to give the instructions I did. I thought I'd just been taken advantage of, and as I'd been warned, I couldn't blame anybody but myself. As I'd had to pay the money I thought that might do; so I put it out of my mind."

" Well, as I say, I did you an injustice, and I'm sorry for it. Still, you'll admit that your way of doing things wouldn't exactly explain itself to anybody who wouldn't be prepared to sacrifice two thousand pounds for making a mistake, and to think no more about it. The whole thing seemed significant. It seems to have put me on to a wrong scent."

" I must talk to my daughter about it. She wanted those rooms exactly as they were, and that was another reason why I didn't mind the price I paid. You say you've talked to her. What did she say? "

" Oh, she was as nice as she could be about it—seems to have taken a fancy to my sister, and wanted to give her everything back—didn't like to think she'd been done out of the things, and of course wouldn't admit that you had been to blame in any way. I don't know that you were. I told her we'd better let it stand now. But if you'd care to sell the things for the price you gave, it would put everything right."

" Certainly I will, if my daughter agrees; and I suppose she will, from what you say. We'll consider that settled then, and it's one misunderstanding removed."

Meadshire was melted. " It's really the only one," he said. " Look here, Mr. Brown, I've become infernally bored with carrying on this feud. I'm not cut out for it. My old cousin, Edward Clinton, went for me the other day about it. I wouldn't let him see that I was sick of it, but I am. I apologise for everything I've done or said against you. Now will you accept that and think no more about it ? "

" Yes, I think I can promise that, Lord Meadshire. I've always been able to make some excuses. If I'd belonged to a place in the way you have, I shouldn't care about seeing somebody else in my shoes."

" That's very handsomely said. But I haven't behaved well, and there's no good denying it. Now you'll sit in the chancel pew next Sunday, won't you? I've been to church six Sundays running, and I want a holiday."

CHAPTER XXIII

SIX MONTHS LATER

" I am thinking of giving a ball here."

The momentous announcement was made by Mrs. Brown to Mrs. Fuller, as they sat at tea together, one late November afternoon, in Mrs. Brown's boudoir. It was received by Mrs. Fuller with complete calm of manner; but her eyes glistened.

" I think it is a good idea," she said. " There is no finer house for a ball anywhere, and done as *you* will do it, it ought to be a great affair."

" There ought to be no difficulty in doing it well in this house. It might have been built for it. It seems a waste *not* to have one."

" Yes; with that splendid ballroom, and everything. I have often thought that Kemsale was just the house to give your genius for organisation full scope."

" I do like organising entertainments, it is true. I like to get people together and see them enjoy themselves. But you know how difficult it has been to do anything here."

The speech showed how far Mrs. Fuller had advanced with her patroness during the past six months. For the difficulties referred to had been those that Mrs. Brown's husband had put in the way of her using Kemsale as the stage for large formal parties. One of the few strains of weakness in this lady's otherwise self-reliant character was the necessity she felt for a confidant. Aunt Millie would not do. She would talk about everything but the

social campaign, and that, to do her justice, Mrs. Brown
had never asked her to talk about. Aunt Millie had never
been to any of her big parties; it was an understood thing
that on that side of their lives each took her own line, and
so they remained fast friends on the other sides. But Mrs.
Fuller would talk about the social campaign as much as
was required. She did it with a constant effort of tact.
Her line was that Mrs. Brown had a duty to perform to
society; no hint was ever allowed to creep out of any question of " climbing." The affair, indeed, was not regarded
as a campaign at all. And she also exercised tact with reference to the difficulties already referred to. She did so now,
as she replied:

"It is only natural that with Katie and Mr. Alfred at
home for Christmas—I suppose you will have the ball about
that time—and I suppose some of their friends here too,
you should get up something to amuse them."

"That is why I want to have it, of course," said Mrs.
Brown. "In fact, Katie said something to her father the
other day about dancing, and he made no objection."

"The last time there was a ball here was in the old
lord's time. He loved gaiety of that sort. It was a very
brilliant affair. But yours, of course, will be just as
brilliant."

"I don't see why it shouldn't be done just as well. I
could hardly expect, I suppose, to get exactly the same
sort of people."

"But why not? It will be chiefly a county ball. You
know everybody around you now. All the big houses will
bring their parties. If you have it, as I should suggest,
in the same week as the Hunt Ball and the County Ball,
you will get exactly the same people, except for those staying in the house."

"I should like to see the house well filled. I suppose

people would come from London for it. We could have special trains for them."

It gave Mrs. Fuller a pleasant sense of superiority when she found her patroness tripping in her knowledge of social habits, which she frequently did when they were based upon country life. But she was careful not to display her superiority. "Wouldn't it be better," she said, "to do as they did here last time—invite people for the three balls. You would be more likely to get the right sort of people, wouldn't you? You know best, but I should have thought that it might be difficult to get them from London at that time of the year, and just for one night."

"That means having a regular house-party for the best part of a week."

Mrs. Fuller had divined the alarm with which a prospect of that sort was regarded. "With the house quite full," she said, "people would amuse themselves. Besides, at this time of the year there would be plenty for them to do. You could arrange the big shoot for that time, and I dare say some of them would hunt. Perhaps you might get up private theatricals, or something of that sort, if there is an evening free."

Mrs. Brown considered this. "Alfred might write a play," she said. "He has often talked of doing it. He might get his party here to rehearse it for some time beforehand. Then it would be natural to get people down to see it. There would be plenty of room for both sorts." Both sorts, as was well understood between them, meant Alfred's and Katie's friends, who would be the excuse for the gatherings, and the most ornamental of Mrs. Brown's acquaintances who could be induced to come. "I think theatricals or *tableaux vivants* are a good idea."

"*Tableaux vivants* would be better still," said Mrs. Fuller. (Irene could pose pictorially, but it was doubtful if she could act.) "Mr. Alfred would be very good at arranging them, and they ought to be well worth seeing and make a considerable stir, done in the thorough way in which you would do them. They had some at Brenchleys a few years ago. They were pretty enough, but they were got up—well, on the cheap, as you might say, mostly with home-made costumes."

Mrs. Brown saw large sums of money spent upon dresses and scenery, the ball-room turned into a theatre for one night, and changed back as if by magic to a ball-room for the next. If spending money could have done every-thing, the prospect would have held nothing but the extreme of gratification.

"It might, perhaps, be as well," suggested Mrs. Fuller, who also had her visions, "to have the *tableaux* performed by the young people, and others, who are at hand here. There are plenty of them, and Mr. Brown likes seeing them about the place, doesn't he?"

"It would give them all something to do about Christmas time. They could come and stay in the house if they wished to, and we could have a series of little dances for them. I shouldn't mind hiring a band for a fortnight or so."

"Oh, what a delightful idea! And how it will wake everybody up! Kemsale will indeed take its place again as the chief house in the county."

"As for the shooting, I really don't know. My husband doesn't care about it. I thought Alfred might, but——"

That "but" meant a good deal. Mrs. Brown had or-ganised one shooting party—or rather the guests for it—and it had been almost a fiasco. When Alfred had heard the names of the guests, he had found it necessary to run over to Paris for a few days, and had, unfortunately, not been able to return in time for the occasion. Time had hung heavily indoors. Armitage Brown, who had always com-

ported himself with affability during the few hours of a
dinner or an evening party, had found the strain too great
when extended to days. His own life had been completely
upset, and he had expressed himself strongly about it. He
had refused to have anything to do with the arrangements
out-of-doors, and Fuller had not been competent to carry
them through. Douglas Irving had saved the situation at
the last moment, and the shooting had gone well; but Mrs.
Brown knew that very few of the men who shot the Kemsale pheasants would come again to a house in which the
host took no interest in their sport, but handed them over
to somebody else, and that she herself had not succeeded
in preserving their womenkind from boredom.

" If you were to make the ball and the theatricals the
chief thing, and were to ask mostly young people—of the
right sort, of course—then the shooting, for the men, would
just be something to do in the daytime, and the women
could go out with them. My husband would have no difficulty in arranging matters satisfactorily for a shoot of that
sort, if plenty of time were given beforehand."

Mrs. Fuller had been furious with the poor little man
for allowing himself to be superseded by Douglas Irving
on the previous occasion, and she knew that Mrs. Brown
had also disliked his being called in. What she had never
been able to gauge, however, was exactly how far that lady
was under the commands of her husband. She seemed to
have extraordinary license to spend money on objects that
she cared about and he didn't, and yet occasionally he put
his foot down, as he had done over this. As people had
been asked to shoot, it was for him to see that their shooting was properly managed for them, and he chose to
delegate his powers to Irving, as he knew nothing about such
things himself. But people like that were not to be asked
again. There were plenty of people about the place who

could be asked to shoot; he wasn't going to have the shooting made an excuse for filling the house with smart Londoners. That was the way he had expressed himself, although Mrs. Brown's guests had not been exclusively
Londoners, but on the whole a very creditable collection of
what she and Mrs. Fuller now always spoke of as "the
right sort of people."

"The difficulty with young people would be that they
might not mix very well with Katie's and Alfred's friends,"
Mrs. Brown said, ignoring the invitation to come out as
backer of Fuller against Irving. "Alfred likes artists and
literary people, and Katie's chief friends are her school
friends. I am pleased to see anybody they choose to ask
here, of course, and to do everything I can for them. I
have never tried to influence their friendships in any way;
but——"

"I have often thought it rather odd that Katie should
have so little of your wonderful discrimination about
people. She is a dear little thing in every way, and anybody would be glad to have her for a friend, I don't care
who they were. See how Lady Grace has taken to her!
And Lord Meadshire admires her tremendously; that is very
plain to see."

"Oh, please don't say that sort of thing," said Mrs.
Brown, in a tone of displeasure.

Mrs. Fuller hastened to amend her mistake. "Oh, I
don't mean in *that* way," she said with a laugh. "I should
never have thought of such a thing. *You* wouldn't care for
it, I know. I only meant that he makes a great friend of
her; and really, I think she has had a wonderfully good
influence on him. That is sometimes the way with a thoroughly nice girl, and a man much older than herself, who
looks up to her as being *good*, if you understand what I
mean, and behaves carefully because of her influence."

" Yes, I understand what you mean; but I don't like to think of Katie mixed up in any way with Lord Meadshire, and I think that what you say is exaggerated. He had a serious break-out not so long ago, and if it were not for Lady Grace I think I should have tried to break off all connections with him definitely after that."

Mrs. Fuller did not believe this, although she thought it quite natural that it should be said. But it was true enough. Mrs. Brown detested Meadshire. For one thing, she knew that he had taken her measure. After his capitulation to her husband six months before, he had not only thrown aside all traces of his former hostility, but had professed an easy intimacy towards the whole family. Katie he delighted in; she had captured him, during their interview in the motor-car, by her sincerity and courage, and by the tenderness she had shown towards Grace. Alfred he liked too, and had begun by apologising handsomely for the way he had treated him on that Sunday afternoon at Little Kemsale. Armitage Brown had been at first rather grimly distant with him, but had found it impossible to stand out against his extreme good nature. He was like a child who has been naughty and wants to " make up." He was like a child in so many ways, inconsequent, undependable, undisciplined, but with the appeal of a child whose approaches cannot be resisted. He chaffed the millionaire about his millions, about his schemes, which he still thought absurd, but did nothing any longer to hamper, about everything that most people would have treated with respectful silence; and the millionaire rather liked it. He had thought that the sudden change from enmity to friendship in a man of Meadshire's history must mean the laying of a train for profit to be presently extracted. He had quite expected a loan to be applied for when the intimacy should be sufficiently established. It is one of the penalties of the rich

man that he must always suspect a proffer of friendship.
But in this case it soon became plain that there was no
design behind the friendly raillery. As long as Meadshire
had any money of his own he would want nobody else's,
and the possessions of another man would cause him no
envy. In fact he would consider himself on an equality
with the richest in respect of money, until his own would
disappear. Armitage Brown had a half-contemptuous regard for him, as a man who had thrown away all his
chances, but retained his cheerful outlook. He was an
amusing companion, of a sort that he had not come across
before; and he was warm-hearted. Armitage Brown's own
feelings with regard to him were beginning to be tinged
with a slight warmth.

But the light raillery which Meadshire directed against
the millionaire was a deep offence to the millionaire's wife.
To be chaffed about her pink saloon and her blue saloon
and her yellow saloon and other marks of her wealth and
state was unforgivable. She was incapable of answering
him in his own vein, and took refuge in haughty silence.
When he saw that his chaff annoyed her he gave it up; but
the occasional twinkle in his eye when he addressed her, as
well as the discontinuation of the chaff, showed her that her
ambitions stood revealed to him. She heartily wished that
his hostility had continued. His frequenting of Kemsale
did her no credit with anybody; she had got beyond the
point at which a much-damaged marquis might have been
desired as an ornament, and her cold correctitude of morals
caused her to shrink from what she had heard about him.
She had from the first disliked the terms of his friendship
with Katie, although she had not made Mrs. Fuller's mistake of imagining more in it than was displayed for all to
see. When the long-delayed "outbreak" had occurred in
mid-summer, and Meadshire had been away from Kemsale

for two months, to return much subdued and much the worse in appearance, her distaste for him had increased to the point of strong dislike. She had told Katie that she must have nothing more to do with him, and her husband that she hoped he would not be encouraged to come to Kemsale again. But Katie would not give up Grace, and as Grace *was* a credit to her friends, Mrs. Brown had not felt able to insist that she should. Meadshire had kept away from Kemsale of his own accord for some weeks, until Armitage Brown, who had been somewhat scandalised by the outbreak, made advances to him of his own accord. He was sorry for him, he told his wife. From all he could hear, he had not kept straight for so long together for many years past, and was evidently ashamed now of having given way. He wasn't going to be the one to show the cold shoulder to a man who was trying to lift himself out of the mire. So they had drifted back to the old conditions. Meadshire was often at Kemsale, and seemed quite to have recovered his spirits and his health. But Mrs. Brown's watchfulness never slumbered, and she disliked him more than ever. If another "outbreak" should occur, she would make a strong effort to cut the tie altogether.

And now, as Mrs. Fuller had given her the opportunity, she determined to express what she felt about it, with no possibility of being mistaken.

"I dislike Lord Meadshire thoroughly," she said; "and I dislike his being as intimate with Katie as he is. The intimacy does her no harm, perhaps, in itself; I will do him the justice to say that I think he is at his best with her; and Lady Grace is nearly always there. I have no fear of anything happening on either side that I should not wish. But it is just because what you have just said others may be saying that I dislike it so. I suppose you would not have said it unless it were the common talk."

Mrs. Fuller was puzzled. Did Mrs. Brown really dislike the idea of her daughter's name being coupled with that of a marquis? The idea was almost beyond the range of her imagination, although she could well understand her wishing it to be thought that she did. And yet there was no mistaking the sincerity of her annoyance. Perhaps there was something behind it that she did not know of.

" *Are* people saying it? " Mrs. Brown pressed her.

" Not in any ill-natured way at all. But you see it is a thing that would be likely to be said anyhow. Katie is looked upon as a great heiress, and a person in Lord Meadshire's position is always supposed to be on the look-out for an heiress."

" I don't know why Katie should be looked upon as a great heiress. She will have some money, of course, by and by, but whatever she may have, she would not have it for many years yet, let us hope. My husband is not so much older than Lord Meadshire, and I should say that his life is every bit as good. Such talk is very annoying; very annoying indeed. I do hope *you* will do all you can to discountenance it. I do think you owe me that, at least."

What Mrs. Fuller actually owed to her was her countenance, which did not help her much outside; some brightening of her own life, for which she paid something on account in an irksome self-control; and an occasional gift of a hat or a gown, which she was glad enough to accept, while she secretly resented the offer. She also resented being reminded of her obligation, but judged their continuance to be worth making due effort for.

" What I shall say to anybody who mentions it to me," she said, " is that you would be very much against it. But, of course, the talk isn't serious. Most people would expect Katie to make a better match than that."

" I have never even thought of Katie making a match at all—in that sort of way. She is very young, for one thing, and she does not care about society. My husband and I would be quite satisfied for her to marry a nice man, by and by, who would not be what the world would call a great match."

This was absolutely true. Mrs. Brown was intent on her own career. Her daughter could neither help her in it nor follow such a career for herself. A " great match," if it should surprisingly come Katie's way, might create complications. Mrs. Brown did not want " greatness " in her private life, of which Katie was a part. The school friends she brought into it gave no trouble. Katie would do very well as she was.

But Mrs. Fuller was quite incapable of divining all this, and thought that she was being " bluffed " or, in other words, lied to. It was part of her game, however, to accept such statements at their face value, and she did so now. " I must say I do admire that in you," she said, " that you are so free from what I call *snobbery*. The way in which you have taken up the Sheards would prove it, if nothing else did. I think they may consider themselves very fortunate to have such people as yourselves here. *They* have certainly fallen on their feet."

" The Sheards are very nice people," said Mrs. Brown quite sincerely. They again were accepted as part of her private and domestic existence, and gave her no trouble in the way of " entertainment." Mrs. Fuller disliked them on that account.

" I hope you won't be offended with me," she said, " if I say that Anne Sheard seems to me to be a little over-free in her manners when she comes up here. I know it is a vulgar expression, but it has sometimes occurred to me that she was setting her cap at Mr. Alfred."

Could it be that Mrs. Brown had also envisaged this possibility, and that it bore no terrors for her? She said at once without flinching: " There is nothing in that. All the young people are very good friends together. It is natural that a young man should be attracted by a pretty girl, and Anne is a very pretty girl, and a nice one, too."

" But, dear Mrs. Brown, surely you would not think Anne Sheard a suitable match for Mr. Alfred!"

" I have not thought about it at all. I don't think there is the least chance of such a thing happening. For one thing, unless I am very much mistaken, young Mr. Clinton and Anne Sheard are in love with one another."

" What, Frank Clinton! Well, I shouldn't advise you to hint that to his father. It wouldn't suit him at all."

" I am not likely to hint it to anybody, and I hardly know old Mr. Clinton. But his son has been over here constantly whenever he has been home on leave, and I think that is the attraction."

" Well, I don't. I think it's Katie. And I believe old Mr. Clinton thinks so too."

" Why do you think that? "

" A little bird whispered it to me. Well, I won't make a mystery of it. When my husband was over at Kencote the other day about this dairying business, Mr. Clinton talked about you all a good deal, and said what a nice girl Katie was. And he seemed quite pleased at Frank coming over here—talked about that too. Even my husband, who is not observant in these matters, put two and two together. And you know that Katie and Mr. Alfred were often invited over to Kencote in the summer, whenever Frank Clinton was at home."

The idea was a new one to Mrs. Brown. " I think it is Anne," she said, but said it doubtfully, as if ready to admit herself in the wrong.

"Should you object to that as a match," asked Mrs. Fuller, "if it proved to be the case?"

Mrs. Brown did not answer for a moment. "Oh, I am not thinking of marriage for Katie," she said with a hint of impatience. "And I am sure she herself has no idea of such a thing."

But in that she was wrong.

CHAPTER XXIV

A COUNTRY WALK

A LONG country walk was not much in Lord Meadshire's way, but that was the form of entertainment to which he was invited one Sunday afternoon at this time, when he and Grace had been lunching at Kemsale. It was a glorious sunny day; they would go up through the woods at the back of Kemsale and along the ridge to where a particular view could be obtained of the two valleys. There was a large party of them: Meadshire and Lady Grace, the Irvings, Frank Clinton, who had come over from Kencote to lunch, William and Anne Sheard, and a friend of Katie's staying in the house. Mrs. Brown and Aunt Millie preferred to stay at home, but Uncle James and Armitage Brown set out with the rest.

They climbed up the hill, some of them walking faster than others, and gradually split up into twos and threes. Presently Meadshire and Katie were for practice of speech alone together.

"There was a time," said Meadshire, "when I liked this sort of thing; and I generally led the party. I had long legs, which I have still, and a thin body, which I have lost. Now I must puff and pant in the rear, and rather wish I hadn't come at all."

"I think exercise is very good for you," said Katie. "You go about far too much in your car."

"My dear child, I am getting old. Exercise is an abomination unto me."

" You are not old at all. You are not much older than Captain Irving, and he seems like a young man."

" He has led a good life, you see, and has therefore preserved his splendid youth. I have not led a good life, and I am old."

" All that is over now," she said with an air of great decision. " It is not to be thought about any more. It is not to happen again; it *will* not happen again."

He looked down at her half quizzically, half tenderly. They made rather a queer couple, he with his great height and heavy shoulders, walking as if walking were not the most natural mode of progression for mankind, she, short and erect, with a step full of spring and energy. " You're very certain of that, aren't you? " he said.

" Yes, I am. You see now what a mistake it has all been, and what trouble it brings to those who care for you."

" Are you one of them? "

" You know I am," she said very boldly. " First of all, I cared about it because of dear Grace; and then, when I saw that it wasn't really part of you, and that it spoilt everything, I cared because of you."

" You wanted to pluck a brand from the burning? "

" I felt that I wanted to help you. One likes to help one's friends."

" You have been a very good friend to me, little Miss Brown. If I had known you, or somebody like you, twenty years ago, things might have been very different with me."

"Well, they are going to be different now. It is never too late to mend."

" I'm not so sure about that. It's all a good deal harder than you think. The spirit is willing, but the flesh is weak."

" Oh, I hate to hear you talk like that," she said. " It isn't the way to do anything. You must make up your

mind firmly; you must stiffen yourself. One can do anything that one determines to do."

He laughed at her gently. "*You* could, I believe," he
said. "But, you see, you have never played with yourself;
you've got your will-power undisturbed; you're young, and
full of energy and confidence. When one has reached my
age, and made such a mess of things all round, there doesn't
seem to be much left to try for. Then when the trouble
comes, one says to one's self, after holding out perhaps for
a bit: 'After all, why shouldn't I? I'm doing nobody
any harm but myself, and what does that matter?'"

"Yes, you have said that to yourself before; but you
are not going to say it any more. It is different now."

"How is it different now, little Miss Brown?"

"Because you have people who believe in you. I believe
in you; and Grace believes in you."

"Poor dear Grace! She was beginning to, before
that little set-back we had in the summer. I say, it
seems rather odd that I should be talking about these
things to you."

"I think it is a very good thing for us to talk about
them. I used to wish I could, when Grace first told me
all about it; and when you came back again I wished it
more than ever. It was one of the proudest days of my
life when we did begin to talk about it together. I felt
that I was trusted, and could begin to do something. I
hate standing by and doing nothing."

"Yes, you're a chip of the old block in that, aren't
you? Do you know that your father also had a word
with me about my little failing?"

"He was sorry about it, I know; and he likes you.
What did he say?"

"I shan't tell you what he said. At least, I'll tell you
some of it. He thinks I ought to do something. He thinks

I'm a pretty useless sort of fellow as I am. And he's not far wrong there."

"I think you ought to do something, too."

"What do you think I ought to do? I'm afraid I don't possess the financial genius of your father. Doing something in these days generally means making money. I've got a genius for spending it, but I'm afraid there's nothing much to be made of that. Besides, I've lost my lavish tastes. They seem to have dropped away from me since I've been living her quietly with Grace. It's a rotten game, anyhow, chucking money away, and the friends you make over it are rotten friends. I think you can trust me there, little Miss Brown. That side of my vivid career is over and done with."

"I trust you in much more than that," she said simply. "What I think you ought to do is to take up some public work. It is what people like you are there for, and your ancestors did a great deal, I know. I was reading about them the other day in a book at Kemsale. They won all sorts of honours for you, and the honours have descended to you, and you ought to show that you are worthy of them."

"*Noblesse oblige,*" he said, laughing at her again. "It doesn't oblige much in these days, and the time has gone by for me. No, I'm a useless sort of fellow all round. I shall do best by living here quietly and behaving myself as well as I can. Fortunately the line comes to an end with me. It's something to my credit that I haven't continued it."

It was true that throughout all his follies and his looseness he had kept to that determination. He had broken up the fortunes of his house, but he would not bequeath the fragments of its ruin to heirs of his body; he would not marry, and share his disgrace with a wife. Did he know now that he might do so, that this brave strong

confident girl walking by his side was ready to join her
clean life to his damaged one, to bear the burden of his
weakness with him, to lift him out of the slough in which
he had involved himself? He knew it very well.

When the difficulties in the way of a friendship between
Kemsale and the Herons' Nest were done away with, the
friendship followed very quickly. The impetuosity with
which Katie cleared out her rooms and transferred their
contents to Grace at the earliest possible moment, and
sent her own warm heart with them to make amends for
the wrong done, left no doubt as to the value of her friendship. She was longing to love Grace, if Grace would let
her, and Grace very soon came to love her. They were
happy together during the weeks of early summer. They
went about amongst the country people, who also learnt
to love Katie, as they had always loved Grace. The two
were a complete contrast, Grace gentle and sweet, but too
yielding, Katie energetic and clear-sighted. Meadshire
showed his liking for his little Miss Brown, chaffed her
and teased her, and sometimes succeeded in arousing her
strong indignation against him. At that time neither he
nor Grace nor Katie herself could have thought of any
closer tie between them.

Then came the time when he began to get moody and
morose. Katie began to dislike him. She knew nothing
of his failing. She saw Grace becoming sadder and sadder,
and thought that there must be some dispute between them,
and he was treating her unkindly. Once she spoke to
him with indignation about it, and he glared at her, and
turned away without speaking. The next day he disappeared, and for a week Grace shut herself up and would
see nobody.

Then she told Katie her troubles, and seemed to lean
on her for support and consolation in her bitter disap-

pointment. For a year had passed since this had happened, and she had begun to think that it might never happen again.

When Meadshire came back, two months later, so much subdued that there was no chaff left in him, and he seemed ashamed to see Katie in the house, and escaped her whenever she came there, ambition awoke in her to show herself worthy of Grace's confidence, to do something to help these kind friends in their trouble. For it seemed to her in her innocence that Meadshire only wanted taking out of himself and showing that his fault was forgiven him to regain his self-respect, and be as he had been before, and better than he had been before. She felt protective, almost motherly, towards him. He was so like a naughty child who must be encouraged not to brood too much upon his fault, but to make up his mind that it should never occur again. So she took much pains to raise him out of his despondency, and presently succeeded.

Then came the time when he talked to her about himself, and she spoke truly when she said afterwards that this was a proud moment for her. She could strengthen and inspirit him now. She knew that Grace had come to feel great confidence in her influence over him, and without any real knowledge of the task before her she thought herself eminently capable of raising him out of the mire.

It is doubtful if she did much more than keep him amused, although his liking and respect for her grew. But to Grace she seemed to be performing wonders. Grace herself had never felt that she had any real hold over him, much as she loved him, and ready as she was to do everything she could to help him. She thought that Katie, with her bright confident strength, could have kept him straight if she had been in her place. And by and by she began to form a hope that she might take a closer place than hers, and give him back some of the years that he had lost.

She waited for a while, and then in her almost feverish anxiety asked him if he could not make up his mind to marry Katie. She put it like that; she thought she knew that Katie would accept him if he asked her.

He laughed at her, as he laughed at most things, but showed that the idea was not new to him. "She's a dear little thing," he said. "I could get on very well with her. If it had been ten years ago, I dare say I might have tried my luck. But it's too late now. I like the little thing too much to want to tie her up to a person like myself, at her age and at mine; or perhaps I don't like her enough. It's a little of both."

Then Grace talked to Katie, and found out that to her the idea was new and alarming. The gentle creature reproached herself for her thoughts about the girl, but her desires were so strong, were indeed heightened by her discovery that Katie's firmness and self-reliance went along with so much innocence and simpleness of mind, that she would not let her alone, the ice once broken. They talked it over together many times, not without tears and strong emotion on either side, and at last Katie said: "If he wants me, I will take him. I will give up my life to save him from himself. I know he is good and kind at heart, but he is weak, and I know that I am strong. Yes, Grace, I will."

She was uplifted by her decision. She had a task to perform. She would not only save and protect this man from his faults, she would make something of him, and be proud of him. Of her own risk she thought nothing, partly because she was ignorant of it, partly because she was so sure of herself.

And so the matter stood on this Sunday afternoon. She

was ready to take him if he should ask her. But apparently he could not make up his mind to ask her. Her
exaltation still held, but it was becoming a little dimmed.
Although she talked to him so confidently and so quietly,
she was not happy, either with him or with herself. Indeed,
her free youthful happiness seemed to be slowly departing
from her. Perhaps she would never recapture it again,
whether she made her sacrifice or whether it should not
be required of her.

There was another couple much interested in one another
who took advantage of that winter walk to secure a practical solitude in the midst of the little crowd. They were
Frank Clinton and Anne Sheard, who had reached the
stage of looking into one another's eyes and finding infinite
meaning there, though the meaning was not yet declared
between them. It was with a delicious sense of hazard
that they had found themselves together and separating
from the rest. Each of them had wanted that, but had
not been sure that it could be brought about, or that the
other wanted it. And now that they were together, and
the rest, though within sight, were not within hearing,
they were so happy that they scarcely knew what to do
with their opportunity.

When Frank's long leave in the early summer had
come to an end, he had been appointed to a ship stationed at Chatham. It was the first time in his naval
career that he had been employed in home waters, and
the number of times that he had been able to put in an
appearance at Kencote, and consequently at Kemsale, if
only for a day, had seemed to indicate that leave was very
easily obtainable for lieutenants in His Majesty's Navy.

He had not for some time admitted to himself that he
was very deeply in love with Anne. He had been encouraged to go over to Kemsale during his leave, and as

it had coincided with Charles Sheard's, he had never gone
there without going to the rectory, unless the young Sheards
were up at the big house, as they often were. A great
deal of lawn tennis was played at Kemsale during that
summer, and a certain amount of golf; Frank liked Katie
and Alfred Brown, and told himself that he would have
gone over just as often if the Sheards had not been there.
Perhaps he might have gone, or nearly as often, for there
were no young people at Kencote now, Joan having returned to her resplendent duties in London. At any rate,
the excuse had been quite satisfactory, and he was enabled
to satisfy his father's curious thirst for news about his
doings at Kemsale whenever he returned from one of his
visits. He never failed to mention the young Sheards when
they had been of the party, and Anne and Charles and
William had been to Kencote with Katie and Alfred on
return visits, and had been affably entreated by the Squire,
who had never, however, broken out into commendation of
Anne as he constantly did of Katie.

It was not until Frank had left Kencote that he discovered how very much he had enjoyed the past few
weeks. It had been the best leave he had ever spent,
and he had never once slept away from Kencote. When
he found how much drawn he was to go back there on
all possible occasions, he could no longer disguise from
himself the attraction that drew him, and being of a
direct habit of mind, and no longer a boy, began to ask
himself whither he was tending.

The result of his self-questionings was that he began
to think about Anne from a slightly different angle. That
the thought of her made his blood run warm was not
quite enough. That had happened to him with other girls,
though never to the same extent; there were photographs
of one or two of them in his cabin, but there was not

one of them that he had studied so earnestly as he did the snapshot of Anne standing on the tennis-court at Kencote that he had taken himself. It did not seem to him possible that this was a passing fancy, to fade away in time like the others. It was of a different quality altogether.

The idea of marriage with Anne gave him a deep thrill, but it could not be admitted without careful consideration. It was only when he told himself that if he was not prepared to woo her in earnest he ought not to be constantly making plans to see her, that he realized what a blank his life there would be if he were not so prepared.

She was very young, hardly more than a child; and he was coming to the end of his youth. It was a disturbing thought that she might not regard him as young at all.

It was quite certain that there would be trouble in the camp at Kencote if he were to announce his intention of bringing home Anne as a bride. That would not worry him much if the reasons for it did not affect him personally, and he had to make up his mind, without blinking facts, whether they did or not.

Anne was the sweetest creature in the world, but she was not sprung from the kind of stock from which brides were sought at Kencote. Did that matter?

No; it didn't matter to him. Anne was Anne, and her " people " were worthy of all respect. Their ways were slightly different from the ways of his people, and that was all. The difference of their ways was almost entirely based upon the lack of money, and he smiled to himself as he invented a question for his father: " What is the difference between the Sheards and the Browns, if you leave money out of account? "

He found that he had acquired a deep respect for Anne's father, and it was based partly upon the very fact of his

not being of a birth and position equal to his own, or
his father's. How many men were there who would have
made of themselves what he had, or having gained his
success would have used it with such singleness of mind,
such entire absence of unworthy ambitions? His was a
fine character; it had gone towards the making of Anne.
If Anne's parents were to be taken into account, her
father ought to weigh the balance in her favour, not
against it, if he were to be judged by worthy standards.
As for her mother, she was more definitely marked of
the origin to which the Squire would make strong objections. But that was all that could be said against her.
She was a good simple-minded woman, unselfish and warm-
hearted. And her character also had gone to the making
of Anne.

Frank had met all Anne's brothers and sisters now, and
had liked them all. John, the Cambridge don, was like
other young Cambridge clerical dons, rather older than
his years in some things, rather young in others. He had
the family sturdiness, both in mind and body. Henry,
the young house-surgeon, was much like him. Neither of
them was in the least ornamental; Henry had not quite
got over his medical student's roughness. If Dick or
Humphrey, or even Walter, had been at the University
with them, they would have left them out of account, as
belonging to the great mass of undergraduates who led
lives quite apart from theirs. But those standards change.
Certainly Walter now, and probably Dick and Humphrey,
would accept men working diligently and successfully at
their professions on their merits.

Frank could not avoid bringing in his brothers to sit
in judgment upon Anne's brothers. They were all some
years older than he, and he had accepted their standards
in his youth—the standards of their schools and colleges,

which were socially narrower than those his own education had taught him; for in the Navy there are real
things to do from the first, and ability cannot be left
out of account. He had been interested to see what Dick
would make out of William Sheard when he took him
over with Charles to fish at Kencote. Dick had been
kind to him and had given him a rod; he had taken
no notice of his deficiencies of costume, or, if he had
noticed them, had not remarked upon them. Dick could
always be relied on to behave perfectly, but Frank had
a suspicion that his courtesy would receive a severe strain
if he were called upon to extend it to Anne's brothers
in any closer degree than as the sons of a neighbouring
parson. But one never knew with Dick. Virginia had
broadened him in some respects; he had a clear brain,
and, for a man of his native prejudices, a tolerant outlook.

Mary Sheard, the elder daughter, was the energetic capable mistress of a class in a big London High School, very
interested in her work, standing no nonsense, a little inclined to be critical of Anne, who was not striving after
scholastic success in the way she herself had been doing
at her age. Perhaps it was on account of this critical
attitude that Frank liked her the least of any of her
family; and somehow, with her half-masculine "sensible-
ness," she seemed more of a stumbling-block in the way
of a complete understanding between his people and hers
than anything else. His young sisters, in the stage of
pupilage, would have "led her a dance." They might
have liked her, as a human being, as he tried now, not
altogether without success, to do. But the schoolmistress
would have been most apparent in her. Still, she was
not Anne, and would not matter much. He wished that
Joan had seen Anne. Cicely had, and had taken to her.

She had even wondered whether it would be possible to get her to Mountfield as first governess to her children. That was the sort of complication that it was impossible to get away from, and made an examination of the Sheards' condition essential, distasteful as it was.

When it all came to be summed up, Anne's extreme youth and the very short time he had known her were the only things that held him back. He was not a boy to rush into an engagement with a pretty girl who had made an impression upon him. He must have more time. But no consideration deterred him from seeing as much of her as he could during that summer and autumn, and now at the end of it he knew that the impression she had made upon him was not a passing one. He loved her deeply and truly, and loved her more every time he saw her. And by this time there was very little doubt that she loved him. Her looks and her words gave him the sweetest thrills when he recalled them in the silence of his night watches, going over every minute of the time he had passed with her, and ardently longing to be with her again.

He was just at that stage when his final word hung upon a chance. He could not be quite sure what the answer would be until he had said the word, and the state of tremulous happiness in which they were living was too sweet to be cut short except at the bidding of strong emotion.

The word was not spoken that afternoon. They talked of everything but their love for each other, but that was implied in everything that they said. The word trembled on his lips many times, but he held it back, he could not have told why. At the end, their solitude was suddenly invaded by Meadshire and Katie catching them up, and he was not alone with Anne again. The chance had passed,

but it would come again. It would come at Christmas-
time, when he would get a long leave, and so much would
be going on at Kemsale that they would meet every day.
And in the meantime this walk had given him a crowd
of sweet memories on which to feed until he saw her again.

CHAPTER XXV

A DIFFERENCE OF PRINCIPLE

ARMITAGE BROWN was angry. Anger was a passion that
he rarely indulged in, and when he did he kept its expression
rigidly subdued, and used other means to make it felt.
It had seldom happened that those means had not been
efficacious in removing the cause of his anger.

But his wife was the cause of his anger now, and he
could not remove her. He must make his will felt otherwise.

They were in her boudoir together. It was a room he
seldom visited. It was not used except in the daytime,
and in the daytime their ways had always lain apart.
They did so now whenever he spent his time at Kemsale.
He had his interests and she had hers. They had never
clashed before, but they were clashing now, and he had
come to tell her that the clashing must cease.

" I thought it was understood," he was saying, "that
after what happened here a month ago, the house was
not to be filled again with strangers."

" But, Armitage, these people are not strangers."

" I call them strangers. At any rate they are exactly
the same sort of people as were asked here before. Call
them what you like. They are not coming here again."

She was offended by his brusqueness. " You have never
spoken to me like that before," she said.

He took a seat deliberately. " It is quite time I spoke
plainly," he said, " and I do so now once for all. I have
never, as far as I remember, once interfered with

your way of living, though it hasn't always suited me.
Since we first went abroad you have spent enormous sums
of money on your parties, and on people that I don't
care a bit about, except one or two here and there, and
I don't believe you care about them any more than I do.
I don't grudge you the money—that's nothing; spend
what you like in any way that amuses you. And I don't
grudge you your parties, as long as you keep them to their
proper place. Their proper place is in London and at
the villa, not at Kemsale."

"Why don't you want people invited to Kemsale? It
is the regular thing to do with a great house like this?"

"What do I care about the regular thing? I'm not
going to give up my home to what you call the regular
thing. I don't object to people being invited to Kemsale
if they are my friends, or yours, or the children's friends.
I like to see them here, and the more of them there are
the better I like it. And I like to see people here from
the neighbourhood. I should like to see a good many more
of them, not only the people from the big houses, but
the others as well."

"What do you mean by the others? Do you mean the
farmers and the tradespeople?"

"I shouldn't at all object to seeing some of the farmers
here. But I think you know quite well what I mean;
and I do mean it. The people I don't want to see here,
and am not going to have here, are the people who come
just for what they can get and are only asked because
they're what's called smart. I'll ask you to accept that
decision and act upon it for the future."

There was a dull flush on her face. It was true that
he had never spoken to her in this way before. But then
she had never given him occasion to. Was it worth while,
for the sake of her ambitions, to hold out against him? She

was a proud woman; she could not give in, in a matter in which he had never before interfered, for just a word from him, not too courteously expressed.

"I think you are taking a very extraordinary line," she said. "Do you really mean, after all these years, that I am not allowed to ask my friends to my house."

He shifted in his seat. "I'll put it more plainly still," he said. "This isn't a small matter; it has come to be an important difference of principle between you and me; and where it is a question of principle I am going to have my way, as head of the house."

"How can you talk about a question of principle in such a matter as this? One would think I was proposing to do something definitely wrong."

"Well, I think it is wrong. You talked just now about asking your friends here. Please tell me this: out of all those people who came here to shoot the other day, how many were really your friends? Which of them would you ask to spend a week with you here alone, as you would ask James and Millie, for instance?"

"That is quite different."

"I know it is quite different. That is just what I am saying. Not one of those people was a friend of yours in any way. You didn't know what to do with them when they were here. They were as much a nuisance to you in the house as they were to me; in fact, more so, for there were one or two I liked talking to, and I don't think there was a single one that you did. The fact of the matter is, my dear, you don't make friends. It may seem a harsh thing to say, but it's perfectly true. You are loyal enough to the few you have, but there isn't a single one of them that belongs to the smart world, and you're really not comfortable with people of that sort when you've got them round you. I'm not either, though, upon my word, I think I'm more comfortable with them than you are. They're just furniture for your smart parties. Keep them so, if it amuses you to have them; I don't complain of that; but don't mix them up with your home life. They only spoil it."

What he had said, though wounding her, was too true to be contradicted. She had not thought he had seen it. She had even thought that he had taken some pride in her social successes, that it had suited him that she should play the part that she had, the part for which he was not fitted himself. She could not even now believe that he was quite indifferent to it.

" I really don't understand you," she said. " I know that there was a time when you preferred to live quietly at Hillgrove, and keep clear of society altogether. But when you became very well known, I thought that you had made up your mind that you could not go on hiding yourself there, that you must mix more with the world. I have done everything for you in that way, taken all the burden of it off your shoulders, and brought you into touch with all sorts of people. I thought that I was helping you, and doing what you wished."

" Well, if I thought you had done it entirely for my sake, I'd say thank you, you've done it very well. But I don't want to be unfair; it suits me all right that I'm known in London not merely as a man who grubs for money in the City. To that extent the place you've made for yourself, and I suppose me with you, is worth something. As far as I'm concerned it's worth just the trouble I take to go out when I'd rather be sitting at home, and not a bit more than that, except that it pleases you. But here it's different. This is my home. Can't you see it? It doesn't seem to me very difficult."

" When we decided on this place out of all the others

we considered, there was no talk of our having a large London house. That came afterwards. If you had said at that time: take a London house to see people in, and a country house to retire to, I should have liked that very well. But we certainly shouldn't have bought Kemsale, which is quite absurd for a place to shut one's self up in. It was to be—or so I understood it—the place in which we were to make the difference. We had shut ourselves up at Hillgrove. There was no idea of our shutting ourselves up here."

" You talk a lot of our shutting ourselves up, and that's the last thing I want, and the last thing we're doing. We must have a dozen young people staying in the house now, and more coming. I like all that. Give them their ball by all means, and all the fun you can. That's all I thought it meant till I tumbled to it that it was going to be made an excuse for another party of the sort we had here a month ago. That will spoil everything, and I——"

"Wait a minute, please, Armitage. I want to see exactly what it is that you do want, and what it is that you are blaming me for. Is it not a fact that when you bought this place it was because you were ready to come out of your shell, and to see more of the world? When we settled upon this enormous house, before we decided to have one in London as well, did you really mean that we were to keep it to ourselves, and to Alfred's and Katie's friends? That is what I want to know."

He had recovered his good humour. He was going to have his own way. He had said the unpleasant thing that he had made up his mind to say; he had no wish to put his wife into a state of antagonism towards him. "Well, you've cornered me," he said. But the facts of the case are these, and I hope you'll accept them and act on them. When we made the change I didn't quite know what I wanted. I suppose I was ready to take up a bigger position in the world than I had done before, and I thought I could do it by buying a fine country house and estate—the finest there was in the market. I had really very few ideas as to what I was going to do with it all. The estate was to be a sort of toy to me, and the house to you. Neither of us knew anything about life in the country, and the trouble seems to me to be that while I've learnt a good deal about my part, you've learnt very little about yours."

"I wish you would say what you have to say without making unkind speeches, Armitage. I am willing to fall in with your views when you have explained them, but I am not willing to accept blame for having misunderstood you. You have already admitted that your views have changed since we came here."

"I don't want to be unkind, my dear, but I think you knew quite well that I should object to what you were going to do, and I am trying to make you see that you have been going on the wrong tack, and to agree with me about it. What has become plain to me since we have been living here is that you are much more mixed up with your neighbours in the country, rich and poor, than you are in London. You can't leave them out of account, and go your own way. I very soon saw that, when I began to get to work with estate business. It's one of the reasons why everybody is up in arms at once when they hear of a rich man like me buying a big estate. They know all about that side of it—people like the Clintons, I mean; even people like Meadshire, who make so many mistakes otherwise—and they think that people like us don't know. Well, they're right. But I tumbled to it pretty quickly, and I believe there's very little feeling left against me on that

score. I'm doing all that the old-established people are
doing, and more besides."

"I really don't see, Armitage, what that has to do with
what we are talking about. You mention the Clintons.
How are they, and people like them, who live about here,
different from the people I want to ask here? We have
known them a very short time. Lord and Lady Dawlish,
and one or two others I had meant to ask next month, we
have known for years, ever since we first went abroad."

"They are different because they are our neighbours.
What I say is that in the country your social life and
even your business is based upon something much more
like friendship than it is in London. You have interests
in common with all the people about you. You meet them
in a more intimate way. Well, take the Clintons. They
call on us and they ask us to dine. They don't give us
a formal dinner-party. They take us into their family.
And it doesn't end there, either. The young people make
friends, and there's coming and going between our two
houses. That's what I like to see. And, mind you, that's
going on always. We're only just at the beginning of
it, you and I. When Alfred takes the reins here after me,
there's that tie, and others like it; and when his children
come they'll be friends with the next generation at Kencote. It's something worth thinking about. You don't
get that sort of thing except in the country. You certainly don't get it with the smart people who come to
your parties in London. They come and eat your food
and drink your wine, and think they're doing you a favour.
They know nothing about you, and you know nothing about
them."

"Why did you say just now that I did not understand,
or had not learnt, what you have just been saying? I
understand it very well. I am ready to entertain our coun-

try neighbours as well as they have ever been entertained, even in this house, where a great deal of state was kept up."

" I should think if you were to make inquiries about the entertainments that were given in this house you would find that they didn't depend upon state at all. A certain amount of state was natural for people like that, and it isn't natural for people like us. If they got big parties of people together they got them together to enjoy themselves, not for the sake of showing off their state. I'm quite sure that the shooting parties they had here weren't like that ghastly affair of ours the other day."

" I wish you wouldn't keep harping upon that. I admit that it was not a success. But that was largely because there was no man to organize it."

" I don't agree with you. The shooting was the only thing that went well, thanks to Irving. The party was a failure because the people you asked to it weren't your friends. And it would be just the same with your ball next month, if I were to consent to your asking people in the same way."

" When the last big ball was given here, not long before Lord Meadshire's grandfather died, the house was filled with people staying here for it. I have seen a printed list of the guests."

" And who were the guests? Every one of them relations and friends of the family, I've not the smallest doubt. It's just what I'm saying. If people like that were to give a big ball in London all the smart crowd would be asked, I dare say. But they would only ask their friends to a ball in the country. Of course their friends would be people like themselves, and I dare say their names would make a fine show in a printed list. Even if you could get a list to look something like it, it wouldn't be the same thing, for they wouldn't be your friends. And I've a pretty strong suspicion, too, that it wouldn't look like the same thing to those who really knew. The people who would go to them wouldn't come to us. Why should they? They don't want anything from us. Your Dawlishes and people like that do, and that's why they come. And we want something from them, or we shouldn't ask them."

"What do we want from them?"

"Their names, in a list. I can't think of anything else."

"Well, Armitage, I think you are unfair to me. I have listened to all you have said, and tried to understand your point of view. I do understand it to some extent and am willing to obey you when you tell me exactly what it is that you do want. But it is very unfair to accuse me of running after people for the sake of their names, as you express it. It is a thing I have never done. It is rather the other way about. People have run after me."

"Well, my dear, if you want the plain truth, I think you have deteriorated in that respect since we have been at Kemsale. You are at liberty to make your own friends, of course, but the only one you seem to have made here, out of all the nice people we have come to know, is a woman I've no respect for at all. If you're not a snob by nature—and I don't think you are—she is, and you have acted more on her ideas than you have on your own."

Her face grew red again. "I can hardly be said to have made a friend of Mrs. Fuller," she said. "She has been useful to me, and I have been able to do things for her. And I am not aware of having acted on her ideas."

"Well, you haven't acted as you did before. It used to amuse me rather to see people running after you. It doesn't amuse me at all to see you running after them."

"I do not run after people, Armitage."

"I call it running after them. How were you going

to ask people for this party? Write first to the biggest of them, and fill up the places of those that refuse—don't think it good enough—by the next biggest. It isn't good enough for us, my dear. We're what we are. Let's keep our self-respect, and ask people to our house that will come because they like us, and not what we can give them."

She thought over it for a moment. Underneath the chagrin she felt at having desires that she had scarcely formulated dragged out and shown up to her, there was a sense of relief at being free of a burden. To arrange her programme for people who would thoroughly appreciate it, and give her no trouble at all by their presence, and let the others go by, was a large relief. And she began to have a glimmering of what lay at the back of her husband's mind, and to see that he was right. Her parties at Kemsale could be as frequent and as elaborate as she pleased, but they must have a different basis from her parties in London. They must draw chiefly from the people around, and there was, after all, a large field to draw from. They could not be as "select" as her London parties, but they would be enjoyed much more, and credit would accrue to her from one form of entertainment as much as from the other.

"Well, I will tear up the invitations I have written," she said, "except to one or two of Katie's friends."

"I don't want you to tear up any to Katie's friends."

"I am thinking of people whom we have known at the villa. Katie has made friends amongst the people you so much object to."

"I don't object to them any more than to any other set of people. If *you* had made friends amongst them you'd have been at liberty to ask them here. Don't let us spar about it. I think we understand one another;

and if you will think it over you will see that I am right.
Now about these parties. You will look after everything
indoors, of course. The young people ought to have a
royal time; and their elders too. The men can shoot,
those of them who want to, and we had better get over a
few neighbours as well—older men, who have been accustomed to shoot here. I don't know anything about it,
and it doesn't interest me, except to go out and look on
occasionally. And Alfred doesn't seem to care for it either.
I propose to put all the arrangements into Irving's hands.
He got us out of a hole last time, and I dare say he'll
like doing it. He has done it for three years, and paid
for it, or his friends have—I don't know. Anyhow, he'll
get just as much fun out of it as he did before."

"Before you do that, Armitage, I wish you would talk
to Alfred and see if you can't induce him to take all that
up as a duty. It seems to me humiliating that we should
have to call in an outsider to do what the men of the
house ought to do. If you do not care to make those
arrangements, Alfred ought to. He does shoot, and it
can't be very difficult to learn what there is to learn.
Let Captain Irving help him, if you like; but don't put
everything into his hands, as if he were master here."

"There's something in that. I'll talk to Alfred. I
should like him to take an interest in all that sort of
thing. He's not too old, as I am. And goodness knows,
he has little enough to do; he doesn't do the work that
he professes to be doing. I've not said anything about
that, because my ideas have changed somewhat since we
came here. It seems to me now that there is plenty for
Alfred to do here, if he'll do it. Captain Clinton keeps
pretty busy looking after property that will be his some
day; and this will be Alfred's in the same way. He
didn't take to my business in London, and didn't much

mind. But there's a great deal of business to be done here that I shall be disappointed if he doesn't take to. I don't want him to grow into a slacker. We have an example of that before our eyes, and it's one that ought to make him careful."

" I am very disappointed in Alfred. I thought at first that he would take an interest in the place. But lately he has done nothing but moon about; and if there is anything that's wanted of him he runs away."

" Well, I don't blame him for running away from what he did. But now we have settled that that is not to happen again, he ought to play his part. I haven't worried him about it yet, because I thought he had better get used to the idea of living here first. He has got used to it, I think. He has been a great deal more at home this year than he ever was before."

" I can't make him out. He seems to have changed. I was prepared to take an interest in the garden with him, as that was what he began with. But he takes an interest in it no longer. He takes an interest in nothing to do with the place. He even told me the other day that he hated the house as it is now. He and Katie are always going off to the Herons' Nest. I suppose Lord Meadshire and Lady Grace have put ideas into their heads. It is a great nuisance. I wish they were out of the place altogether."

Armitage Brown did not take this up. He was thoughtful for a moment. " Well, I'll have a good talk with Alfred," he said.

CHAPTER XXVI

FATHER AND SON

IRENE FULLER came down to breakfast twenty minutes late, in motor-cap and coat. Her mother, who had been only a quarter of an hour late, exclaimed in vexation. "Surely you're not proposing to go trapesing off for the day when there's everything to be settled this morning up at the house," she said.

"It's a fine day," said Irene carelessly, "and I thought I should like to go with father. They won't want *me* up at the house."

"You can make yourself very useful there. I told Mrs. Brown particularly that I should like to bring you. I take all the trouble I can to get you in to things, and you haven't got the sense to lift a little finger for yourself, even when everything's made easy for you. There's that Anne Sheard in and out of the house as if it belonged to her, and you might be the same if you'd just exert yourself a little. As it is you're just like a stranger there."

"They don't care for me and I don't care for them," said the girl. "What good should I be to help settle things?"

"Really, you'd try the patience of a saint. There are the parts in the *tableaux* to be finally settled, and the costumes. If you're there, you'll get the good parts you ought to get. If you're not, I've got to do it all for you, and I'm not going to. It looks as if I was always trying to shove you in."

"Well, that's what you always are trying to do, isn't it?"

"When you've had breakfast, you'll just go and dress

yourself properly and wait till it's time to come with me.
I've had enough of it. You're always wanting to go off
with your father now, and you never used to before. What
you've got in your head I don't know. But you've got to
drop it and do what you're told. I'm sick of you and
your ways. All the young people in the house will be
there this morning, and Alfred will be making his final
arrangements. I'm not going to have you out of it. If
you don't know where your bread's buttered, I do."

"Alfred won't be there this morning," said Herbert
Fuller. "He is coming with his father to meet us at
Points. I wish you'd told me you wanted to come last
night, Irene. I said I'd take William Sheard."

"Oh, if it's only William Sheard," said Mrs. Fuller,
"he can sit up behind, as he's done before; good enough
for him too. The way those Sheards poke themselves in
everywhere—well, I should be ashamed to do it in that
bare-faced way. I wonder why Alfred has changed his
mind. I quite understood that there was to be a meeting
to decide things this morning at half-past ten. He doesn't
seem to be taking the interest in the *tableaux* that Mrs.
Brown hoped he would. Did you tell him that you were
going to Points this morning, Irene?"

"No. I haven't seen him for nearly a week."

"Well, you can go this time; but next time you'll please
ask my leave beforehand. You seem to think you can
do exactly what you like. Now mind you talk to Alfred
about the *tableaux*. Make some suggestions, and show an
interest in them. See that you get some good parts.
For goodness' sake try and do *something* for yourself, and
don't leave it *all* to me."

"I shall be starting in a quarter of an hour," said Fuller,
rising from the table, "with you or without you, Irene."

Herbert Fuller was a busy happy little man in these

days. The alterations that he had made in his house during
the summer pleased him greatly, and fortunately they also
pleased his wife, who had now resigned herself to a permanent occupation of Barton's Farm. Armitage Brown,
always intent upon time-saving, had bought him a two-
seated car for estate work, which he drove himself. It
had been one of his ambitions to have a little car, but his
wife's expenditure had hitherto stood in the way.

William Sheard made his appearance just before the
time appointed, and hung about in front of the house, much
to Mrs. Fuller's annoyance, who, however, did not ask
him in. She hated all the Sheards, and usually referred
to William as "the hobbledehoy." But William's appearance had quite altered since he had first come to Kemsale,
and his outlook too. Armitage Brown had suggested that
he should be taken into the estate office. He had paid
Fuller a premium to teach him his work, on the understanding that the Sheards were not to know of it. An
outlook almost too rosy for belief was in front of the
boy: in the foreground a life for which he was eminently suited, to be lived entirely in the country, which
he was getting to love more and more, and in the distance
the practical certainty of succeeding to the Kemsale agency,
if he showed himself competent. He was showing himself
exceedingly competent; Fuller had never had a pupil or
an assistant so keen and immersed in his work. Every bit
of it was a delight to him; he could think and talk about
scarcely anything else. As he waited on the gravel, an
offence to Mrs. Fuller's eyes, even she could hardly find
her excuse in his appearance. He was dressed in rough
brown tweeds, very different from his shabby school clothes,
and if he did look like a farmer's son, as she remarked
disgustedly to Irene, he looked like a very contented and
prosperous one.

He did not mind at all sitting up on the little perch behind, and told Irene that he was glad she was coming with them, in a way with which even Mrs. Fuller could have found no fault. He had dropped some of his shyness and awkwardness; he had found his niche in the world and was gaining confidence in himself and his abilities every day. He leaned over the back of the car as they ran along the muddy roads, and talked to Fuller about the land they were passing through and about the work there was in hand that morning, and Fuller treated him as an equal, and sometimes deferred to his opinion. Irene sat silent for the most part, but showed some interest when they talked about the dairying.

They arrived at Points Farm rather before the time at which Armitage Brown had appointed to meet them there. They did not go to the house, but stopped opposite to where the new buildings were now all ready for the work in which Points Farm was to lead the way.

Mr. and Mrs. Davis and their son were waiting for them at the gate. Mrs. Davis had lost some of her air of melancholy; she was now as interested and as optimistic about the project as anybody. She gave Irene a warm greeting. "Well, now, this is a pleasant surprise, my dear," she said. "Will you come into the house and take a little refreshment, or would you like to wait and go round the buildings with the rest of us?"

Irene said she would go round the buildings. She was a different girl from the one who mooned about at home, taking no interest in anything, as her mother so often told her. She even wanted to begin the inspection at once, and John Davis took her off for a preliminary view without waiting for the rest. The two of them seemed to have plenty to say to one another, but as a matter of fact Irene had been to Points Farm with her father several times of late, and scarcely needed showing what had been done.

William Sheard found himself talking to old Mr. Davis, who had taken a fancy to him.

" It's a fine thing to make your living out of the land, and to live on the land," said the old man. " Times are changing all round us, but the land must always go on. If you study it diligently it won't fail you. You may not make so much money as in other pursuits, but you live the best sort of life. You are fortunate to get your chance, and I think you will do well with it."

" I shall try my best, Mr. Davis," said the boy. " It's the one thing I really like, and feel fitted for. It's Mr. Brown who has given me my chance, and I feel very grateful to him."

" Mr. Brown is a good-hearted man," said the old farmer, " and I believe a far-seeing one. I am not yet convinced that all his ideas are right, but my son is quite sure that we shall all do well to follow him, and I am ready to fall in, for the few years longer that I have before me. The old people are gone, or going, and those of them that are left must try and keep step with the new ones."

Armitage Brown's car came up at that moment and he and Alfred alighted from it. Alfred looked a shade dispirited, but cheered up as the little party came together, and showed more interest in the subject in hand than might have been expected of him.

The inspection did not take long. The chief object of Armitage Brown's visit to this part of his estate was the farm that was being cut up into small holdings, and the buildings that were being adapted or newly erected on it. When a move was made away from Points Farm, Irene elected to stay behind and talk to Mrs. Davis. Her father was to pick her up on his way back. Mrs. Fuller would not have been pleased if she had known that her inter-course with Alfred had been confined to a few words of greeting and farewell.

The expedition ended with a visit to the new factory, now nearly completed. Alfred and his father went on to Kencote, where they were to lunch. As they shut them-selves in at the back of the car, out of hearing of the *chauffeur,* Armitage Brown began at once: " Now there it is, Alfred. You've seen it all, and heard a great deal about it. It's all interesting enough, but as far as I'm concerned I want to go on to the next thing, now I've once put it in hand. Can't you make up your mind to take it up? "

Some suggestion of that sort made on the way out had induced that air of depression in which Alfred had reached Points Farm. " I really can't see that it's in the least in my line, father," he said plaintively. " It's all business, you know, just as it was in Lombard Street, and I thought we had agreed that I am not cut out for business."

" I don't mean that you should take it as business, except to get a general idea of the financial side. It's using the land to the best advantage, and settling as many people as possible on to it that is the chief thing in this scheme. It isn't money-making—at least not for us. Just a fair return; that's all I want from it."

" Well, what do you want me to do? I was interested in the new cottages—rather wished I'd had a hand in designing them. I think I could have made one or two improvements."

His father turned to him eagerly. " Now that's exactly the sort of interest I want you to take," he said. " You've shown so little, that it never occurred to me to talk to you about that particular detail. Look here, my boy; let's have it straight out, you and I. I've made the money; there's no necessity for you to make any more. But you've

got to use what I've made, you know, sooner or later. Most
of it will come to you. And this place will come to you.
Whatever I do here, if I live another thirty years, I shall
just be the rich stranger, who knows nothing about it all.
They'll say that of me, if I coin gold out of the land. I
shan't belong. But with you it's different. It's different
already. They'll make friends with you in a different sort
of way to what they will with me. In a few years you'll
be one of them. That's what I want you to see, and to
play up to."

One would have thought by his face of misery that the
young man was being told that expectations of wealth
were to be disappointed, instead of being begged to take
advantage of them.

"Surely it's not so very difficult," his father said with
a touch of impatience. "You've got one of the most beautiful homes in England. I'm just asking you to take an
interest in it. I bought it partly for you."

"You never told me so. I didn't have much to say in it."

"You might have had all the say you wanted. What's
wrong with the place, Alfred? What's wrong with *you*?"

"I don't know that there's anything wrong with me,
except that I'm the son of a rich man. I don't seem to
have been cut out for it."

"I don't know whether you think you're cut out for the
son of a poor man. I don't. You've done exactly what you
liked; you've stuck to no work. You haven't spent a great
deal of money, it's true, but you've had all that money
could buy you in your home, and you've lived just as it
suited you outside of it. A poor man's son couldn't have
done what you have."

"I'm afraid I'm rather a useless sort of fellow, father;
but I can't help thinking that, if I hadn't had any money
at all behind me, I could have made enough to live pretty

much as I have—except, of course, when I've been at home."

"Yes, and for how long? It's been all very well so far. But you're getting on now. You're twenty-six. You might have wanted to marry before this; I hope it won't be long before you do marry. You couldn't offer a wife the sort of life you've been living abroad, even if you'd made it pay for itself, which you haven't. I've never bothered you about all that wandering of yours, but of course it has been a great disappointment to me. I always wanted you to do something. I didn't care what it was; but so far you've only enjoyed yourself."

Alfred sighed. " I suppose I've enjoyed myself more than most fellows," he said. " I've got that to look back upon; and you've been very good about it, father. If you want me to settle down now, I owe it to you to do what you want."

Armitage Brown felt baffled. " I wonder if there's any other young man in the world who looks at things in the way you do," he said with an affectionate but irritated smile. " What am I asking you to do? Any one would think I wanted you to shut yourself up in a prison. You can go abroad whenever you want to, as long as you don't stay away too long. You needn't go in for London society, if you don't care about it; I'm glad you don't; I shouldn't have left you so free as I have if you'd been a young man about town, or a loafer, as I prefer to call it. I quite thought you had taken to country life at one time."

" So I have to some extent. I've been here at Kemsale more often and for longer than I've stayed in any place in England since you let me off Lombard Street."

" Well? "

" The place is too big, too rich. It oppresses me. We don't seem to belong to it. It fitted the people who

were here before; it doesn't seem to fit us. All the time
we're trying to live up to something, something we don't
understand."

"There's something in that, Alfred. I'd no idea of it
before I came here. I suppose you saw it all along, and
that's why you took no interest in it when we first talked
it over."

"It may seem odd, but I never thought of it as a place
that had anything to do with me at all. I certainly never
thought of it as a place that would be mine some day, as
you say it will."

"A father has no right to grumble at that, my boy.
And I hope it will be a good many years yet before you
have to take it over from me."

"So many years that one needn't think about it at all,
need one?"

There was silence for a time. Then Armitage Brown
said: "These people we're going to—the Clintons.
There's the old man, bred up to it all. They say he's
hardly left Kencote since he inherited it from his grandfather. And there's his eldest son. From what I hear
he has been about a great deal more than his father;
but now he has settled down there too. You might say
that the old man was the narrow-minded country squire
that one reads and hears about, though he has his points
too, and he's not a man to be despised. But his son is
different. He's a man of brains, of a sort. He could
never have done what I have; very few men could. But
if he'd been born to a big position in the financial world
—the son of a big banker, or something of that sort—
he'd have made good. He'd have carried on. And he's
seen the world. Yet there he is, quite happy in living
the best part of his time here in the country, and looking
after his father's interests, that will be his by and by."

" Isn't that because he was born to it? "

" I suppose so, partly. But it's a lot that most young men wouldn't ask to be born to, if they had it offered to them young enough. I shouldn't. It's too late for me now to change my interests altogether. I want to be doing bigger things than I could do here. But I think if I were to be offered my life again, beginning at your age, I should choose your chance rather than my own. I can never be a satisfactory squire of Kemsale, as old Mr. Clinton is of Kencote. But you can. And Kemsale wants its squire. I've come to see that."

Alfred laughed. " Fancy me a squire! " he said. " And as for that, father, I think you have turned yourself into a squire in a thousand. You're not cut after the pattern of Mr. Clinton, of course; but you bring a new mind to it, and a mind that's able to take up anything that it sets itself to. If I tried to follow you, it would be just Lombard Street all over again. I haven't got it in me."

" Haven't you got it in you to do something or other with your father, Alfred? I've done everything alone, all my life."

Alfred was touched. The words, and the tone in which they had been spoken, revealed something in his father that he had not suspected hitherto.

" Do you feel like that about Kemsale? " he asked.

" I'll tell you exactly what I feel about Kemsale. It's a much bigger thing than I thought it was when I bought it. When I was making my plans about running the estate, not to pay handsomely, but to pay as a business proposition, I was constantly getting little warnings that it couldn't be treated just as any other business proposition. I was impatient of them. I thought it was all old-fashioned feudalism, that a go-ahead modern man would just get rid of. Now I look upon it differently. The

feudalism can be overdone. It was here. It's good neither
for landlord nor tenants that one man should be looked
up to as of different clay from all the rest, or so it seems
to me. The way I look at it is that they ought to be all
in together, with the landowner as the guiding spirit.
Perhaps they would say—the old people—that that was
their way. Well, according to their lights they act up to
it, the best of them. They know their people and they
are ready to help them in all sorts of ways. It isn't
like a big business in London where you've got hundreds
of people dependent on you, but know no more about
most of them than if they were strangers. That's the
side of it I should like to see you take up. You're fitted
for it. You can make friends; people like you. They
like you already, the people here, and little Katie too;
she's doing just what she ought to do, and no old-fashioned
squire's daughter of them all could do it any better. The
people look on you and her in a different way from what
they look upon me; I can see that. If you ask me what
I want you to do, I want you to live in the place—make
your home in it."

"It isn't much to ask of me, I'll admit," said Alfred.
"It's what I have done for the greater part of the past
year."

"Well, perhaps I want a little more than that. I want
to be able to talk to you about what I do myself here,
when I come down. I shan't be here quite so much after
Christmas. There's a big affair on that will occupy most
of my time for some months to come. I don't find that
this place gives me enough scope. I've been very interested in this dairying business, and I think it will turn
out all right. But to tell you the truth, it was a lucky
chance, to begin with. I might have taken up some other
scheme that wouldn't have had so much promise. I didn't

know enough. I shall go slower in the future, do what I can to get the place up gradually, working a good deal more on the old lines, unless I see a brilliant opening. I want to come down here and have things to interest me, but not work at in a big way. It's to be my recreation. But I should like it to be much more than that to you."

"If it is to take an interest in the people, father, I think I can do that; and as for model cottages and that sort of improvement, if you want it, I could take an interest in that too."

"Well, think it over, Alfred. Do what you like in the place, but let us talk over what you do together. I shall enjoy the place more than I do now, if I can feel that I'm helping you to make what you'd like to make out of it. I'm not bad at putting ideas into shape, you know. It's what I've been used to."

Alfred laughed at him. "Dear old dad!" he said. "You're a perfect marvel. I wish I had it in me to do you more credit. But I'll do my best, now I know what you want."

CHAPTER XXVII

THE PICTURES

DOUGLAS IRVING was in luck again. His friend Bradgate told him so, and his friend Wesbrook endorsed the statement, as they sat in Douglas's room after the first day's shoot, in that blissful sportsman's hour between tea and dinner, when easy-chairs seem easier than at other times, firelight brighter, and tobacco sweeter.

"You always do fall on your feet, Duggy," said Bradgate. "From all I can see, the millionaire has taken you to his bosom, and as for the shooting, you have as much to do with it as you've had for the last three years."

William and Mrs. Bradgate, Charles Wesbrook, and some young cousins of Beatrix's, now amusing themselves in the drawing-room, had come down the day before for the Meadshire festivities. They had attended the South Meadshire Hunt Ball at Bathgate the night before; they had shot to-day and were all to dine at Kemsale presently and view the *tableaux* afterwards. On the morrow there was to be a lawn meet at Kencote, and in the evening the Bathgate ball. On the day after they were to shoot again, and the proceedings would end with the ball at Kemsale.

"Armitage Brown wanted me to take over the whole management of the shooting a month ago," said Douglas. "I was to have the big days when I wanted to, and ask who I liked. He didn't care about it himself and he didn't suppose his son would."

"His son seems to have bucked up about it," said Wesbrook. "He's a nice fellow that, and makes an excellent shooting host, though he doesn't know much about the game."

"I told Brown that Alfred ought to look after it. It wouldn't look well for me to take it on, and ask people just as if it were my own. I said I'd do all I could to help him, and it's turned out very well. I don't think he'll ever shoot for nuts, he's not keen enough on it; but he's trying to be a good boy and please his papa. I'm glad you thought he did well to-day, Charles. We all like him here. He's different from other fellows; but he's one of the best."

"I suppose papa wants him to take his place as a future county magnate," said Bradgate. "It's not a bad sort of billet, either. Mr. Armitage Brown shows up rather well as a country gentleman, Douglas. We had a little conversation together to-day, and got on very well. Nobody would have thought that either of us had ever heard of the City. I should have liked to ask him one or two questions—seemed sort of queer to be talking to a man like that and not extracting a bit out of him. He seems to think a lot of you, by the by. Have you ever got him to talk?"

"I haven't tried. I've left it to him. He did say something the other day about having something on that would keep him pretty busy in London for the next few months."

"By Jove, that's interesting. Can't you get early information? It might be worth a lot to you."

"I asked him if he couldn't put me into it. He laughed and said he didn't know I wanted money. He thought I was one of those fellows who had everything he could want."

"You're on those terms with him, are you? What did you say?"

"I said that most of us could do with a bit more. I said: 'You'll do me the justice to observe that I've never mentioned the word money to you, but naturally when one's in your company, one can't help thinking about it sometimes, and if there's anything good going you might let your friends have first chance!'"

"Capital, Duggy! You're quite a diplomatist. That's the way to treat him. What did he say?"

Douglas hesitated. "Well, I can't tell you exactly what he said, Bill. I wasn't to. But when the time comes I think I shall be able to do something for my pals. I can't say more than that at present. You must leave it to me."

"Right you are, my boy. You seem to have played your cards well. And whether you make anything out of him or not, you've got him as a neighbour, and he seems to be a fairly useful one."

The dinner-party at Kemsale ought to have brought some consolation to Mrs. Brown for opportunities denied her. Meadshire, who had to take her in, and regretted the necessity as much as she, told her that not even when Royalty had been entertained at Kemsale had there been "a finer show." "Except in the matter of plate," he said. "I'm speaking the absolute truth, so I'm bound to say we beat you there. We had some magnificent Tudor plate. It was the first thing I got rid of. But I doubt if my old grandfather gave them a better feed than this, Mrs. Brown; and as for the flowers, we never had anything like 'em."

Mrs. Brown suspected that she was being laughed at, but answered with cold propriety, and made a mental note to the effect that still more plate was wanted, Tudor if possible.

If this was the largest dinner-party that Mrs. Brown had ever given, as it was, for the great room would have hardly taken another table anywhere, and was at least double the size of any she had had to fill before, it was also by far the merriest. It is to be doubted whether the majority of the guests would not have enjoyed themselves just as much if the viands and the wines had not been of such super-excellence, or the accessories of the feast so elaborate. They were for the most part very young people staying in the house, some of them drawn from circles in which such displays of wealth were not unknown, but more still quite unaccustomed to them. When the chatter and laughter was at its height, Armitage Brown, who had been talking quietly to Lady Grace on the one side of him and Virginia Clinton on the other, looked round him with a pleased smile. It was the first time in his life that he had enjoyed one of his wife's parties, or felt that the lavish display of hospitality that marked them had its reward. "We can hardly hear ourselves speak," he said, "but I shouldn't mind if they made more noise still. I really believe they're enjoying themselves."

"Mr. Brown, it's the loveliest dinner-party I've ever been to, if you'll excuse my lapsing into American," said Virginia. "If you make a joke, I shall laugh so that I shan't be able to stop myself. I feel like that, with all these young people about me."

"We're all young people to-night," said Grace. "It takes me back to the time when I was just grown up, and my grandfather gave me a ball and filled the house with my friends. Those are by far the best sort of parties; and this is going to be a very successful one, Mr. Brown."

Armitage Brown experienced a thrill of pleasure at these

words. He had been right in standing out for his ideas against his wife's. To get people together to enjoy themselves—that was the kind of party-giving that brought satisfaction to host and guests alike. It seemed fairly obvious, but it had certainly not been his wife's idea. He glanced at her as she sat stiff and stately between Meadshire and a young man whose ancestry had brought him the honour of supporting her on her other side. Neither of them was talking to her at the moment; she was isolated in the midst of all the gaiety and friendliness. But as she looked round her, and especially at the tables where Alfred and Katie were sitting, her face changed ever so slightly, and took on that look of satisfaction which meant that things were going well, and she was priding herself on a success. It came to him then that she was beginning to see. This sort of gathering, which brought pleasure to many whose opportunity for pleasure was small, whom it was so easy to please because of their youth and large capacity for enjoyment, was the right sort of gathering, in the country, and for people such as themselves. Its selection was based upon exactly the same principles as the bright gatherings that Kemsale had seen in the past; the great house was being used up to its full capacity. And there was nobody here who was not a friend, or at least a neighbour.

The *tableaux*, like most entertainments of their kind, were more amusing to the performers than to the spectators, although there were some in the audience to whom they seemed as remarkable as anything they had ever seen. The audience, in fact, was more " mixed " than Mrs. Brown liked, and Mrs. Fuller had told her quite plainly that it "would never do." Armitage Brown had required that some of the tenants should be asked. Mrs. Fuller had said, though not to him, that such a thing

couldn't be done; the county people would be up in arms
at being asked to meet farmers and their wives. She had
hinted, with what had seemed to her infinite tact, that
the Browns, being themselves, so to speak, on their trial,
couldn't afford to make such innovations. But the tact
had not been enough to cover the impertinence. She had
at last succeeded in offending her patroness. Mrs. Brown
had not been unmoved by her husband's accusation that
she had made her sole friend at Kemsale of a woman least
deserving of friendship. Her pride was on the alert; Mrs.
Fuller, if she had known it, was no longer in a position
to offer any advice as to what ought to be done, without
giving offence. She did not know yet that she had given
it, and had postponed the realization of a change of attitude towards her from Mrs. Brown, by giving way instantly when she discovered what that lady's intentions
were. The " county " was to be represented at this particular entertainment by those of its younger members
with whom there was already some intimacy, and these
were to be asked to dinner. For the rest, the ball must
suffice, and another dinner-party before it for the county's
biggest wigs, or such of them as would be likely to accept
an invitation.

A stage had been erected at one end of the ball-room,
an orchestra had been engaged, the scenery and the costumes were the best that could be procured for money,
and the men who had come from London to see to every
detail were enough to obviate the long waits that the
form of entertainment chosen is liable to when undertaken
by amateurs. Alfred had grumbled at the elaboration
brought to bear upon his ideas. It would have been so
much more fun to have painted the scenery and made
the costumes themselves. He and his friends and Katie's
friends had done this for a few of the pictures, and

enjoyed themselves greatly over it; but there had not been time to do it for all, and he was not sorry at the end to leave the management in the hands of the experts.

The pictures followed one another in quick succession. It must be confessed that those which followed the stories displayed in the popular print-sellers' shops were more vociferously applauded than those invented and carried out by Alfred and his artist friends, fresh and charming as some of them were.

In one of the former there were two couples in eighteenth-century costume, engaged in a beautiful garden at a game of cross-purposes. Alfred and Anne Sheard, apparently betrothed to one another, and Frank Clinton and Irene Fuller, in a like predicament, were all four gazing not at their own companions but at the opposite partners. It was agreed on all hands that Frank and Anne put a marvellous amount of expression into their looks, and this picture was demanded three times. Mrs. Fuller was one of the most energetic in her applause; and indeed Irene looked very well.

Armitage Brown had asked Mrs. Fuller to pay particular attention to Mrs. Davis. Mrs. Fuller had gracefully accepted the charge, while feeling annoyed that it should have been given her, for she had thought that her fitting place was exclusively with those of the house-party, and those who had been asked to dine, and had had ideas of showing condescension to the people who had come afterwards. She had, however, escorted Mrs. Davis to a seat in the front rows, next to her own, and patronised her affably, while occasionally turning from her to talk in markedly different tones to her neighbour on the right, who was of the elect.

" I can't help fancying," said Mrs. Davis, when the

curtain had gone down for the third time on the picture of the two couples, "that there is something between young Mr. Clinton and that pretty daughter of the Rector's. Their looks were almost too natural not to be true."

Mrs. Fuller laughed, not very amiably. "There would be a pretty to-do over at Kencote if it were so," she said. "I think myself that it was a mistake to give that girl such a part. She did make eyes at him, I admit, and there may be something in what you say as far as she's concerned. It shows the danger of taking people out of their places."

"The other two did their part just as well, I thought," said Mrs. Davis. "Your daughter is a pretty girl, Mrs. Fuller, and a nice one, too. We always like to see her over at Points when she comes with her father."

Mrs. Fuller was not at all pleased with this compliment. If Mrs. Davis thought that a daughter of hers came to Points Farm as an equal, as seemed to be indicated by the tone of her speech, she had better be disabused of such an idea. "She likes going round amongst the tenants," she said, "and often does it when she's wanted elsewhere. They make a lot of her here, as you can see by her being chosen for a part like that."

Mrs. Davis was meek and proud at the same time. She grew very red and said: "That is an insulting speech, Mrs. Fuller. I do not consider that your daughter is conferring a favour upon me by coming to my house occasionally, though as I say I am pleased to see her for her own sake."

Mrs. Fuller thought that perhaps she had gone too far. After all, the Davises were very "good people," and not to be confounded with the ordinary run of farming tenants. "Oh, please don't think I meant anything of that

sort," she said. "When she does go round with her
father, yours isn't the only house she goes to, you know.
If it were I shouldn't mind in the least—naturally
not."

"I think you have an unfortunate way of expressing
yourself," said the old lady, only half-appeased. "I think
I will go and find some of my friends elsewhere if you will
kindly allow me to pass."

"Oh, please don't move," said Mrs. Fuller, in great
alarm. Armitage Brown was standing with his back against
the wall at the end of the row in which they were sitting.
If the offended lady should take it into her head to tell
him why she was thus changing her seat in the middle of
the performance, Mrs. Fuller was aghast at what might
be the result. "Please stay," she said in an urgent, hurried whisper. "I want to tell you something. You must
forgive my not being quite myself to-night. You remarked
yourself how well Irene and young Mr. Brown played
their parts. Well, you can guess *why*, perhaps. It has
been going on for months. I wouldn't breathe a word
except to an old friend like yourself, and I'm sure you
won't repeat what I say. But you can see how it is with
me, can't you? I'm in a state of excitement. I can't
be responsible for everything I say."

"I don't think you can," said Mrs. Davis drily. "And
as for our being old friends, Mrs. Fuller, I have never
flattered myself that you looked upon me with any friendship. You have always considered me beneath you, and
it may perhaps surprise you to know that I don't consider
myself beneath you at all. It so happens that I have
always known exactly what you were before your marriage, and that Captain Fuller descended a good many
steps to make that marriage. I have kept what I know
to myself hitherto, because your husband is a gentleman,

and I have a regard for him. I have a regard for your daughter too, who takes after her father in the main, which is why I——"

The ringing of the bell on the stage and the sudden lowering of lights cut short the discourse, which had been delivered in a low, even voice, and seemed as if it would have gone on forever. It may be imagined that Mrs. Fuller, during the respite that followed, deeply regretted the ill-advised speech which had brought it upon her. It was eminently disturbing too, just at this time, to discover that her past was known, and to some one whom she had succeeded in offending. There was nothing disgraceful in her past, but the penalty she had to pay for the position she claimed in the present was that she could not afford to have it generally known. Or so she thought, being unaware that it would have caused more surprise amongst her neighbours to have proof that she was what she claimed to be than what she was.

When she could talk again, under cover of the music, she said at once: "When you talk of what I was before my marriage, Mrs. Davis, I should like to tell you that in my eyes poverty is no disgrace to anybody. You may tell all the world, if you please, that I was poor as a girl, and had to work for my living. I have never tried to hide it. I have even told Mrs. Brown the facts of the case."

"I don't suppose for a moment you've told them all," said Mrs. Davis, in the same low persistent tone. She also had been thinking, and had apparently made up her mind to have it all out.

"I was not very happy at home," said Mrs. Fuller, faltering, "and I worked at dressmaking until I married. Lots of ladies of good birth have done the same. There is nothing to be ashamed of."

" No, but you're ashamed of it all the same," pursued the terrible quiet voice. " Besides, you weren't a lady of good birth, whatever you may pretend about yourself. Your father was a regimental bandmaster, and married your mother out of a little sweetstuff shop in a back street in Portsmouth, where you were brought up. My own father was chaplain to the same regiment, and I remember you very well as a forward giggling girl, with the worst possible manners and not the best of reputations, though I don't say that you couldn't look after yourself even at that age. How you managed to get hold of poor Captain Fuller I don't know, as it was long after I married myself and left the place; but I recognised you directly you came here."

It was much more terrible than anything that Mrs. Fuller had imagined. She had thought that all traces of her life before the dressmaking period, which was the one in which she had met her hsuband, had been covered up and forgotten. She could only abase herself and beg her tormentor to keep her information to herself. " You can't be surprised," she pleaded, " that I shouldn't want the facts of my childhood known. I shook myself free from them as soon as I could. I have made a good position for myself, and it would be a cruel thing, for my good kind husband and for my daughter, if——"

" Oh, you needn't alarm yourself," interrupted the relentless old lady. " It was for the sake of your good kind husband, whom you've never valued as he deserves, that I held my tongue, and I shall continue to hold it as long as you behave properly. But it was just a little *too* much to have you, of all people, setting me in my place. As for your silly ideas about your daughter and young Mr. Brown, I've no doubt you've worked hard enough to bring something of that sort about, but there's nothing in it, and you only succeed in blinding yourself and making yourself look ridiculous when you talk about it."

The conclusion of the performance brought the painful interview to an end. Mrs. Fuller emerged from it much battered, and her equanimity was not restored during the dancing that followed by the fact that Irene favoured John Davis as a partner above others, and did not dance once with Alfred.

CHAPTER XXVIII

MORE FESTIVITIES

KEMSALE turned up in force the next morning at the lawn meet at Kencote, chiefly in motor-cars, but partly on horseback. At the last moment Mrs. Brown drew back from the party, on the plea of a headache. Her headache was of the slightest; she could not bring herself to appear at an important house as introducer of the motley-looking cavalcade that had already ridden off.

Horses had been supplied for everybody who wanted them, and most of Alfred's friends did. They were chiefly artists or students of art, some English and some French, ready to get the utmost fun out of everything that was going on, and not to be deterred by deficiencies of costume or ignorance of the art of equitation from taking part in an English fox-hunt. It is doubtful if such an appearance as they made in the aggregate had ever been seen in a South Meadshire field before; it was a miracle that every member of the party eventually found his way back sound in limb; but the stiffness induced by the unwonted exercise gave Kemsale the appearance of a home for cripples on the day after.

Alfred's ignorance of horsemanship was not so great as he had pretended. He had had his own pony as a boy, and had been as ready to take to a horse on occasions as most vigorous young men. During a spring sketching expedition in the New Forest he had even taken rather keenly to hunting with the stag-hounds, but he had kept this fact dark for various reasons. His chief objection to hunting was that it was the sport of people amongst whom he was not accustomed to find kindred spirits, but he was not sure that here in Meadshire that objection might not be overcome. There were young people from neighbouring houses whom he was beginning to know very well, and some of them had been staying at Kemsale during the past week. There had been a tendency to form two groups amongst the guests assembled. Alfred had not been altogether at his ease in his duties as host. On the one hand, some of the young men from the country houses, and those whose presence derived from acquaintance made on the Riviera, had been inclined to treat coldly the artistic contingent; and on the other, sundry members of that contingent had shown themselves affected by their situation in such a way as to give cause for the coldness. As light-hearted Bohemians they had been all that could be desired as companions; in rich and conventional surroundings they had not all been able to behave as if a happy poverty were not a lot to be rather ashamed of. Alfred was beginning to suspect that he should have to choose between one way of life or the other, or at least that the mixing up of the two ways of life in this manner would not give satisfactory results. What he hated more than anything was to feel that the wealth whose evidences were so apparent in his home affected the attitude of others towards him. The young men of recognised parentage did not show that they were affected by it, though this might only have been because their code did not permit them to show it, and it was probably owing to the wealth that his status was accepted by them. But at least they were at their ease at Kemsale. So were the majority of his other friends, especially the Frenchmen, who took all the unaccustomed luxury and ceremony as a piece of good fortune and good fun, and

were not otherwise impressed by it, or inclined to alter
their views of Alfred because of it. It was just the one or
two who would never be the same towards him again,
however much their friendship might appear to have increased. It spoilt everything, gave him an ugly view of
human nature, and made him feel cut off from the free
and careless enjoyment of his artist life. There seemed
to be a fate pushing him towards rich conventional respectability, and in spite of the many attractions that life
at Kemsale held out towards him, as well as the fact
that his duty seemed to lie there, his inclination was to
resist the compulsion.

Arrived at Kencote, most of the artist brigade declined
to go into the house for the refreshment hospitably offered
to all comers. The reason given, amidst much laughter,
was that if they once got off their horses many of them
would find great difficulty in getting on to them again,
but it is probable that a hint had been given to the rest
by one of their number who shrank from the sensation
that their appearance would occasion. Alfred felt some
relief at not having to head a procession of them into the
house, and hated himself for the feeling. But he was
wavering between two opinions.

The Squire greeted him and those who went in with
him cordially. " But why aren't you in pink? " he asked,
in his loud and confident voice. " We've got to thank
Kemsale for a handsome subscription," he said, lowering
his tone a little. " Very glad indeed that the South
Meadshire is going to be supported from Kemsale again;
it hasn't been for years, at least not by people hunting
from there. You must come out with us regularly now
you've once begun, and you must get your coat. I dare
say it will be a lot smarter than mine—ha! ha!—haven't
bought a new coat for years, and don't suppose I shall ever

buy another now. Well, I've had my fun; time to make room for the younger fellows now, I say!" He lowered his voice still further into a confidential whisper, and took Alfred's arm to lead him to the comparative privacy of a window. "There's a little matter I want just to mention. There's a rumour going about that your father has an idea of keeping the hounds off that dairying land of his, when everything gets into order. That won't do, you know—make a lot of trouble. Besides, it isn't necessary. I can satisfy him as to that if he'll come and talk it over with me. Is he coming to-day, by the by?"

Alfred said that he wasn't. "But he told me that he had given up that idea of his," he said. "I think John Davis persuaded him that the hounds would do very little damage."

"Well now, I'm very glad to hear that. Of course John Davis knows all about it. I suppose they've hunted from Points as long as from anywhere. George Davis used to come out with us regularly years ago. He's a younger man by three or four years than I am, but he gave it up earlier. Couldn't mount himself so well as he used to, I fancy; but I hope all that's going to be changed for them now. He'll have to thank your father for that. He's getting in to things in a wonderful way —your father, I mean. I'm glad this rumour of interfering with the hounds isn't true. It would never have done. He'll learn all that sort of thing by and by, and as for you, young man, why, when you're as old as I am, you'll forget you've been anything but a country squire all your life. Gobblessmysoul! What are all those ragamuffins doing here?"

The artistic contingent had drawn nearer to the house, on the wide stretch of parkland that lay beyond the drive. They presented a sufficiently remarkable appearance.

There may have been two or three pairs of gaiters amongst
the dozen or so of them, but as a general rule their trousers
were either rucked up to their knees or in process of becoming so. There were velvet coats amongst them, flowing
ties, and an assortment of brigand-like felt hats; the youngest of them all wore a long yellow beard.

On ordinary occasions Alfred would have laughed heartily
at their appearance and at the Squire's face and exclamation of horror. But he was ruffled at the speech that had
just been made to him, and at other things, and said stiffly:
" They are all friends of mine. I'm sorry they are not
ornamental. I'll go out and tell them to move farther
off if you like."

But it was the Squire who laughed heartily, and insisted
upon the whole party being fetched indoors. With unwonted sharpness he perceived that some of them were
French, and as he had been nurtured on stories of Frenchmen in the hunting-field, he took their presence as a tremendous joke. Alfred's French friends had no reason to
complain of their glimpse of British hospitality, and if
some of his English ones suffered from *mauvaise honte*
in being dragged in amongst a crowd of sportsmen and
sportswomen, it was not because they were not given a
welcome. The Kemsale brigade became a famous catch-
word amongst the followers of the South Meadshire after
that day, and the Squire was furnished with a new stock
of Franco-sporting stories, drawn from his own observation, which lasted him for the rest of his life.

But it was not everybody who accepted the Kemsale
house-party as merely providing a fund of amusement.
It not only invaded the hunting-field, and interfered considerably with the proceedings of the day, but was large
enough to make itself felt at the two Bathgate balls.
These, like other hunt and county balls, were the preserve

of the country houses around, with the usual sprinkling
from the families of country parsons, doctors and lawyers
and the like, and were merry and sociable within those
limits. But merriment and sociability from outside their
accepted limits are apt to be looked upon coldly in such
circles. It was thought to be a very queer lot that had
come from Kemsale, and there was some resentment and a
great deal of criticism brought to bear upon the new
people who were responsible for its introduction. They
ought to have known better, since they were only on
probation themselves.

This feeling in the air caused Mrs. Brown, who divined
it readily enough, untold agony of mind. She sat stiffly
on the dais at the end of the Assembly Rooms, wonderfully gowned, wonderfully jewelled, and wondered how
she could ever have consented to be responsible for such
a motley crew. As long as they had been confined to
Kemsale, their unstinted enjoyment of the entertainments
provided for them had caused her to regard them with
indulgent eyes. But to see them making themselves bois-
terously at home here, to compare them with the smart
young men of the county, with their red coats and their
sleek heads, and painfully to collect the glances of distaste and the smiles that followed disparaging comment,
was purgatory to the poor proud lady. Her husband's ideas
simply would not do. She saw it quite plainly now, and
she had an idea that her son saw it too. It was some
relief to the acute distress of mind which she underwent
on that first evening—she could not face the second, and
stayed at home—to believe that Alfred was coming round
to her way of thinking. He did not wear a red coat, but
any one who observed him would certainly have put him
down as belonging to the " county," and not to the awful
crew that he called his friends. She was assured of that,

and she watched him constantly. He did not look as if he were enjoying himself, as he had done the night before at Kemsale. Surely he had come to see at last that he had made a mistake in bringing these terrible people to Kemsale, a mistake in making friends with them at all when the right sort were so ready to welcome him as one of themselves!

She was quite right in supposing that Alfred was not entirely happy, and quite wrong in everything else that she supposed about him. He did see plainly that " it wouldn't do," but it was not against his own friends that his annoyance was directed. All but a few of them were tried and trusted companions, with whom he had enjoyed some of the best days of his life. Until this public appearance he had rejoiced in being able to give them an unaccustomed pleasure and rejoiced in the free and happy way in which they had accepted it. It was what they were doing now, and what they were being criticised for. Hadn't they as much right as anybody else to enjoy themselves? Wasn't it what ought to be expected of clever gay young men, who had spurned the path of money-making in order to devote themselves to a glorious art, that they should not show themselves impressed or oppressed by the smug self-complaisance of well-endowed respectability? He resented on their behalf every shrug and smile and whisper. His heart warmed towards them. He made himself one of them, and towards the end of the evening his mother had the additional mortification of seeing him shrugged at and whispered at with the rest. She had dreadful visions of her own ball-room deserted by the people she wished to see there, and Kemsale marked forever as outside the pale of " county " sociability altogether.

When the night of the Kemsale ball arrived, however, she was consoled to find that none of those who had accepted her invitation had stayed away. She had been rather surprised at the way things had been " done " at the Hunt Ball. The eighteenth-century Assembly Rooms in the George Hotel at Bathgate had harboured these annual gatherings for many years past. They had been considered extremely handsome at one time, and were so still in a faded old-fashioned way, with their panels of worn crimson brocade, and their lustre chandeliers and sconces. It had never been considered that they needed any special decoration, except that of flowers, and these had been provided on a comparatively modest scale. The floor was excellent, and the supper good, and that was all that was wanted for an evening's enjoyment amongst neighbours.

But then Mrs. Brown had never been accustomed to think of a ball as an opportunity for enjoyment. She had not been in a position to go to balls in her young days, and thought of them now chiefly as affording opportunities for display. If the people who were apparently contented to disport themselves in such surroundings as those of the Hunt Ball would come to Kemsale and hold over their opinion of its owners until they saw the kind of thing that would be provided for them there, she thought she could make them open their eyes. And this anticipation had greatly consoled her during the miserable hours she had spent in the Bathgate Assembly Rooms.

And indeed, except for the absence of the Tudor plate, which still rankled with her a little, there could have been no decorations in Kemsale's most palmy days to equal hers. They were entirely floral; Kemsale had been so abundantly decorated already that there was no opportunity to do more than cover up its decorations with flowers. The supplies offered for the purpose by Mackenzie, who had thought that at last there was a chance of showing what he could do with his great range of glass-

houses, were rejected as quite inadequate, and he himself
was swept contemptuously aside as decorator-in-chief, and
told to put himself and his stock at the disposal of the
London florists who were summoned to do their utmost,
regardless of expense. Mrs. Brown received her guests
in a forest of great palms and orchids; the walls of the
ball-room were trellised with pink roses; all the rooms of
state had their lavish and appropriate decoration; the scent
of flowers was everywhere. The numbers of the band
were limited by the space afforded by the musicians' gallery; otherwise she would probably have made overtures
to the full Queen's Hall orchestra; but it sent down its
swinging strains in a way to set the heaviest foot tripping
on the almost too polished floor. Of the supper it need
only be said that the young people who wanted to dance
all the time hurried away from it as soon as possible, and
the older people lingered over it more than they were
accustomed to linger even over ball suppers, which are a
solace to those whose dancing days are over and a not-
to-be-despised part of the entertainment to some others.

And yet there were criticisms—ungrateful it must be
allowed, since all the lavish expenditure did make this
particular ball something exceptional in the way of country
balls, and to be talked about afterwards. It seemed to
be a "try on," an attempt to take by storm a citadel that
prides itself on not lowering its flag to money. The Browns
had been "taken up" already; there was hardly any one
of importance of "the county" that was not represented
at Kemsale on this night. But the county was not to be
shown the way to do things; it was quite satisfied with its
own way, and a considerable part of it was quite as well
aware as Mrs. Brown of how "things" were done, in
great London houses for instance. These elaborate floral
decorations would have been suitable for one of the rec-

ognised London palaces on an occasions of great state;
they were hardly suitable for a country house, even when
it was as large as Kemsale, and the unsuitability was all
the greater when it represented nothing that the county
was inclined to respect, except unlimited wealth. Mrs.
Brown had, in fact, made the same sort of mistake in over-
elaborating her ball as her husband made in going to church
in the country in his best London clothes. Neither of them
knew their way about yet.

In ordinary circumstances, the county's cause of complaint would have been felt, and probably expressed, by
no one more exhaustively than the Squire of Kencote. It
would take a good-sized pamphlet to explain what accessories of life and what standard of behaviour would have
been considered to be fitting to the various social states of
which he had knowledge; and it is doubtful whether the
explanation would then have satisfied anybody who did
not stand exactly where he stood himself. But the principle behind its subtleties and self-contradictions would
have been fairly plain. In spite of his own dignity as the
head of an ancient line, and the wealth that more than
supported it, he had always clung to an essential simplicity
of life. It was the things one did in the country that were
of importance; the end must not be obscured by the means.
And the end was a healthy useful life, spent as much as
possible in the open air, and with neighbourliness to rich
and poor alike to colour its pleasant activities. Its full
fruition could be attained by means of a moderate degree
of wealth, and an over-application of wealth to its nicely
adjusted parts would throw the complicated machine out
of balance.

But the Squire's critical faculty was asleep on this
occasion. He even defended the profuse spectacle against
disparaging comment. " What are a few flowers more or

less to people like this? Very pretty and bright I call
the whole thing; rather a compliment that we country
bumpkins are considered worth such a show, I think," was
the line of his defence. And to one or two of his particular cronies there would be a confidential " They tell me
this man's worth——" The figures were only indicated in
a roundabout way, but the fact plainly emerged, for those
who knew the Squire, that he felt some personal interest
in them, and his pride that aped humility set tongues wag-
ging in a way that would have offended him deeply, only
that he had no idea that his most secret desires were, as
it were, cried aloud by himself.

He had not been present at either of the Bathgate gatherings, and would have considered that his age absolved
him from attending this one, if he had not wished to see
for himself how affairs were progressing in a certain
quarter.

Frank had secured a fortnight's leave over Christmas,
and had spent the preceding week of it at Kemsale. He
had also visited Kemsale, as has been said, on every occasion that he had made a flying appearance at Kencote, and
those appearances had sometimes been of such short dura-
tion that it was only natural to suppose that a very strong
attraction had led him to make the journey down to Meadshire when most young men in his position would only have
used the opportunity for a little jollification in town.
Surely by this time something might be expected to come
of it! The Squire, remembering his own youth, had a
strong suspicion that such an occasion as this would be
very likely to bring matters to a head.

And so it did. Frank had spent the most blissful week
of his life at Kemsale, and this was to be the end of it.
Anne, who was now a prime favourite in the house, had
been caught up and enveloped in all the excitements of

the time. He had been with her every day, and often for the whole day. They had floated with the glamourous tide, understanding one another perfectly, and being understood and abundantly sympathised with by most of those who had such frequent opportunities of observing them. They were constantly left together. No one would have thought of claiming either of them for anything separately. The young man was so gallant and handsome, the girl so pretty and sweet, that it was felt to be an idyll to be treated with tenderness, not to be too much talked about. Probably Mrs. Brown was the only one of all the large company who did not know what was going on under her eyes, and even hers could hardly have remained blind to it if on the night of the Hunt Ball she had not been so immersed in other thoughts, and had not stayed away from the ball on the night after. By this time it was well enough known to " the county " at large, and it was a little ill-natured of some of the Squire's more intimate friends not to give him a hint of it, but to wait and see the realization of the truth, and what should follow it, break in upon him gradually.

The poor old man, so confident and self-satisfied in the early hours of the evening, provided all that could have been desired in the way of entertainment to the cynics as the truth did gradually dawn upon him. As is the way of young men in his case, Frank made his concessions to what he conceived to be his duty at the outset, so as to be able to give himself up more completely to his inclinations later on. He danced twice with Katie, and the Squire beamed each time, did not know he was beaming, but was closely observed. Then came a dance with Anne, during which he made some of those observations already recorded. This dance was followed by a prolonged period of absence, during which he began to show himself somewhat puzzled and disturbed.

And so the game went on, until, finally, after a much longer period of absence, the two of them came back into the ballroom, and their faces showed as plainly as faces could show anything that amidst all the troubles and misunderstandings of the world here were two young people who feared nothing of what might come as long as they could meet it together.

CHAPTER XXIX

THE OLD AND THE NEW

" I CALL this the haunt of peace," said Alfred. " After the turmoil we have been living in it's like coming to a delightful rest cure."

He and Katie were lunching at the Herons' Nest with Grace and Meadshire alone. The spacious dining-room, with its oaken floor, old panelling, and fine furnishing, might have been in some ancient peaceful house that had known no change for generations. The winter sun flooded the room, and through the open windows nothing could be seen but the massed ranks of the pines on the other side of the gorge, and nothing could be heard but the music of the water on the rocks below.

But if the scene was quiet and untroubled, the faces of the four who sat at the table were not. Alfred showed his disquiet less than any of them, and perhaps his disquiet was less than theirs. But he was feeling dispirited and out of gear, and in spite of his words he was gaining no solace from this companionship of four.

Meadshire was in a frowning discontented mood. He sat for long periods saying nothing, and when he did speak had nothing to say that had any effect upon the general depression. He was drinking nothing but water; otherwise, Alfred, who became more and more irritated with him as the meal progressed, would have suspected him of being on the road to one of his periodical breakdowns. Grace looked at him sadly every now and then, but tried to keep the ball of conversation rolling. Her face was thin and her eyes heavy. Alfred wondered how he could ever have thought her young.

Her face kept its sweetness, but it was that of a middle-aged woman.

Little Katie made valiant efforts to be bright and talkative, but her efforts were not a success. She looked as if she had been crying. She and Alfred had not been much together while Kemsale had been full, but now all the guests had departed it had come to him that she had not shown that happy gaiety that might have been expected of her, with so many of her friends around her and so much to occupy them. He had asked her, as they had walked to the Herons' Nest together, if there was anything the matter with her, and she had denied it vigorously. He had not pressed his inquiries, thinking that he might have been mistaken as to the past, and that the reaction from gaiety to dullness might account for her dejection of the present. Now he thought that there must be something—something between her and Grace; but he did not connect it with Meadshire's lowering state, except so far as he made everybody in his presence uncomfortable.

They were talking of Frank Clinton and Anne Sheard. Sympathy with those happy lovers brightened the faces of three of them until Meadshire struck in.

"You don't suppose Edward Clinton is going to allow that, do you?" he asked; and his eye rested for a moment on Katie.

Grace spoke hurriedly as if to prevent him from saying more. "He may be a little disappointed at first," she said. "But he can't help loving that sweet little Anne when he knows her. He is much more soft-hearted than he gives himself credit for."

"He's much more soft-headed," growled Kemsale. "But there are two gods he worships, money and birth, and as your sweet little Anne has neither he'll kick up a devil of a row about it."

" Yes, perhaps he will make a fuss—poor Cousin Edward! He did about Dick and Virginia; but he adores Virginia now."

" That's very different. Virginia had money; and she was a beautiful woman—an American, and you don't ask for birth from them. I don't see Edward welcoming a pretty little girl out of a country parsonage whose parents are—well, we all know what they are—as good as they make 'em. They'll do for us, but they won't do for Edward."

" If Frank Clinton has any pluck," said Alfred, " he won't take much notice of all that nonsense. He'll just take her out of her country parsonage, and be happy with her. Who's Mr. Clinton, that he should turn up his nose at a girl as charming as little Anne? "

He spoke with some contempt. The cause of his present ill-humour was precisely " all that nonsense," which had been bothering him as he had never allowed it to bother him before. He was going to make a stand against it, to make it quite plain what his own position was; and Meadshire, who seemed determined for some reason or other to show his disagreeable side, should have something definite to be disagreeable about if that was what he wanted.

Meadshire turned his frown upon him. " Edward Clinton is my cousin for one thing," he said.

Alfred laughed constrainedly. " Does that mean I'm not to take it upon myself to criticise him? " he asked.

" Oh, we all criticise dear Cousin Edward," said Grace lightly. " But we love him all the same. I'm sure he won't stand out long, if he stands out at all."

Meadshire went on as if she had not spoken. " Edward Clinton is the head of a family that has been at Kencote for something like five hundred years. That's a record that very few people in England can show. I don't blame him for holding up his head about it and wanting to keep his line what it's always been."

"But you said just now that he thought too much about birth and money," said Katie. She spoke with a little air of authority, as if she wished to recall him to himself, and had a right to do so. And he smiled at her as if he accepted her right.

"I don't say that I agree with him," he said, more amiably. "But when I'm asked who Edward Clinton is, I'm giving an answer. He's something quite recognisable, and has been all his life."

Alfred was about to pursue the subject in a way that would probably not have tended to preserve Meadshire's slight improvement in manner, but Grace prevented him by talking about something else, and the rest of the meal passed more easily.

They drank their coffee outside in the sun, and presently Meadshire, who seemed to be unable to sit still, and had been walking up and down the terrace with his hands in his pockets, puffing at a cigarette, asked Katie to go to the upper rocks with him. She arose at once, and Grace and Alfred were left alone together.

"What's the matter with Meadshire?" Alfred asked. "He doesn't seem to be in the best of tempers."

She laughed at him. "I have been thinking the same about you," she said. "I suppose we are all feeling a little off colour after our excitement of the last few weeks."

"It isn't that with me," said Alfred, after a pause. "I'm very glad the excitement is all over. It wasn't a success, and I hope it won't be repeated."

"Not a success!" she exclaimed. "I think it has been the most brilliant success. Everybody is feeling extraordinarily grateful to you for giving them such a good time. It has been quite like old days at Kemsale."

The last sentence had been divided from the rest of the speech by an appreciable pause. Alfred smiled at her. " It is like you to say that," he said. " You make the best of us, and you're generosity itself. All the same, I think your chief thought must have been how very unlike it all was to the old days at Kemsale."

She was too truthful to protest that she had meant exactly what she had said. " In many ways," she amended her statement, " it was like our gay times. But, of course, my grandfather was very old already when I was just grown up; the gay times were not so frequent as they had been, and it is natural that I should remember best the happy quiet times."

" Yes, I know," he said. " And your quiet times were very different from ours. You belonged there, and we don't. Unless we are making a noise and spending vast sums of money on amusing ourselves and other people, we don't know what to do with ourselves. My father is tired of the place already; my mother is dying to get away from it now, and will be off directly, with Katie. And if you want the truth about me, I've had as much as I can stand of it for some time to come, and I'm going off as well, if my father will let me."

" It isn't like you to talk like that of your father and mother," she said gently. " They have both been very kind, and have given many people a great deal of pleasure. And your father, especially, has shown himself to be a really good and considerate landlord."

" I'm not saying anything against either of them, and perhaps I wouldn't say what I have said to anybody but you. It is when I think of you in connection with Kemsale that I see how unsuitable all of us are to be living here."

She saw that he wanted to unburden himself, and though she did not understand the springs of his discontent, she liked him well enough to be interested in them. "Tell me why you say that," she said. "I shouldn't have thought that your father was tired of Kemsale, as you say he is; and I don't see any reason at all why you should be."

"I don't suppose my father does know that he is tired of it. Perhaps he isn't altogether. But ever since we first came here he has been trying to make Kemsale his chief interest, and he can't keep that up any longer. It isn't enough for him. I suppose he has made a great deal more money than he knows what to do with, and I believe he had an idea of leaving off money-making and settling down here, if it suited him, though he has never actually said so. I suppose he wanted to see how it turned out first. Well, he has one of his big affairs on in the City, and he's just as pleased to be getting back to it as if he were a boy going home from school. You won't see much of him here for weeks to come. He may be down occasionally on Sundays, but he won't have much attention to spare for Kemsale affairs when he does come down. He'll just want to rest."

"It is very curious," she said. "But I suppose every man is most interested in the things he does best. Kem never really cared about estate work. If he had been an engineer, or something of that sort, I expect he would have worked hard at it. Still, he was fond of Kemsale when it was his, and I think your father is too."

Alfred had not yet forgiven Meadshire his fractiousness.

"I dare say my father will be as fond of it as he was," he said. "But he thought he was going to be fond of it in a different way. He thought it would give him something to do all the time. Now he finds it won't, he wants to shift it off on to me. He sees well enough that it wants taking care of—that it's too big a thing to leave to agents and business people. Old Mr. Clinton taught him that, I think. He has been rather impressed by the way he has stuck to his land, and his eldest son sticks to it now."

"Yes; Kencote is enough for both of them. Why isn't Kemsale enough for you? I thought you had been happy here. You told me before Christmas that you had never stayed for so long in one place. What has happened since to make you want to leave it?"

"Oh, I've had my eyes opened; I expect you know why."

She looked at him in surprise. "Indeed I don't," she said. "I thought that having so many of your friends here would make you like it more than ever. Katie told me that you had never had such an opportunity for hospitality before you came to Kemsale."

"It doesn't seem to have brightened Katie up much. It was all right until one made the discovery that one's old friends weren't considered good enough for one's new ones."

She cast down her eyes. She had expected nothing of this sort, and was not altogether guiltless of having thought some of his old friends not quite good enough. She thought he was accusing her, but could not remember that she had given the slightest occasion for accusation.

He was not looking at her, and went on: "I can see it all now. I suppose I've always known in the back of my mind that I could get into any society I cared about because of all the money. It doesn't seem difficult to buy your way anywhere nowadays, even amongst the people who pride themselves on respecting something besides money. But I've hated the idea of it so much that I've sunk the beastly money as much as ever I could. I've made friends amongst people I've really liked, and I've had a royal good time. All those fellows who were down here—clever and amusing fellows—took me for myself, not for my money, or my father's money. Now, even with one or two of them it's different already. They think of me not as a fellow like themselves, as they used to, but as a chap who is plastered with gold. I hate it; it humiliates me. I'm like Crœsus, who ruined everything that he touched."

"I think it is rather fine that you should think about money like that," she said. "I can understand it. There are people in the world who are affected towards rank in the way that you hate. One has to guard one's self against false values. It is the penalty one pays for being a little different from others. But still, I don't see why what you have said should make you turn against poor Kemsale. One's rank was in its right place here, while we had it, and I think your father's wealth, which he spends here so generously, is in its right place, too."

He smiled at her again. "You always calm one's ideas," he said. "But I don't think you really believe that money is a good substitute for rank at Kemsale. You make the best of us, as I said before, but you stood out against us for a long time, you know. I don't think you've changed all your ideas since we became friends."

"I have changed a great many of them," she said simply; "and I suppose it is because both you and Katie are so little affected by——"

"By the money. Yet it's the money that has put us where we are. When we lived in a big house in the suburbs of London you wouldn't have thought us fit people to know."

"Oh, you mustn't talk like that. You're muddling things up. I should always have thought you the nicest people to know, if I had once got to know you. So does everybody about here. I don't think you have any reason to complain of lack of friends here. No one could have made themselves more liked in so short a time."

"Well, if people have taken us up, I say it is because of the money. I thought at first, as far as I was concerned, it was because of myself. So it may be with a few, but with the majority it's because of the money. And I've found it out. That's why I'm longing to get away, and be myself again."

She did not speak at once. Then she said slowly: "If you think about it like that, it is of no use simply to say that you're wrong. But I think you are wrong all the same."

"I'm sure I'm not wrong. Any number of the people who were at Kemsale the other night were turning up their noses at us all the time, and they were turning them up still higher at Bathgate. And why?"

"Well, why?"

"Because we had the impudence to be ourselves. If we had filled our house with people all cut after one pattern they'd have passed us—of course as long as we behaved ourselves humbly and gratefully for being taken notice of. It would have been better than they would have expected from people like us, and——"

She would not let him go on. "Oh, but I think you're talking a great deal of nonsense," she said. "If you want the plain truth, your friends did make a good deal of noise, and they weren't the kind of people we're accustomed to. Most people were rather amused at them, and if there were some who took it all too seriously, you can surely make allowances. If a lot of fox-hunting young Englishmen took charge of an artists' ball in Paris it would have been just the same, the other way round."

He was already inclined to be a little ashamed of the

division he himself had tried to create at the Bathgate balls, and she had spoken with more decision than she generally used. " Well, all that isn't of much importance," he said, rather grudgingly. " It isn't really what I'm up against. I suppose these people here have a right to have their own show run as it pleases them. Well, let them run all their shows as it pleases them, and I'll keep outside. I don't belong to them. I belong to the other lot, and it has been made plain to me that the two lots don't mix. I've made my choice now."

" Have you got a right to make your choice in that way? " she asked him.

" Why not? I don't belong to the fox-hunters. I don't care for them, as a body. Of course I like one or two here and there. I like Irving; I like Frank Clinton; I like a few of the fellows who have been staying with us. But that's only because they're something more than fox-hunters."

" It's because you know them. Nobody likes all the people whom they have to live amongst. I'm sure you don't like all the artists amongst whom you have lived. You pick and choose, and the rest you tolerate. But in a city you have more choice. In the country perhaps you have to tolerate more than you can make friends with. It's the same for all of us."

" What did you mean when you said I hadn't a right to choose for myself? "

" I asked you whether you had. I had a little talk with your father the other day. He wants you to settle down here. He told me that Kemsale would be yours some day. He doesn't want you to do what some of us have done—look upon a great country estate as so much property, providing an income to be spent, and carrying with it no duties or responsibilities. He told me that he had come to see that that was not the way that land should be held—at least not in England."

"Oh, yes, he's got hold of all that, the dear old dad. There's nobody like him for seizing the salient point. Only, unfortunately, he isn't going to bother himself with holding land in what he sees to be the right way on his own account. I've had it all out with him, and I did make up my mind more or less before Christmas to give it a fair trial. But what he doesn't see yet is that it takes the right man to do it. You don't always find the right man amongst the people that you come from, and you're less likely still to find him amongst the people from whom I come. You may. I believe my father would have been one of the right men if he'd taken to it early enough. But I'm not. It would suffocate me to live down here all my life—even going away a good deal, as I should— amongst all the people who think themselves so broad-minded and are really so narrow."

"Well, I've lived amongst them all my life," she said, "and I don't believe they are more narrow than others. I think it is the happiest life there is, to live most of your time quietly in the country, and do the work and take the pleasures that lie close to your door."

"I like to think of your doing that. It seems to suit you. When I go away from Kemsale I shall often think of you living here in this pretty place—so much nicer than Kemsale is now, in the way we have spoilt it with our money. Ah, if Kemsale had been what it was before! If it could have gone on somehow with no change, I don't think I should have wanted to leave it. When I first came down, your influence seemed to be over it all, though the changes were beginning to be made then. I loved it; it was something that I had never known before. But we seem to have rubbed it all off now—all the romance of it. I don't know that we're more vulgar than other people of our sort, but we do seem to have vulgarised Kemsale. It can never be again what it was when you lived there."

She was a little abashed by his speech, and did not quite understand it. But she recognised him for a young man of originality, who could say things that other people would not say. It was difficult to answer him. She thought of him and Katie both as quite unspoilt by their upbringing, but she did also think that Mrs. Brown had vulgarised Kemsale, and she could not commend them without criticising her.

" It is kind of you to think of me like that," she said. " I am a little part of Kemsale still, and if it is any pleasure to you to know it I am much happier living here with you as neighbours than I had thought at first that I could possibly be—with any new neighbours, I mean, at Kemsale. So you see, the way it all seems to strike you doesn't strike me."

" Well, how does it strike you exactly? You can't help seeing that we're different from the people in all the other country houses. I don't mind being different, you know. What I hate is to be in a place where one isn't allowed to be."

" It doesn't strike me that you are so very different. We're not all cut after the same pattern, as you seem to think. I don't believe you do think it really. There's as much room for your tastes in the country as for anybody else's. And some of your tastes are the same as those of all the rest of us—more of them than you're inclined to admit just at present. I will tell you what I think about you, as we're friends, and I may speak my mind. The life you have been living has been delightful to you while you have been quite young. But it couldn't go on in exactly the same way; you wouldn't be satisfied with it. It is not as if you were preparing yourself to be a great artist; you have only taken the amusing parts of an artist's life, just as other young men take to other amusements before they settle down to the life prepared for them; or as my cousin Dick Clinton, for instance, took to soldiering for a time, not as a serious profession. You've had your fun out of it all, but it would be wasting yourself to go on with it much longer. We all have something to do in the world. I think your duty plainly lies here, as your father wishes it; and you couldn't get rid of Kemsale if you wanted to."

He sat silent for some time. Then he said: "It all comes back in the long run to the money. Money is a dreadful tyrant. You work for it as my father does, and it isn't like working for other things which are satisfying in themselves. When you have worked to make it, if you have made so much that it is beyond anything a man can want, you have to work to use it; or it mocks you. He sees that, as he sees most things; but he has the genius for making it, not for using it. Whatever he tried to do with his money he would make more of it. He couldn't help himself. This scheme of his that he has started here—no doubt it will benefit the estate, and the people on it, but the end for him will be that he will make money out of it; it wouldn't be his scheme if he didn't."

"He told me that he didn't want to make much money out of it—a fair return on his capital he said. It was for the benefit of the estate and the people chiefly. I think that is just right. It is what landholding has always been at its best. The Clintons think it is right, and they say—or Dick says—that it is a good thing to get new blood and new ideas into it."

" But don't you see that he's got beyond the point at
which he can satisfy himself with working for those objects?
The stakes aren't high enough. He's as little of a gambler
as anybody. I don't believe he has ever won or lost a
penny on cards or horses, and I know enough of his business to see that there is as little speculation in it as possible. It's all sheer knowledge and calculation. But the
stakes have got to be high all the same. That's why
he's going back to the City now. No, it's I who have
to bear the burden of all the wealth he's rolling up; and
I'm not fit for it. It oppresses me. I can't leave it lying
idle any more than he can. I've got that much of his
blood in me."

" There are so many ways of using money to benefit
the world."

" Are there? I've often thought of that. The people
who give away enormous sums don't seem to me to make
much of a hand of it. I think it's enormously difficult to
find a way, when you have to dispose of a great overplus."

" I suppose it is only of late years that individual men
have become so rich that they have to dispose of millions
by giving them away. It used to be easier. Men were
rich because of their land, and their land gave them all
that they wanted. Now rich men turn their money into
land, and gain new opportunities. I think that is the best
way. I think that is the way marked out for you at
Kemsale."

" It looks like it," he said. " I'm afraid so."

CHAPTER XXX

HELP IN TROUBLE

WHEN Meadshire and Katie had left the terrace, Meadshire said: " There's very little to see in the garden now. We'll walk up to the heronry. The fact is I want to get away from your brother. He's in a devilish irritable mood, and I don't want to quarrel with him for your sake, little Miss Brown."

She made no reply. She was thinking how she should open what she had to say to him.

" What's the matter with you both? " he asked her. " I can't say that *you* are irritable, for you never are; but you're not very cheerful."

" No, I'm not," she said. " I'm very miserable."

" Poor little girl! Why are you miserable? Tell me about it."

" I'm miserable about you."

The dark look which had lifted from his face returned to it. " You needn't worry about me," he said.

" How can I help it? You know how I love Grace, and she's as unhappy as she can be. She sees what is happening, and she feels that she can't help you. She thinks I can. Oh, I wish you'd let me. You have let me talk to you about it before. Can't you talk to me now? "

He turned round on her suddenly and glared at her. She stopped, and looked up in his face, half frightened, but plucking at her courage. " Can't you see I'm making a fight? " he asked gruffly, and then turned and went on again.

She was conscious of a great sense of relief. The ice was broken; she could talk to him now. " Oh, I know you are," she said, " and I'm so glad. It isn't only for Grace's sake. It's for your own, too. You know how I want to help you, if I only can. It will help you to talk about it, won't it? If one is fighting against something, it does help when your friends know it, and are thinking of you all the time."

They had come to a broader part of the path, where there was a seat facing a gap in the pines, through which the sun shone. He sat down heavily, and she stood by him looking down upon his face, which was in pain.

" I've never fought against it so hard before," he said. " I've never fought at all, except a little, last year. I'm going through hell, little girl."

He looked up at her with a glance half-whimsical, but looked down again immediately, his face reverting to its expression of dark struggle. But there was something in the glance that pierced her through and through. She sat down beside him and her breath caught in a sob. " Oh, I wish I could help you," she cried. " I wish I could bear it for you."

His face cleared a little. " You have helped me, my dear," he said. " At least, it's because of you I'm putting up a fight. If you hadn't shown me that you thought I could—and hoped I would—— But it's too much for me. Ten years ago, perhaps, I might have won through. It's too late now. I shall fight as long as I can; then I shall have to give way."

" Oh, no. You mustn't say that. You *can* struggle through if you make up your mind."

He smiled at her again. " You don't know what it is," he said. " Nobody can, unless they feel it themselves. It comes and goes. At it's worst you can hold out, unless the stuff is actually there, and then when the craving dies down a little there's another sort of impulse pushing you on. I can't explain it, but it's stronger than the other. It's like your will turning traitor on you. When I do give way this time, it probably won't be when the craving is on me. I shall do it deliberately when I needn't—physically. I shall go dead against what I want, and I shan't be able to help myself."

"Oh, but you mustn't talk as if you were going to give way. If you have held out so long—surely it passes, doesn't it? It is months since you had any desire to give way. It can't last forever."

"I don't know how long it can last. It seems to me now that it will last till I do give way. I only know that I can't hold out much longer. My will is slipping away from me. I seem to be caught in a net. I've reached that stage where there seems no reason for holding out. You'd better forget all about me, little girl. I'm past caring for. I shan't risk it coming on here again. I shall go away, when I know I'm in for it. You needn't know of it any more. When I'm down here I shall be all right, and we can be friends, as we've always been."

She wanted to cry, but held back the tears, and put all the strength of her clear firm mind into her determination to stiffen his resistance. "If you think of yourself like that," she said, "of course you won't hold out. I don't understand all about it, but I *know* that it can't be necessary for you to give way. There must be things you can do."

"There are said to be cures. I don't believe in them much, and if I did I don't think I'd try them. The only reason I should want to get the better of myself would be because somebody believed in me—or wanted to. Grace—and you too. Oh, you've put a little bit of your pluck

into me. I'm more of a man now for holding out as long
as I have, even if I can't hold out much longer. If one
put one's faith in a medical cure, and ran to it every time
one had need—well, I don't see that it would be much
better than running to the other thing. One would be
no better in one's self."

"Oh, yes, I see that," she cried. "It's yourself you
must conquer. But I didn't mean that sort of cure. Perhaps there is no actual cure and you would have to fight
always. But I believe if you fought and won, the times
when you would have to fight would get less, and the
fight would be less hard every time. When you talk about
it—when you talk to me—doesn't that help you? It isn't
strong enough to make you want to go away now, and
leave me—for it?"

"No. At this very moment I've no actual craving. I'm
not sure that the worst of that isn't over. I wouldn't let
Grace have only water on the table at lunch, but I didn't
mind drinking only water myself."

"Oh, then, I do hope you are getting over it this time.
Perhaps you will only have to struggle on a little further
to be free again. And then you will feel ever so much
stronger, having got over the desire."

"Yes, but I've tried to tell you that that isn't the worst
danger. The struggle plays the devil with your will—
seems to turn it all topsy-turvy. When you want it most
it's there, and when it seems to be wanted less, you find
it gone altogether."

"That is where a friend ought to be able to help you.
If your own will is damaged for a time, you ought to
be able to depend upon another will."

"If the friend were always there! That's the trouble,
little Miss Brown. It's when one is by one's self that
the perverse devil gets hold of one. Well, it's on the

knees of the gods. What will be will be. We needn't
spoil this lovely afternoon, anyhow, by dreading what's
going to happen. Let's go up across the hill. Perhaps
a long walk will do me good. And at least I'm safe
while I'm with you."

He took her assent for granted and started off up the
rocky path. She followed him. She had made up her
mind now what she was going to do. It was not easy
to do it, with his back towards her, and both of them
walking fast, but it was not easy to do it anyhow, and
the additional discomfort would not deter her.

" If you'll let me, I'll always be with you to help you."

He didn't catch what she had said, and called out a
question over his shoulder.

" Please stop," she said. " I have something to say
to you."

He stopped and faced her. Her face was pale and
her eyes were on the ground, but she raised them to his,
and spoke in a clear voice. " Let me stay with you always
and help you," she said. " I know I can."

His face grew wonderfully soft. He put his hand on
her shoulder. " You're a dear good little girl," he said.
" You've done me an honour that I shall never forget.
By Jove, I will see it through this time, for your sake.
But you shan't sacrifice yourself for me, my dear. Come,
we'll go and sit down again, and talk."

They went back to the seat, and she said in a voice
that trembled a little: " It wouldn't be sacrificing myself.
It would make me happy to know that I was helping
you through the bad times. I should feel that I was
helping to save your soul for you. It isn't given to many
women to do that for a man."

He took her hand in his. " Supposing it went wrong,
my dear! " he said. " At first it wouldn't go wrong. But

afterwards—when we had become more used to one another! I'm not altogether a brute. I should be very
grateful to you—always—even when the bad times came
on me; but I'm grateful to Grace, and it doesn't prevent
me from showing myself a brute to her. I daren't risk
it, Katie."

"I would risk it," she said. "I'm not afraid."

"I know you're not. You're the bravest, best little
soul in the world. And you'd never reproach me, whatever I did. You'd stick to me through thick and thin.
Perhaps you might save my soul for me, as you say. I
should have to be a lot worse than I am if I didn't fight
tooth and nail against myself for your sake, even when
it didn't seem worth doing for my own. Oh, we'd make
a great fight of it, together. Perhaps we should win.
It's a great temptation, Katie. But I'm not fit for you,
my dear. I'm too old. I've played the fool with myself
and my chances too long—not only in that way, but in
every way. I've nothing to offer you in return for all
you'd do for me. If I'd known you ten years ago—but
you were a child then, and I was already a blackguard
and a waster. No, my dear, it isn't to be thought of."

It was she who felt weak now. She had offered herself
to him, but she could not plead with him to take her.
She could only show him how ready she was to give herself; and that was difficult.

"I don't want you to think of me," she said; "I mean,
I don't want you to think for me. I've done all that; if
I hadn't thought it all out again and again, and made up
my mind, I shouldn't have dared to say what I have. I
said it because I thought you wouldn't; and yet I thought
that you would want me, if you knew I was ready to
come to you."

A feeling towards her that he had not had before was

creeping into his mind. He had thought of her cool loyal strength as something to lean on, as a refuge from himself; she could be like a kind devoted little sister towards him—like another sister, stronger and more resourceful than Grace. And he was fond of her, and liked her as a companion; it would not be irksome to be tied to her for life. They would get on very well together. But now he was beginning to see her as a woman whom he might desire for a bride. She had shown tenderness, not merely kindness and courage. She had no beauty except the freshness of her youth, and the beauty that shone through her from her fine true nature; but that was more than enough to make a man desire her for a mate. It made it harder for him to stand out against her; but he was determined to stand out.

He still held her hand in his. "Don't think I don't want you," he said. "God knows I do. If I could think only of myself, it wouldn't have been left to you to speak, as I love and honour you for speaking; I should have asked you long ago. But it's the one thing in all my rotten life that I've put away from me. From the first, I've said to myself that a man like me had no right to marry and share his disgrace with others. It's true I never thought of any one like you, who knew the worst about me and was ready to share it and to mend it. If I'd known you when I was young, Katie, I think I'd have let you risk it for me. I can't let you now, my dear. You don't know the risk. I'm not fit for you. I should be more of a blackguard than I am if I spoilt your youth and goodness in that way."

She was crying softly, but left her hand in his, and made no attempt to wipe away the tears. "You're not a blackguard," she said. "If I didn't know that, I might want to help for Grace's sake, and a little for your own, because we're friends; but I shouldn't have said what I have to you. I know of your faults, but I know what you are beneath them."

" Ah, but you don't know. How can a young girl, good and innocent like you, know all that there is in the life of a man so much older, who has done what he pleased, never held himself in, thought of nobody but himself and his own gratification? "

" I know that there is much that I can't know. But I look behind all that. I don't fear it. Love casteth out fear—such fear as that."

He was profoundly moved by the word. Yes, it was love that she was offering him—the noblest kind of love, which thinks no evil. Might he not take the great gift, and be healed and raised by it?

If he could give love in return! That would balance the account, weighed down so heavily by his sins as against her purity.

They sat for a long time in silence. Her hand rested in his, as a token of her quiet and willing surrender. Its touch.soothed his troubled spirit, and whatever there was in his thoughts that lay outside the great fact of her love for him, and her readiness to share with him the burden of himself, was swept away.

He turned to her and took her face between his two hands and looked into her eyes. Then he kissed her very gently on the forehead, but said nothing. She did not know, when they walked on together, nor when they parted, whether he had accepted her offer of herself or not.

CHAPTER XXXI

AN ENGAGEMENT

IT was the morning after the ball at Kemsale. Frank
Clinton was closeted with Mr. Sheard in his room where
the picture of the clipper sailing-ship *Orion* hung amongst
the dull-bound books on theology and Biblical study.

Mr. Sheard's face was serious. " I can't say this has
come upon me as a surprise altogether," he was saying.
" But I'll admit that I didn't think it was coming so
quickly, if it was coming at all."

" Well, you can't have expected that it wouldn't come
to Anne sooner or later," said the young man.

He looked confident and happy. It is to be supposed
that his happiness was so gloriously new to him that an
interview which most young men in his case look upon
as a necessary but irksome interruption to more pleasant
interviews was not even irksome. He could talk about
Anne and take a delight in the open recognition of his
love for her.

" Sooner or later, yes. But aren't there some difficulties
in the way, Mr. Clinton, that we have to consider? "

He raised his honest eyes to Frank's face. They held
nothing but liking for him, as he sat there handsome and
strong, with the glow of his happiness on his face. If he
must lose his little daughter he could not wish that a more
proper man than this should take her from him—other
considerations apart.

" What difficulties? " Frank asked.

388

"Does your father know of your wish? Would he approve of your marrying a daughter of mine?"

Frank's face fell a little. "My father has had a sort of idea that I wanted to marry somebody else," he said. "I've given him no grounds for it; in fact, I've taken some little pains to make him see which quarter the wind was in. But he hasn't seen it before last night, and at present he's suffering from disappointment. It won't last long when he knows Anne."

"Well, it's natural that you should think that. I shouldn't like you to think otherwise. But there are questions which young people in your state of mind can't be expected to give much weight to, and they are just those that parents have to think of most. Let's be honest about it—you and I. Isn't your father, being what he is, likely to object very strongly to your marrying a daughter of mine? You needn't be afraid of answering. You won't hurt my feelings. I'm what I am, and I'm not ashamed of it. I *should* be ashamed of myself if I pretended to be something else—something like your father, for instance."

"If you want a perfectly plain answer, I don't know how my father is likely to take it, when he has got over his disappointment. He won't hear about it now, and that's the truth. But it doesn't follow that he won't do everything that's wanted of him when he gets used to the idea. He's like that. You know my brother Dick's wife. Well, he nearly disinherited Dick, as far as he could, because he insisted on marrying her. They didn't meet for nearly a year—Dick and he—and Dick gave up the Service and took a job till he came round. Now he thinks there's nobody like Dick's wife. I don't suppose he'd act in the same way again. He's had his lesson, and there's a lot more sense in him than you'd sometimes suppose from his way of talking."

Mr. Sheard may have been somewhat surprised at this very outspoken summing-up of a father by a son, but he did not show it. " I don't know anything about the circumstances of your brother's marriage," he said. " But I've been told that his wife was a lady of title before he married her. Your father's objections to her can't have been the same as they might be towards my little Anne."

" She was the widow of a fellow with a title. That's all. She wasn't of the sort that he expected his eldest son to marry. He didn't know her, mind you. When he did, he came right round. You see, he's lived tied down to Kencote for the whole of his life. He can't forget he's a big man in this little corner of the world, and that our family has been here for hundreds of years. Perhaps it's all more important to him than it ought to be."

" Well, Mr. Clinton, I've no fault to find with a man who prides himself on his birth and his position, as long as it leads him in the paths of honour. And I can't say that I think it's wrong for him to wish that his children should marry into families something like his own. That's his side of it. But we've got our side too, you know—we people without birth or wealth. As far as you're concerned you've put that aside. I'm not ashamed to say that you do us honour by treating us as equals. If Anne marries you she marries into a family that's a good deal above her own, and I don't pretend it wouldn't be a gratification to us, if it could be happily brought about. But we have our proper pride as well as those above us. It wouldn't be for us to aim at such a marriage for our daughter. If what we are, and what she is, is enough,

on both sides, no one's pride suffers. But if it isn't, then
my objections would be as strong as your father's, and
they would come from the same source."

"You mean that ——"

"I mean that before I consent to a marriage between
you and Anne, your father must consent to it. It's for
him to take the first step, because it's for him to waive
the difference between us, not for me."

Frank was conscious of a drop in his happy confidence.
He knew enough of the man before him to recognise that
he said nothing that he did not mean, or was not prepared
to act on. "I'm long since of age, you know," he said.
"And I'm not dependent on my father altogether, though
I should expect him to make provision for me when I
married."

"But Anne isn't of age. In any case, I shouldn't want
her to marry until some little time had elapsed; but we're
not ready to talk of that yet. And I say nothing of provision for marriage. My ideas of a suitable provision
would probably be different from yours; they would certainly be very different from your father's. I married
on a hundred and fifty a year, and I should let Anne do
the same, if I trusted the man who married her. I should
trust you; we needn't talk about that side of it at all.
She'd go to you with nothing; she'd be one with you,
whether you were rich or poor; you'd work it out together. I sometimes think that the start in life of a young
couple amongst the people I belong to—where they take
their risks together—is a happier thing than what you are
accustomed to in your circles, where all is made easy for
them from the beginning. But that's going too far at
present, too. I just say it, so as to make it quite plain
that I'm asking for nothing for Anne, except that she
shall be received as a daughter in your father's house.

That I have a right to ask for her, and I can't give my consent without it."

"Yes," said Frank slowly, "you have every right to ask for that; and I shouldn't be satisfied for her without it. I wish I could take her over to get it now. She'd get it from my mother, and my sisters—I think from every one except my father. And she'll get it from him by and by. Perhaps I ought to have made more certain of him before I came to see you, before I spoke to Anne. I don't like to think I can't take her to my home, proud as I am of her."

"Well, it's one of the little complications that come from the differences we've been talking about. I shan't allow it to vex me, and if I were you, I shouldn't take it too much to heart. Little Anne won't, I know, as long as she's sure of you."

"Then you don't forbid me to see her, until I've settled up with my father, or to write to her?"

"Oh, no. It's you I'm ready to give her to, and I'll give her to you gladly when the time comes. If it doesn't come before, it will come when she's of age, and can choose for herself. I shouldn't consider I had the right then to stand on my pride. I'm afraid that's what it comes to now, but I think I'm right to do it."

As Frank rode home that afternoon, with Anne's kisses warm on his lips, he asked himself whether he was not better off in having found her where she was, than if she had been of some great house, kept and guarded from him until all the tiresome side-issues of betrothal had been settled for them. Their love for one another was so fresh and still so wonderful that it was enough for them at present to spend those blissful hours together, to feed on them in memory, to look forward with keenest delight to letters, when they should be parted, and to

meeting again; always with the bright hope before them
of a time when they should be together for always. A
long engagement! It was a more common experience
amongst Anne's people than amongst his. Lovers' inter-
course was founded on it; their freedom was not affected
by difficulties in the way of an early marriage, and if
those difficulties were not as a rule of the same kind as
the difficulties that confronted him, still, Anne's parents
had treated them in the same way—as presenting no
obstacle to a complete understanding between him and
her. Within due limits their affair was their own. They
might not marry till the way was clear, but they were
not forbidden to be happy in their love for one another,
or to plight their troth, as if the obstacles would never
be overcome.

Frank had found it difficult at first to talk to Anne of
what had happened since he had parted from her the
night before. He was so afraid of hurting her, so ashamed
of having to make her understand that he had not yet
been able to make a welcome for her in his home. But she
was so young, and so shy with everybody but him—and
with him she was adorably shy, but in another manner—
that she rather dreaded having to face his people at
Kencote, and it was an actual relief to her not to have
to do so while the wonderful thing that had happened
to her was still so new, and what should come of it was
hardly yet in her thoughts. She wanted no one but him
at present; she liked to feel that she was "engaged";
but marriage was a long way off yet. They would come
to that slowly, after long happy months, perhaps after
years. It didn't matter now how long it would be, since
Frank was hers to love and to think about, and had promised to write to her every day.

So his task was easy, after all, and he had to thank

the ideas to which Anne had been brought up for it; or rather the ideas to which she had not been brought up. His father was not ready yet to sanction their marriage. Anne saw nothing much to trouble her in that, though she was a little surprised that Frank said nothing about his sanctioning their engagement, which to her was quite a different thing. But she saw that in respect of the sanction it was to be considered the same thing, by the way Frank spoke of it, and she was quite prepared to leave it to him to remove the difficulties, all in good time. He found that it was not necessary to explain to her what they were. In his relief he made some slight sacrifice of filial affection. Anne was left with a vague idea that the Squire was rather a tiresome old gentleman who would come round all in good time, and she displayed much more interest in whether Mrs. Clinton would love her, and whether Frank's sisters wouldn't be too " grand " for her. He was able to reassure her on both these points, from his own convictions on them, but it was represented to her that until his father " came round " there might be some difficulty in their all coming together happily. He had left her a little sad, but more because he was going away the next day and did not know when he should next be able to secure a leave, than because of what he had told her about Kencote. She would wait for him, in her happy home-nest, and dwell on her thoughts of him there. She was not ready to leave it yet; it mattered little that the doors of Kencote were not yet open to her.

There was an agreeable surprise waiting for Frank when he reached home. Joan and her husband had arrived, on their way from one country house to another. Or rather, as one country house was in Norfolk and the other in Hampshire, and they had had to pass through London, they had filched a day from the second of their visits, and turned aside into Meadshire. It was a source of gratification to the Squire that Joan had made so many opportunities of coming to Kencote, and that her young husband was always ready to accompany her, if the numerous calls on him permitted him to do so. Although the Squire considered himself " as good as anybody," because of his ancient birth, and the wealth that enabled him to support it in honour, and had had his taste of social eminence in his youth, he had lived his retired life at Kencote for so long that visits from members of the most exalted aristocracy, to which young Inverell belonged, were not quite like other visits to him. Viewed as a country gentleman, living in comparatively simple style in his large house all the year round, he was in fact rather more outside the orbit of his daughter and son-in-law than the Sheards were outside his. Frank thought he might draw advantage to himself out of this timely visit.

Joan was considered to be rather spoilt when she came to Kencote, but all her demands were based upon her love for her childhood's home, and gave pleasure to her parents as well as to herself. One of these was that she was always to have the old schoolroom, now disused, as her special sitting-room, and one of the first things that had been done on the receipt of the heralding telegram was to prepare it for her use. So it was as they sat together on the old sofa, covered with faded chintz, in front of the schoolroom fire, with no one to disturb them, that Frank told Joan of his love and of the difficulties in the way of his marriage.

" I think she's a darling," said Joan, looking at Anne's photograph. " Dear old Frank, I'm so glad. I was beginning to think you'd be left, out of us all. Really, she's awfully sweet. I'm sure I shall love her."

"She's ever so much prettier than that," said Frank, and Joan laughed at him, and gave him a sisterly hug.

"I wonder if I should have time to go over and see her to-morrow before we go," she said. "If father is tiresome about it, it might soften it down a bit for her. I know how much I felt it before it was all made right for me and Ronald. I'll tell you what I'll do—I'll say I must go over and see Grace. Then I'll go there on my way. I'll take Ronald too. He'll come if I tell him why. I never feel of much importance when I come back to Kencote; but Ronald's different."

"You're a good girl, Joan. I thought you'd take it like this, but I wasn't quite certain."

"Why, how did you suppose I'd take it? Whoever you married I should try to love her, if she'd let me. And it oughtn't to be difficult with a sweet thing like that. Let me look at her again, Frank, if you can spare her. Yes, she's a real lamb, as Nancy and I used to say."

"Well, Joan, it's no use keeping things back. I don't think you quite understand how it is, though I've tried to tell you. It's difficult, because whatever I say about her people it looks as if I were running them down, and I like them too much for that, especially her father. I should like and respect him if there were no question of her at all. It's natural that you should think of them as ordinary rectory people, and father unreasonable to object. But they're not quite like that."

"Oh, but I know, dear Frank. I was here when Uncle Tom came and told us about them, in the spring—when he first knew that Mr. Sheard was going to Kemsale."

"Yes, of course you were. I'd forgotten that. He told us that Sheard had been a curate at Melbury Park, and I think he said he had been a mate on a merchant ship before that. Well, he was the skipper of a crack sailing craft, as a matter of fact; but that doesn't make much difference. He's a very fine fellow—simple and honest and good right through; if you said that he wasn't a gentleman you'd feel ashamed of yourself when you once came to know him; but with the ordinary meaning that people like us give to the word, that's what it amounts to, and that's all that father can see. It doesn't affect Anne. I'm quite sure it doesn't. I've had my eyes and my ears open. I couldn't very well help it, under the circumstances. She's just what you'd want her to be, wherever you put her. I think you'd be rather surprised if you saw her mother, after you'd seen her. She's a dear kind soul, as good as gold. If she weren't, I suppose Anne wouldn't be what she is, as she's always lived at home. But there's no getting over it that she'd be out of place dining here, for instance. Oh, it seems beastly to say such things of Anne's mother, and I do like her, and can get on with her, though she's not equal to her husband. You see, Joan, I'm not quite like the rest of you. You've always lived amongst people of our own sort, and you're inclined to think that they're the only ones in the world— at least, father is. But one meets all sorts in the Navy, and knocking about the world as I've done. You don't think so much of position and all that sort of thing. You take people for what they are in themselves. I tell you honestly that I like being with people like the Sheards, when they're as straight as they are, better than with most people of our own sort. They've got their job to do, and it's what they're thinking about. They're more serious than us, but it's the right kind of seriousness and doesn't make them less cheerful. And their lives are much simpler. I've come to like that rather, too."

"You know," said Joan, after a slight pause, " I think we've all got something to thank father for in that way.

I was talking to Nancy about it the other day. I suppose you couldn't call our life here simple exactly in the way that you mean. There's a lot spent on it; father has always lived like a rich man, and you boys, especially, were brought up to have everything that other rich men's sons have—all the healthy things, I mean. But still, the life at Kencote is simple compared to that of most other houses one goes to. It's why I like coming back to it; and Ronald likes it too. When you live as we do, and see so many people who think of nothing but spending money and amusing themselves from morning till night, you have to take hold of yourself a little, and say that you're not going to make amusement the chief end of your life. Perhaps we owe more to darling mother than we do to father —we girls, I mean—but, in spite of all his funny little ways of looking at things, he has stuck to his simple old-fashioned manner of living. We used to grumble at being dull here sometimes, but we love to think of it all now, and to come back to it."

"Well, I haven't had as much experience of the other sort of life as you have. I dare say you're right though, and compared with that this is quiet, and perhaps dull. But it seems to me pretty complicated. When I went to stay with Humphrey in Australia, we took a trip out west and stayed for a week with a pal of his. There wasn't a servant within miles, and we did every mortal thing for ourselves. Humphrey said it was the only life worth living, and he hadn't a care in the world; and you know what Humphrey used to be—couldn't shift a yard without his man, and would have thought that a fellow who didn't dress for dinner every night was beyond the pale altogether."

"Humphrey had the right stuff in him all along, and now it has come out. Father was always against his

extravagance, and his fashionableness, when he was young
—poor Humphrey!"

"He was against a lot of things. I suppose he has
always had his fixed ideas, and they're not those of the
smart world. But they don't help me much now. He's
just as much against the far greater simplicity of people
like the Sheards as he is against the extravagance on the
other side."

"But it isn't because they live simply that he's against
them."

"Oh, well, we know why he's against them. They're
not good enough for him. But I say it is really because
of their simplicity. Their ways are different from ours.
That's all there is to it. He doesn't know what good
people they all are. He doesn't want to know; that
doesn't count."

A gong boomed through the house. It was the second
that had sounded, and denoted that half the time appointed
for dressing had passed away. Joan sprang up. "I really
must go," she said. "Dear Frank, it will come all right
in the end. I am going to see to it for you. I believe I
know father better than you do."

CHAPTER XXXII

THE SYNDICATE

THE Irvings were sitting at breakfast. The happy month of June had come round again. June was a glorious month at Little Kemsale because of the roses, which were the Irvings' specialty. Neither of them liked to be away for a night while the roses were in their full glory. There was a great bowl of them on the breakfast-table, and another on the sideboard. The room was scented with them. And new beds had been dug the previous autumn along the lawn in front of the house. These were filled with the newer varieties, and the first thing to be done every morning was to go and see what new treasure had unfolded itself during the night.

But during this May and June Douglas had been a good deal in London, running up one day and coming back on the next or the day after to his roses. He had gone up on business. He was in a big affair with Armitage Brown, he told Beatrix, and he had been able to do Bill Bradgate a good turn, and put business in his way. Things were developing extraordinarily well, but there were all sorts of difficulties to be overcome one by one. Armitage Brown had been working steadily at them for the last six months. It was wonderful what a genius he had for getting things through; Douglas could see now that there was a good deal in that definition of genius being an infinite capacity for taking pains, or whatever the phrase was. Armitage Brown brought his mind to bear upon each tiny detail, and left nothing to chance. He was really a wonderful fellow, and it was an extraordinary piece of luck being allowed to go into a thing with him.

He talked a great deal to Beatrix in this fashion, but gave her no details of the scheme. He wasn't allowed to say a word about it yet, and she wouldn't understand it if he did. She must be careful not so much as to mention outside that there was anything on, or that he went up to London to see Armitage Brown.

As a matter of fact, his visits to London were not quite the important affairs that Beatrix imagined them to be. He would go to Bradgate's office in the City, to find out what was going on. Sometimes Bradgate had a little piece of news for him, sometimes nothing whatever had happened, and he had not had word with the financier since Douglas had last been up. Bradgate, indeed, had little to do with it at this stage, though he expected it to bring grist to the mill later on. But he was kept informed from time to time of the broad aspects of the affair, and the progress that had been made, and it was actually from him that Douglas got all his information. He got none at all from Armitage Brown. He would call in at his office, and sometimes he would be admitted, but not always. There would be a word or two about Kemsale; Douglas generally prepared himself with something to say about the game, which he now looked after entirely. Then Armitage Brown would say: " Well, I'm very glad to see you, but I'm frightfully busy. I may be down on Sunday; if not, give me a look in the next time you're up. I like to hear what's going on." So the door was kept ajar; but the only time he had ventured to ask a question about the great scheme, Armitage Brown had said: " Oh, that's going on all right. I haven't forgotten that you want to take a hand. When I'm ready for you I'll let you know."

Then Douglas would go to his club and play bridge

after luncheon, until it was time to go home. Sometimes he would stay up for the night and go to a play. And once he dined with the Browns in Berkeley Square, filling a place at the last moment in one of Mrs. Brown's big parties. But he had scarcely a word with his host.

They were talking of the Browns now, over the breakfast-table. Kemsale had been shut up since the beginning of the year. Armitage Brown had spent some of his Sundays there, sometimes alone, sometimes with his brother and sister-in-law. Neither Mrs. Brown nor Katie nor Alfred had been down, and there was no immediate prospect of their coming. Rumour was rife as to the reason.

" They're not much good to us after all," said Douglas. " I did think Alfred was going to stick to the place."

" Grace thought so too," said Beatrix. " He talked to her about it just before he went away. I'm afraid he's rather a harum-scarum creature. He's very nice, though. So is poor little Katie. Douglas, I wonder if it's true about her and Lord Meadshire."

" I'm pretty certain of it. Why should she have been hurried off like that, all of a sudden. We know that Mrs. Brown hadn't been meaning to go for another day or two. And she never came to say good-bye."

" She wrote though; and said she hoped to see me when they came back from the Riviera. She never has come back."

" Well, I don't know that she hasn't. Mrs. Brown said she was at Venice with Alfred a month ago. She wasn't inclined to be communicative. I'm afraid the poor little thing's in disgrace. I think it's a beastly shame of Meadshire to make up to her. I suppose she got carried off her feet. You can't think that a nice little thing like that, and as young as she is, would really want to marry a

fellow like Meadshire. However, I suppose she fancied
herself as a marchioness, and——"

"Oh no, Douglas. I don't believe she'd care a bit
about that. She's not like her mother."

"Well, her mother doesn't seem to have cared about
the idea. Or perhaps it was Armitage Brown who put
his foot down. He looked pretty glum after Mrs. Brown
had whipped her off. So did Alfred. He hates Meadshire."

"He did at first. I don't think he did after they all
made friends together."

"He did at the end. He said so. I expect what happened was that he'd heard about his trying to get hold
of Katie. He was very strong on people being after
them for the sake of their money. Of course that's what
Meadshire wanted. I don't blame Armitage Brown for
turning him off with a flea in his ear."

"You don't know that he did that."

"I can guess. Meadshire was furious with him, before
he went off; and when I mentioned Meadshire's name to
Brown he looked as black as thunder."

"I do feel most awfully sorry for Grace. She thought
he was getting over his bad habits at last, and had settled
down quietly here. Now he's worse than ever—drinking and spending money again; and never comes near
her."

"Oh, he's a rotter. Can't help it, poor fellow. The
best thing that could happen for everybody would be for
him to drink himself into his grave. He'll never be any
good now. I wonder that he managed to keep himself
steady here for so long. I suppose he knew he wouldn't
have a chance for Katie if he didn't."

"If it's true that he wanted to marry Katie, I expect
he proposed to her on the night of the Kemsale ball. So
did Frank Clinton to Anne Sheard, and young Davis to

Irene Fuller, and there have been difficulties about all three proposals."

Douglas laughed. "Tottie's rage!" he said. "I can't help laughing whenever I think of it. Of course it's a very good match for Irene. She's turned out to be much more sensible than her mother. But poor Tottie! And she'd quite made up her mind that she'd caught Alfred for Irene. Really, Bee, if you were to put that woman———"

"Into a book, nobody would believe she could be true," Beatrix finished the sentence for him. "That's one to me, and wipes off yesterday's."

"I wasn't going to say that at all."

"What were you going to say?"

"Never you mind."

"Oh, you're not playing fair. But Tottie has come round now. I didn't tell you; I met her yesterday, and she told me that she'd decided to make the best of a bad job. She talked a lot about Point Manor; Points Farm is going to be dropped entirely. And it seems that the Davises are, after all, a rather aristocratic family. One of them married a baronet, about a hundred years ago I think it was, and they've been 'seated' at Points Manor for two hundred years."

"She's a record, isn't she? Never disappoints expectation. What did she say about the Browns? Everybody knows Mrs. Brown gives her the cold shoulder now."

"Oh, they are hopelessly vulgar, in spite of their money. But I wasn't to say she said so, for goodness' sake. People in their position had to serve people of all sorts, and keep in with them to a certain extent, but for the future she thought that she should let Herbert bear the brunt of it. She'd done her best to make a friend of Mrs. Brown, and put her up to things, but she got little thanks for it, and she should leave her to take her own way for the future, and make all the mistakes she was liable to."

"Bursting with spite! I wonder if she really thinks she deceives a living soul by talking like that. She's jolly lucky to have the Browns at her silly back. Little Herbert has been treated remarkably well. He might quite easily have been sacked, at his age, and he wouldn't have got another job; but he's making more than he did before. I must say Armitage Brown is a generous fellow when he likes anybody; and he doesn't buck about it either. I bet you what you like he paid little Herbert a premium to take young William Sheard into the office and teach him his job."

"Do you think he did? I don't believe Mr. Sheard would have allowed that. He's very independent."

"He wouldn't have known anything about it. He wouldn't know it was usual. He'd think that as it was Brown's office he had a right to put young William into it."

"He would, wouldn't he?"

"It wouldn't be usual. Fuller has to teach him his work. He'd have a right to a premium. Young William's doing very well. Did you ever see such a change in a fellow? It's just what he's suited for."

"All the Sheards are good workers. Isn't it funny, Douglas, what a success they've been? I wish Mr. Compton would come and pay us a visit, and see how it has turned out."

"I shall write to him directly it's fixed up between Frank Clinton and little Anne."

"If it ever is fixed up. Mr. Clinton won't hear of it at present, and he's an obstinate old gentleman."

"Oh, he won't hold out when they show they're in

earnest. There's nothing against the child. Frank doesn't want to marry her family."

" I like her family; they're so straight about things. They never try to disguise the fact that the Clintons are higher up in the world than they are, or blame Mr. Clinton for objecting."

" They allow Anne to consider herself engaged to Frank, though."

" Well, I rather like that, too. Mrs. Sheard told me how they felt about it. They think Anne is quite good enough for him, and they are not going to take a humble line about that. But they won't let her marry him till the Clintons think so too; and say so. And Mrs. Sheard believes in long engagements, and thinks Anne is too young to marry yet, anyhow. The idea is that they are to have a year's probation. So it really doesn't work out badly. Mr. Clinton ought to get used to the idea before the year is up. The rest of them are on Frank's side, and I expect they'll work it between them."

" I know Lady Inverell is. It was rather nice of her to go over and see the Sheards. But I doubt whether Dick Clinton is, and he has a good deal to say to things over at Kencote."

" Mrs. Dick has a great deal more to say, in the long run. She's rather amusing about it. She says that she thought she had got to the bottom of all British prejudices, but this beats her altogether."

" Well, I can't see that it's so unreasonable as that. Anne is a charming little creature, of course; any man might be proud to have her as his wife."

" That's just what Mrs. Dick says."

" But the Sheards—in a way—well, you know what I mean."

" Of course I do. You're British. So am I, I suppose.

But I do see a little what nonsense it all is; and of course to an American——"

The morning post, brought in at that moment, closed the conversation for the time being. There was a letter for Douglas, directed in a large firm hand, which he opened first.

"Good business!" he exclaimed, when he had read the few lines it contained.

Beatrix looked up from her own reading to see his face radiant with satisfaction.

"Dear old girl!" he said. "Our fortune's made. Armitage Brown has put it through. I'm to go up and see him as soon as possible. I'll go to-day. I can catch the eleven o'clock train."

"What does he say?" asked Beatrix.

He glanced at the letter, hesitated a moment and then handed it across the table to her.

"Dear Irving," it ran,

"I have secured the concession and arranged for the consolidation of all the properties. I understood you to say that you wished to take up shares in the preliminary Syndicate to the extent of £20,000. If you still wish this I shall want a cheque from you within a week from to-day, but I should like to know your decision at once, as there are others anxious to come in. Before deciding you had better come up here to have full details.

"Yours truly,
"Armitage Brown."

"Oh, but Douglas! Surely you are not going to risk twenty thousand pounds! Why, it is more than half that we have."

He had known that the protest would come, but felt

irritation at it none the less, which, however, he succeeded in keeping under.

"My dear girl, I don't know all the details of the business, but I know enough to say that it's an absolute certainty. It is one of the biggest things Armitage Brown has ever taken in hand; and as far as his work is concerned he has finished it. What it comes to is that he has bought something that he can sell again for anything up to ten times its value."

"But you can't possibly be certain of that, Douglas!"

She was greatly distressed. She had had no idea that he had been meaning to risk a very large sum of money in what looked to her like nothing but speculation, and said so, while he felt more and more impatient with her, but still carefully refrained from showing it.

"Well, dear," he said, "I suppose it's natural that you should think of it like that. And if I were to put in this money, or any money, into the company that will be formed when these preliminaries are put through, it *would* be a speculation, though a good one, I believe. But this really isn't. What do you think Armitage Brown is putting in himself?"

"Oh, I don't know. But——"

"Half a million. Five hundred thousand pounds; and he's the cleverest financier in London, perhaps in the world. Honestly, Bee, it's a real kindness on his part to let me go in with him at this stage. He wasn't a bit keen that I should. Good heavens! why, there are people tumbling over one another to get the chance that he's giving me. He only did it because he thought he owed me a good turn for looking after things here. I said I wouldn't take a salary from him, but he could put me in the next big thing he took up."

"Why didn't he want you to go in with him?"

" He said he didn't like to mix up business with friend-ship."

" Then he must have thought there was some risk."

" I'll tell you exactly what he said. I don't want to hide anything from you, my dear, and I suppose it's natural that you should think one risks money when one invests a great lump of it at once."

" Let's talk about it in the garden," she said. " I must just go up to the children, but I'll come down again in a quarter of an hour."

He saw that he should have to convince her fully, if he were to be able to go up to London later on with a clear mind. He thought over how he could put it very carefully, for he was absolutely convinced himself.

What Armitage Brown had said to him in answer to the request he had mentioned was: " I don't usually do that sort of thing, because if I want money for anything now I can always get it without any difficulty, and if any-thing goes wrong afterwards I'm not bothered by thinking I've let in my friends. But I have something coming on that seems to me to have practically no risk whatever if I can get it up to a certain point, and if you like to chance a thousand or so I'll make an exception for once, as you have been very good about lots of things down here."

There had followed certain explanations, but actually until this very day Douglas had never been told more than that it was a question of securing a concession from a foreign power, and buying up scattered properties of great value, for which a large sum of money would be required, but which could be put on to the market for an enormously large sum. He was given to understand that the difficulties lay in the securing of the concession, and in getting all the properties together. When this had been done practically everything would have been done. There would be some technical work to do which would take a few months, and then the members of the original Syndicate would receive their enormous profits. Bradgate knew a little more, but Bradgate was forbidden to open his mouth about what he knew, even to Douglas. All that he had been able to tell him during his visits to London was that details were being gradually overcome, and their talk had been chiefly of the companies that were to be formed later, and the profits that were likely to be made by the members of the Syndicate.

Douglas felt that this wanted a great deal of explaining, and he realised, as he thought it all over, that Bradgate, his particular friend, had been rather adroit with him, in keeping back so much, while being so ready to talk. At the same time he had never said anything to dissuade Douglas from taking his chance, and he had always advised him about his business affairs, and done well for him. That would be a point. Beatrix knew how careful old Bill was.

When Douglas had mentioned the sum that he wanted to use, Armitage Brown had demurred to it. It was then that he had let out what interest he was prepared to take himself. " I wouldn't risk a sum like that," he had said, " unless I was pretty certain of getting it back, with a good deal more besides. But if I were to lose even as large a sum as that it wouldn't make a poor man of me, and I should make it up later. I don't want to pry into your affairs, but can you say the same of what you want to risk? For I'm not going to say there's no risk in *any* business proposition, though I shouldn't let you go into this one at all if I could see any."

That had been enough for Douglas and he had given the required assurance; but this was a point in the conversation that he did not propose to tell Beatrix. It would give her a wrong impression. Armitage Brown had, of course, felt obliged to give him a conventional warning.

That it was merely conventional was proved by the way he had taken Douglas's reply. " Very well," he had said indifferently. " Nobody else will come in under twenty thousand. It will make it easier. I should have let you have some of my own shares if you had only wanted a thousand or so, as I thought, and I don't particularly want to part with any of them." Beatrix could be told that. She would only misunderstand the preliminary warning.

It practically rested entirely upon Armitage Brown's honesty, and really there couldn't be any question of that. It didn't even rest on his capacity, because if he did not succeed in bringing off his *coup*, no money would pass. He was bearing all the preliminary expenses, which would be by no means light, himself. Surely Beatrix would admit that Armitage Brown was absolutely to be trusted.

She did admit it. But Douglas, after all, did not feel that he was justified in holding back from her that word of warning, and naturally that loomed larger than anything with her.

She cried—amongst her roses. " We've been so happy here," she said, " and you have said again and again that nobody could want more than we have, Douglas. Why risk it all, even in the slightest degree? "

It appeared that he had only said that nobody could want more than they had when there seemed to be no chance of getting any more. There were lots of things that they could spend a great deal more money on, if they had it— a house in town, for one thing; a country house, not perhaps larger than Little Kemsale, but belonging to them instead of rented, with land going with it; perhaps a villa in the south of France, or a moor in Scotland—oh, lots of things! Not worth risking Little Kemsale for, of course; " but on anything you like to swear me by, Bee, I'm not risking anything. It really is so, if you could only see it."

She gave way at last. He promised to ask Bradgate fairly and squarely if he thought he was justified in risking so large a part of his capital. If Bradgate said no, he was to cut down his risk to five thousand pounds; they haggled about the precise sum for some time, but Douglas said that it was absurd to make a mere word of Bill's outweigh all his own convictions.

What Bradgate did say, when the question was put to him, not quite in the form suggested by Beatrix, was: " I'm not going to take any responsibility for it, Duggy. As far as one can humanly see, the risk isn't there. The thing is done when the papers are signed and the money is paid over. All we have to do then is to sell to the public, and that there'll be no difficulty about whatever. At the same time, I'm with our friend Armitage. I don't personally put more money into anything than I can afford to lose."

" But you're putting a lot more into this than you want to lose."

" If I did lose it, it would give me a nasty knock, and we should have to lie low for some time, the missus and I. But we should have enough left, and I should make it up again. You wouldn't have enough left, and you couldn't make it up."

His last words were: " I'm not going to advise you to do it, because if you did lose your money, I should feel I'd been partly responsible. And I'm not going to advise you not to do it, because if it comes off, as I believe it will, you'd never forgive me. You must make up your own mind."

So Douglas made up his mind, and instructed Bradgate to sell out securities to the extent of twenty thousand pounds.

CHAPTER XXXIII

THE END OF A DREAM

ALFRED was closeted with his father in Armitage Brown's business room at Kemsale. It was mid-July, but the rain was pouring down outside, and there was no relief to the spirit anywhere: certainly none in the room itself, which had taken on more than ever the appearance of an office.

Nor was there any in the hard bearing of the millionaire, who had not seen his son for six or seven months until the evening before, and was now delivering to him an ultimatum.

"My patience is at an end," he was saying. "You've had your fling, and now you've got to settle down to do what I tell you. I'm very disappointed with you. When we talked it all over last year I put it to you in such a way that I thought you would take up your life here so that we might have more in common than we've had before. I thought you were ready to do that, partly out of affection to me, partly because you'd come to see what a good thing I was offering you. But all you do is to rush away from the place without a word, and stay away for seven months. I don't know how much longer you'd have stayed away if I hadn't insisted upon your coming home. I'm not going to put up with that treatment any longer."

"Oh, well, father, you know why I cleared out. I really wouldn't put up with living in the same place as that fellow, after what had happened."

"If you mean Lord Meadshire, that had nothing to do with you at all. I was quite prepared to deal with him, and did so. Besides, he went away himself within a week, and hasn't been back since. You're talking nonsense. We got on very well here when we first came, and there was definite hostility between him and us for some time. I don't want to have anything more to do with him, but I'm certainly not going to let him drive us out of the place. But I'm not going to argue about it. I've treated you as a man of sense, and that treatment has failed. You haven't shown sense or duty or affection or anything else that you ought to have shown. You've just gone off and amused yourself, on money I've supplied you with. Now you have to do what I tell you."

Alfred's father had not spoken to him like this since his boyhood, and very seldom then. He did not like it, but felt no resentment against him, nor any sense of fear. He did feel, however, in spite of his twenty-six years, that he would have to do what he was told.

"Well, I'm sorry you're not pleased with me," he said. "But I haven't really lost sight of all you said last year. I've been thinking about it ever since. Can't you take my absence as a last good long holiday before I have to settle down to the serious business of life?"

Armitage Brown was rather taken aback by the free amiability of this speech. His annoyance against his son had been growing ever since his absence had begun to lengthen itself beyond all reasonable limits. He had made up his mind to have no more nonsense, and was ready to deal with Alfred as he had occasionally dealt with an unsatisfactory subordinate, shortly and sharply. After a time, if he behaved well, he would take him into favour again, but at first he would be kept strictly up to the collar.

But subordinates under rebuke had not been wont to treat matters in this way, and he did not quite know how to take it. Also he was fond of his son, and already softened

by the news that he had not simply ignored all that had
been said to him.

"I can't understand you," he said. "I don't believe
there's another young fellow in England who would want
to run away from what I'm offering you. One of the
finest houses in the country, with everything in and about
it to amuse yourself with, in a healthy sort of way, opportunities for seeing all the friends you want here, plenty
of nice people all round you, a fine estate—and all you're
asked to do is to spend the greater part of your time here
and look after it all."

"Oh, I know, father. I suppose I am a bit of a freak.
It's not my line in life, but I suppose I can make it so, if
I take pains about it. What is it you want me to do
exactly?"

Armitage Brown stiffened himself. He had laid down
in his mind a course for his son to pursue. That should
be kept to, for a time at any rate. Concessions might be
made later. "I want you, first of all, to go into the estate
office for a year. I shall article you to Fuller in the ordinary
way, and you'll work at it just as if you were any other
young man learning estate agency. You can take regular
holidays—not more than three in the year, and not more
than six weeks in all."

"All right," said Alfred resignedly. "If I'm to do it at
all, I may as well do it thoroughly. I suppose I shan't
have to stick in the office all day, as I did in Lombard
Street."

"You'll have to do what Fuller tells you. As you have
mentioned Lombard Street, I should like to say this. When
you were in my office you did what you were given to do,
but you took no interest in it whatever. When you left,
you knew no more what all your work tended to than you
did when you came. You didn't work intelligently. Now

you're four years older, and I hope you'll be ashamed to treat your work in that way. You'll go there for a definite object, and you must keep that object before you."

" I'll try to. What is it? "

" Are you trying to annoy me; or do you really mean that you don't know what it is? "

" I have my own ideas, but I should like to be sure of what yours are."

" I've already told you. If you want it again, put into a few words, what you have to do is to fit yourself to run this place, as an enlightened landowner ought to run his property. You have to take your place in this part of the country as the owner of Kemsale ought to take it. Live like your neighbors do, and, if you can, take to the same pursuits. I don't want you to hunt and shoot just for the sake of doing it, if you don't care about it, but because it will bring you into the right relations with them, and they're both healthy amusements that I expect you can take to with a good deal more pleasure than you pretend. The fact is, Alfred, you've been keeping up a pose, and you're old enough to drop it now. You're not a great artist or a great anything; you're just an ordinary young man, quite fitted to lead the life of other ordinary young men in your position. For goodness' sake drop your nonsense once for all and behave like the rest."

" It's an awful outlook," said Alfred. " But I'll do my best."

" Get Irving to teach you what he can about game-preserving, and managing the shooting. I shall expect you to take that over next season. It's absurd to pay all the money I do to preserve game and hand it over to somebody else. I might just as well let it; but of course I'm not going to do that. Shooting parties are a very good way of getting people together in the country. I enjoy them myself, though I don't shoot. I didn't mean to say anything about my part in the whole business, Alfred, as I've said it already, but it does seem to me that you might do something of your own free will to make this place an attraction and a recreation to me. I work very hard; I'm too old now to do without my work, and give myself up to an easy life down here. I haven't fitted myself for it. But I could enjoy the place if you would only do your part in connection with it."

"Oh, I'm going to, father. I've made up my mind about it. I'm going to begin a new life altogether."

"Well, I hope you really mean it. I think the life will be pleasant enough for you, and you'll come to enjoy it. You ought to. If you do your duty by me and by the place, I hope to have a good many years yet in which to enjoy it myself. I should like to see you married before very long. There's no hurry for that, but——"

"Well, if I'm going to settle down here for life, and become the right sort of country squire, I think the sooner I get married the better."

His father stared at him. "Do you mean that there is some one you want to marry?" he asked.

"I've been thinking about it ever since I was here last. I shouldn't have said anything to you about it before trying my luck, but for what happened with Meadshire and Katie. But if you approve I'm going to ask Grace Ettien to marry me."

"Grace Ettien!" Armitage Brown looked thunderstruck. "What on earth are you talking about? Are you trying to play with me?"

"No, I mean it. There's no contact in my mind with Kemsale—at least as regards the life you want me to take up here—except through her. Otherwise, it's just a great overgrown place in which we spend a vast amount of money and get very little in return; almost nothing that *I* care about. It's just a heavy burden. But ever since I first came here, I've felt that there was another side to it, and it has always been represented to me by her. If she'll marry me, I can go into it all with some chance of settling down to it happily, and taking the sort of place you want me to take here. If I've got to do it all off my own bat, well, I'll do my best, but I shall never feel that I'm in my right place."

Armitage Brown was simply bewildered by this. "Are you in love with Lady Grace?" he asked.

"I like her better than any woman I know. I should be very glad if she said she'd marry me. It would make all the difference to me, settling down here for good."

"She's years older than you are."

"Five years older. That's nothing."

"Have you any idea as to whether she——"

"As to whether she'd have me? No, I should think it's quite likely that she wouldn't. But I should like to ask her."

"It's a new idea to me altogether," said his father, after a puzzled pause. "I can't understand what you're really thinking about. Of course, she's a very charming woman, different altogether from her brother. There might be difficulty there, though, if you're really serious about this. But somehow I can't think you are, Alfred. I wish you'd tell me what's in your mind about it. It isn't a subject to treat lightly."

"I've tried to tell you what's in my mind, father, as far as I know myself. I've thought about it ever since I went away from here after Christmas. I had a talk with her, just before that; it was on the same afternoon that Meadshire spoke to Katie. She understands all about Kemsale, and what's wanted here; she's part of it—has been

all her life. With her as my wife, I could do exactly what
you want me to do, and take a pride and pleasure in it."

Armitage Brown sat at his desk looking down upon his
blotting paper, still with the same puzzled frown upon his
face. " Well, it isn't for me to settle," he said. " If you're
in earnest about it, I shan't say no. It seems to me odd.
It wouldn't be at all the sort of marriage I had thought of
for you. But I don't know that it would be any the worse
for that. You'd better think it over very carefully before
you do anything. She seems much more than five years
older than you. You don't seem to be in love with her, by
the way you talk, and it's a dangerous thing for a young
man to marry a woman he isn't actually in love with. Still,
you're old enough to know what you want now. If you do
want this, and Lady Grace wants it too, I shan't stand in
your way. That's all I can say at present. Except that
I won't have her brother in this house. He's done a cruel
thing upsetting poor little Katie. She pretends to have got
over it, but it's plain to see that she hasn't. I wish I'd had
my eyes open to what was going on. When you do see Lady
Grace, I wish you would talk to her about that. I should
like to get to the bottom of it."

Alfred went to the Herons' Nest that afternoon. He was
in a curious exalted mood as he walked there. He had
not answered his father's challenge as to whether he was
in love with Grace. His feelings towards her had small
resemblance to the feelings that he had once or twice in
his life experienced towards certain attractive young damsels
with whom he had been thrown in contact; but he regarded
it as all the more likely to be the real thing on that account.
For it was touched with emotion. She did stand for something that was desirable to him—a unity of life, and a
purpose, which he seemed incapable of realising by himself.
He was convinced that, with her, the life that his father

desired him to live at Kemsale would satisfy him, and satisfy him in a way that his present life had ceased to do. Her companionship would be sweet to him; they would have very much in common; he would be proud of her as his life; their days would pass in a quiet happiness that seemed to him to promise just that permanence and security that married life ought to hold. Since he had seen her last he had thought of her constantly, and wished to see her again.

And yet, when he found himself in her presence, he was conscious, not of elation, but of a feeling more like cowardice.

She looked pale and sad, and hardly smiled as she greeted him. When he had told her that he had come down to Kemsale the evening before, she asked at once whether Katie was there, and he said that she had come down with her mother on the day before he had.

" She hasn't been to see me," she said. " Isn't she coming? "

The question put him to constraint. Katie had not mentioned Grace's name to him for months past. She had wrapped herself in complete silence about what had happened to her. It was understood that it was not to be touched upon between them. He had no idea of how she stood towards Grace, or indeed of how she stood towards Grace's brother, who had asked for her in marriage.

Grace did not press him for an answer, when she saw that he hesitated. " I suppose you know," she said quietly, " that my brother went away directly after your father treated him so badly, and has not been here since."

It was like taking a plunge into very cold water. He had never thought for a moment that she would speak of this at all, still less she would speak of it in that way.

" I heard that he had gone away," he said awkwardly;

and then more gently: " But I don't think my father behaved badly towards him."

" If he had known what he was doing," she said, as if she had not heard him, " I think he would not have behaved as he did. Poor Kem was getting over his troubles. For a year, with one short lapse, he had been a new man altogether. Katie had very much to do with it. With her he would have conquered his old self altogether; I feel sure of it. So did she, the dear girl, when she promised to marry him. He was full of gratitude and affection for her. He was strong and resolute, and happy in a way I have never seen him before. Humble too, about himself, but with the right kind of humility. Oh, it was a wicked thing to treat him as your father did. He pushed him over the brink—pushed him to his ruin. It is all over with him now. I've lost my brother. I shall never have him with me whole and sane again."

She burst into tears. It was as if she had been saving herself until she could bring her indictment, and not till now had lost control over herself.

Alfred felt horribly uncomfortable. The feelings towards her which he had nurtured for so long crumpled up and disappeared. He was not touched to sympathy or tenderness by her tears, as he would have been if his sentiment for her had been based upon a genuine love, of whatever quality. He was simply distressed at finding himself plunged into a scene with a woman. And he was against her in what she had said, and was bound to combat it. But, of course, he would do so gently, so as not to disturb her still further.

" None of us thought that it would be a suitable marriage," he said; " and my father felt strongly that, under all the circumstances, Meadshire ought not to have made love to Katie before asking for permission."

"Made love to her!" she echoed. "Oh, how you misunderstand everything! Dear Katie didn't misunderstand it. She knew everything that she was doing, and would have been happy in doing it, for the rest of her life. Is she happy now? Will you tell me that?"

"No, she isn't," he said, with the risings of indignation in him, but keeping a level voice. "It has upset her altogether. She is a different creature. If she weren't so young, I should say that it had spoilt her life for her. If you can see our side of the question at all, I think you ought to be able to forgive my father for anything harsh he may have said over what brought that upon us."

"And I suppose his view, and your view, is that my brother so worked upon her that she hardly knew what she was doing; and that it was a righteous act to save her from his clutches, for which she would be grateful to you when she came to her senses."

It was exactly what they had thought, but he did not feel inclined to acknowledge it in face of the contemptuous tone in which she spoke. He was feeling more and more uncomfortable in her presence, and even hostile towards her. He had never thought of her as possessing the qualities which she was showing now. She was gentle and sweet and quiet, and would always be so, under whatever provocation, he had thought. But this was not the woman whose image he had cherished in a corner of his heart.

"Does it look like that now?" she went on. "Is she grateful to you? Has she acknowledged that she made a great mistake? If a girl is saved from the sort of man you think my brother is, would you expect to say of her six months later that it has seemed to have spoilt her life?"

A glimmering of doubt came to him. He was so constituted that the other side of a question was bound to

have weight with him. But hitherto he had thought that
there was no other side to this question.

But as he was gathering his thoughts together to reply
to her, his ordeal came suddenly to an end. " I won't talk
about it any more," she said, in a quieter voice. " She
might have saved him; she would have saved him; and
he would have made her happy. Now it is too late. When
I see Katie, as I hope I shall soon—tell her that I want
to see her—I will do what I can to help her out of *her*
trouble. We shall be sisters, always, she and I. And as
we all have to live our lives here, close together, I hope
we shall none of us feel enmity towards one another. I
shall never talk of this again to you; nor to your father
when I see him."

This was once more the Grace whom he knew, and something of sweetness and serenity had returned to her face
as she spoke.

" If we are never going to speak of it again," he said,
" I wish you would tell me why you look upon it so
differently from what we do—from what, I think one might
say, nearly everybody would be likely to."

" I think I will say no more about it," she said, after
a pause. " It is over and done with. If your father
were to withdraw his opposition, it would make no difference now. But yes, I will just say one thing, which you
may think over, if you like. You talked of my brother
making love to Katie. You must believe me when I tell
you that he had never done that. There are many kinds
of love, and the love that there was between them was of
the highest kind, short of the love one owes to God. It
would have healed him, and it would have given her a
very noble kind of happiness and satisfaction in life. You
know, women don't demand that life shall be made easy
for them, as men do. They can find the best that is in

them through sacrifice. I hope that dear little Katie will get her happiness back in time, and that she will marry and have children to spend herself on. But she was ready to rise to great heights. Whatever she does she will tread a lower path now."

He was chilled by this. He did not think that his sister would have risen to great heights in marrying a drunkard and a waster, even if she should succeed in making him drink and waste less, or not at all. He had his facile perceptions, and an idealism that had its practical results on his own conduct, but they did not lead him to look upon self-sacrifice as anything but a means to an end, and the end here seemed worth so little.

They sat for a time in silence, and then talked of other things. He told Grace that the fiat had gone forth that he should settle down at Kemsale, and turn himself into as near an approach as he could to the average country gentleman. He was rather amusing about himself, and she was able to treat the subject lightly, though not without some effort. They parted half an hour later, quite good friends.

CHAPTER XXXIV

THE WAR

THE month of July wore itself out. To most of those
with whom we have had to do it was a time of waiting,
with expectation for some, but for others no lightening
of the atmosphere, which contained many elements of discomfort.

Armitage Brown's long period of work was done. The
Anglo-Moravian Syndicate was in being, and the consequent public companies were in process of formation, with
every indication of a most successful launching when the
time should come. But their broad details had long since
been settled. The actual work in connection with them
was being done by smaller men. He could now stand aside,
and count upon taking his enormous profits.

He was conscious of no elation. The profits would be
of no advantage to him, except to use for further efforts,
each one of which must be bigger than the last, if he were
to employ his millions, and gain satisfaction from employing them. His life would be changed by them in no smallest
particular. There was nothing that they could give him
that he wanted, or could not have had before. It was
some satisfaction to have put through a big thing like this.
But against that was the drop that came from losing the
consuming interest that had held him for the last six months.
He had worked as hard as if his whole income depended
upon it, and was ready for a short rest; but he knew that
the rest would soon become irksome to him. Even the
interests of Kemsale would not hold him for more than a
few weeks.

Mrs. Brown knew now that she disliked Kemsale. The life that she lived there had no salt for her; there was no progression in it. She saw that other gifts than hers were wanted for playing a leading part in the country, even with Kemsale at her back. She had resigned herself to treating it as a house of rest, conserving her energies for London and the Riviera. But its unwieldliness and the sense that it was being wasted, with only a few of its great range of rooms occupied, made it sit like a burden upon her. It was a humiliation to her to feel that she was incapable of using any house, however splendid, up to its full capacity. There was some consolation in Alfred's having taken up his work in connection with it. Through him Kemsale might come, in time, to be considered again one of the social centres of Meadshire. But Alfred was moody and depressed. He had his regular work, and did it, but he seemed to be more at a loose end than before. She doubted whether he would ever come to take a real pride in his position, or in a future that might be so full of dignity and honour, if only he would use his opportunities. She saw that he had just the qualities that she herself lacked, to make himself prominent in country society, if he cared to use them. He made friends easily; he could attract anybody to him with what he had to offer them, and treat them on a basis of hospitality that was beyond her powers altogether. She was ill at ease about him, but could only wait and see how his new and enforced attachment to Kemsale would turn out, hoping for the best, but suffering many hours of uneasiness and boredom in the meantime.

Towards Katie her feelings were those of impatient disapproval. Her husband had forbidden her to talk to the girl of what had happened in the winter. He had dealt with it himself. Katie was to be treated with affection

and helped to forget it. He was peremptory; nothing was
to be said to her at all; it would do no good. So the girl
and her mother had drifted apart. There had never been
much confidence between them, and now there was none. If
Mrs. Brown had loved her daughter, even as much as she
loved her son, it would have been impossible for her to
keep the silence that she was instructed to keep. But it
suited her to do so. Except for some curiosity as to
exactly what had happened, which she knew that Katie
would not have satisfied in any case, she wanted to forget the
disagreeable occurrence herself. It reflected no credit upon
her to have had her eyes closed to what her own daughter
might be subjected to, especially as she had been warned of
it; and her husband had blamed her for not looking after
Katie, and had said things that she also wanted to forget.

But Katie made it difficult for her to forget anything.
She was obviously trying her best to be exactly what she
had been before, and outsiders might have seen no difference in her. But those of her family could not help noticing
the change in her, try as she might to hide it. She had
been a young light-hearted girl a year ago. Now she was
a saddened serious woman; no effort of brightness could
disguise it. She was a standing reproach to her mother,
who could only wait for the time when she should recover
from her disappointment, but in a constant state of wonder that she should have felt disappointment at all, and
should take such an extraordinary time to get over it.

At Little Kemsale there was no increase of happiness
over the coming fruition of Armitage Brown's great *coup*.
Beatrix no longer expressed doubts as to the result, for
Armitage Brown had said a word or two to her, at Douglas's request, that had made her doubts seem unreasonable.
The thing was practically done. The launching of the
companies was a matter of a few weeks only, and then

the members of the original Syndicate would take their extremely handsome profits. She and Douglas would not be millionaires like Armitage Brown, but they would be rich. She never heard it talked about in any other way than as if they were rich already, but she felt at the bottom of her mind that she would never consider themselves so until the money was actually in Douglas's bank.

Douglas was already talking of leaving Little Kemsale, which they had thought themselves so fortunate to find, and to which they had done so much to make it still more to their taste. His pleasure in it had departed. It had done splendidly for them as long as they could not afford something better, but it had many disadvantages, and now they would be able to look about for something very much nicer. His chief occupation at this time was to study house-agents' catalogues, but it did not save him from the weariness of waiting. The garden was at its ripest, but he took little interest in it, nor pleasure in the long summer days, but only wished that they would pass away more quickly.

At Barton's Farm there were already beginning preparations for Irene Fuller's wedding, which was to take place in November. She was to live at Points Manor, where there was plenty of room for the old couple and the young couple too. Mrs. Fuller had strongly objected to this arrangement. She had previously strongly objected to every other arrangement, important and unimportant, that had been suggested, including the central one of Irene marrying John Davis; and at last Mrs. Davis, who had been politeness and patience itself ever since her encounter with Mrs. Fuller at Kemsale, had once more expressed herself forcibly.

She was in a position to make an ultimatum, and its terms were that Mrs. Fuller should henceforward behave herself and give no more trouble. "You're perfectly at liberty," said the quiet terrible old lady, "to go about

telling everybody that it's a great come-down for your
daughter to marry my son. Nobody will believe you, but
that's your affair. You please yourself and you don't
hurt us. But we are going to take Irene away from all
the lies and nonsense to which you have brought her up,
and make a nice good useful woman of her; and we are
going to do it in our own way. Thanks to you, she
knows nothing about housekeeping, or anything that a coun-
tryman's wife ought to know, and it will be a benefit to her
to have me at her back, at least for some time to come.
She's sensible enough to see it herself, or the suggestion
would not have been made. Peacock about as a fine lady
as much as you like, but don't forget that I know all about
you, and can tell others what I know if I'm driven to it."

So Mrs. Fuller had capitulated, and was busy with
Irene's trousseau, for which her husband had produced
a sum of money exceeding expectation. He had not told
her where it came from. He was far more independent
and authoritative in the matter of money than he had
been at any time since their marriage. He had a grip on
his affairs at last, and intended to keep it. The fact
was, that after nearly two years of the new ownership of
Kemsale, he had proved himself the right man in the right
place, and enjoyed the fullest confidence and liking of his
employer, while she had overshot the mark, and had lost
the confidence she had first enjoyed. Mrs. Brown's coldness towards her rankled deeply; she was by turns contemptuous and waspish about that lady, and her amiability
in her own home was rather less than before. But its
absence was less effective than before. Her husband had
a great deal to occupy him outside, where everything, including the dairying scheme, now in full working order,
was going so well; and her daughter was looking forward
to getting away from her. Barton's Farm was not exactly

a happy home, but its unhappiness recoiled chiefly upon her who created it.

Happiness, indeed, was not the note of Kemsale at this time. Even little Anne Sheard, living in the glamour of her first love, was beginning to feel that the delay in her recognition meant something more serious than the year's probation which it was represented to be. And yet none of all the company of neighbours, except Grace, who mourned for the downfall of her hopes, and Katie, who was slowly recovering from a shock, had anything serious to complain of in the complications that touched their lives. Those complications came from sheer artificiality. A breath from the real world of struggle and passion might have been expected to blow them all away.

And the breath came.

There were rumours of war. Almost before those who were not particularly interested in foreign politics had gained an idea of what it was all about, there was war itself. Before they had become used to that sudden and surprising fact, the net had dropped and caught them all. War for them meant fighting, and men to fight, this time, not reading about it in newsapers. It came home.

The news that England would certainly go in was sent to Kencote a few hours before it was known to the country at large by Dick Clinton, who always seemed to be able to get inside knowledge of anything that was going on. He had gone up to London on the first serious rumour, and when he returned it was with a budget of news. He was to rejoin his old regiment, and it was believed that it would be one of the first to be sent to the front. John Spence, Nancy's husband, was to rejoin too; he had rushed down from Yorkshire with the same eagerness as Dick. Both of them held themselves fortunate, at their age, not to be left out of it. Young Inverell, serving a few years

in the Household Cavalry, would also, probably, be amongst
the first to go. Dick had seen Walter in London. He had
already volunteered for Red Cross work. Dick had been
able to pull strings at the War Office; he would certainly
be accepted for work at the front.

This was his news, as it affected the immediate Clinton
family, with much more as to what was going on behind
the scenes to give it point. Including Frank, serving in
the Navy, it accounted for all the sons and sons-in-law,
except Humphrey and Jim Graham. Both of them had
held commissions as young men in the Meadshire Yeomanry.
Within a week Jim Graham had found his way back to
them, and a cablegram had been received from Humphrey
announcing that he had secured a commission in the Austra-
lian Expeditionary Force.

The Squire's first state was one of bewilderment. England was being hurried into a catastrophe on no clear
grounds that anybody could take hold of. Why should
we go to war for the sake of Servia? His opinion of
Servia, which changed completely at a later date, may be
suppressed. He suspected the Radicals of muddling the
affair, but this suspicion was balanced by the fear that
they might keep a dishonourable peace. He had no particular opinion of the Germans; they were a beer-swilling,
sausage-eating nation, who committed numerous absurdities,
such, for instance, as crying " Hoch," when an Englishman,
if he cried anything, would cry " Hurrah! " But, on the
other hand, he had no particular opinion of the French; he
had lately seen some of them in the hunting-field; and they
ate frogs.

He came to anchor on the invasion of Belgium, and
read the full reports of speeches by Radical ministers,
which he had never done before, preferring to take them
for granted as a pack of nonsense. He admitted that they

read well. He had never denied that the Radical ministers were clever fellows—the trouble with them had been that they were too clever by half; and now that they saw their duty plainly he hoped that they would do it. They seemed to be doing it, so far, and he for one was quite ready to let bygones be bygones, and support them freely. We must give the Germans a lesson that they wouldn't forget in a hurry. We must teach them this and that, and the sooner we did it and got it over the better.

But underneath all his confidence in England's being able to do quickly what was necessary—aided, of course, by France and Russia—there grew upon him in those early hurried days of preparation a blank feeling of dread at the payment to be demanded from those who by inherited tradition would have the doing of it. Dick had served in the South African War, and had come through it un-scathed, with a D.S.O. to his credit. There had been long months of anxiety, but they had never darkened to fear. The chances had been that one out of so many would escape. What were the chances of seven escaping, in what was soon seen to be a far more serious matter? He put the fear from him, and was upheld by the pride of knowing that all the younger men of his family and those connected with it had answered at once to their country's call, as he would have answered himself in the good days that were behind him. But he knew that there were dark times coming to him and the women who would be left behind, when once the days of preparation were over, and they should be left alone to wait, and perhaps to weep.

Dick brought the reality close home to him when he told him that he ought to give way at once in the matter of Frank's marriage.

" I've had a letter from him this morning," Dick said. " He can't say where he'll be sent, of course, and there's

no such thing as leave now. But he may possibly get
a few days later on, if his ship is anywhere about—that
looks as if he were going to be kept in home waters—
and he wants to have everything prepared for a quiet wedding at a few days' notice."

" A wedding! " exclaimed the Squire, much startled, and
inclined to be offended. " That's going ahead with a vengeance. I told him definitely I wouldn't hear of his marrying this girl. It isn't a suitable marriage for him. You
said so yourself."

" I didn't altogether like it. I don't think it is particularly suitable. But, after all, he's made up his mind; he's
quite old enough to do it; and she's a nice girl enough."

" She's a mere child with a pretty face. And her people
are not the sort that a son of mine ought to marry amongst.
Why should you want me to change round now all of a
sudden and give way? "

" Oh, because that sort of reason loses its weight at a
time like this. He won't be marrying her people, and we
needn't see more of them than we want to. Anyhow, I
don't think they'll do us much harm. Her father is a
good enough sort of fellow, and he's behaved well about it."

" I don't think he's behaved particularly well. He has
allowed Frank to consider himself engaged to the girl
against my wishes."

" He's said he won't let him marry her till you give your
consent. That's straight enough. Look here, father, I
don't want to rake up bygones, but you took just the
same line about me and Virginia, and you know what very
nearly happened. What did happen has made this difference, that I'm going out with the regiment as a captain
instead of in command of it."

" I don't think you ought to bring all that up, Dick,"
said the Squire in a pained voice. " I've not said I won't

give way, but you can hardly expect me to go back on the position I've taken up in a few minutes. And your marriage and Frank's are very different things. You are my eldest son, and——"

"Well, but my dear father," Dick interrupted with a laugh, "that makes it all the easier to give way. It doesn't matter so much whom Frank marries, as the youngest of us. What I meant by reminding you of my marriage was that there's very little time. We have heaps of other things to think of and settle up in the next few days, and we don't want to keep this hanging over our heads as a question to be worried about. We had quite enough of that in my case."

"Well, I don't like the idea of this marriage, and I say so plainly; and I've seen the girl; it's quite different from Virginia's case. I might give way if Frank had set his heart on it, and felt the same in a year or so's time. But when you talk of an immediate marriage—rushing into things like that—it doesn't seem to me reasonable. I don't understand why you press it."

Dick stood up and lit a cigarette from a match-holder on the mantelpiece. Then he turned round and looked down at his father, who sat at his big writing-table, half facing him. "This war is a very serious business," he said. "We're all going. I don't know how many of us will come back. If Frank doesn't——"

He broke off; the old man gave a stifled cry of pain. "You won't want him to be thinking bitterly—about anything," Dick said.

There was a pause. "One of her brothers is a sailor," said Dick; "and another one—the boy who has come over here sometimes—is enlisting. That's two of them in the same box as the rest of us."

"I don't see what that has to do with it," said the Squire.

"It seems to me that it has, in these days. We're all going to do something that matters more than anything we've done before. People like that are doing it as well as us. We're not thinking much now of the little differences between us. They don't seem to be of such importance as they did."

"I think you're right, Dick," said the old man, slowly and painfully. "After all, we're giving up a lot more than that. There's you, and John Spence, and young Inverell. I wish to God all those rascally Germans were at the bottom of the sea. Well, I won't hold out any longer. You do think she's a nice good girl, don't you? Virginia likes her?"

"Oh, yes. So does Joan. She and Ronald Inverell went over to see her, you know. If they can do with it, I think we can. They're ready to treat her as a sister. So is Cicely. And mother would have had her here before this, if you hadn't objected."

"I rather wish I hadn't objected," said the Squire. "Frank has always been a good boy, given no trouble about money or anything else, and liked to come home whenever he could. I don't like to think of the boy going into danger, and thinking bitterly of his father, as you said. Perhaps I've treated him a bit harshly over this."

"I only said that because I wanted to bring it home to you—what he might think if you stood out. All you have to do is to write to him and tell him that it's all right. You'll make him happy, and the girl, and yourself, too. There's not too much happiness to look forward to just at present."

The Squire sighed deeply. "I'll write to him," he said. "And I'll ask your mother to go over to Kemsale with me to-morrow. It isn't a time to hold up your head now, except over what you're doing to put things right."

CHAPTER XXXV

THE OLD IS BETTER

"Well, Mr. Brown, I hope you have brought some good news. One wants it in these times."

The Squire had been sitting in his room, with the *Times* on his knee, long after he had finished his first reading of it. His windows were open to the hot August air. He would go out presently; there were many things to see to, now Dick had gone; but it was difficult to bestir one's self about ordinary duties when all the world was changed about one.

Armitage Brown did not look as if he had brought good news. His face was dark, and he did not smile as he accepted the Squire's greeting.

"I thought I had better come and tell you myself," he said. "You know we have declared war on Austria at last. That puts our business off indefinitely, and most likely loses us our money for good."

Some months before the Squire had asked him in his bluff half-condescending way if he could make use of a couple of thousand pounds he had lying idle. He had been good enough to say that he didn't much care about speculation, but with a famous financier living next door, so to speak, if he didn't try his luck now he never should. There were the two thousand pounds, if Mr. Brown could do anything with them. If they were lost, he shouldn't grumble; if they were doubled, he should think very highly of the capacity of "you gentlemen in the City."

It may be imagined that Armitage Brown was not accus-

tomed to be approached with offers of this description, but
its calm assurance caused him a grim amusement, and he
told the story afterwards to some of his business associates,
with considerable success. He could hardly have explained
why he allowed the Squire to take up two thousand of the
shares he had reserved for himself in the Syndicate. From
his point of view it was pure benevolence, and yet it would
not look at all like that to the Squire. But the aristocratic
old country gentleman had touched his imagination in a
curious way. He was inclined to admire his magnificent
ignoring of all standards but his own. And in Meadshire
there was no doubt which of them was the bigger man.
Armitage Brown felt it no less than his neighbours, and
did not mind feeling it. His amusement at the request
that had been made to him was directed partly against
himself, for being actually rather flattered by it. And it
would be gratifying to turn the Squire's two thousand
pounds into five or six at least, and probably very much
more, and so exhibit himself as able to do something that
the Squire, for all his beliefs in himself, could not do.

But all those ideas were very far from his mind as
he sped over to Kencote in his fast car. He was furious
with himself. Never before had he allowed motives of
friendship to influence him in matters of business, and
now this affair, out of all the others in which he might
have given his friends an interest, greatly to their benefit,
must needs go wrong. Douglas Irving, his nearest neighbour, had virtually been ruined by it. He was going back
to his regiment, leaving his wife to move into a cottage
and live on a few hundreds a year. That was what had
come of doing him a good turn, though he had not known
that the fool had put the greater part of his capital into
his hands, or he would not have accepted it. And this old
Squire—he supposed he could afford the loss, but if he had

judged him aright, he would not take it quietly. He rather hoped he wouldn't. It was with the idea of relieving his mind that he was going over to Kencote to tell his news by word of mouth instead of writing it. Irving had taken it well, had apparently seen clearly, what was quite true, that the factor which had come in to upset everything could not have been guarded against, and that Armitage Brown was not in the least to blame. It had been a painful business, all the same, and he wanted to get the taste of it out of his mind. He might do that if the old Squire gave him the opportunity of stating—with some indignation—exactly how each of them stood in the matter.

As for his own loss, it disturbed him greatly. It was the first serious set-back he had ever had. The loss of the great sum of money, and the dislocation of the money market which would occasion him the loss of much more, appeared to him in the light of a disaster, and he had not yet begun to recover from it. It was of no use at present reminding himself of the fact that whatever happened he would still be a very rich man, and that the universal change of values would give him opportunities in the immediate future for the profitable use of his financial acumen. While the great majority of people would lose heavily, he would gain, and the longer the war lasted the richer he would be at the end of it; for he could hold out, and others couldn't. But it was not enough. He felt like a man who had been made poor, and his impulse was to draw in everywhere, to put down all unnecessary expenditure, to lie low and wait for the better times to come. He had gone back, when he had never thought to do anything but go quickly and steadily forward. He cursed the war, and all the disturbance it had brought him. It was in no complacent mood that he prepared himself to listen to the Squire's remarks on his loss—the Squire, to whom the war had also brought considerable disturbance of another sort.

The Squire's face darkened when he brought out his news. " I haven't been thinking much about that sort of thing," he said. " Well, it's another blow; I suppose one can put up with it. I was a fool to risk a sum like that. It's a thing I've never done before in my life."

This was what Armitage Brown wanted. It turned the point of his anger away from himself and gave him a certain satisfaction in being free to give vent to it. He was thoroughly angry, in a cold self-contained fashion that left him fully capable of expressing himself in the most disagreeable way he could find.

" You weren't a fool at all," he said. " You would have been a fool, under the circumstances, not to take the chance I gave you."

The Squire looked up at him in some surprise at this method of address. But he did not understand that he was being invited to a quarrel, or he might have chosen his next speech with more care. " If the chance has resulted in my losing two thousand pounds," he said, " it doesn't look as if I should have been a fool not to take it. However, it's no good crying over spilt milk. If the money's gone, it's gone. I shall be wiser the next time."

" What do you mean exactly by that, Mr. Clinton? "

There was no doubt now that the man was in a disagreeable frame of mind. The Squire had become accustomed to something like a deference from him, and had rather lost sight of his eminence in another sphere. He was reminded of it now by his hard expression and short aggressive speech. But he was not in a quarrelsome mood; he was too down-hearted for that. " Oh, of course, I don't blame you in any way," he said handsomely, " and speculation is your business, I suppose. You've done extraordinarily well with it, I know. But for people like me, it's better to give it a wide berth. That's all I meant."

"Speculation isn't my business," said Armitage Brown, "any more than it's yours. My business is to get together all the knowledge I can, and use it. I gave you all the information I had myself about this particular business. It was buying properties of a definitely known value at much beneath their value, and selling them again. Where was the speculation in that?"

The Squire was not prepared to say. But he felt it rather hard that, having lost his two thousand pounds, he should be browbeaten about it. "I suppose the trouble is that we can't sell them again now," he said. "Perhaps we didn't think enough about that risk."

"What you mean, I take it, is that *I* didn't think enough about it. I thought about nothing else, until I'd gone over every possibility. It was the central point of the whole thing. I won't take a particle of blame for what has happened, Mr. Clinton. It was I who was the fool to take your wretched little bit of money. I didn't want it. If this business hadn't been stopped, like hundreds of others, by what no man at the time could have foreseen, you would have had handsome profits out of something that I should have done all the work for; profits that I should practically have given you. And you'd have taken it as a matter of course, with perhaps a thank you thrown in. That's what I should have got for going past my rule not to let my friends into my business, and it's all I should have got. It is I who was the fool."

"Well, perhaps you were," said the Squire drily. He had been offended at the reference to his "wretched little bit of money." Two thousand pounds was not a sum to mention in that way, by anybody, and the fact remained that the man who so mentioned it had lost it for him.

" Still, I haven't grumbled yet at the result, and I've said expressly that I don't blame you. I suppose you couldn't foresee the war, any more than any of us. Is the money gone for good, or shall we get it back, or some of it, when the war is over? What's the situation? "

He was taking it more reasonably than Armitage Brown had anticipated. He had been intending to work up to a little effect. The outbreak of war between England and Austria was just the one thing that could have ruined this wonderfully engineered and consolidated piece of business. Was there anybody in England who could have foreseen, at the time the money was called up for the original purchase, that in the course of the few months that must elapse before the companies could be formed, we should be at war with Austria? Had the Squire himself had the slightest suspicion of it? That was to have been the poser; because any one could have seen that that would ruin the scheme as it had been explained to him, and he could not shift the responsibility of ignoring the risk on to anybody else.

But apparently he did not wish to shift the responsibility. It was with a drop in his tone of aggression that Armitage Brown said: " My loss over this is very heavy, because it was about the safest proposition I've ever tackled if I could once bring it off, and I put a very large sum of money into it. I'm not even going to say I risked it, because if one took into account such risks as have spoilt this business, there would be no business done at all. I'm sorry to have lost your money, but you had exactly the same opportunities as I had of taking this risk into account, and you didn't see it as a risk any more than I did. Nobody could have seen it. I don't know whether the money is lost for good or not. I'm advised that the Austrian Government is quite as likely as not to keep the money we have paid over to them, and resume the properties too.   We shall certainly be able to do nothing with them until the war is over, and I suppose whether we shall be able to deal with them then will depend upon a good many things— who wins, for one."

"Well, there isn't much doubt as to who's going to win. They seem to think it will be a longer job than we thought for at first, but we shall get the better of them in the long run, the lying dishonest blackguards.   I don't know much about the Austrians.   I believe they are a bit above the Germans; but they have gone in with them, and they'll have to be trounced for it together.   Of course the Germans would think nothing of selling you something and sticking to it after they had taken your money.   We'd better consider it as lost, I think.   If we get some of it back by and by, so much the better.   I can't help wishing I'd got this money in hand now.   I think I should have sent it all to this fund they're starting.   That's something we stay-at-homes can do to help.   It'll come hard on a lot of people who haven't got much.   It's wonderful how the whole nation has come together over this; makes you proud of being an Englishman.   By the by, Brown, if you haven't sent your contribution to the fund yet, you might do it from Meadshire, not from London.   We want the county to show up well in whatever is going on.   I'm sending a thousand pounds as a first contribution.   I expect you'll better that by a long way; but I thought I'd wait to see if money is wanted particularly for something else."

"Oh, I've not begun to think about that yet," said Armitage Brown.   "The war has knocked everything sideways.   I shall be kept busy for a long time to come, trying to make up what I've lost only within the last week or so. The war!   Who would have thought at this time of day that half the nations in Europe would be at each other's throats, and about nothing that anybody cares a pin about? "

" It's a sad business. I don't suppose the world will ever see the same again—not in my lifetime. Still, it gives us something to think about, and something to do. I'm cutting down everything I can here. It's made it easier—the servants enlisting and the horses being taken. We've sent off nine men from the house and gardens and stables alone, already. Not bad that; but everybody is doing his best in his own sphere of life now. Are you making much difference at Kemsale? "

"I shall make all the difference I can. It's no time now to spend money on keeping up a great empty house. I should let the place if I could find any one to take it. I shall be pretty busy for some time to come, looking after my business. I shan't be down here much. I shall leave my son to do what he can to keep things together at Kemsale. He won't mind living in a few rooms, and I can shut up the rest. I've given half the servants notice. If the men like to go and enlist, they're welcome."

" Your son isn't going, then? "

" Going? Going where? "

" Why, Gobblessmysoul, to fight, like a man! We want all the men we can get."

" Well, we shall have to do without him, then. No, he's not going to fight. Why on earth should he? He's the only son I have. He'd be no better than any young ploughman at fighting, and he's heir to all I've got. I'll keep him out of it."

The Squire gulped down his growing disgust. He had something to suggest, and wanted to be persuasive. " I've an idea in my head," he said. " I don't know whether you've thought of it, but you talked just now about shutting up Kemsale. What about turning it into a hospital? I and one or two more have been going over the houses in Meadshire that are suitable, and the fellows that can afford to equip them. Naturally we thought of you first, as you have the biggest house of the lot, and I suppose more money than any of us. If we could get up a committee, and you could come forward with the first offer—we'd arrange that—it would give it a good lead. How does it strike you?"

Armitage Brown rose from his chair. "It doesn't strike me at all," he said. "I'll say good-bye now, Mr. Clinton. I'm sorry to have had to bring you bad news, but——"

"Sit down," the Squire interrupted him. "I've got something to say to you. What *are* you going to do towards helping in this war?"

Armitage Brown did not obey the peremptory order. He showed frowning offence at the tone in which it had been given. "What am I going to do?" he repeated. "Pay taxes through the nose, like everybody else. I shall have thousands to pay in taxes; and I shan't squeal at it. I'll pay my share, and more than my share, because they'll come down on me for more, but——"

The Squire stood up himself, and interrupted him again. "When you go out of this house," he said, red in the face with anger and contempt, "you don't come into it again. I'll have no dealings with a man who behaves like a mean and selfish cur. And I'll take good care to let it be known far and wide what sort of a man we've got amongst us at Kemsale, which used to take the lead in every good work in the county."

Armitage Brown's brain cleared as if by magic. Many thoughts passed through his mind, and he saw many things he had not seen before. He sat down again and said: "I'll ask you to explain what you mean by that, Mr. Clinton."

The Squire's strong indignation winged his utterance. He spoke with more than his usual clarity, as he bent his white brows upon the man sitting before him, and addressed him as if he were some culprit amongst his own people, who had incurred his heavy displeasure. The text of his discourse was that people who owned land and lived on it had duties to perform, and if they didn't perform them when the call came they were shirkers and cowards, not fit for honest God-fearing people to associate with. " You have a young unmarried son," he said. " Why aren't you sending him with the rest? Because he's your only son! I've got four sons, and they're all going, and three sons-in-law, and they are going too, and leaving their wives and children. I'm proud of them; I wouldn't keep one of them back. Your son has to stay behind to look after your property. Property! That's all that a place like Kemsale means to you—the money it has cost you. I'm an old man; I'm the twenty-second Clinton to hold Kencote, and I'd go to-morrow if I could be any use. My eldest son, and all the others, have gone. All three of my daughters' husbands are men of property, two of them men of large property. Young Inverell—you know all about him; I suppose he's about the same age as your son, but with a young wife and child, and everything in the world—name and wealth and a great future before him— that a young man could have. He's leaving it all; glad to take his chance of coming through, just like the young ploughman you talk about. Who are you, I should like to know, that you should skulk behind your money-bags, and men like that should go out and do the fighting for you? We've given you your chance here of coming in and being one of us. You've had a welcome; we've put aside the fact that your birth isn't the same as ours. But, by God Almighty, if you're going to show that you've got no honour and no pride in yourself and your country, your name will stink among us, and your precious son's after you."

Armitage Brown had sat quite still during this indict-ment, with his eyes on the ground, and no change on his face. It was in a voice quite level and free from offence that he said: "Well, Mr. Clinton, I've made a mistake. You've shown me that. But I'll ask you to remember that I've just lost half a million of money that I know of, and a lot more that I don't yet know of. A man that that's happened to isn't likely to have his thoughts free for other matters, till he's got over it a bit, and begins to see his way."

The Squire's indignation was not softened by this speech. He had more to say yet.

"We give our sons when our country wants them," he said, "and we give ourselves if we're young and strong, as I wish to God I was. We love our homes and the land that's been ours for generation after generation, in a way that a man like you, who just buys them for money, can't know anything about; and we leave them as if they were nothing. If we've got money we're ready to give that. What are you ready to give? Nothing! Nothing in the world. I say that men like you who rake great fortunes together that do no good to anybody but them-selves are a pest on society. You're not brought up to give your manhood to your country. The gentlemen of England—and the ploughmen, too, by George—yes, they can do that. But you can't even help with your money. It's all there is to you, and it gets you where you've no right to be, nine times out of ten; but we've got to do that as well, because you won't. Taxes! You'll pay your taxes! Pah!"

He had been standing on the hearthrug, and now threw himself into his chair again, somewhat exhausted by the harangue he had delivered, but still flaming with anger and contempt.

Armitage Brown spoke with the same absence of offence as he had used before. "It's a strong accusation," he said, "and if it were true, I should have nothing to say. I should get up and go. The men like me—the rich business men—do give our money when there's a call on us. We give more than anybody. I've subscribed many thousands myself, at one time or another."

"You said just now that you hadn't even thought about subscribing to this fund that's been started, and——"

"I said I hadn't thought of what I should give. I didn't mean I shouldn't give anything. Of course I shall. And I admitted just now, before you began to rub it in a second time, that I'd made a mistake. My mistake has been in not seeing what was wanted quick enough. You must make some excuses, Mr. Clinton, for a man who has just lost getting on for a million of money. That is how the war has touched me personally. It has touched you in a very different way, and it so happens that your personal interest in it is a more patriotic one than mine. But that's not to say I shouldn't have come to take the right views, and do the right things, when I'd had time to get over what has so upset things for me. You've brought them home to me, and I don't resent your plain-speaking at all. About this hospital plan now—what are you doing about it yourself? Are you going to turn this house into a hospital?"

Was all this quite sincere, or was it a clever attempt to avert retribution of an awkward kind by disclaiming an attitude that was seen to be indefensible? And was the question at the end an attempt to turn the tables? Nothing had been said about turning Kencote into a hospital.

The Squire, at any rate, was suspicious of such a sudden surrender. "I shouldn't have asked you to do something I wasn't prepared to do myself," he said, with little change in his tone of indignation. "My wife and I are going to move down to the Dower House to be with my daughter-in-law. I am going to offer this house. There's a lot of room in it. Whether I can fit it up as a hospital all complete I don't know yet. I shall have to see what it means and exactly what is wanted. And I don't want to do anything till I've seen others about it. I should like to make it a county business—or South Meadshire, at any rate."

"Well, whatever you do with Kencote, I'm ready to do with Kemsale. It was a new idea to me altogether, or I wouldn't have spoken as I did about it, when you first mentioned it. I didn't even realise that private hospitals would be wanted. But I suppose they will, and you have thought about that as you've thought about other things. I'm willing to follow your lead, Mr. Clinton. I know I'm a new man here; I'm not so anxious, perhaps, to cut a figure in county society as you might imagine; what you threatened a while ago wouldn't bother me much if I didn't think what you proposed was right. I've done a good many things since I came here that I hadn't thought of doing before; I've tried to be a good landlord according to my lights, and if I haven't understood everything at once, it has been because it's not my way to do things just because other people do them; and as you pointed out, I wasn't brought up to it."

The Squire began to be mollified. The man talked a lot, and seemed able to change his views and intentions more quickly than an ordinary mind could follow him. But he was not altogether untried. It was true that he had not shown himself unduly anxious to curry favour with the more important of his neighbours. He had taken his own line about many things, and he had also shown himself ready to learn from those who knew better than he did. And so far he had proved himself an exceptionally good landlord in everything that really mattered. If he was ready to do his duty now, and spend money, which others who were more than ready to do their duty could not afford to spend, he might still prove himself a strong support to whatever should be done in the county; and it would be a feather in the Squire's cap to have him brought to a right way of thinking.

"Well, I'm glad you're inclined to look at things in a better way," he said. "What I should like to do would be to call a meeting of the people who are ready to offer their houses at once. My own idea is that any money we can collect besides, for equipment and so on, had better be offered at the same time, as a lump sum, and let the proper authorities deal with it, and with the accommodation."

"I think I may say—now you've given me the idea—that I should be ready to equip my house completely, in any way they might direct."

"You can make that offer if you like. What I'm trying to explain is that some people might be willing to give up their houses, but couldn't afford to do more than that. Personally, I should feel that if I offered to do that with my own house, it would look as if I were trying to gain credit over other people who were just as willing as I was, but couldn't afford to do so much. That's why I should like to make a county business of it. I should pay what it would cost me to fit up this house into a general South Meadshire fund, and the proper people could use it as they pleased."

Armitage Brown felt abashed. The old man still had something to teach him in unselfish neighbourly feeling. "That would be far the better way," he said. "If you will call your meeting, I'll be ready to attend it. And I'll undertake to subscribe at least what it would cost to equip Kemsale."

The Squire was conquered. This was tangible. His hostility to the man who had revealed qualities that he had not suspected in him dropped away, and he saw again the man whom he had liked, approved for the respect he had shown to himself and his opinions, and been ready to accept as a desirable neighbour, in spite of obvious differences.

" It's very good of you," he said. " I'd better call the meeting, because I know the people and have sounded some of them. But you're the owner of the biggest house. You'd better take the chair."

" No, I won't take the chair," said Armitage Brown. " You shall do that. But I dare say my business experience will come in useful in working out a scheme, and helping to run it afterwards, if that's necessary. There may be other things we can do in South Meadshire. I'm ready to give time to them as well as money, Mr. Clinton. It will take my attention off disagreeables that aren't perhaps so important, after all. I've got to thank you for showing me the way."

CHAPTER XXXVI

THOSE AT HOME

As Armitage Brown sped back from Kencote to Kemsale he felt as if a heavy weight had been lifted from his mind. He no longer thought of his losses; they seemed to be as nothing. They were, in fact, nothing in respect of any practical effect that they need have upon his actions. He had been shown his duty, and he was ready to do it.

He was more than ready to do it. He had come into line, and whatever he could do now, by wise use of his money, and still more of his organising ability, he would do, with as much energy as he had brought to bear upon his financial adventures, and as much satisfaction as he had gained from them.

For the old Squire had brought him to himself, and the real man was not the selfish money-grubber who had brought down that indignant fulmination. His vision had been obscured for the time, but the idealism was there, and the spark had been kindled that had made it glow. The quick change that had come over him was characteristic of the man. His son had remarked, with another reference, upon his genius for seizing the salient point. He had done it again and again in small matters since he had turned himself into a landholder, and largely under the influence of the old man who had been a landholder before he himself had been born, and had now shown him so plainly what fine ideals of loyalty and service lay beneath all the easy stereotyped course of life led by men of his order.

He had seen it all, as in a flash. These men might be

stiff and prejudiced against change, reactionary in some of their ways, a hindrance here and there, perhaps even as a class, to the march of liberty and progress. They had more than others, and were jealous of all interference with what they looked upon as their rights. But when the call came they were ready to give themselves, eagerly, without waiting to be called, without taking or seeking credit for it. It was not simply because the higher ranks of the fighting services were chiefly their preserve, nor from the young man's love of adventure, that they went so readily. Those reasons counted; but what counted more was the instinctive inherited response to the call of honour. The old man had made his claim. He had pointed to his eldest son, and to his sons-in-law. They had more than others, and they gave more; their great possessions would not hold them back for a moment. It was true that others were now coming forward who had less to give, but who gave all they had. Patriotism and self-sacrifice were not the monopoly of one class. But if the Squire was to be taken as representing the old order of English wealth, and Armitage Brown himself the new, then there was no doubt as to which of them had shown up better hitherto.

Armitage Brown went over in his mind the hard things that had been said to him, but with no bitterness. His mind was large; it had only been narrowed where it had concentrated itself upon piling up money with no wide view as to its proper use. He even thought with something like affection of the righteously angry old man blazing out his wrath at him. He had not understood everything, he had not made enough allowances; but his readiness and rightness had stood out in such contrast to his own failure to grasp the true proportions of all that was happening around him that there was no combating them. He was not a man who saw things clearly and without prejudice,

as a rule. He had lived for many years in an old-fashioned
feudal backwater of his own, while the great river of
progress had flowed past him. But he had seen clearly here,
and acted rightly, even down to that detail of sinking
his own importance so that he should not appear to be
taking credit that would not be wholly his. It was a
fine touch that; it had come after Armitage Brown had
capitulated to him, and was ready to bring a more trained
intellect than his to bear upon his schemes; but the simple
man had thought of it, not the clever one.

Well, he had been shown the way; he would not be
behind now in treading it. He liked the old Squire's idea
of organizing his county of Meadshire. They had talked
of other things that could be done; the Squire was watching the recruiting figures with pride at the response of
the county, but some jealousy because other counties were
doing still better; he knew personally every man who was
serving or ready to serve on his own estates, and many
outside them. Armitage Brown knew scarcely anything
of what was going on at Kemsale, and yet he had prided
himself on the things that he had done to make it a model
estate; he had thought himself far better fitted to advance
the welfare of his tenantry than the owner of Kencote, with
his old-fashioned views.

As for his own son—he could not quite make up his
mind there. Was it really necessary that a young man
of such value should offer himself as food for cannon? He
thought of young Inverell, the Squire's son-in-law, who
had been brought up as an answer to that question. There
was not much doubt which of them the world at large would
consider to be of the higher value; but Alfred was his son,
his only son. The comparison did not convince, but only
dejected him. Did Alfred want to go himself? He had
said nothing about it. But they had not talked much

together lately. Armitage Brown had been gloomily considering his affairs; Alfred had been busy with the work he had taken up, or at least, kept a great deal away by it.

But when he reached home he found that the decision had been taken out of his hands. His wife met him in a state of perturbation. Alfred had received a telegram and had already gone up to London, leaving farewell messages. There was a good chance of his getting taken on as an interpreter. Captain Clinton had worked it so far for him, and had wired him to come up without delay.

To Armitage Brown's recovered vision his wife's annoyance seemed unreasonable. Alfred's decision had cut the knot of his own hesitations in a very satisfactory way. He was glad that he had wanted to go, and relieved that his going would not involve the greater dangers. " I think he might have told us what he was thinking about," he said. " But I'm not sorry that he is going to do his share. I shouldn't have made any difficulty—if that's why he kept quiet."

" Oh, I think it is dreadful," said poor Mrs. Brown. " He couldn't deny that there was danger, though he pretended to make light of it. He hopes to be sent right to the front, and he thinks that the men who do the interpreting work will be expected to make themselves generally useful. Whether that means fighting or not I don't know, but I'm sure Alfred hopes it does, though he only mentions Red Cross work. He actually said that if there had not been a chance of his getting an interpretership he would have enlisted at the very first."

Armitage Brown was conscious of a glow of pleasure. He wished he had known of that before, so that he could have told old Mr. Clinton. It had still rankled a little, after he had come to his own senses, that the Squire and his belongings had not needed bringing to theirs. But

here was his own son who had been as ready to offer himself as any old-fashioned gentleman of them all.

" It makes me proud of my boy," he said. " I suppose he will let us know when he is going. If he can't
come down here we'll go up to London and give him a
send-off."

She had expected that her husband would regard the
matter in the same light that she did. It was some time
before he could get her to listen while he told her of the
change that had come over his own views. He did not do
so directly. While he appeared to defer more to her wishes
in certain matters than the Squire deferred to those of his
wife, he was actually far more independent of them; for
the Squire always appeared to get his way in everything,
while Armitage Brown actually did so. The decision he
had formed on his way home was that Kemsale should be
given up at once for its new use, and that he would rent
Little Kemsale back from Irving, furnished.

Mrs. Brown was startled by the proposal. If economies
were to be made, as she had already been told they were,
she would be glad enough to get away from Kemsale.
If the knowledge that the house was not actually being
used was galling to her, it would be still more so to make
the fact apparent, which would be done by shutting up
most of it and dismissing half the servants. But she wanted
to live in London. " What is the object," she asked, " of
tying ourselves here, to a small house, if we must leave
the big one? "

" You'll be much happier in a smaller house," said her
husband, who knew more about her likes and dislikes than
she suspected. " You'll get rid of a lot of bothers, and
I shall get rid of a lot of expense. I don't want the
Berkeley Square house opened up this year; just keep a
few rooms and a couple of servants there for when we

want to go to London. There's a great deal of work to
be done here; we shall be able to do it conveniently at
Little Kemsale, and the house is quite big enough.   It
will do Irving a good turn too, to take it off his hands in
that way; unless he's made other arrangements, which I
hope he hasn't yet."

Douglas had made no other arrangements. He was glad
enough to consent to this one. He and Beatrix were sitting together in his room when Armitage Brown went down
to them. Douglas had returned from London that morning.
He was to rejoin his old regiment on the next day. Bradgate was going back to it too.

Douglas was not particularly disposed to welcome this
visitor. He had had a very bad quarter of an hour with
Armitage Brown some days before. He had seen in him
what he had not seen before—the hard ruthless man of
business, to whom the losses and distress of other people
were matters of annoyance, so far as they affected his
own ease of mind, but not matters of sympathy. He had
felt like a culprit before the man to whom he had entrusted
his money, when he had been obliged to confess what
the loss of it meant to him. He did not blame him for
its loss—he could hardly do that—but he did not want
to talk to him about it again.

But Armitage Brown had apparently reverted to his old
state of mind, which had not been destitute of sympathy
and kindness towards his nearest neighbours. When they
had talked a little about the war, and Douglas's probable
movements, he made his proposal, offering a very handsome rent for the use of the house exactly as it was. " All
your things will be looked after well," he said, " and perhaps you can leave them more as they are than if you
were to let the house to strangers; you'll be able to come
back to them when all this trouble is over."

" I'm afraid we shan't be able to come back to them,'
said Douglas. "We were just talking of that. But I'm
very much obliged to you for your offer. Of course we'll
accept it gratefully, won't we, Bee? "

She was sitting on the arm of his chair, her hand in his.
She looked as if she had been crying, and there were
signs of emotion on his face too. But she spoke lightly
enough. Their troubles were between them; no outsider
was to know how deeply they had been hit. " It's a splendid chance," she said. " Thank you so much, Mr. Brown;
it will make things ever so much easier for what we want
to do. I am going to offer myself for hospital work, when
Douglas goes. I had some training before I was married.
I shall hope to get taken on somewhere at once."

"What, Red Cross work? " he asked.

Her face fell a little. " I should have liked that," she
said. " But with Douglas away we can't make up our
minds that I should leave the children."

" You'll have to leave them, won't you, if you go nursing? " His voice was gentle. He saw what they must
be suffering. If Douglas had not risked, and for the
present at least lost, the greater part of their income, he
might have gone off to his duty, and left his wife and
children behind in the home that they had so loved. He
could have thought of them there safe and sheltered while
he was undergoing the dangers and hardships of war; he
could have inspirited himself with the happy anticipation
of returning to his home, far dearer in its expression of
his tastes and affections than it had ever been.

" We are going to send them to a friend of mine,"
Beatrix said, with a catch in her voice. " When Douglas
comes back, we shall all be together again, somewhere."

" Well, now," Armitage Brown said, " I think I can
suggest something better for you than that." He told

them of his plans for turning Kemsale into a hospital.
" Why shouldn't you do your work here? " he said. " We
can find you a pretty cottage somewhere handy, and you
can have the little ones there with you. We don't want
more partings than are necessary at a time like this, do
we? When men are going off to fight for us all, those
who are left behind ought to stick together. You are part
of Kemsale, you know, Mrs. Irving. I don't want you to
leave us. There's plenty you can do here."

He left them a good deal happier than he had found
them. Beatrix could not restrain her tears, but they were
tears of joy this time. " It would have been dreadful
to have sent the darling children away," she said. " I have
tried ever so hard to get used to it; but it would have
been the hardest thing of all, except your going, dearest."

" It's the first bit of comfort we've had," said poor Douglas. " Oh, what a fool I've been; and all through not
knowing when one was well off. How on earth I can
have looked forward to leaving Little Kemsale, I can't
think. Now we're going to lose it, it seems to me like
Paradise. And it will be worse for you than for me, Bee.
You *were* contented and happy here, and warned me against
my folly. Why didn't I listen to you? I shall never forgive myself."

" I have, long ago, if there was anything to forgive,"
she said. " And you must forget it all now, Douglas dear.
We shall have enough; we shall all be together, when you
come back, and you'll get such a welcome, darling."

" You're very sweet and good about it, Bee," he said,
pressing her hand. " I shan't mind so much now, if I
can think of you and the kiddies here somewhere. He's
a good fellow, Brown; I know he'll do what he can, and
perhaps things won't be so bad after all, in the long run.

But it doesn't seem of such importance now, how one is going to live, as long as one has a home of some sort."

"That's what I feel," she said eagerly. "There is so much to do, for both of us, for all of us. Perhaps in the past we have thought too much about enjoying ourselves. We shouldn't be happy now, doing that, if we could."

"I have thought too much about enjoying myself," Douglas said. "I don't think you have, my dear. Well, we've both got our job now. I shall do mine with a much better heart, thanks to friend Armitage. He's going to do his, too. Somehow, I didn't think he would take it up like this. However, we're all going to do what we can, and there's no need to think about what is coming after, until we've got through. Old Bill feels that; his business has been knocked endwise, besides what he's lost in the Anglo-Moravian; but he says he doesn't care, as long as he can leave Mrs. Bill fairly comfortable; there's something quite different to think about, something to do. After all, we're all of us better with something to do, and when it's as important as this war is, it doesn't leave you much time to think of your amusements."

"One gets down to realities," she said. "We shall both be better and stronger for it, when it's all over, if we have done our best. We shan't think so much of what we've lost; we shall have something to put in its place. So don't worry any more about what has happened, Douglas dear. It can do us no harm, if we don't let it."

Douglas went off the next morning, and a few days later the Browns moved to Little Kemsale. A cottage was found for Beatrix on the outskirts of the village. It had a large parlour and a large garden. With a little alteration it would make a charming home; but nothing was to be done to adapt it at present; it would do for

her and the children and two maids, as it was. It was
furnished from Little Kemsale, and the gaps there made
good from Great Kemsale. Armitage Brown had succeeded in mending the damage done to the lives of these
friends of his by no more than a little thoughtful kindness. Whether or not they would ever get back to something of their former prosperity seemed at present to matter
little. Their way was clear; they could leave the rest.

At Kemsale Rectory there was deep seriousness in these
days, heavy with fate for so many. Charles was in his
ship somewhere on the other side of the world; young
William had joined the Meadshire Hussars, and was busy
with his training; John, the Cambridge don, was hoping
to get a chaplaincy at the front; Henry, the doctor, had
already gone out to a base hospital. But little Anne
had been made happy, though her fears for her lover
were not small. The Squire and Mrs. Clinton had driven
over to Kemsale with their treaty of alliance. Frank was
employed in home waters; his letters gave no information
as to where he was or what he was doing, but he had
expectations of a week's leave later on in the year, and
preparations were to be made for a wedding upon the
first opportunity.

The Squire, having once given in, behaved handsomely.
Frank's allowance was to be increased to a thousand a
year, and they were to occupy a snug little Georgian house
in the village of Kencote, where Anne would be under
the fostering eye of her new relations when the lot of a
sailor's wife left her alone. Her parents would have
preferred that she should stay with them until she and
Frank could settle together in whatever home the exigencies
of his profession would allow. But they accepted the
arrangement philosophically, as part of the price they
must pay for their daughter marrying outside of their

station. Anne was to be a Clinton, and it was for the
Clintons to say what was suitable for her, not the Sheards.
She would not be far off, and would often be with them.

But the differences between Clintons and Sheards, in
these unsettling days, seemed much smaller than at other
times. Even to the Squire, the dignity of his house seemed
of less importance, except in so far as it was upheld by
the services it was rendering so willingly; and taken on
that ground the Sheards, who were rendering their services too, were not devoid of dignity. The Squire recognised it, as he sat in Mrs. Sheard's drawing-room, which
was furnished now, though sparsely. He recognised it
in the Rector's upright direct manliness, which met the
same qualities in himself, and made the unessentials with
which they had been overlaid shrivel away from him. Still
more did Mrs. Clinton recognise it in the simple-minded
woman who was moved by the same fears and sorrows and
pride on behalf of her sons as she was herself.

The Squire made no patronising speeches. " Well, Mr.
Sheard, my boy wants to marry your girl; we've got to
put our heads together and make it easy for them." That
was his opening, and nothing was said throughout the
interview that followed about his own previous unwillingness to make it easy, or even possible, for them. When
little Anne came in, blushing and smiling and rather frightened, he kissed her and said: " My dear, we're going to
take care of you while Frank is away; and when he
comes back to us again, we're all going to be very happy
together."

When Mr. and Mrs. Clinton drove away he said:
" That's a very dear little girl. I'm glad she's young
and pretty. She'll cheer us up at Kencote. God knows
we shall want it, with what's coming." There was no
word of criticism, no reference to those differences which

had bulked so largely with him, and, if he had been thinking of them now, must have made themselves in some ways apparent during the visit. But Mrs. Clinton had known how he would take it when it came to the point. She had kept quiet and not hurried to intervene. She wanted her boy's happiness, and had known that his love for this good sweet girl was not a mere passing fancy. In time she would have moved; but there had been no necessity, and she was glad that her husband should have shown himself what she knew him to be without pressure on her part.

"I am sure we shall love her," she said. "Frank has chosen well."

There was another marriage to be celebrated at Kemsale, quietly and prematurely because of the war. John Davis was in the Meadshire Yeomanry, as all his forbears had been since his family had first settled at Points Farm. He and Irene were to be married in September, and she was to go to her new home to wait for him there.

Mrs. Fuller was relieved from certain mean anxieties by the arrangement. A "grand" wedding, to the carrying out of which she would have brought every faculty that she possessed if Irene had been marrying what she would have called well, would have presented difficulties under the circumstances. She had already begun to dread them. The Davises would have brought to the ceremony many friends and relations of the utmost respectability, but of the kind at whom she had been accustomed to turn up her nose. But she on her side could not even have done that. Her husband had scarcely any relations, and while she had plenty, she would have died rather than produce any one of them.

But a quiet wedding! It was being done now, under similar circumstances. It was "the thing." Even presents

were to be discouraged—not strongly discouraged from
immediate neighbours; but there was to be no display of
them. This got over another difficulty that had kept Mrs.
Fuller awake in the night; for there had been nowhere
for presents to come from, apart from immediate neighbours, or, at any rate, none that could be displayed with
advantage.

Poor little Herbert was pleased enough to be rid of
the fuss. His mind was greatly exercised over what was
happening. He mourned his advancing years as he had
never mourned them before, even when he had thought
that they might bring him to penury. He thought about
the war night and day, and envied from the bottom of his
loyal little soul the men who were young enough to go off
and fight. Mrs. Fuller gave him no sympathy, until, stung
by her sneers, he began to consider seriously whether he
couldn't be of use in training new troops, and talked of
sending in an application. Her sympathy was not remarkably soothing then, but she managed to put a stop
to his designs. He was wanted where he was; and what
should she do, pray, if he were to go off and leave her?
And he wasn't strong enough for it either; he was very
proud of appearing younger than he really was, but his
years were beginning to tell on him, and he'd better not
put himself in a position where that would be made plain.

Thus did this amiable spouse refuse to be parted from
her supporter. She cut out and made up a few suits of
pyjamas for the Meadshire Yeomanry later on, when she
found that that sort of thing was "being done," and
pushed herself on to one or two Meadshire ladies' com-
mittees. Otherwise, the war made no difference to her.
" If only one could send a few women to the front," said
Armitage Brown, with reference to her, " one wouldn't
so much object to the phrase ' food for powder.' "

CHAPTER XXXVII

FAREWELLS

"IF you care to go back that way, we might all go and
have a last look at the house."

It was Alfred who spoke. Grace and Meadshire had
been dining at Little Kemsale, and the three of them,
with Katie, set out under the harvest moon for the great
house, which was now fully transformed into its hospital
state.

During the early days of the war Meadshire had come
down to the Herons' Nest, for the first time for eight
months. He was sobered and sad, himself again for a
time at least, but showing the signs of his long bout of
intemperance as he had never shown them before. On
the morning after his arrival he motored over to the
headquarters of the Meadshire Yeomanry, with which he
had served as a young man, and his offers of renewed
service were promptly rejected. He went straight up to
London again without returning to Kemsale, and Grace
heard nothing of him for some weeks. Then he wrote to
say that he was to be allowed to take a motor-car over
to Headquarters, and make himself generally useful. He
was coming down for a night to say good-bye. He wanted
also to say good-bye to Katie, and to the Browns, and
asked her to arrange it. Armitage Brown need not fear
any renewal of the request that he had rejected so intol-
erantly. He should like to leave England in a state of
friendship with them all.

Armitage Brown consented at once. He did not regret

having refused his consent to a marriage between Meadshire and Katie; but he was inclined to regret the way
in which he had intimated his refusal. He did not now
understand all that had led up to the proposal, but was
no longer disposed to think of it as a dishonourable attempt on the part of a middle-aged wastrel to capture an
heiress. He had never talked to Katie about it at all;
she had shown him no less affection than before, and
had been docile and companionable whenever they had
been together. But the change in her had been marked,
and had continued. After some months it was no longer
possible to think of her either as a girl who had been
rescued from a danger into which her youth and inexperience had led her, or on the other hand as one who was
grieving over a broken love-affair. Her father did at last
mention Meadshire's name to her when Grace had asked
him what she had been told to ask.

"Lord Meadshire is coming down to-morrow, Katie.
He wants to say good-bye to us—to you. Will it distress
you to see him, my dear?"

Her face did not change in the least as she lifted her
eyes to his and said: "Oh no, father. I should like to say
good-bye to him before he goes. Grace told me he was
coming."

He said no more, but was as puzzled as ever, and inclined to sadness, because his girl was now sad, or at
least subdued, where she had been so gay and bright.
He made up his mind to get Meadshire by himself, if he
could, and get out of him what it was that had happened;
to ask him, if he had now given up the ideas he had
formed, whether he could not do something, or say something, to release the burden from Katie's mind, and give
him back his daughter restored to her former self.

It was not unreasonable, considering what had passed

between them, and the anger in which they had parted, that he should ask Meadshire for a few words before he received him again amongst his family. The interview was short. Meadshire came in looking grave, but already more recovered in health and bearing than he had been on his last hurried visit to Kemsale. "This will very likely be the last time we shall meet," he said, as he shook hands. "I wanted to tell you that I bear you no grudge now for what happened the last time we met. You were right, in the main. Where you were wrong doesn't matter now. Let's forget about it and part friends."

"Oh, don't speak as if you weren't coming back," said Armitage Brown. "We shall hope to see every one back before many months are past. And I want you to tell me, before we forget it, as you say, where I was wrong in what I said to you."

"I've a feeling that I shan't come back," said Meadshire. "I'm not sure that I want to. I've made a hideous mess of my life, and it's past mending now. If it's ended while I'm doing something at last that's worth doing, nobody need be sorry for me. Well, as you've asked me, I'll tell you that it might have been mended last winter. That dear good little girl would have kept me straight. I should have been so proud of her trust in me that I don't believe any temptation that might have come would have been strong enough to break me down, or to break us down together. I don't think she'd have suffered for it either; there would have been a good deal more to bind us together than with most. I'd stood out against it; I'd thought it wasn't fair on her. But we had a conversation together, when I was just getting over a very bad time, thanks to her influence over me, that took me out of myself. I felt then that I could get the better of myself with her to help me, and that I shouldn't be taking everything from her and giving nothing; and I knew the way in which she looked at it, too. We had come together on higher grounds than a man and a woman do where there's no suffering and no repentance between them. So you see, when I was tackled by you about wanting that brave good healing little soul for the sake of your money, it was as much of a shock to me as if I'd never thought about money in my life. I hadn't thought about it in connection with Katie, not once, believe me or not as you please. I believe I said some rude things about your damned money; but you must balance them against the things you said to me. I suppose you can't help your money colouring everything you have to do with, and you couldn't be expected to see what an outrage it was to bring it up against me in the frame of mind I came to you in."

Armitage Brown let most of this pass, but he looked very serious. " I'm willing to admit that I misunderstood the situation to some extent," he said. " Of course I completely withdraw all I said about money; I've come to see that that wasn't at the bottom of it. Still I can't regret—especially after what has happened since—that I refused your offer for my girl. I wanted to ask you now, before we spend our last evening all together, if you can't do something to put things right for us all. You said, in your letter to Lady Grace, that you had given up——"

" Oh yes," Meadshire interrupted him, not altogether without impatience. " You won't be bothered with me again. Whatever I might have been—whatever she might have made of me—eight or nine months ago, I've put it out of my power to be anything to her now. Poor little soul! She was ready to do the biggest thing a woman could do—save a man from himself, and I think she'd have done it. It's too late now—for her. But there's another factor that has come in since. Lots of us fellows who can't do anything for ourselves can do something for our country. I've got another chance, thank God. I should like to say something to her about that. I'll try and put her right with herself, if I get the opportunity before I go off. You needn't be afraid of my saying anything to her you wouldn't want to have said."

"I'm not," said Armitage Brown stoutly. "I've misunderstood you in some things. You're a better man than I thought. Still, I can't regret refusing you my daughter, though I'm sorry I used the rough way I did."

"We were both of us pretty rough," said Meadshire, with a smile. "I hadn't meant to say what I have to you, but I'm not sorry it has been said. We misunderstood each other before, and made friends to some extent after it. I hope we can part friends now. You've taken my place here; you'll fill it better than I did. You've done much better than I did already, and you'll do better yet. The old blood is worn out. It's just as well that it shouldn't be continued. I've come to see that. But you've got something to see too, Brown. You can't replace blood by money. I believe you're beginning to see it; and your son saw it long ago. Well I'm not the fellow to preach to you, but I'm glad we're going to part friends."

The four of them walked up the long east drive under the moon, Grace and Alfred in front, Katie and Meadshire far enough behind to be out of hearing.

Not a word was said between Meadshire and Katie as to what had happened when they had last met, and she knew that not a word would be said. And yet she was quieter in spirit, happier almost, than she had been at any time during the past nine months. He was talking to her as he had never talked before, not even on that winter afternoon when they had both been so much moved out of themselves.

"There were older men than I," he was saying, "who had gone back to their regiments, and they'd been glad to have them. They wouldn't look at me. Oh, then the iron entered my soul. What good was I in the world, if I couldn't do that? I went through black days and nights. The devil that's ridden me ever since I was a boy took hold of me, though I'd been giving him rein for months past and thought I'd worn him out. I wouldn't give way to him, though. I felt if I did I should be damned and lost to all eternity. Then I got my chance—my last chance, and the devil slunk away. I don't believe he'll worry me again now till I've done what's laid down for me to do."

"I shall be thinking of you always, out there," she said, in her young clear voice, which never hesitated to say what was in her mind. "I shall be full of fear—a woman can't help that for those she loves—but I shall be full of pride, too. I suppose I shan't be happy again till it's all over; but I shan't be unhappy in the way that I have been."

"It is I who have made you unhappy, my dear. I have made every one unhappy who has ever had anything to do with me. I've had everything given to me that a man could have had, and I have thrown it all away."

"No, you have kept the best. Those who have loved you have loved you for that. And now there will be nothing but the best to think of. All the rest is blotted out. It wasn't really you. It will never again come into my thoughts about you."

"God bless you, little Katie," he said. "I shan't fail you in your trust again."

Alfred was also going off the next morning. His mood was light-hearted, almost merry. It was as if a burden had been removed from him, and he had at last found his true vocation. It jarred somewhat upon Grace, who was weighed down with fears and sorrow.

" I can't look upon the dreadful war as a chance for adventure," she said at last. " It is too much to hope that all of those whom one knows, and loves, will come back from it. Some have been killed already, though none as yet who are nearest."

He became graver at once. His feelings towards this gentle creature, older than himself, still held some tenderness, though the fact that he did not feel quite at his ease in her presence, and talked more lightly on that account, proved that he had awakened from his dream.

" I don't look upon it only as an adventure," he said. " It is a very serious business, for all of us—much more serious than anything that has ever come into my life before. But it cuts so many knots for me. I shall be doing something to make myself useful at last."

Her thoughts were upon the two behind them; and she felt some impatience with him for returning to a subject which they had discussed before, but which seemed to have little importance in these heavy days.

" There is no one who could have better chances of making himself useful than you," she said. " You can't cut knots by running away from them. Oh, but I don't mean that. You are right to go, of course, but you will come back. Pray God you will come back, and your place will be here for the rest of your life."

" When I come back," he said, " if I do, everything will be different. I feel that, though I don't exactly know how. That is why I'm not worrying about the future. I

have something to do now, and all I have to think of is
how to do it as well as ever I can."

She thought she had spoken with undue asperity, and
said gently: " I'm sure that is the way to think of it.
The call has come for all of us, and we need not think
of what will be after it. And, of course, it is right for
those who are young, and are going to face hardship
and danger, to keep a brave heart. You will know that
those who are left behind are thinking of you all the
time."

" I shall like to feel that you are thinking of me," he
said simply. " I shall think of you too, very often. I
have always thought of you whenever I have thought of
Kemsale. You have seemed to belong to it, and we never
have. But even that is altering now. We could never
be what you have been here, however much we tried.
That is why I have so kicked against being pitchforked
into a position I could never fill. But nothing will be
quite like it was when the war is over. The changes
have begun already, and they will grow bigger. That's
what I feel about it, though I don't know what they will
reach to. But one can leave all that for the present.
There are things to be done. When I do come back, if
I do, there'll be other things to be done, but they won't
be the same as before. When the time comes I'll try
to do them, too."

They came to the great house, with all its uncurtained
windows staring nakedly. Old Mrs. Parmiter let them
in, and showed them over some of the rooms, swept clear
of trappings and furniture, ranked with white beds in
unending rows, all waiting clean and bare and sad for
what should come in the near future. Never had Kemsale looked like that before, never had its innumerable
rooms been so full of meaning. The graciousness of the

old life and the empty show of the new had alike been swept away. It was shortly to become a home of pain, but a home of healing too. What it should become hereafter could not yet be foreseen, but it would never again be quite what it had been before.

THE END.

www.ingramcontent.com/pod-product-compliance
Lightning Source LLC
Chambersburg PA
CBHW020920020726
47495CB00002B/264